I0721993

ZORTEGA'S QUALUM

— AND THE —

SHADOW WALKER

D.G. JOHNSON

ACKNOWLEDGMENTS

We want to say thank you to everyone who believed in us as we wrote this novel. To all our friends and family who gave us so much support. To the people in our lives that are based on our characters. We want to thank our illustrators, who worked tirelessly to bring our characters to life. We appreciate everyone who gave us unbiased feedback and continued to push us to make this dream a reality. Without you, we never would have made it this far. We also want to thank our fans for joining us on this adventure. As we go forth, rep your Zodiac and support your line.

The Prologue

The Fight

On one seemingly quiet night, Johnathan was about to join Elizabeth for a nice glass of wine and a bubble bath. Before joining his wife, he took a minute on the back porch to have a cigar with his father, Keith Braymark. Laughing at the great conversation his dad was having about his late mother spoke volumes as to how he felt for Elizabeth.

Feeling the dewy air blow around outside, he looked up to the sky and knew he was surrounded by love and family. His loved ones were a small group, but he would do anything to protect them and keep them safe. Still listening to his dad go on about himself back in his day, he heard a ringing in his ear.

"Hunny, come in. The kids are asleep, and I got the grapes," messaged Elizabeth telepathically. Johnathan and his family weren't normal humans; they were

actually from another world with magical powers. They moved to earth because of the rules and his wife's human work, which he didn't mind so much. However, he knew he should hurry upstairs before she used some magic on him. Grinning from ear to ear, Johnathan hopped up and told his old man not to stay up too late.

On his way upstairs, he noticed the office light was on, but couldn't recall the last time someone had been inside there. Attempting to go in and take a look, he felt a cold chill, similar to that of a fall morning.

"Hey, who are you?" Shouted Johnathan. In Johnathan's office was a masked man standing next to his bookshelf, tearing through his books.

The man noticed him in the doorway, and before Johnathan could make a move, the figure casted a line of fire across the room. He did not want to be disturbed by Jonathan's presence, so the intruder continued his search a little faster. Jumping back from the fire, Johnathan became furious that he couldn't just tackle the man, but a quick thought came to Johnathan. He blasted a gust of wind at the corner of the room that allowed him to run by. Frantically scanning the room, he located the figure and tried to restrain him. Flipping him around, he stared into his glowing eyes, and muttered, "You're a royal?"

Not fazed by the notion, the figurehead butted Johnathan, causing him to fall backward. When Jonathan regained himself, he wound his arm back enough to punch the figure in the stomach. Barreled over in pain, the man retaliated by blasting balls of fire at Jonathan. When the golden flames began to engulf the office from the line of fire, he casted. Johnathan managed to dodge another blast of raining fireballs that were aimed at him. The gray smoke filled the room, so Johnathan called out for backup to help. Ebon, Johnathan's familiar, darted out to protect his Niyor in any way he could while trying to see which direction the figure could be coming from. Shortly after entering the room, Ebon realized his Niyor, and the intruder were not the only ones in the room. Shuffling through the smoke, Ebon found himself wrestling with a dark shadow.

With both him and Ebon fighting to win dominance in all the commotion, Johnathan hurried to the painting of his lost mother reading him a bedtime story as a child. Johnathan figured that since he knew the man was a royal that he was only here for one thing. Placing his hands on the portrait, he removed the book from her hands. "Geairco Los Pricela." Turning around, he witnessed the man's eyes glow with delight. "Very sneaky, I would have never thought to have looked there. Now, hand it over!" Hearing this, Johnathan realized that he made a fatal mistake. In his hands, he held the Qualum, a book that contained the most powerful magic of the thirteen zodiacs'. As he blocked the intruder with his counter moves, another thought crossed his mind that filled him with dread. His wife was going to kill him for begging her on where she kept the book.

Meanwhile, Elizabeth the Libra, was the keeper of the Qualum and she grew annoyed with her husband's absence on their date night. She drained the bath and was saddened by her husband not joining her. After her failed date, she began washing up in the shower. Through the water, she heard a loud commotion as her lungs filled with smoke. She ran out of the bathroom, frantic to clothe herself. Terrified that the house was on fire, she managed to crawl to the children's wing. She knew she needed to protect them with a powerful shield. Who on earth could be attacking us? And why? She thought to herself. Unable to leave her children, she begged her Niyor to go help her husband protect the book and locate her father-in-law.

Elizabeth's familiar was Uni; he was a miniaturized panda. He transformed out of her charm bracelet and dashed off into the cloud of smoke. Uni had army crawled down the stairs to the burning office with his stubby panda legs and was in dismay by the sight he saw. Trying not to be detected, Uni went transparent and slid along the wall to maybe see if the man was unguarded.

"Raquise!" Johnathan cried out as he shot out more fireballs. With one hand tightly wrapped around the Qualum, Johnathan became blindsided by the light reflecting off the mirror. Taking that moment, the intruder attacked him, causing him to fly into his bookshelf of military awards and medals. He laid on the ground dazed and in pain, as he began to feel every hit Ebon had obtained

in his fight with the man's companion. Severely injured, he attempted to defend himself from the intruder long enough to escape. He looked around for the exit, but only saw darkness. Trying to devise a plan to escape with the book, he worried if others had accompanied the man. He thought of using his weapon to level the playing field in case there were more in the house.

"The Qualum will be mine!" He said with a sinister voice as he yelled through the flames. The masked intruder ran towards Johnathan, only to be tripped up by Uni's paw. Afraid of what he'd do next, Uni did the only thing he could think of and grabbed a hold of his arm to stop the onslaught of attacks toward his Niyor's husband. With a moment of time granted to him, Johnathan hobbled to his feet. He was still cornered by Ebon, the shadow, the intruder, Uni, and a grand old antique cherry desk. "Get off me, you peasant animal!" Shaking him around, Uni was thrown off of the man on to the ground. Feeling the pain Elizabeth's familiar had just received, she knew that it couldn't be going well.

"Aduka!" Shouted the intruder, as beams of light shot at Johnathan. The fire continued to rage around them and threatened to consume them both. Taking his shot, Johnathan ran at him, picking him up in the highest body slam, and tackled him to the ground. As the two men wrestled for dominance, the man soon realized the book was still in his hand, so he tried to grab it. Johnathan rolled the intruder onto his back to hold him down, but he was one-handed and badly hurt. The intruder knocked the Qualum out of his grasp and threw it to the far wall where Ebon laid injured. With both Niyor's badly hurt, Johnathan fought with both hands to unmask the intruder. Uni could see the struggle Johnathan was having and managed to get up and lend help. After tugging and yanking, Uni pulled the mask off.

"You!" Cried out Johnathan as the man rolled backwards knocking Johnathan off him. Covering his face, he flung Johnathan over his shoulder and onto the desk. Hitting the desk with so much force made him crumble to the floor in a heap. Uni was horrified that he might have been dead and ran off to go find help in all the flames. Holding his paw over his mouth to breathe, he managed to find Keith stumbling around the house, screaming out to find his son and

daughter-in-law. Uni was unclear if he had just left Johnathan for dead and the book to be stolen, but he finally reached him in all the confusion. Keith was unable to see anything below eye level, so Uni tugged on his pants legs.

Almost firing at poor, shambled Uni, he climbed onto his back and handed him the mask he brought with him. *"Hurry, he's dying, I think, Johnathan is dying!"* Said Uni while he showed him the way. Keith immediately rushed to the office. Beyond the smoke, Keith recognized the tall statured man like it was an unwelcomed reunion. Befuddled, he manifested and twirled his staff out on the defense, ready to fight.

Looking around the room, he became anxious, so he yelled out, "Johnathan, are you okay? Get up boy!" Keith shuffled around the room, as the tall man retrieved the book from Ebon. The intruder was eager to find a particular page, and when he did, he began to read the spell. Not wanting him to read out another word, Keith fired at him.

"Requise!"

Even though he missed his target, Keith had fortunately made the intruder mess up the words to his spell, which created a pocket hole in the room. As the orangish-blue glowing hole appeared behind the shadowed man, it grew from a small circle to a doorway-sized hole. Waking up slowly, Jonathan sees that the hole was swallowing books off the shelves and smoke from the air. It grew vacuously and started sucking in everything in its path.

Axer, Keith's fox familiar, charged at the man to grab the Qualum. Frazzling the man and before it sucked in Axer, he leaped for the staff that Keith held out for him. Pulling him in and placing him behind pieces of the furniture. Keith jammed an anchor into the ground with his staff, then placed a shield up so the vortex couldn't pull them in any farther. Frazzled by the book being stolen from him and the vortex, the man yelled out, "You will regret this, Braymarks! Mark my words, I will free myself!" He frantically tried to grab the floor for leverage, but the man decided to grab Johnathan instead as he was being sucked in. Johnathan tried to fight him, but he was weak from the injuries he sustained. As they slid closer to the vortex, he clung to the leg of the desk only to be knocked back by Ebon. Screaming in fear, the intruder and Johnathan disappeared into the void.

As the orangish-blue light appeared, it cleared the room and filled the hole. Axer, the fox, walked over to Uni. *"Sorry, I was late. I was on the porch. This coat won't clean itself. Plus, it looked like you had it all under control,"* smirked Axer.

"Axer, you just love showing up at the last minute too, "Save the day, don't you?" Said Uni, hobbling to his feet after laying down in a moment of relief.

"Rollinka!" Keith chanted as he began to put out the golden flames. "Rollinka!"

"Uni, stop standing around and go give the Qualum to Elizabeth." Said Keith as his face filled with dread and concern.

With a salty look on his face, Uni thought about how he was just as rude as his fox. A bruised-up Uni took the book from Axer and walked out of the burned-up room. Climbing up the flight of stairs and down the hall to what looked like a dead-end was a closet door.

Knocking on the door, Uni said, *"Lizzy, it's me. I got the book, and there's something I need to tell you."* With her two children tucked behind a dresser, Elizabeth let's the shield fade. Hesitant, she stood in a defensive stance to make a quick fire just in case it was a trick. With Harley and Bowen not old enough to create their magic, Elizabeth feared for their safety. Years away from their ceremonies, with no familiars of their own to help, she felt unmatched.

"Uni, if that's really you, show me the book, please!"

Uni stepped in with his injured panda like walk and held the book up in front of him, hoping she didn't shoot.

Poking her head out was Elizabeth's youngest, Harley, "Mom, it's Uni. Don't hurt him!" Before Elizabeth could even stop her from coming out, she rushed over to bear hug the panda. Relieved and horrified, Elizabeth said, "I'm so glad you're okay Uni! Are you hurt? I felt your pain." Shaking his head, he pointed to all the cuts and burns and asked her to heal him as he sat down.

Scaring everyone in the room, a man knocked on the door to announce himself, Mr. Dominic Cade, their longtime butler. "Ma'am, Sir Braymark wishes to see you." After bowing, the slender figure disappeared down the stairs into the kitchen to fetch a mop and broom.

Questioning for a minute where he was during all this, Elizabeth sends Harley and Bowen off after him to get warm chocolate milk. "Come here Uni," said Elizabeth as she picks him up. "Go rest. You deserve it, Leapa." She then transforms him back into the beloved charm bracelet that she had received on her thirteenth birthday.

"So, are we going to just stand around here giving hugs to Uni, or are you coming downstairs? I mean, I did save us and all, so shouldn't I get the hug?" Said Axer striking a strong muscle man's pose. Ignoring him, she picked up the book and made her way to the office where Senior Braymark stood. When Elizabeth entered the room, she stood next to her father-in-law, staring at the scene before her, hardly believing her eyes at the carnage and destruction. The antique desk was charred black, the windows shattered, along with books and papers all over. The photo from her wedding day was on the floor in a broken frame with her husband's face half-burned off.

She turned to Keith and asked, "What happened here?" Stunned after putting out the fire, he simply stared at the spot where his son and the intruder both disappeared. Tears of anger began to well up in his eyes. If he hadn't gone to work on his welding in the garage, he would have seen the smoke and rushed right over to help sooner. If it hadn't been for Axer thinking they knocked over a candle; he wouldn't have entered the house for a while. He tried not to blame

himself for giving his son space on his date night with his wife. Snapping out of it, he turned to Elizabeth, who was still waiting for him to answer.

"Someone tried to steal the Qualum," he replied. Elizabeth stared down at the book in her hands, happy that it was safe once again under her guard. She then looked around the room, searching for the one missing occupant.

"How did it even get out of the painting? Do you know who it was? Where's Johnathan?" She asked Keith franticly. Her father-in-law could only stare at the lonely spot on the floor with no response. "Keith?" She said again, "Where is Jonathan?" A hint of hysteria began to enter her voice when he wouldn't answer her. Finally, he looked at her as the tears started to fall down her face.

"I'm sorry, my dear, but he's gone. I did what I could to save him, but it wasn't enough; he pulled him into a spelled vortex. I had to make a choice to save the book."

"Do you know who did this? What am I going to tell the kids? How could this happen?" Said Elizabeth with a choked-up voice.

Keith embraced her firmly. "He's a strong boy, and I've taught him well. I'm sure he's not dead, but right now we have to alert the council about Xalucard."

XIV

CHAPTER 1

It was a fall like afternoon in spring, and Deveraux Vanseal was heading out for his first chance to get an actual girlfriend. He was slightly nervous because it was a date with a human girl, not a Zortegan. Zortegan's are magical people, like Dev and his family. There were a good deal of on earth, but he didn't know any personally. For as long as he could remember, it had only been them in this city and state, but he really didn't know. Dev's parents said he wasn't allowed to know if there were others for his own safety. Driving to meet up with everyone, Dev wondered if having this date would make him feel more human, or would he totally blow his cover by stopping time as he went in for a kiss.

Shaking it off, Dev pulled into the parking lot. He looked left and right for a parking spot but had to wait in line as the cars moved forward. *"Put your ear to the floor and shake your waist! Now clap on the legs! Clap! Clap on the legs!"* Sang Dagon.

Dev looked down at his necklace and asked, "Are you singing the song on the radio?"

After a moment of quiet, Dagon said, *"What? It's a catchy song."*

Laughing at his buddy, Dev looked up and noticed there was finally a car pulling out so he could park. Pulling into the space, Dev turned the car off and attempted to fix his tie and vest. He nervously looked at the clock radio and seen it said 6:45 pm. He stared into the rear-view mirror, attempting to get ready for his date.

"All right man, you got this. Be yourself, Dev. Be yourself. It's just a first date, no pressure," said Dagon, giggling.

Contemplating sending his familiar home, he sat outside the Rollie. He took a deep breath in as he stepped out of his dad's Gray, four-door Tonka truck. Every Saturday night was teenager night at Rollie's. Every teen hung out there or down at the slides. Tonight, was different, Dev had a date with Remy Phillips. She was a girl Dev had been crushing on for years. She was on the dance team at his school. Anthony had done the impossible and gotten her to say yes to going out with him tonight. He and Anthony were supposed to go on this crazy double date, but Anthony's date couldn't make it until after she got off work. Taking a moment, he started walking up to the door and heard someone shouting his name.

"Dev, over here!" Dev turned to see his best friend standing in line to get in the door. He was kind of relieved that Anthony was at least in line because it looked like it was going to be a packed night. With the music blasting, Deveraux's heart started to beat faster because technically, this was the only date he had ever been on.

Relived to have seen him first, Dev walked over to greet him. "Man, over here. Come on! Remy is already inside. Don't make her wait. Do you know what I had to do to get Olivia to get her to agree to a double date?" Said Anthony. Anthony was an interesting character. He stood at six foot one and looked like a

cross between a stripper's body, and that one brown-haired, laid-back member of a boy band. His hazel eyes accented his cream-colored skin. Even though he had the angelic face of an angel, he acted as crazy as a hyena on a good day.

"Man, if this is a pity date, Anthony, I'm out. You know the last thing I need is for my powers to act up because I'm nervous. It's my bloodline's pre-year, and we get a surge in power, just to stay balanced or some mumbo jumbo like that. My dad said I gotta be careful not to freak out, so I don't turn the streamers into snakes or the rink into ice," said Dev. Dev began to feel his powers rise with his nervousness, but he forced it down and tried to focus on having a good time.

"Dude, you need to relax. We are just gonna head inside, meet up with Remy, and show off our moves on the rink. Who knows? We may even get you laid. Or at the very least, get you a girlfriend, hint-hint, wink-wink." Said Anthony. Dev looked at him and almost hopped back in his truck and drove off after he made that comment.

"Next! That'll be seven-fifty each." The cashier said, and like clockwork, she punched in two tickets and rang up the receipts.

The Rollie was a big rectangular building lit to the max with multicolored strobe lights flashing in all directions. They aimed multiple headlights at the two disco balls hanging on either side of the rink, flashing thousands of bright diamonds over the floor, the walls, and the ceiling. The employees had even turned on the fog machines located on the outer rim of the rink. A low cloud of fog was slowly billowing over the floor.

It had given the rink a rave-type atmosphere as a pulsing beat blasted over the many speakers placed throughout the building. Looking around, Dev could see kids of all ages skating and dancing to the music, waiting in line to get skates, or to get food from the concession stand. He saw the others sitting at tables, laughing with each other while having a good time. At times like these, he kind of wished he was just a regular human who didn't have to worry about magic, or training, or any other crazy aspects that were the norm for his life. Dev wished he could just be a regular guy with regular problems like everyone else.

He pushed these thoughts to the side as he grabbed ahold of his wolf pendant that housed Dagon, thankful to have him as a partner. A familiar is a magical entity that is bonded to people like Dev. He felt Dagon respond to his thoughts with his own affirmations. He smiled as he continued to scan the room for Remy. Anthony noticed her sitting at a table near the DJ booth and lead him that direction.

She was wearing a red top, a jean jacket, and jean shorts. She was lacing up her skates and chatting with the other four girls from the dance team. Remy was so pretty. She had long, flowy afro braids, and her makeup always looked like she was a model on the cover of Atlantica Magazine. With his smoothest swag walk, Anthony headed straight into the gaggle of girls with Dev in tow.

"Remy? How are you, darling? It is absolutely fabulous to see you again. You look amazing, dear. So much better than your rather..." He looked at the other girls with mock contempt, "... drab companions." He said with a laugh. The girls cried out with mock outrage, laughing and hugging him in greeting. Dev stood back and watched with a hint of jealousy as his best friend mingled so easily with the group. He wished he wasn't so awkward and shy around the opposite sex. Anthony walked back over to him, put his arm around his shoulder, and walked him up to the group. "Remy, this strapping gentleman is my friend, Deveraux Vanseal, and he will be your escort for the evening." He gestured at Dev with an exaggerated flourish, then clapped him on the shoulder. He whispered in his ear, "Go get her, pal."

Dev glared at his best friend and repeated him, "Go get her, he says. I hate you so much right now." She was the co-captain of the dance team, and he had maintained a crush on her since elementary school. When she walked up to him in her yellow and grey striped dress, he noticed her darker-toned skin and chocolate brown eyes. It was the first day he realized she knew his name. Dev thought she was so nice when she gave him a get-well-soon card. He had

broken his ankle teleporting for the first time because he had landed outside the treehouse that he and Anthony had built when they were seven.

Salena, Dev's Mom, tried to train him how to navigate through a portal, but he wasn't very patient and just jumped. Dev couldn't wait to jump through it, and because of it, Anthony had to help him hobble along for two weeks on crutches. Then just to teach him a lesson, his Mom wouldn't let him use a feather to heal himself because of all the injuries he had. She worried he would run out before his adult ones grew in. That Valentine's day in class was the best day ever because even though everyone got a card, that message made it feel even more special. He had waited for eight years for this moment.

Anthony just laughed and said, "Love you too, sugar," as he walked off with the other girls toward the concession stand. He looked back and yelled across the room, for all to hear, "I slipped a condom in your back pocket just in case, wink-wink!" Immediately Remy looked straight at Dev as he checked his back pocket, hoping he was kidding. Annoyed with the joke, he decided to remind Anthony that he had the power to hurt him. With a flick of his fingers, Dev tied his shoelaces together. Anthony fell with a loud thud while the other kids around pointed and laughed at him. He looked up from his shoes to Dev and flipped him off. Brushing himself off, he pulled his shoes off and walked over to pick up his skates.

"I'm so sorry," Dev said, putting his head in his hands.

"It's okay. I know Anthony is a prankster. How are you?" Said Remy.

"I'm good. You look beautiful tonight. I bet you wake up like that," said Dev, sort of whispering.

"Well, thank you. You look nice as well. You really make the vest and tie thing work," Remy said with a smile.

Yawning rather loudly, Dagon said, *"Ook.... now that the small talk is out of the way, say something. Dev, this awkward silence is making me wanna pull my fangs out!"*

Looking around for an empty bench to go take a seat, Dev placed one hand in his pocket and one hand on Remy's back and led her towards the arcade room. He had a few extra coins in this pocket and felt maybe winning her a stuffed bear or something first might make the date start off right. "Do you wanna play a shooting game with me? Anthony and I play Braver one all the time. I even have one of the highest scores." Rolling over to the game as best as she could on the disco shag carpet to the game, she shook her head no. Grabbing the controllers, Dev said, "Here I'll show you." Placing some money in the machine, the game booted up and began to play. One by one, Dev was knocking down apocalyptic zombie soldiers while Remy did her best to stand up straight and aim. Dev noticed his enthusiasm was a little louder than the rest of the people in the area after Dagon had almost popped out for a victory high five. Putting the gun down, Remy asked, "Can we go get your skates? They are playing some really good music and it's hard to stand on this carpet. I wanna sit down on the bench and take a break."

Thinking it might be a good idea to do what she wanted, he cringed at the fact that he had to slowly let the zombies eat him so the game would kill him. "I'm going to help you over to the bench and then I'm going to grab some skates," said Dev. Reaching out for his hand, Remy tried to stride over to the bench with him. "Hey, I know I got a little excited on the game, and I know I didn't personally invite you out myself, but I'm glad you decided to come out," said Dev, smiling at the fact she was holding his hand. Now that she was sitting on the bench, he turned and headed for the skate counter.

"Next, can I help you, what size?" Said the man at the counter check.

"I'll take a size eleven since my shoe size is a ten and a half."

"Okay, give me one second."

Handing him his skates, Dev said, "Thank you for your help."

Hoping he didn't take too long getting his skates, he hustled back over but not without Dagon's input, *"I'm so glad you came because I dream about you day and night, and drool over all the babies will have, and the life we'll live together..."*

Placing his hand over his necklace, he ignored Dagon and sat down next to Remy and asked, "Do you skate here often?"

"My adopted mom used to bring me and my brother Josh here to make us smile," said Remy.

"Oh, that's interesting, but I will let you know I'm going to out skate you." He said with a laugh as he went to pick up his skates to put them on.

"Oh? You think so? Someone is confident." She said while twirling around him in a dizzying display to show off her moves.

"Most definitely, my lady. Would you like to bet on it?" He stated as he skated backwards towards the rink without looking.

"Hmmm. A bet, eh? What exactly did you have in mind, good sir?"

"If I win, you allow me to take you on another date."

"Okay, and if I win, you have to dress up in a shark uniform and do a performance with us." He stopped short and gasped at her, wondering not for the first time what he was getting himself into.

She laughed at his shocked look. "What's the matter? Can't handle the humiliation if you lose?" Dev felt his wolf charm necklace grow warm and heard Dagon's voice in his head.

"Psst. You got this, bro. Show her your moves."

With a smile, Dev accessed a small bit of his magic and launched himself into the air over Remy's head. He landed lightly and smoothly skated backwards around the rink, amongst the shocked skaters. The only one not shocked was Anthony, who was clapping and cheering Dev on from the sidelines. "Yeah! That's my boy! Show 'em what you got!" Dev continued skating backwards around the rink until he pulled up in front of Remy, who was still shocked by his opening move. He held his hand out to her. "Would you care to join me?" He said with a smile. She smiled back and skated around him onto the rink. While pushing off the edge, she coasted around him while dancing to the music before deciding to speed off.

"Catch me if you can," she said with a wink. Dev looked back at the wall and laughed when she sped out onto the rink. Taking off after her, he caught up with her rather quickly. Wanting to make her laugh, he grabbed Remy around the waist and lifted her off her feet. She squealed with delight and terror, kicking the air. "Set me down now!" She said with a laugh. He brought her down and smiled while still carrying her, her feet barely an inch off the ground.

"I told you I would out skate you tonight." He whispered to her. While she was still in his arms, he lifted her up and began to spin on the tips of his skates. While still holding her above his head, he broke into a split and still kept moving forward.

"Okay, okay, okay! You win. I surrender. You can take me on another date." She said with a laugh. He laughed and began to set her down. As her feet touched the ground, she slipped and fell with Dev dropping with her. They landed in a heap with Dev on top, with his face planted right in between her breasts and his hands slightly lower then her hips. After sharing a blushing embrace, Dev looked up at her as others just skate on by them.

"Go in for the kiss. Now's your chance! Just let me lay on those hilltops for a quick minute. I'll tell you how they feel," said Dagon. Laughing at his familiar's antics, he pushed himself off Remy and helped her off the ground.

"Deveraux! It's time to go!" Said a voice inside his head. He looked around to make sure he wasn't imagining his nanny ruining his date by whispering sweet nothings in his ear. *"Hunny, can you hear me?"* Gabby whispered again.

In the middle of the most perfect moment he was having with Remy, Gabby, Dev's nanny started to summon him. Dev tried hard to ignore his nanny while trying not to look like he belonged in a psych ward.

"No comprende, mind- whispering. Please leave a message at the sound of the silence."

Squirming and singing shoo fly don't bother me under his breath. Remy squinted her eyes at him.

"Hunny, your dad needs you home. Your aunt is coming into town with some essential news, and she wants the entire house there."

Dev accidentally shouted instead of messaging back. "Like, really Gabby? Can't you see I'm trying to become popular by getting a shark girl as a girlfriend?" Remy looked at Dev in total confusion. They had been having such a good time, and then he started acting strange.

"Why are you singing that song? Did I do something wrong because you fell on me? Why are you shouting, and who is Gabby?" Said Remy.

Realizing he had no actual way to explain that answer, Dev messaged Anthony. *"Help!"* With a moment of awkwardness, Anthony turned and saw his friend in major Mack Daddy trouble with his lady.

Smack!

Remy had slapped his arm as she looked at him. "There's no way I'd ever be your girlfriend when you're talking about other girls on a date. Like, why are you acting so weird? Are you talking to yourself or me?"

Seeing the anger on Remy's face, Anthony rushed over to help. "Okay, okay, love birds. We were having a good time, so what happened?" He asked.

"Dev mentioned a girl named Gabby, while talking about making me his girlfriend and talking to no one," Remy stated in a huff with her arms crossed. Anthony looked at Dev with a slight look of alarm and then started to laugh.

"Oh, don't worry, Remy. Gabby is his nanny. He has been in love with her since he was a kid," chuckled Anthony.

"You're in love with your nanny? That's creepy!" Remy said, looking at him.

"I'm not in love with my nanny!" Denied Dev at that moment, Dev was just over this whole situation and was more concerned with getting Anthony to shut up.

Now that the DJ was playing Remy's jams again. She was ready to go skate, and forget the whole thing, only if he stopped acting so weird.

Dev pulled Anthony aside, "Dude, you're not helping! Now I look like a damn grave robber," said Dev.

"I wasn't trying to make you look like a grave robber, but you clearly asked for my help, and it worked. She was ready to vanquish you by the look in her eyes."

While pretending to pay attention to Dev's rants about how she was out of his league anyway, Anthony grabbed his shoulders and turned him around. He pointed him toward the DJ booth.

"Dude, it looks like you got bigger problems to worry about. Is that Mable?" Frozen in fear, he slowly turned around. He was just hoping this night would just end because it wasn't about to get any better.

CHAPTER 2

Staring at him from in the corner of the DJ booth was Mable. She was a grand, eight-foot brown bear that liked to stand on her hind legs. As he stood there in disbelief, Anthony started whispering jokes. "Dun ta dun dunt. Dun ta dun dunt da, da, dead man walking." Almost drowning in embarrassment, Dev looked away to make a clean dash for the front door.

"I didn't know ignoring a person you're on a date with was the gentlemen thing to do. What are you two talking about? You are both losers, and just when I thought you were cool," said Remy. Very annoyed with how the boys had started to act, she began to skate off over towards the other girls. Watching her skate off, he realized that the date was over. His nanny had sent her personal guard bear out on him to ruin everything.

"Did you know she was coming? You didn't miss curfew tonight, right?" Dev shook his head no. "Okay man, just go get your stuff. I'll cover for you," said Anthony.

Dev hung his head down slightly and skated over to go get his shoes and keys. Remy was staring at him while trying to get pep talks from her friends, as she had explained how she thought he was charming but really weird. Anthony skated over, still trying to help, but the other girls treated him like he was the one that ruined the date. As Anthony tried to smooth things over, Dev packed his stuff up and walked over to turn his skates in at the counter.

Mable growled with an angry look in her eye, *"Do you know why I've been sent here?"* Dev tried not to look at Mable where everyone could see him, so he quickly put on his shoes. *"Boy, I know you hear me speaking to you. Talk when your elder speaks to you."*

Speaking to her with his mind, Dev responded, "I can't just openly talk to you right now. Not with all these people here. Look, I heard what Gabby said, but I was trying to enjoy my date if that's alright with you."

"Boy, you better watch your tone when you speak to me before I knock you to the ground." She growled back to him. Dev's wolf necklace grew hot, and Dagon appeared next to him, growling at the bear in front of them.

"You may be older than me, but remember no one harms him while I am here! So, bring it on, old lady!" He growled.

Dev held him back with one hand, *"Calm down, both of you. Let's just get out here and head back to the house so we can see what my Aunt wants."* Dagon growled one more time at Mable. She proceeded to get down and backhand him before he was able to disappear back into Dev's charm.

"That wolf is getting too big for his britches. Let's go, boy." Looking over her shoulder, she saw Anthony standing behind her. *"You may as well come with us too."*

Anthony walked up to Dev and whispered, *"My money was on Dagon, but that bear has got some guns on her."* They walked towards the truck when they heard someone call out to get their attention.

"Hey, Anthony. Where are you going?" He turned to look at who called his name and was relieved to see it was Olivia. Smiling at the fact that he had a reason to stay, he began to back up.

"Um, well, my date is here. So I'ma go this way, away from the family drama," giggled Anthony with much amusement.

Dev looked at him. "So, you're just going to leave me to my aunt's madness?"

"Yes, yes, I am. Let me see, pretty high school date or angry spirit bear? Here I come Olivia!" Said Anthony as he fist-pumped backwards.

Mable walked up to Dev on all fours, *"Don't even think about going back in. We have to go. Now, don't let me beat you home because if I come back, I'm bringing your aunt, and you know how she likes to be the center of attention."*

Definitely not wanting his party animal aunt to come and embarrass him. So, he hopped in the truck, turned over the key and began to follow Mable out of the parking lot. He watched as all his classmates showed up to hang out while he was being dragged back home for some dumb gossip his aunt was probably overreacting about. Driving with the music turned up loud, Dev sat and imagined what it was going to be like to go to Zortega for the summer. According to the rules of the councils, the royal bloodlines have to train in secret on earth. Then they return for honor training during their sixteenth year.

Turning the corner, he started reflecting on how great the beginning of the date was, but he knew he wasn't getting another one. Dev knew he should have gone in for a kiss. At least he could have said he had gotten one, but it's hard to kiss a girl with your familiar being a pep-talking perv. Then your nanny summoning you every ten minutes to come home and deal with your crazy Aunt.

Changing gears, Dev wondered what was so important that his date couldn't have survived two more hours at least. The twins' Kaloke ceremony wasn't for a few weeks, so she was kind of early. Everyone was on their way for the whole magical Vanseal family rite of passage spectacle, but who knows what Aunt Lesley wanted.

Getting closer to his home at the bottom of the hill, stood a very grand, but well-kept larger-than-average Victorian-style home with white trim and a golden door. Dev could always see his house from the hill because it was the one on the corner surrounded by a grove of trees that he and his siblings would climb on. The two-story home towered over its neighbors with modern windows and an almost regal feel from the gated fence out front. Dev's dad Rodney took great pride in making it the standout home on the block. Typing the gate code in the front gate of the wrought iron bars, Dev drove up the five-car curved driveway and parked behind his Mazda. Dev heard Aunt Lesley from inside the house, talking loudly to everyone in the room. He sighed loudly and headed for the front door.

Walking into the house, Deveraux was hit with the very overwhelming smell of his Aunt's pungent floral cherry perfume. Placing his stuff down in the hallway, he heard, "Devy-Poo!" His Aunt cried out as she gave him a crushing hug. Being so close to her made him immediately lightheaded and overwhelmed by her perfume. Aunt Lesley was an all-natural, black-haired beauty. She was very gorgeous for her age, but she would never take off her party makeup from the night before. Aunt Lesley also liked to try to be hip with her clothing that was sometimes a size too small. She was about five-six, a little taller than Dev's Mom, and she had a daughter named Autumn. However, no one ever saw that much of her because she wasn't the mothering type.

"Boy, look at you growing up like a weed. How's your magic training coming? Are you helping the twins? I mean, no matter how much you train, you'll never beat your auntie because you should never curse a lady, right.... Devy?" Said Aunt Lesley.

Dreading every second, he had to be in the room, he replied, "Yes, Auntie," as he looked around for the nearest exit. They said I had to be home, not that I had to be in the room, he thought, but no luck. Mable was standing guard by the

stairs because she knew he wanted to disappear up there. Gabby wasn't the type of nanny you said no to because even though she was the sweetest nanny ever, for some reason, she gave Dev the feeling that he didn't want to make her mad. Her look told him he wouldn't want to see that side of her. With Gabby's dreads so neatly pulled in a bun, she gave Dev the stare of his life to come join them in the living room. On her face was a special marked tattoo that she displayed when her eyes glowed a piercing white color. The look was terrifying to him, so Dev just went to the couch and sat down. The room was filled with boredom, so he waited to hear what was so important that it couldn't have waited until later.

He looked around the room at his assembled family members and their familiars as they all gathered to hear the news. His twin brother and sister were sitting around the table, trying to practice this new spell that their mom was teaching them. Ezekiel, the family science and stars nerd, and Eland, the overwhelmed and very emotional athlete, watched their mom as she effortlessly made the air dance with her magic. Gabby was dusting the bookshelf while Mable stood guard at the door, blocking Dev's first escape. His father walked in with his goat familiar hot on his heels, agitated by this early summons from his work. He took a seat next to his wife and kissed her on the cheek.

"What's this all about?" He whispered.

"No idea with my crazy sister," replied Selena.

"So, gather around everyone, even you, Gabby. I just returned from Kalebulax City, and I heard from Stella's Aunt, that heard it from Char's parents, that received word from Geno, that Renee and Levi the elders... that would be so drop-dead juicy if they were secretly dating, or, ooh, what if they are having an affair? I'ma have to talk that theory over with Stella."

"Lesley! Focus! Let's bring it back," said Rodney.

"Oh! You're so by the book! Can't a lady have a real live soap to entertain herself? But... ummm... Oh, yeah... they were whispering about some evil familiars who were targeting different places. The human break-ins and mysterious deaths are somehow connected. So, the council might summon you for an early emergency meeting, Rodney, oh brother-in-law of mine. There, you happy this family is always ready to shoot the messenger?" She said as she got up to pour herself another Cosmo from the bar.

"Did you hear what they were looking for? Or who sent them? Or why?" Said Rodney.

"Honey, do you think this is related to the bloodlines or just rogue familiars, and if so, who let them out of the black hole? Because if it's true, the twins are in danger. They don't have their familiars yet, and the ceremony can't happen for another few weeks," feared Salena.

"Babe, hopefully, it's all just human-related because if it's what I think it is, those deaths weren't random," said Rodney.

Ring! Ring! Ring!

"I'll get it." Gabby implied as she dashed off to go get the phone. "Well, the beauty of twins is if you lose one, you always have a backup," said Lesley.

"Hey!" Said the twins simultaneously as they pointed at each other on who should be the one to go. That just made Salena's energy boil as she got angry at her sister's comments. Tiye, Salena's familiar, leapt out of her lynx tattoo and jumped at Lesley. Tiye aimed only to spill her drink on her, which made Lesley really frustrated, which made the twins snicker at the look on her face. Tiye looked back while laughing as she made her way to protect her Niyor's twins from their crazy Aunt.

"Ugh... really, sis? Just cause you're older does not mean I won't have Eve claw that cat's eyes out. I was just playin', and you ruined a perfectly good Cosmo. I'm not cleaning that up, and I hope you have dry cleaning." Gestured Lesley half-way joking. Laying down next to the twins, licking her paws, Tiye said, *"I liked to see her try it. I've only had crow, but there's always room to try owl."*

"Hoot, hoot," said Eve at the whole situation. Eve, Lesley's familiar, felt it best to fly up on the bookshelf before things got worse.

Dev just sat there looking utterly confused as to why his mom and Aunt had started acting like bickering teenagers. Was this really what his aunt had ruined his night for? A rumor she had heard from four people that had heard it from the pope, who had tea with Santa, who saw Genghis Khan kissing the tooth fairy.

With everyone bickering, Gabby re-entered the room. "Sir, you've been requested by the elders on the Universal mirror." Stunned by the sudden emergency, he thought, maybe Lesley was right. He looked at the kids and told them to go upstairs, but they just stared right back. "Okay, I'll take it in the office. Thank you, Gabby," said Rodney.

"Ladies, would you like some tea?" Suggested Gabby softly. Laughing to himself, Dev knew the only reason they said yes was because Mable was standing behind Lesley with Eve in her mouth and Tiye under her paw. Gabby had been around the family for a long time, and she always made Mable put the family in time-out when they couldn't act like adults. Everyone knew if their familiar was hurt, they were hurt as well. So, as long as Mable had his mom and Aunt Lesley's familiars in check, they would act right without even laying a finger on them. It was kind of a funny thing that happened when it happened to them. It was like watching two bad kids act like angels when they were on the verge of a whooping. So, they did what any kids would have done, they grumbled and sat and drank their tea until the, "parent" left the room.

Dev just shook his head and tried to help the twins learn the basic drawings for casting. They were pretty much cramming for their Kaloke final. It wasn't enough to just get their magic. They would have to prove they could control it. Plus, his dad wasn't going to be back for quite a bit if he had to go to Zortega. Unfortunately, in Zortega every two hours there was four hours here, so it was going to be awhile before they'd hear the big news.

AQUARIUS

CHAPTER 3

Closing the door behind him, Rodney sat down at his desk. He pulled out his celestial Capricorn mirror and placed his palm on it. He was spiritually shifted away to the Slaven. The Slaven was a council room in the Nova castle, located in the center of Kalebulax City. The city itself was located in the heart of Zortega. It was surrounded on all sides by separate regions representing each bloodline. They represented one ruler each as a council member, even though the world mingled amongst each other. It was a beautiful place with stars from the night sky as bright as day. Kalebulax City was actually cloaked from the earth, along with all of the planets of Zortega. There were many portals around the earth that humans didn't know about. Also, what the humans didn't know is, the earth orbited Zortega like a moon.

Rodney looked out the window at the Northern Lights filling the skies, flowing over the white mountain tops and the majestic coral lakes. The Maroon Valleys grew the tallest trees and the tastiest Mangleberry fruit. For him, it was as magical as a Nebula cloud. Music and laughter filled the air with the euphoria of its people, along with the magic of the Zortegans and familiars training in every region. Unfortunately, there was one region that had become forbidden. It used to belong to the Ophiuchus line, but after the war, they nicknamed it the Blackhole region. This region was a very dark one, because that's where the Kantors were kept. Kantors were rejected or bad familiars that came from Zortegans that couldn't pass their Kaloke ceremonies. Once a familiar is brought into this world, they are bonded to their Niyor. Their bond is one that can never be broken by anything other than a wrongful death. Another kind of a Kantor is a familiar that has had their bond broken and is unable to move on. Their heart is consumed by their rage and loneliness and they become creatures of darkness.

Walking away from the window, Rodney's body began to transform. His eyes began to glow, his royal color and his talon tentacles behind his ears became present. Thunderous and beautiful, his wings extended from his thighs from knee to hip bone. They were three to four feet in length and as white as snow. He flapped them a few times before tucking them in around his waist. Taking a second to scratch his neck where his Capricorn symbol laid. He took a second to transform into his robe. This was the form of all Zortegans, but only the royal ones' eyes glowed as a symbol of power. Everyone else's eyes were shaped like diamonds.

Rodney wished he could visit more often because this was his home. His dad had grown up here alongside many others before they had decided that royal families were to live on earth. Royalty meant they were next in line for the throne of that zodiac. Every line was represented by a gemstone, and every stone was made of distinct elements. Even though the bloodline stones were different, the lines were placed into four groups: Fire, Earth, Wind, and Water. These elements fueled their powers, but also allowed no one bloodline to overpower the others.

After transforming, he walked down the main hallway and ran into Scorpio. He was dressed in his official robe that was dyed his bloodline's gem color. The robes the council wore were a mark of the head of each line, and each one was very ornate. Scorpio's robe was a deep topaz that seemed to absorb all light around it. The black cuffs and the collar sparkled with the yellow topaz gemstones that marked the Scorpio line. Rodney clothed himself in a similar style. His robe was a bright turquoise blue, but he often wore the deep ruby red to represent his birth month of January. However, the turquoise robe also had blue topaz sewn into it, as it sparkled when he walked down the hall.

Scorpio was talking to Aries, who was also in her royal gown covered in crystals all over her aquamarine robe. Taking a glance at her he thought she looked very breathtaking. Although, she was young for her age, she had a level of intelligence that spoke of wisdom beyond her years. Her mocha-colored skin glowed in any light. She had an athletic build that bespoke of many hours spent in a gym. Her hair was always done in curls that bounced whenever she moved her head. She was considered to be one of the most gorgeous women around. With almond-shaped eyes that sparkled, a smile that lit up any room, and a laugh that sounded like the tinkling of bells. However, when she got serious, she was a force to be reckoned with. She was always ready to argue her point and stand her ground against anyone who slighted her. Her magical abilities were truly awe-inspiring or terrifying, depending on if you were watching her or on the receiving end of her attack.

Rodney walked past them to enter the Slaven hall room, where they always met for meetings. Opening the doors, he waited for every single one of the eleven leaders to arrive. As he waited, he stared around the conference room. It was a large room with high vaulted walls and thirteen stained glass windows. Each window had an animal depiction of each lines symbol etched into them. The ceiling looked like one giant night sky filled with the constellations of the zodiac. At the moment, it showed the Taurus constellation to symbolize that it was their time as the head of the council. When his time was done, the constellation in the sky would shift to the next leader.

In the middle of the room was a large oval spiral-shaped table with twelve high-backed thrones seated around it. They shaped it like a giant spiral slide with blades on the two sides. The thrones were an equal distance apart from each other in descending order, as if they were in a jury courtroom. In the middle of the oval at the very bottom was Taurus's throne. Each throne was cut from the same gemstone that was specific to each line. Then the thrones were placed in front of their own respective windows. Although it was supposed to be a high honor, sitting in those thrones was the most uncomfortable thing about being on the council, thought Rodney.

Floating around the room were creatures called Epsis', they resembled tiny planet like galaxies with ears, arms, and legs. Their primary purpose was to see to the needs of the council members during the meetings. Rodney called one over and requested a Mangleberry juice to sip on. He was displeased about all the theories and gossip of why they had been summoned. As he sat by himself, contemplating the reason for the meeting, the other council members began to assemble. He watched as all of them walked in, carrying their own celestial item that allowed them to travel between realms.

Wanting to be left alone, Rodney knew that was to be soon outlived. With the heckling he heard in the hallway, he realized was right. He could feel a headache coming on as Gemini and Libra walked into the room.

"Hey look, Libra, it's the all-powerful baahh and his baby sheep," said Gemini.

Humored by her joke, Rodney knew she was referring to him, so he stood up to greet them. "Oh, look who's here. I thought for once they would leave the unimportant lines out of the superior line's work," said Rodney, smiling.

"You're such an ass, Capricorn," said Gemini.

"It's okay, Gem, He knows the only reason he's an ass is that he's so apologetic for what his line did to ours back during the Zodiac Wars. I mean, it's a step up from evil," said Libra.

"Now, Libra, can't we be friends? The wars were thousands of years ago. You're supposed to be the one that keeps us balanced and balance ladies don't get wrinkles over thousand-year-old wars," said Rodney, who was very angry with what Libra said.

Gemini's power level rose, and just like that, he was standing next to a mirror image of her. Adare was weak on her own, but once her other half appeared, she was like fighting a woman on her monthly. Which reminded him that all men are better advised to roll over and play dead rather than face two angry women, thought Rodney.

"See, for once, you're right, Capricorn. I am the balance, and if it wasn't for the fact that we need your line to maintain it, I'd eliminate you myself," said Libra.

"Sounds like there's a hint of sexual tension for my line. How long has it been since hubby walked out on you? Cause I'm married," said Rodney.

"Let me at him. I'll naw his little goat tail!" Messaged Uni.

Pisces gathers them to sit with a loud bang of the celestial bells from the tower behind them. "LET'S ALL GATHER," said Pisces. With disgust in Libra's eyes, she picked up Uni and went to sit at her place at the table.

With all the council members present and familiars in tow, they all sat in their designated places. While also fighting and bickering, they demanding to know why they had been summoned so early.

"Silence!"

Taurus stood at the head of the table and yelled as he addressed the other members. He was an elderly man. Although he was rather thin, he seemed to radiate an aura of strength. He stood tall and straight despite his age, and he watched over the table with piercing blue eyes that took in every detail. "Now, I know this is not ideal, but I'm head of the council at the moment, and we won't get anything done listening to theories. Cancer has been looking into some

magically related deaths, and it looks like someone or something is targeting bloodline familiars, killing them, and turning them into Kantors," said Taurus.

Everyone around the table stared at Taurus in stunned silence. They knew there were deaths, but to hear that familiars had been turned over to the dark side was truly unexpected and terrifying. This meant that the enemy, whoever it was, was extremely powerful, and that meant they truly had a problem. In their entire history, there had never been a situation as dire as this.

The head of the Scorpio line was Nikolai. He was a smooth, short mohawked, gentleman with a sharp tongue that charmed all the ladies and a football player shaped frame. His clean features and personality entertained all the valueless ones. His dark chocolate covered skin and strong jawline attracted females for miles. He decided to sit forward with his scorpion familiar crawling around the table. "How is that possible?" he asked, "Our familiars are parts of us. I thought that they only ceased to exist after we ourselves passed on into the void."

A slight cough drew everyone's attention as Geno, the head of the Pisces line and currently the oldest member on the council, stood. "Technically, that is true," he stated. "However, under certain circumstances, familiars can remain in this world after their partners pass on. The best example of this is our very own familiars given to us after we took our position on this council. Each and every one of them was passed to us from our predecessors when we took over as the head of our line. They hold the knowledge and memories of the generations that can be traced back to our very beginning." He looked at his own shark familiar, as it swam around his head while he spoke. "On the note of them being turned into Kantors, it only happens when some sort of negative event turns the hearts dark. They are beings made of pure spiritual energy mixed with our own souls. So, either we ourselves have to become sinister, or they have to witness an act of pure evil that will blacken their hearts completely. In this case, I would assume that the murder of their Niyor is what turned them into Kantors." With that being said, Geno took his seat, looking truly troubled. The others looked around, some looking worried while others drew their familiars closer to them, terrified of ever losing them in such a way.

A thought occurred to Rodney as he took in all this information. He cleared his throat to speak. "Usually, the Kantors are wild spirits and uncontrollable. So how is it that this mysterious figure is able to bend them to his will?"

There was a snort sound from across the table as Taylor-Rose, the head of the Aquarius line, looked up from her phone. She was an older lady with black and green-haired dreads. Her smile made people feel warm, but she always liked to absorb everything around her. Most didn't approve of her brash ways, but she didn't care as she adjusted her body around in her chair while pushing up her reading glasses. "Well, if you knew anything at all, you would know that there are forbidden spells that allow such control." She said, looking at Rodney with disdain for his lack of knowledge. "If any of you ever cared to open a book and learn your elder history, you would know they had banned these spells at the end of the Zodiac Wars." With that statement, she went back to her phone and continued scrolling through whatever app she was currently on.

Rodney rolled his eyes at her statement. "I'll have you know I am rather well read when it comes to our history. However, that doesn't explain how this person knows these forbidden spells that give him this level of control. Also, how do we free the familiars and stop this man from causing more trouble? Who is this mysterious person in the first place? Where did he come from? And most importantly, what does this person want?" Rodney asked. Everyone looked around at each other as they pondered these questions and tried to come up with solutions to prevent more disasters.

"Has anyone pondered the thought that this mysterious figure maybe someone in this very room?" All heads snapped in the direction of the person who had voiced an absolutely ridiculous thought. Nikolai looked back at them, unashamed at his statement. "I'm not accusing anyone directly." Looking directly at Sagittarius, he stated, "However, think about it for a second. Who else would have the knowledge and power to pull a stunt like this?"

Aries chimed in, "You know he has a point." said Aries, "I believe it's Leo." Pointing her finger at the head of the Leo line. "We all know he works as a

mobster and drug kingpin. Killing someone would be easy for him, and then he could just take their familiars for his own."

"Yeah!" A few in the crowd cheer in agreement.

"Cancer, contain him, and then hold him at The Dipper until we can hold an eclipse!" Shouted Aries.

"Wow... Just because I control crime doesn't make me a killer. A Leo has to be a king at something, and I'm a boss at money, I only take lives when they steal from me. I don't kill any Zortegans, only worthless humans. I know killing our kind is a celestial crime. I'm not trying to be black holed for anybody," said Donavan, leader of the Leo line.

"Enough! This is embarrassing. These spells are dark magic, and we banished the only line that used it for it, and we don't ever speak of them. I mean, really. We eliminated them a long time ago," snarled Sagittarius.

Raising her hand, Gemini said, "Mathematically, it makes sense, but that would mean there was a descendent over the course of a thousand years we never eliminated."

Silence froze the room. Most of the former elders had evaporated in their own element style because one only lives up to three hundred years old. Most of the elders in the room had only heard rumors of the past.

"Order in the room!" Shouted Taurus. "We will not be containing anyone, we will not point fingers, and will not assume that anyone from the thirteenth line survived the black hole banishment. Cancer will do a full investigation, and we will go to the caverns and question the python ourselves. Until then, ward your homes with meteors and proceed with your lives as normal. Keep your families close. Because most of our children attend the same schools, Gemini, Libra, and I will go about setting up defenses there as well to ensure their safety. Please, everyone, be on your guard. This is a powerful magic we haven't seen in years."

Taurus then adjourned the meeting. Frustrated, with no real conclusion, Aquarius had to get the last word. So, she grabbed her familiar and stomped out the door, shouting. "If I was head this time, I would have gotten results today before we had wasted everyone's time!"

Everyone looked around and followed suit on getting ready to return home. Aries, annoyed by everyone's loud outbursts, she rushed over to offer her help with spreading the word. She ran over to Sagittarius, who was a humanitarian and had her own following in both worlds. They both put their heads together and began to brainstorm ways to spread the word about this new threat. Sitting back, Taurus watched the others leave in a bit of a panic. He could feel his age catching up with him dealing with all the different opinions and knew it was almost time to move on.

Rodney walked over to Nikolai and asked, "Do you really think it's a member of the council?"

Nikolai looked at him seriously. "I can't say for sure. I only made that comment to observe the reactions of the other members so I could see who acted suspiciously."

Rodney nodded at the smart yet subtle tactic to weed out any possible suspects. "Did anyone stand out to you?"

Nikolai looked at him. "No one acted out of the ordinary when I made the accusation. So no, but I will keep watching and see what happens." With that notion, he grabbed his celestial item and traveled home. Rodney looked around at the last few stragglers, wondering if it was possible for one of them to be committing these despicable crimes. He saw Libra glaring at him from across the room. Rodney winked and blew her a kiss before he grabbed his mirror and traveled home. He landed in the middle of the living room, surprising everyone. Immediately, he was bombarded with questions about the meeting.

"Look, everyone, it's just a lot to deal with. We will discuss this later. For right now, please just give me a chance to process it. Gabby, could you please get

the kids ready for bed? I need to talk to the adults alone. Dev, I need you to help train the twins this weekend. I'm going home to figure some things out, and I have a few ceremonies to perform."

Dev chuckled to himself. "So, what you're really saying is, "Dev. You will be training the twins, due to the fact that I won't be home much," right?" Rodney laughed out loud and said, "I would really appreciate it, son."

Dev nodded as he headed up the stairs. "Okay, Dad. I've got it." He said. Looking at the twins, he beckoned them upstairs. "C'mon, you guys, let's get ready for bed."

"Why do we always miss the juicy stuff?" Said Eland. With Gabby ready to unleash Mable off of Lesley and Selena and onto the kids, they all realized she wasn't playing and scurried upstairs for bed.

CHAPTER 4

"Gabby! Turn off the water cloud!" Shouted Dev. In an attempt to wake him for school, the twins had practiced casting magic on their brother.

"DEV!!! Deveraux Vanseal! It is 7:20 am. I have called your name three times for breakfast. Now, you're going to be late dropping your brother and sister off for school. Get up and get dressed before I cast my own spell that will be worse than a water cloud." Shouted his mother.

"Okay, already! I'm up, jeez. I can't even dream about my date last night." Waving his hands, he quickly stopped the downpour of the clouds and laid there in his soaking wet pajamas. Fortunately, the best part about being a magical being is using magic for personal gain. Dev got up, looked at his closet, and a dry pair of pants and a polo shirt floated out. Standing in his bathroom, he took a moment to look at himself. He was a five foot-nine average teenage boy with caramel color skin and a wrestler-built body with a slim frame. He stood there admiring himself as he put his clothes on, while a brush smoothed out his waves when he applied some hair grease. With a touch of deodorant and some lotion applied to his baby face, knees, and toes, he was ready to go.

"Dev, don't you leave your room all wet. Gabby is not a maid!" His Mom shouted from downstairs. So before leaving the room, Dev cast a cleaning spell. Once done, he headed downstairs to grab the keys to his Mazda. Giving his Mom a hug and kiss as she sat on a kitchen stool, they wished each other a good day. He headed towards the door, grabbing a bun cake from Gabby on the way out. As he started to bite into it, he looked back at Gabby with a mischievous glint in his eye. "Hey, Gabby?" He called. She looked up at him, "Cousin chase called and said he can't wait to get a bite of your bun cakes." He laughed as he dashed out of the kitchen door before, she could respond. Looking back for a minute to see if she was coming after him, Dev grabbed his backpack from the family room. After discovering he was safe, he went to locate the twins and noticed his aunt leaving the study looking for something.

"Where is the wine? Haven't you heard of mimosas with your bacon and eggs?" Lesley asked as she rushed around the kitchen in a bathrobe. She was searching high and low for wine, not knowing Gabby had locked it all away.

"Haven't you heard of alcoholics anonymous? Selena, just how long is your sister staying to drink me out of house and home?" Rodney asked as he set his cup on the table and looked up from his paper. While walking out the door, they heard, "Lesley! Your familiar just stole my bacon. I swear I am going to turn her into a coo-coo clock if she touches my plate again!"

"Come on, dweebs, we're late for school," said Dev, laughing hysterically.

He rushed the twins to the car while resisting the urge to leave them both. Once everyone was buckled in, he turned the car over and burned rubber down the driveway. "Dev, could you slow down a bit?" Ezekiel asked from the back seat. In response, he pushed harder on the gas, reducing the drive from fifteen minutes to five.

Driving up to the middle school, Dev shoved the twins out of his car so he could haul ass to the high school before the home period ended. Mrs. Jones loved to give out detention slips when anyone was late to her math class. Dropping them off, he sped out of the parking lot and down the road, thankful that his school was only a few minutes away. As he raced the clock trying to make it to school on time, he failed to notice the police motorcycle idling on the side of the road, clocking his speed at twenty miles over the legal limit.

Soon, all Dev saw in his rear-view mirror was flashing lights as the cop tried to flag him down. "No, no, no..." He moaned in despair as he pulled over to the side of the road to wait for the officer. While he waited, he pulled his license out of his wallet and grabbed a copy of the registration and insurance. He sat back, watching as time ticked by, drawing closer to the first bell. When the officer arrived at his window and asked for his documents. He handed them over and watched as he walked back to the car at a leisurely pace. Dagon giggled, *"Oh, you're so dead when your mom finds out you were speeding, and you got a ticket."*

"Dagon, you're so not helping. This has been a crappy day already, and now I look like I'm talking to myself." He said. Waiting for the cop to return with his stuff, he wished for a time-traveling spell that could rewind time to when he woke up.

"Son, do you know how fast you were going? I clocked you at forty-five in a twenty-five, and this is a school zone." Said the officer to him.

"No, officer. I was just focused on getting to school before the first bell. If I don't, I have to run extra laps at track practice if I get a detention." Pleaded Dev innocently, in hopes that he would be understanding.

The officer looked him over with a piercing stare and gave him his stuff back. "Son, this is your only warning because I could take you to jail for this. Watch your lead foot next time or get to class earlier, so you don't have to worry about being late." Nodding his head in joy, Dev put his things in his wallet and then placed it in his back pocket. Dev thanked the officer and slowly pulled off.

He turned down the hill to the Reda Miles Magnet High School parking lot. The school was a large building made of different sections. It had a modern yet futuristic look to it, but it was a random shaped building with four floors and an open courtyard in the middle. A pathway on either side of the main building connected the gym and performing arts area. The courtyard was open to the elements for days of pleasant weather, and with a retractable ceiling for rainy days. Throughout, it was a large garden used for various classes to identify different forms of plant life. It also hosted a recreational area, where the students could come to do their homework or eat lunch. His school had the most state-of-the-art equipment in every department. Each classroom held fifteen to twenty students; this set up had given the teachers better chances of interacting with each student. Due to its stellar curriculum, it was one of the top schools in the state in academics and sports. In the back of the school was a large stadium that was used for all sporting events and festivals.

Hopping out the car after parking, Dev ran to the front door, but tripped and landed in the bushes. Now beyond frustrated, he walked in the door, only to be stopped by Principal Weber. "Hello, Deveraux. Good morning to you. Nice job, last weekend on the four by one relay. The team is looking good. Keep up the excellent work. The first bell just rang for the first period. So don't let me keep you. Better get to class."

Groaning out loud, Dev began walking to his class, dreading what was about to happen. While he was walking, a thought occurred to him. Lately, his father had been teaching him how to influence the minds of those around him, but only after he swore not to use it for evil reasons. At the moment, to avoid detention and extra laps, it seemed like a good reason for trying. He figured he would compel his math teacher to make it seem that he had been in class on time. So, with that thought in mind, he walked into Mrs. Jones' class, clearing his mind and accessing his magic to accomplish the task.

"Well, well." His teacher crawled from her desk as he walked in. "Mr. Vanseal, how nice of you to join us finally. Please come get this detention slip before you head to your desk." Dev walked up to the desk, confident in his abilities as he let the magic flow through him. All he needed to do was make eye contact and use the magic to implant an image of him being on time.

He leveled his gaze and stared into her blue eyes, slowly pushing the image into her mind. As he stared at her, her eyes became slightly unfocused, and Dev smiled. His first attempt at compulsion seemed to be working. Then the unthinkable happened. From out of nowhere, he felt a presence push back on his mind, and the magic stopped.

Mrs. Jones' eyes became sharp and alert, and she thrust the detention slip at him. "Take the slip and go to your desk right now, Deveraux Vanseal."

His limbs seemed to move of his own accord as he took the pink slip from her hand. He strolled over to his desk and sat down. Only after he was in his seat did the alien presence leave his mind so that he could think clearly. Mystified at what had just happened and slightly terrified from the event, he quietly sat in the back of the class while Mrs. Jones droned on about equations. He only snapped out of it when Harley poked him in the arm with her pen. She was one of his best friends. He couldn't remember how Harley came into his life, but she had always been there. He saw she was eyeing him from her seat with her big round baby eyes.

Her new amber colored haircut went great with her dark brown complexion, Dev thought. Most guys only noticed her full-figured body, but she was more than that. She made all the guys in the class feel dumb, so no one ever looked at her as anything other than a walking answer sheet. While he was looking at her, she slipped a note into his hand. Trying to hide it under his desk, he opened it and read it.

Are you okay?

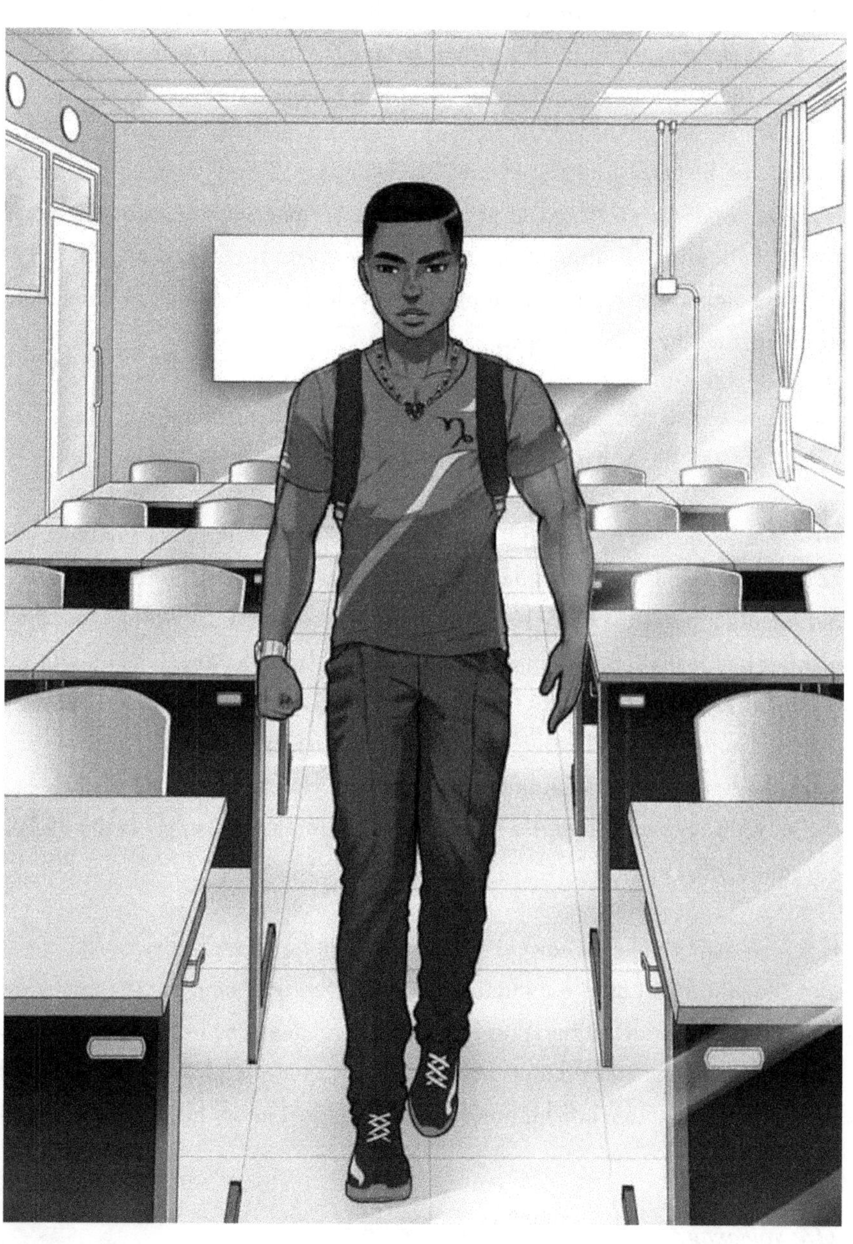

With a small smile, he wrote: *Yes, I'm fine, just irritated at having detention. Thanks for checking on me.* He handed the note back and watched the teacher again, wondering why the spell didn't work. From Harley's desk, he heard her say. "Anytime."

"Quiet!"

Dev and Harley both jumped at the command. "Since the valedictorians in the back are talking about how they love math so much. Surprise chalkboard pop quiz! Harley, you first." Said Mrs. Jones as she cleared the board for Harley's problem. Everyone in the class turned around to give them the death stare. Dev sank in his desk as Harley stood up in the front of the class to answer the question, "What is (6!)?"

Doing the math rather quickly in her head, she said, "Um (6!) is seven hundred and twenty."

"Shockingly, you are correct, Miss Braymark. I guess your chatting has helped you retain some of my teachings. Now Mr. Vanseal, your turn."

Walking up to take his turn, he heard Dagon say, *"Man, human school is so boring. I hate staying in this pendant all day."*

"Okay. Dev, what is the answer to (7+ (36/8))-14?"

With the class looking at him to get it right, Dev started to panic because he clearly didn't know the answer. So, he took a moment to look over at Keaton's desk. She was the best in the class. When he glanced, he could see the answer on her paper, so he did what most teens backed into a corner would do. "-2.5", Dev said as he looked at the stunned teacher.

"Well, congratulations, that's correct. How did you get that answer?" She asked.

Dev just stood there and said, "It's all up here." He smiled faintly, tapping his head. Then he headed back to his seat and sat down, trying not to give away the fact that he really didn't know how to do it.

She looked around the room for her next victim, and after calling name after name, the bell rang, saving all that was left in the room. "I want pages thirty-eight to forty-five read and all twenty-six questions done by tomorrow!" Mrs. Jones called out. Everyone grabbed their books and backpacks and headed out the door.

Dev chased down Harley and wrapped his arm over her shoulder to act like he was injured and needed help to his locker. Laughing, she wrapped her arm around his waist as they headed to their lockers. "So, Mr. Vanseal, would you like to tell me the real reason you were late this morning?" Harley asked as they swapped their math books out for their history ones.

"I was pulled over by a cop for speeding, I fell and tripped in the bush out front, and then stopped at the door by the principal." He said with a sigh. "Now, I'm stuck in detention with Mrs. Jones." He groaned, still confused by the strange occurrence when he tried to compel her.

Harley looked at him. "What was that longing look into the teacher's eyes for? I thought you liked Remy, not cougar math teachers."

Dev looked at her and smiled, "The teacher looked at me, and my alluring brown eyes electrified her. So get it right."

"Yeah right, you wish. I know you like them, older ladies." Harley said as she grabbed the last of her books.

"No, those older ladies like me. They are always looking for reasons to keep me after school, to have their way with me. It takes all my willpower to resist them. I know I'm a stud, which is why they try to make me their boyfriend." Dev replied with a smug grin.

Dagon chose that moment to pipe up. *"You wish you were a cougar chaser. Them women would eat you alive. Just remember how well your date went with Remy."* He quipped.

In the back of his head, Dev replied, *"Quiet, you, or I will leave you at home next time."*

"Ha! You wish you could leave me at home, but I would just find another way to follow you here and keep an eye on you," messaged Dagon back to him.

Dev had to stop himself from responding out loud to prevent himself from looking crazy in front of Harley and everyone else. Closing his locker door, he swung his backpack over his shoulder and headed to his next class with Harley in tow. "Hey, I am heading to the gym. I'll see you at lunch," said Harley.

Walking down the hall, Dev wondered if he could smile his way out of extra laps with the track coach for being late. As Dev sat in history, he blanked out, thinking about the day he could go to Zortega. He wondered what it was going to be like over there. What the trees looked like and the way the animals roamed around that weren't familiars. Oh, he even dreamed about getting to join his dad in the royal Slaven hall as he picked up his backpack to head to English.

Maybe he would get a robe too. Maybe there was like a predecessor day, and he would get to rule over his dad's region in Zortega. As the bell rang for dismissal of English class, he became unhappy that he had a book report to write on The Outsiders. He wondered why teachers always assigned homework over the weekends. There already wasn't enough time in the day to think about schoolwork, training, track practice, and trying to have a life.

Dev headed out and put his backpack in his locker and strolled over to lunch, "Dude, I heard they're having meatloaf surprise, my favorite. Did you know it's not real meat? The lunch lady told me it was squirrel from her homeland of Britain. It's called Burgoo," said Anthony, walking up to him.

Dev looked like he was going to puke as he called Anthony a sick man. "Like, how could you? Why would you? How am I friends with you?" Dev muttered as he looked around the corner to see what was on the food line before he chose the salad bar. He was struggling to hold down the chunks he would blow if he saw the meat. With Anthony in front of him in line, he slid the tray across the two silver bars, waiting to be served. He hoped the lunch lady was giving out spaghetti so Anthony wouldn't have ruined meatloaf for him for the rest of his life.

When he got to the lunch lady, he was relieved to see that there were sub sandwiches and quickly grabbed one of them to place on his tray. Happy with his choice, he headed back to the table and sat next to Anthony, who had saved him a seat next to him.

"So, what do you want to do after we get out of practice today, bro?" Anthony asked as he took a bite of his mystery meat lunch.

Dev just groaned in response and went on to tell him about getting detention from Mrs. Jones. He would also have to do extra laps for being late to track practice.

Anthony looked at him with mock pity and rubbed his forefinger and middle finger together. "I feel for you, bro. I really do. See how I'm playing the world's smallest violin for you?" Dev knocked his hand away and went back to his sandwich. He thought about being late to class and wondering why his magic hadn't worked. For the life of him, he couldn't understand it at all. It honestly scared him to think that there was something out there powerful enough to turn his magic against him. Or maybe he wasn't ready and had done it wrong. He really didn't know.

"So, what is up with you, lames?" Harley asked as she put down her lunch tray.

"We were actually talking about that one time at summer camp where you tried to cross the zip line and failed." Anthony said with a grin.

"Shut up, Anthony. At least I didn't end up upside down like some people we know." She said as she pointed over Dev's head. Sitting down, Dev glared in her direction.

"As both of you well know, that equipment was faulty, so any of the incidents in question were not my fault," said Dev.

Anthony laughed at his best friend's dark mood. "If I recall, you were calling for Gabby the whole way down."

Harley was laughing so hard she couldn't breathe as she remembered Dev flying down the zip line upside down and screaming in fear.

"I looovvvee you guys too," Dev said as he finished his sandwich. "Also, I didn't cry out for Gabby. I was saying how happy I was that they picked that activity. There's a difference."

The lunch bell rang for the second lunch period, and Dev realized it was time to go. It always seemed like it was never long enough to eat anything. Throwing away his tray, he joins the rest of the students as they walk out of the cafeteria.

"Man, can't this day be over." He heard Dagon say in his mind as he walked down the hall.

"Relax," he sent back. *"It will be over soon, just a few more classes, then we are done."* He smiled at the thought until he remembered the dreaded detention, as well as having to explain to his coach his reasons for being late to practice. With a sigh and a shake of his head, he headed to the basement for his weight training class.

ARIES

CHAPTER 5

ev grabbed his bag as the final class bell rang. His arms, back, and legs were still slightly sore from his earlier weight training class. Never again would he put three plates on a bar and lift it as a bet. He groaned inwardly as he walked up the stairs to his locker. He was in so much pain that he was almost glad for the quick break in detention before he had to go to track practice. However, he felt like a boss for being able to lift the weight, not just once or twice, but three times before he had to set it down. He smiled at the memory. He was so proud that he dropped the weight and strutted around the room, flexing his little muscles and posing in front of the mirror. As Dagon howled and messaged at him, *"Get it, muscles, get it! Drop that bead of sweat for all the ladies!"* Ignoring him, Dev's teacher called for the last round of maxing out. Out of time, he had to finish leg day on the squat bar. Dreading the last few minutes of class, he grabbed the homework from his math class and headed to detention. He winced in pain from the abuse his muscles had taken. He closed his locker and headed for his last class of the day. He really just wanted to get detention over and done with, so he no longer had to worry about it.

He reached his economics class and found his seat before the bell rang. As his teacher began to drone on and on about the latest project, Dev's eyes glazed over as he stared at the clock, willing it to move faster and end his misery. Before he knew it after many pencil taps and head nods, the final bell was ringing. His classmates were grabbing their stuff and racing for the door and the sweet freedom it promised. Grabbing his bag and slightly shocked that he had zoned out like that, Dev headed for Mrs. Jones' classroom for detention.

When he reached the classroom, Dev was surprised to see Harley and Anthony sitting at their seats, seeming to studiously work on their homework assignments. "Aww, Mr. Vanseal," said Mrs. Jones from her desk, "Nice of you to finally join us. Please take your seat and no talking." With that, she turned her attention back to grading the stack of tests on her desk. Dev headed to his desk, but not before he stopped in front of the two of them. They smiled at him from their seats.

"What are you guys doing here?" He said in alarm. They both just laughed at him, Harley responded, "You didn't think we would just let you rot in here on your own, did you?" Anthony, still chuckling, chimed in, "Yea, so when you left after lunch this afternoon. I headed back to the cafeteria, and with Harley's help, managed to start the greatest food fight ever seen! I heard Remy Phillips talking about you, still upset about your date, and calling you a loser. So, I made it my personal mission to smear chocolate pudding and hot mashed potatoes all over her hair! She tried to get me back with her smoothie while her friends started throwing food off their trays at me. Harley yelled for me to duck and then threw her entire tray of spaghetti high into the air, causing it to rain down on all of them! That was all it took for the other kids to start taking shots at each other. Food was flying everywhere, and I had to duck under the table to stay clean! From what I hear, they're still scraping food off the ceiling. With that stunt, we managed to score ourselves a one-way ticket to detention city. Population us!" Anthony finished his statement with a broad grin and pointed his thumbs at himself and Harley. It shocked Dev that his friends had gone through such lengths to get themselves stuck in detention with him, their loyalty really moved him.

"Mr. Vanseal, if you would be so kind as to go to your seat. This is detention, not a social hour." They all jumped as Mrs. Jones began to reprimand them, so Dev rushed to his seat. Walking in the door stood Remy, she was covered in stains from the food fight that his friends mentioned. She looked like someone who had been in a car trying to enjoy her fast food and shake when the driver suddenly slammed on the brakes. From the look on her face, she was dying inside. She always worried about being clean and presentable to the world.

"Miss Phillips, I do not want my desk looking like a napkin. Please go change into your gym clothes and report to the other detention class," said Mrs. Jones.

Laughing at how annoyed she looked, Dev pulled out his homework and tried to focus on finishing it. However, no matter how hard he tried, he couldn't concentrate and kept focusing on the clock, wishing and willing it to go faster. While he stared at it, a thought occurred to him. He would just use his magic to make it seem as if time had sped by. After thinking it over, he accessed his magic and nudged the hand so that the clock read 3:55 pm. Smiling, he looked at Mrs. Jones and cleared his throat. "Mrs. Jones?"

"What is it, Mr. Vanseal? Shouldn't you be focusing on your work?" She asked, with a glance in his direction.

"Yes ma'am," he said with a smile. "I just wanted to point out it's about time for us to leave, is all." Harley and Anthony looked up in surprise, and Mrs. Jones raised her eyebrows slightly as she stared at the wall clock.

She turned back to Dev with a glare and said, "I don't know what you're trying to pull young man, but it won't work. As you can see, it has only been ten minutes. You still have fifty minutes to go. Now, if you are done wasting my time, please return to your work." Dev looked at her in shock, not believing what he was hearing. He then turned his head to the clock on the wall and almost stopped breathing. The clock somehow had been turned back to its original time, despite the magic he used. He couldn't believe what was going on and began to slightly panic at the thought that maybe there was something wrong with him.

"Yo, Dagon, why can't I use my magic? Did you turn the clock back? I mean come on man, I can feel my calves burning now from all the stadiums I'm going to have to do if I don't get to practice," messaged Dev.

As Dagon was letting out a big yawn, he said, *"Nope, not me. I was sleeping, and, FYI, if your powers weren't working, I wouldn't be able to hear you message me."*

Looking around the room, Dev tried to think of one more way to try and get out of detention. A light bulb went off in his head. Everyone couldn't do their homework if the lights went off. Dev focused really hard, connecting with his powers, and messaged Anthony to tell Harley to get ready to run for the door on his signal. Anthony looked at him and seen he was focused, so he started tapping kids on the shoulder, one by one, to get them to put their books away. Holding his hands apart on his desk, he begins to close them. As he closed them, the lights flicker like the bulbs were dying. When his hands finally met, the lights went out. Mrs. Jones looked stunned that he had managed to poke a hole through her magic free zone after his clock stunt. When the lights went out, Anthony and Dev dashed for the door and everyone that wasn't stunned bolted with them. "Class, come back here!" Mrs. Jones said as she stood up to command the room, but before she could blink, most of the class was gone, so she just let the other three go early as well.

After booking it to the gym, Dev threw his books in his gym locker and changed his clothes. Before running out of the room, he swiped a glance at a mirror and noticed his shirt was on backwards. He was frustrated with trying to hop on one foot to put his shoes on like a retarded kangaroo. He snapped his fingers to turn his shirt around before hitting the double door. Afterward, Dev busted through the doors and ran down the hill, like someone had set off a rogue firecracker near him. He fell and stumbled on to the track into the back of the coach's legs.

"Um, hey there, Coach Hunter! How are you doing?" Slightly chuckling at Dev's grand entrance, Coach Hunter helped him to his feet. As soon as he made sure his star runner was okay, the coach lost all humor.

"Don't bother coming up with any sorry excuse for being late. I already know exactly where you were, Vanseal." The coached growled as he glared at him. "So, for getting yourself into an unacceptable situation and having everyone wait for your pretty self to show up. You will be running the stadium from now until I get tired. Oh, and after every fifteen steps, I need twenty good leg squats." Dev looked at him in absolute shock and terror at the thought of all the running he would have to do. "Now stop gawking at me and get moving now! Drop down into starting formation! Go, go, go!" He blew the whistle as Dev grabbed his block, turned it towards the stadium stairs, and then got in his stirrups. Coach Hunter had timed his release. As the whistle blew again, he takes off running to the first step of the forty rows of seats.

While Dev begins his grueling run, he saw Harley was at the top of the stadium watching him, still amused by the crazy escape they had made from detention. Looking around the field, she saw the other sports teams practicing and the cheerleading team working on their new routine. Harley glared down at the squad as they practiced different moves and stunts for their next competition. Not a single member of that squad had ever treated her kindly, even going as far as to ban her from tryouts only because they thought she was weird.

Thinking back to when she had first started high school, all she had wanted to do was join the cheerleading squad. She had watched every routine from the past six years and practiced every move until she had memorized and perfected all of them. When the day of tryouts came, she walked to the gym only to see the whole team standing at the doors, almost like they were waiting for her. The captain and co-captain, who just happened to be sisters, stood with their arms crossed, smirking at her as she walked up. Marie and Stephanie James had made it their mission to give Harley as much trouble as possible from the moment they first saw her. Marie, at the time, had been a senior getting ready to graduate. She was easily one of the tallest girls in school at almost six feet.

Marie had long black hair, fair skin, and cold hard green eyes. Even when she smiled, it seemed dark and threatening. However, for some reason, all the boys swooned over her at every turn. Stephanie was a smaller version of her sister except with hard blue eyes instead of green and very heavy set.

When Harley saw them standing there, she groaned inwardly, already gearing herself for a fight. "Where do you think you're going, freak?" Marie snarled at her as she approached. Harley had never been one to back down from a challenge, so she walked right up to them. "I heard cheerleading tryouts were today, so I wanted to participate." Stephanie started to laugh, as did the other girls who wanted to get into her good graces. "We don't have any room for freaks and weirdos like you. So, why don't you just go on and leave." With that, all the girls turned and headed into the gym. When Harley tried to follow them, Stephanie and Marie blocked her path and pushed her to the ground. With one last look of contempt, they turned and walked away, locking the gym door behind them.

"Move, Move, Move! I'm not seeing too much hustle, Vanseal! Pull the lead out, or I'll add jumping jacks to your caseload! Move them buns private, faster!" Yelled Coach Hunter from the stands as he tried to watch Dev while still conducting relays.

As Harley snapped out of it, she realized Dev's labored breathing as he ran past her and on to the next set of squats. She decided to help Dev put himself out of his misery, but she couldn't let anyone see. Harley had to do something quickly because Anthony was coming. He always came to sit with her while she waited around for her brother Bowen and his best friend Marcus to get done with Rugby practice, so they could walk home.

Raising her hands halfway to the skies, she softly whispered a few words to make the clouds start crying. Hell, it was fun to rain on her brother's parade and ruin the cheerleader's day in the process. With rain coming down, Harley took much pleasure in making it almost look like a hurricane. The cheerleader's skirts were blowing upward for all to see while they slid in the mud, trying to find shelter.

"Oh no, your weenies, don't. If it ain't raining, we ain't training, and Dev, for you, ain't no rain, ain't no muscle gain," Yelled Coach Hunter over the thunder Harley had added. Since he had insisted on still making the teams run, she decided to throw in some artistic lightning that had very particular targets.

Soon, jagged blue-and-white bolts of lightning began flashing down on the field. Most of it seemed to be aimed at the cheerleaders, but they were ducking and dodging them while also screaming at the top of their lungs for shelter.

Coach Hunter had to dive to the side to avoid an unusually large bolt that left a significant black burn mark where he had been standing. "Okay, okay! Time to go, everyone inside. DOUBLE TIME! MOVE!"

Everyone was already moving towards the gym to take cover from the barrage of lightning raining from the heavens. The coach took one more look around to see if anyone was left. His eyes bugged out when he looked towards the top of the stadium.

"VANSEAL!" He roared. "WHAT ON EARTH DO YOU THINK YOU'RE DOING?" Harley looked around and saw Dev practically flying up the steps. Harley didn't understand why he wasn't heading down towards the gym. It became clear where Dev was going when he reached the top of the stairs. He raced straight towards her at an inhuman speed. When he reached her, without even stopping, he scooped her up and headed for the next set of stairs. However, instead of running down the stairs, in an amazing acrobatic move, he jumped up and landed on the railing, surfed the entire way down with Harley clutched to his chest. When they reached the bottom, he executed a triple somersault and landed on the track. Without breaking stride, he raced towards the doors of the gym where Coach Hunter was waiting with the door open. As soon as they entered the hall, Harley released the magic, and the storm immediately dissipated, much to the shock of everyone.

"Are you okay? Why were you just sitting there?" Said Dev.

"The storm wasn't that bad. I had an umbrella, plus you know I like thunderstorms. I was fine." She said as she shoved him away from her.

"Fine. Next time, I'll let you become Albert Einstein's sister," Dev said. He was grumpy because he was soaking wet, and he could feel the cramping in his legs. He went to sit down next to Anthony as he tried to catch his breath.

"Yo, Torte, let's go! Mom says we have to be home because of the warning!" Bowen shouted over the crowd. Turning to face her brother, she looked super annoyed to see Marcus, his sleazy know it all best friend. He was always hitting on her behind Bowen's back, and when she tried to tell him, he always told her that his friend was off-limits, like she wanted him.

"I'm coming. Let me grab my stuff and tell Anthony were not walking home with him," messaged Harley to Bowen.

"Hey, did you hear that?" Said Anthony.

"Hear what?" Said Dev.

"I don't know. It sounded like someone was talking to me, but no one's here but you and me," said Anthony.

"Dude, you're losing it, but go walk Harley home. Imma get home the expressway," said Dev, picking up his bag and in full aches and pains.

Dev walked down the hallway and then slipped into the music hall. He pulled out his pocket watch and opened it. Summoning his power, he flashed into the mirror that was locked inside of it. Appearing in the walkway of his home, Dev hobbled to his room and plopped face down on the bed, crying out, "Gabby! Come heal me, please! I've been in a fight with some stairs." After a few moments passed, his door opened.

"Dev? Honey? Are you alright?" Asked his mother. He tried to turn to look at her, but every movement caused him immense anguish. So, he just spoke into his pillow.

"I'm fine, Mom, just in a lot of pain," Dev murmured.

"What's wrong with my baby? Where are you hurting? I will heal you."

"I just lost a fight with some stairs is all. Nothing serious."

Gasping, Selena went to his side. "Did someone push you? Tell me who it was, and I will tear them apart." She growled.

Dev almost laughed, but even that made him groan in pain. "No one pushed me. I just had to do extra laps because I was late for track practice." He said.

"You must have been running really hard to be this worn out." She took a whiff of his clothes and pinched her nose. "You definitely smell like it! Why didn't you shower when you got home?"

Dev rolled his eyes. "I barely had the energy to make it to the bed. A shower really wasn't on my list of priorities. Can you please heal me?"

"Okay hold still." His mother said as she grabbed one of her feathers and crushed it between her palms. Her palms began to glow with a soft white light as they hovered over Dev's body, and he could feel the pain lifting. "You really should make your personal hygiene a priority."

"Yes, yes, Mother, I know. I will take a shower as soon as you're done, okay?" He closed his eyes and relaxed as his mother healed him. Soon, he could sit up without an ounce of pain and gave his mother a hug in thanks. I don't know what I would do without you, Mom," said Dev.

Selena smiled at her son's compliment, then snapped her fingers. The next thing Dev knew, he was in the shower fully clothed with ice-cold water splashing down on him.

"MOM!!!" Cried out Dev.

"Make sure to wash behind your ears, son." His mother called out as she walked out the door with a laugh.

CHAPTER 6

While Dev's school days repeated throughout the week, Dev was excited to finally be able to turn his alarm clock off because today was a teacher workday. This meant a day of no homework other than his English paper and plenty of time to sleep in. Soon, the aroma of pancakes, fried and scrambled eggs, and Selena's famous Zortegan coffee filled the home. Smelling the food through the cracks in the door made Dev slowly began to wake up to a hungry stomach.

Tiye was sent to wake everyone up, so she banged her tail on every child's door like an annoying alarm clock. "Kids, come eat! Gabby made breakfast!" Shouted Selena as she took more sips of her coffee.

"Family meeting!" Messaged Rodney to everyone in the home. It was time to discuss the warning and what this meant for the family.

"Oh, come on, Dad! It's Friday. There's no school, and I just wanna relax before the track meet Sunday," messaged Dev back.

"You can rest later, I promise. Right now, there are important matters to discuss. NOW GET UP!" The last command was roared into Dev's mind, and he almost jumped out his skin and right on to the bedroom floor.

Rubbing his head, Dev sat up and groaned at the injustice of his day off being interrupted in such a messed-up manner. While rubbing the sleep out of his eyes, he heard a soft crunching noise. He removed his hands and looked around the room and saw his father's familiar, Yendor, with his back to him and his head in the closet as he chewed on something. With a sick feeling of dread, Dev walked over to the closet to see the blasted goat chewing on a few specialized magazines that Anthony had managed to obtain for him. Dev looked in disbelief and fear at the shredded pieces that fell from Yendor's mouth and landed on the floor. He was shocked at the fact that the goat had found the magazines in the first place. More fear came from the fact that if Yendor had seen them, his father had seen them as well. He looked down at the floor again, trying to make out the smiling faces of the swimsuit-clad or semi-undressed women, finding only saliva-covered scraps of paper. Yendor eyed him with disdain as he let out a loud bleat, then floated through the window.

Picking up the pieces and placing them in the trash, Dev looks out the window. In the tree was Eve, who was just looking at him with her piercing blue eyes, while her head was tilted to the side. Walking over to the window, he shuts the blinds as loudly as he can. "Can't a teenager get any privacy around here?" Grumbled Dev. Heading back to his closet, he pulls out a pair of black-and-red sweatpants and a black sleeveless hoodie and puts them on. Once dressed, he headed down the stairs and towards the dining room.

Walking in, he looked around at his family, who are all seated and enjoying the amazing spread that was placed on the table. Dev could see pancakes and waffles stacked high, bowls of light and fluffy biscuits smothered in butter and honey, plates of sausage, bacon, and eggs with steam rising from them. Bowls of fresh fruits, like strawberries, apples, mangleberries, grapes, and blackberries, were all over the table.

Taking a seat next to the twins, who both seemed to be scarfing down a cinnamon roll the size of a frisbee, he grabbed a plate and began to pile it high with food. As his mouth became dry, he grabbed a glass of apple juice for himself. Looking up, he saw his mother and aunt bickering back and forth over some topic he couldn't understand. Both were still dressed in silk bed robes, looking radiant in the morning sun.

Gabby was bustling around the kitchen, sending more floating dishes out to replace ones that had been emptied. Gabby's kitchen was her domain. It was a chef's kitchen with a huge island and the cleanest pots you could lick off of, even though Dev wouldn't dare try to. The walnut wood panel cabinets towered to the ceiling, and the island was always topped with goodies for the family to eat. Some days she would be dancing on the mop and singing to the broom while cleaning after every meal. After finishing a new batch of goodies, Gabby came out of the swinging door, asking if the family wanted thirds.

Dev was digging into his meal, trying to make more room as he heard his father clear his throat. He looked up at him and saw him staring back with a gleam of amusement in his eyes. "So, Dev, Yendor here tells me he found something exciting in your closet." A small smile slowly played across Rodney's face as Dev's eyes widened in fear.

"I don't know what you're talking about." Dev replied, while shoveling food into his mouth, trying not to look guilty.

Rodney chuckled softly to himself at his son's discomfort and decided to drop the subject for now. He decided now was a good enough time to let the family know what had transpired at the council meeting. He placed his drink down and softly tapped his fork on the plate to get everyone's attention. "Can I have your attention, please?" Said Rodney.

Everyone had almost ignored his first request as some continued eating. Eland had made it her mission to sign across the table at her brother about why he was ignoring her message. Ezekiel was clearly messaging his mother to get her to stop. Lesley sat in pure boredom as she tried not to say a quickly witted comment to his question. While waiting for the family to listen up, Dev looked at his Mom, trying to tell the twins to stop silently messaging across the table. Scowling at the kids, Selena said, "Children, I need you to listen to your dad!"

"Last Friday, I was called to a council meeting, and it seems there're some bad things are happening in this realm. They are Zortegan-related, and it's becoming pretty dangerous. So, the council has decided that all Zortegans be on high alert and to set all their wards. We will place a curfew on the kids, especially the ones with no familiars," said Rodney.

Laughing with much joy, Lesley took another gulp of her mimosa. "See? I knew it."

He waved her off. "Lesley, no one was ever going to take your little gossip travel club seriously. From now on, the twins will not go anywhere without a chaperone, and Deveraux will be home immediately after track practices. All familiars will take turns on guard till after the Kaloke ceremony. Whatever this thing is, or who these people are, they want to gain power. That ceremony is one of our most powerful exchanges of magic energy. Also, son, if we are called to fight, I will have to go, so your successor training starts now. Meet me out back after breakfast."

Dev looked up from his fully loaded plate only to have fear cross his mind. His dad was going to have so much fun torturing him with the Zortegan way of battle fighting. Suniva is the casting of spells in the physical form that his dad was teaching him. Suniva consisted of high intensity moves while simultaneously casting elemental spells. His dad had upped his training when he was about the twin's ages, but even more shortly after forging his own weapon. Dev was determined to learn his own style similar to his dad's, so he could beat him at his own game one day.

"Don't worry, son, I promise I might go easy on you," Rodney said with a small, evil smile on his face.

Dev tried to continue eating his food, but couldn't manage to swallow another bite. The thought of his father's training running through his mind made him lose his appetite. For as long as he could remember, every Saturday and Sunday morning, he and his dad would head out back to train in magic and combat.

Over the years, he had gotten pretty good, but he knew he was still no match for his dad. He could recall so many times where his dad had used his training as a way to just beat him up until he learned to defend himself. He remembered one particularly bad day after he had gotten a few bad grades. He had spent most of the day upside down, hanging in midair while his dad just made him bob up and down around the room.

Shaking his head to remove that thought, he continued to try to focus on his breakfast. After finishing up, he headed to his room to change into his training clothes. His father always liked to wear the more traditional outfit, which looked like a karate outfit from an old television show he used to watch. It consisted of a sleeveless black silk shirt and pants set with a blue stripe going up the seam of each leg and on the lapel. He had a blue sash tied around his waist and a white cloak like shawl over his chest.

He remembered the first time he had seen his father in that outfit. He loved seeing the moons on his cloak that represented the many battles he had fought while training to be the head council member of the Capricorns. He had laughed so hard thinking his dad was going to attack him, but he had stopped laughing, however, when his father gave out a shout. Right before his eyes, he released his magical power. It circled around his feet like smoke. It was all so reminiscent of watching the characters from TV shows release their own energy when they began fighting. Dev had to put his arm in front of his face to shield himself from his dad's crazy magic power as it pulsed off him in waves.

After about thirty seconds, Dev couldn't stand it anymore and fainted from the sheer force of it. The next thing he knew, his dad was standing over him, looking concerned while shaking him to wake him up. Groaning as he sat up, he looked at his dad. "Jeez, dad, I didn't know you could go crazy like that."

His father laughed at that and said, "Where do you think those old TV shows got the inspiration from? When we first visited Earth, we weren't cautious like we are now, and they became obsessed, so we had to use the Legions powers to help humans forget us." Dev looked surprised at that piece of knowledge.

"You can't be serious," said Dagon.

His dad just shook his head. "The magic we have is limitless. We can do just about anything, so most of the anime shows you see literally are inspired by the powers and abilities that we have. It's called unleashing Novalo Gama. Which borders on the point of an atomic bomb because our power are just as destructive."

Dev smiled at the memory as he finished changing into his workout clothes, which for him was a sleeveless T-shirt and basketball shorts. Once fully dressed, he headed out back to the training area.

Standing in the backyard, he portaled through two distressed trees outside in the yard. The training grounds were an area of woodlands about the size of a football field ringed with gigantic boulders. The only way to enter was through a small tunnel hidden behind a door like rock. Every time Dev would enter the grounds, he felt like he was entering an ancient world. The slate gray boulders were at least fifty feet high, all ending in jagged points on the very top.

Stepping out from the tunnel, he saw his father standing at the other end, meditating peacefully. Dev wasn't fooled by any of this. He could feel the power radiating off of him. There used to be one point in time when Dev couldn't even begin to stand up against this level of power. He knew his father was barely using half his magic.

Stretching his arms over his head one by one, making sure to crack the neck muscle in-between, Dev then jogged in place for a second or two. Squatting down, Dev then decided to make sure his legs were limber and up to the task of exchanging blows with his dad. Feeling the earth through his hands as he

concentrated his reserve toward the fight, and it made Dev feel a little more confident.

Walking towards his father, he stopped a few yards away from him and began to release his own magical energy until it was at the same level. Slowly, his dad opened his eyes, and the two stared at each other. Their energies raged against the flow, with sparks flying in the air. The wind howled around them without any kind of warning, Rodney sprang forward and pulled his fist back for a punch, putting as much power as possible behind it. Just as he was about to connect with Dev's face, he was suddenly gone.

Without skipping a beat, Rodney landed and threw his arm up to block the roundhouse kick aimed at his head. The amount of power behind it was staggering and almost caused his arm to go numb from shock. Fighting against the pain, he grabbed his son's foot in one hand and his leg in the other and threw him across the field. As soon as he released him, he bolted after him, ready to throw another attack as soon as Dev touched down. However, Dev was ready for the move that was coming as soon as his feet touched the ground.

Using his momentum, he threw his back over and began to execute a continuous stream of backflips. Dev traveled further down the field until he was almost at some boulders. Dev had devised a plan while continuing to dodge his father's attacks. Focusing his energy to his feet, he shot forward when he touched the wall, ready to unleash his own attacks. Rodney was slightly taken aback at the abrupt change, but he still braced himself for the collision. Rodney sidesteps and reached out to grab Dev's hand, but to his shock, he felt himself being grabbed. Using the force of his jump, Dev grabbed his father around the wrist and while, placing his other hand on his chest, threw his dad back the other way down the field. Knowing better than to let his father have any room to breathe or think, he sprang after him, ready to deliver another blow while his dad was disoriented. As he charged forward, he felt a shift in his father's energy, and he stopped short of attacking him.

A second later, in the spot where he would have been, a massive lightning bolt blazed from the sky and struck the ground, leaving behind a ten-foot-wide circle of blackened earth. Staring in disbelief at this raw display of power, Dev looked up to see his father on his feet and staring at him. However, where his eyes used to be a dark brown, was only two spots of lightning. The very force of nature seemed to have adhered to his body with little streaks sparkling from head to toe. His hands were also no longer empty. Now he held his signature weapon that he used only when in intense combat. They were a pair of Sai knives, sharp on all three points, and imbued with his father's magical energy and lightning powers.

His father was one of the most powerful earth elementals that could use lightening that had never been born according to many. Very few could stand up to him when he was like this. Dev had absolutely no fantasies of being able to defeat his father when he was all charged up. Despite the fear coursing through him, he felt great pride that his father had deemed him worthy enough to use this form against him. Instead of backing down, it was only fair that he began to raise his power level so that he was at full strength. Even though he was still working on it, he released his own unique ability. Where his father could control earth and lightning, he could create and control earth and fire. As his power began to rise, balls of fire fell to the earth. Dev was engulfed in a blazing inferno that caused him no pain. He did, however, refrain from calling forth his own signature weapon. He wanted to test himself to see how long he could last at this level. He had no illusions of winning, but he would not go down without one hell of a fight.

Again, the two warriors stared at each other as their energies crackled around them, wrestling for dominance. Then with a signal that only they acknowledged, they had sprung at each other, howling to the skies. They met in a clash of blazing heat and blinding light, throwing punches and kicks. They continued many combos only to be blocked and dodged from one another. Both flew around the field, trading blows of various intensities to the point that it seemed the very grounds would be destroyed.

As Rodney took a chance to lunge at Dev to plunge a Sai into his side, Dev dropped down and, using his legs, swept his father's legs out from under him. Using his hands, he pushed up and spun in midair to scissor-kick his father to the ground. As Rodney hit the ground, he sank into the earth and moved himself to a different part of the field. He knew that Dev couldn't find him because once a member of his house used this move; they were completely invisible and tough to detect. Earth was his family's natural element and could be used at any given time for attack or defense. Rodney watched Dev turn in small circles, trying to pinpoint his location while also composing himself for the next attack. As he watched, he swelled with pride at how powerful his son had become, how determined and brave he was to continue this bout.

Most others would have tucked their tail and run as soon as Rodney had released this power. His son, however, had stood tall and made himself ready to face whatever was to come. He was truly shocked at the level Dev was currently at, especially since Dev could almost match him move for move. Dev's flame made it almost impossible to really attack him, and if it wasn't for Rodney's lightning, making him faster, he would have taken a lot more hits to the face and body.

Rodney was pretty much camouflaged by the rock. So, he decided to have a little fun with Dev, which meant dodge ball, lightning-style. Moving the ground of the training field at his command, Rodney made the ground uneven while Dev jumped from spot to spot, keeping his balance. Rodney gave him a harder task by shooting continuous bolts of lightning at him. Dev thought his dad was rather mean for playing this dirty trick and decided to return the favor.

Using his flames, he heated the ground to an unbearable level. Rodney shot into the sky like a rocket to escape the heat. When his father flew into the air, Dev raced after him, ready to land a blow to the back of his head. However, Rodney had other ideas. He flew towards the ground, and with Dev in tow, he struck his foot down and used the ground to form hands to trap him.

With Dev pinned, Rodney took his Sai and slashed his own son across his back with no remorse. Screaming out in sheer pain, Dev's eyes glowed green, and he released an explosion of power, and the earth's hands crumbled. He dropped to the ground and landed in a crouched position, tired and wounded. That move had taken a toll on him. He was losing strength and was struggling to keep going at this level.

His father shouted, "Had enough, boy? I will not go easy today!"

Trying to stand up, he looked around for his father. He spotted him shooting across the field with his knives, ready to plunge them into his chest. Dev raised his arms as his father struck, and there was a clang. Rodney's knives clashed against Dev's own signature weapon. In his hands was a sword that was black as night, but it was also known as a Japanese Katana, except the blade was ringed with black flames. The hilt wrapped in white cloth was the only bit of color on it. The pommel had a black golf ball-sized diamond attached to it.

Jumping back to try another angle, Rodney glanced at Dev's blade and how strong he made it, before disappearing into the Earth. "Bring it on, old man!" Dev said with a cocky teenage strength in his voice. Kneeling on the ground, Dev took a silent stance, waiting for his dad to reveal himself so he could strike.

"Oh, gentlemen? The lady of the house said to come eat. Training time is over," messaged Gabby to both men. Even while training, the men still had to be available if there was a strike on the home. Gabby was like everyone's message board, roaring out updates. With both men pretending like they were too busy to speak up or too sneaky to give their location up, neither one answered her.

"Found you!" Dev said as he slashed his sword through the air at what looked like dust clouds. It would have almost connected if it hadn't been a decoy.

"Know your enemy, son." Rodney aerial flipped backwards and kicked him into the air, but as he flew, Dev rolled over and darted back at him with the sword in full swipes. From the far distance, he heard a whisper and a clap that echoed through the arena. A force field dispersed around them, stopping them

in their tracks. They look over and saw Gabby walking toward them with a very annoyed look on her face. Her eyes were fully electrified white with her face tattoo just as vibrant.

"Why do you make me repeat myself?" Gabby asked. She was no ordinary nanny. She was a Legion. Legions possessed the powers of at least four or five zodiacs lines combined. It was like the story of how humans came from Adam and Eve. The Zodiacs came from the Legions, even though all of their ancestors weren't all extinct. The few that were left chose a zodiac family to guide and raise. Some got lucky like the Capricorns, and some didn't, like the Geminis. That was why they said Geminis were so crazy. All of them swore to limit their magic and just have a simple life, but that didn't mean she was one to mess with. Taking her on was like a car on a train track, which was suicide because everyone knows who wins that fight.

"I SAID DINNER IS READY!" Gabby said as she whistled one more time, which broke the force field. Wrapping vines around their legs, she dragged them down and outside the portal door. "I want you inside and cleaned up! That will be enough magic for this evening!" She said as she kissed both men on the cheek while dropping them on their feet. Scurrying off, she then walked out of the tunnel to go fix the twins' plates.

"Dad, you just let an old lady punk you like that?" Said Dev.

"Umm, son..." Before he could warn him, Gabby was behind Dev like a ghost fully geared up in a terrifying magical display.

"You wanna repeat that, boy?" Gabby said, snapping her fingers. She programmed him for after- dinner bunion duty.

Rodney walked past to go clean up, shaking his head. "You still have so much to learn about life, son. Oh, and remember to clean up the shavings when you're done."

CANCER

CHAPTER 7

The next morning, Dev woke up with a strong smell of lavender oil all over his hands. He shuddered at the memories of the night before, rubbing Gabby's crusty feet as punishment for his rude comment. He swore from that moment on, he would never call any woman old again. Trying to clear his head of the overwhelming scent that plagued him, he rolled out of bed and began to get ready for the day. He had to meet up with Harley and Anthony at the mall to get tuxedos and to find a dress for Harley. With the date slowly coming closer, he knew that he should really start getting his stuff together, sooner rather than later.

"Hey, buddy. How did you sleep?" Dagon asked as he floated through the air behind him. Dev grimaced as he recalled the horrifying dreams of being stuck in a land of crusty feet with no escape.

"Not as well as I would have liked, but I'm okay." He grabbed a pair of faded black jeans and pulled them up, along with a black hooded sleeveless shirt. He ran a brush over his head, washed his face, and then headed downstairs to grab a quick bite to eat. As he entered the living room, he saw his father sitting on the couch, reading a newspaper. His dad chuckled when he saw him enter.

"I could smell you as soon as you entered the hall. So, how was your first time?" He said with a laugh. Dev glared as his father started to crack up.

"You know, you could have given me a warning." He said as he watched his dad almost die from laughter.

"I tried to, but it was too late. You had already sealed your fate." His father responded as he held on to his sides. Shaking his head, Dev walked towards the kitchen, mumbling about the injustice of the entire situation. Grabbing an apple and some orange juice, Dev headed out the door and started walking around to the front of the house. When he saw his dad's truck blocking him in, a thought occurred to him. With a dark smile, he backed up to around the side of the house so he wouldn't be seen by anyone who just happened to be walking by. Doing one more check to make sure no one was around, he pulled out his pocket watch. Closing his eyes, he focused only on Anthony's room and teleported himself there. The sight that greeted him when he materialized would forever be locked in Dev's mind.

"Gaaahhh!" He screamed as he covered his face with his hands, trying to banish the demonic sight before him.

"Dude!! What the hell are you doing in here?!" Anthony screamed. Dev slowly pulled his hands away from his face to see if he was really seeing the frightening image before him. There, in all his glory, was Anthony in a leotard, wearing a headband and wristbands in front of his television. He was following a female aerobics instructor move for move. At the moment, he seemed to be trying to tie himself into a pretzel.

Dev took all this in and did the only thing he could do. He fell to the floor, laughing and banging his fists. He laughed for so long; it became hard to breathe, and tears were streaming down his face. Finally, when he had managed to calm himself down, he risked another peek. The horrible sight of his best friend still

in that position was too much to handle at the moment, so he burst into laughter all over again.

Dagon took this moment to come out of his charm. *"What on earth is all this racket about? I'm trying to..."* He paused in mid-sentence as he took in the sight before him, not truly understanding what he saw. He shook his head back and forth, trying to make sense of what he was seeing. This only sent Dev into more hysterics. He then began to howl, almost like a wolf himself. He was laughing so hard his sides began to hurt.

"Okay, okay, if you're done enjoying the show, do you mind not laughing so hard at my exercise routine?" Said Anthony.

Dev finally calmed down and took in large gulps of air as he sat up. "I'm sorry, bro. I just can't believe what I'm seeing." He said as he wiped his face. "What on earth are you doing?" Said Anthony. Taking advantage of this opportunity, he pulled his phone out and quickly snapped two pictures of Anthony before he could move out the way. He swore that he would show Harley these photos when they got to the mall.

After disentangling himself, Anthony stood up and stretched, then headed to his closet to change. "If you must know, it's my daily workout routine. It helps me stay fit and flexible for the ladies." He said as he grabbed clothes to get ready. "I thought we agreed you would warn me first before just appearing in my room all willy-nilly."

Dev thought about that for a second and realized they had. "My bad, I forgot. I was just ready to get moving so we could get to the mall. Harley's called me five times today already to make sure that we would be there to help her pick out a dress. So, I figured I could just teleport us both there. That way, it would be faster, and we could beat the rush."

Anthony had changed into a thin hoodie and jeans. "Okay, I see your point, but next time, seriously, warn me first before you jump into my room, or I may be liable to beat you over the head," Anthony said as he grabbed his wallet and keys off the desk in the corner of the room. Dev chuckled at the empty threat and again apologized before grabbing Anthony's shoulder and flashing them to the mall.

He transported them into the men's restroom by the food court. Taking a look around, he was glad to see that there was no one around to see them. He pulled out his phone to find that he had missed another three calls from Harley. Growling in annoyance, he called her back to let her know they were in the mall. As soon as his phone made the first ring, Harley answered, and Dev had to pull the phone away from his ear.

"WHERE THE HELL ARE YOU?! GET DOWN TO THE FOOD COURT NOW!!!" She screamed.

"Okay, okay, we are here in the bathroom, and we are coming out now. Where are you located?" Dev asked once she had finally calmed down. He heard her take a breath and release it before responding.

"I'm standing next to the escalators near the Burger Fool. Please hurry. There are so many students here, and I want to find a decent dress before they are all gone," said Harley.

"Dude, how do you do that without barfing? I feel like my stomach is being put back together in pieces," groaned Anthony.

Dev grabbed Anthony and dragged him out from the bathroom stall and over to the escalators where he saw Harley standing. Shuffling from foot to foot with anxiety, she grabbed them both by the hand and pulled them to the first floor. They were floored by the number of students there were in every shop that sold any kind of dress or tuxedo. Dev began to despair that he would ever find anything decent enough to wear for prom, let alone find anything for Harley. He could see fights breaking out over dresses between girls, and students being thrown out of the stores for misbehaving. He was half tempted to place a shield spell around the three of them to keep them safe from the craziness.

Walking into one of the most popular discount department stores, Harley looked around, and instead of backing down, she got a determined glint in her eye. Grabbing both boys by the arm, she dragged them into the mass of flying limbs and screaming girls. While trying to escape for the next three hours, Anthony and Dev were subjected to everything from swinging arms to sharp manicured nails. Kicking feet, and all other forms of bodily harm at the hands of hormonal teenage girls trying to find that perfect dress for their perfect night.

It was shockingly funny to the boys that Harley was one of the wildest of them all. She was a force of nature, grabbing every single dress that caught her eye. On at least two occasions, they could see her staring down other girls reaching for the same dress. It didn't make any sense that she was so hostile.

Harley doesn't even have a date, Dev thought. But there she was, rolling on the floor with another girl, trying to rip an outfit from her grips. After about the sixth dress, Harley finally landed on a maroon and gold full-length dress. It was stunning and kind of hugged her in the right places.

Clapping his hands, Anthony said, "Yes, we have chosen the gown. Now can you pay for the sugarplum fairy dress so we can go eat? We've been here for hours, and that orange chicken smells so good."

Harley rotated in the mirror again, staring at herself. She loved how the dress hugged her body, and the color complimented her skin tone. Smiling to herself, Harley decided that this was the one. After taking it off, she headed for the counter. Once it was her turn, Harley paid for the dress, praying she would get a date to wear it for. After completing her purchase, she grabbed Dev and Anthony and walked toward the food court for lunch.

Walking down the hall, passing the watch kiosk, they headed for the food court. It was your typical dome-shaped room with high ceilings and lots of tables and chairs set out so neatly by the janitors of that workday. On each side were different food stands ranging from Chinese to soul food. It also had a play area that was chained off for the kids, so the Moms could eat in peace. On the right side was Red Jackson's famous BBQ, Dev's favorite.

Dev looked around, glad to be done with the hunt for Harley's dress. He could see classmates hanging around the mall. He happened to spy Remy dashing down the hall. He headed in her direction, hoping to apologize for the way their night had ended, as he drew closer to her. When she noticed him walking towards him, she stopped in her tracks. Even standing there she was still one of the most beautiful girls he had ever seen. All Dev wanted to do was make up for what had happened and hopefully earn another chance. As he walked closer, she noticed Harley right next to him and curled her lip up in disgust. Harley sees Remy glaring at her and wraps her arm around Dev and places a kiss on his cheek. All the while, Remy never stopped looking in Harley's direction. Remy flips Dev off as she passes him and moves on to the nail shop. He laughs at Harley's antics and continues to walk with his friends to grab some food.

Trying to decide what they wanted to eat, Anthony just complained about his stomach growling. Dev headed for Red's, in hopes that he could get some lemon pepper wings. Harley was lagging behind them, tired from all the wrestling she had done to find her dress. She looked around for the nearest hoagie place. She wanted to find something healthy to eat to keep her from gaining weight. Anthony groaned at the fact that all he could think about was the orange chicken. The fact that he couldn't get a plate saddened him because it was either buy some food or buy his tux.

Finding a table, Harley and Dev began to chow down on their food. After a while, Dev noticed that his friend didn't have anything in front of him. "Anthony, why aren't you eating, man? You were the one who was dying to get in here."

"My mom hasn't given me my allowance yet, so I only have enough for either food or my tux," frowned Anthony. Looking at his plate, Dev decided to be a good friend and gave him the other half of his teriyaki wings.

"Here you go, bro. Enjoy," He said as he slid his tray across the table. Anthony smiled gratefully at him and dug into the wings.

"So where to next?" Harley asked as she took a bite of her hoagie. Dev and Anthony looked at each other while finishing off the rest of the wings.

"Well, all we need to do is head to a tux shop," Dev said as he put his tray away.

"Yeah, I'm trying to look so fresh and clean for prom for all my ladies," Anthony said as he wiped the sauce off his face.

"You're such a pig!!!" Harley shouted, "And not in just the eating way either."

Dev stood up from the table. "Let's go. We can talk about all of Anthony's imaginary girls later." They walked towards the nearest shop that sold suits and tuxedos for all ages to wear.

Amir, the store manager, walked over to them with a smile on his face." How can I help you?" He asked.

Looking around the store, the boys each searched for a tux that suited their style. Anthony asked for a dark gray suit with a black shirt and a white vest and tie. Dev didn't know what he wanted because he hadn't asked anyone to go to prom with him yet. Dev knew the color was supposed to compliment the girl's dress. Maybe if he just went simple, it wouldn't matter if they matched.

Pulling a measuring tape out, the clerk asked Dev to stand up straight and hold his arms up. After a very uncomfortable pat-down, the clerk ran over and pulled out a clean and straightforward white suit. Brushing off the jacket, Dev slips his arms in the vest and then the coat while looking at himself in the mirror. Completely bored, Harley laid on the ottoman watching Anthony try to use a pimp cane. Wanting to have a little fun, Dev puts on a top hat and begins to pose with Anthony. Strutting their stuff as if they were in a best-dressed competition, Harley joined in by pretending to take photos with an imaginary camera.

"Okay, ladies and gentlemen, this is not a dress-up store." The manager huffed. Stepping back in front of the mirror, Dev asked the clerk for a gray vest and a white bow tie before heading over to pay. On his way up to the counter, a display case full of cufflinks and watches distracted him. He walked over and took a look inside. The glistening jewels shining in the light slightly mesmerized him. Dev smiled as he saw a set that he immediately knew he had to have. Walking over to the counter, he asked Amir about the collection in the case.

Looking him over, Amir asked, "Are you sure you want that set?"

The question slightly confused Dev, but he responded that he really did want it. A condescending look entered the clerk's eye as he continued to look at him. "Young man, as I stated earlier, this is not a dress-up playroom. I will not remove items from their place just so you can take a picture with them and not buy them."

Slightly annoyed by the accusation, Dev calmly looked at the man and said, "I assure you I will buy them. So, if you could please go and grab them, I would greatly appreciate it."

Amir continued to stare at Dev and then finally walked over to the case and pulled out the set that Dev wanted. He rang it up and smiled at the price, waiting to see what Dev would do next.

Looking up at the cash register after all his items had been scanned, Dev pulled out his wallet. He flipped through it until he found his debit card and then put it on the counter. "Here you go," Dev said, not even fazed by the price as he swiped the card and provided the pin. The manager grabbed the receipt and was surprised that the payment hadn't been declined. After ringing up Anthony's rental tux and placing the suits in hooked bags, they headed out. "You really showed him. Hint-hint, wink-wink money bags," laughed Anthony.

Walking around the mall, they began to window shop some of the new video game stores. Dev contemplated the thought of asking his mom to buy him the newly released Braver 3, when Dev heard a noise.

"Oh, look, it's the dwarfs," Bowen said as he wrapped his arm around Dev's head. Standing behind Harley was Marcus, looking ever so determined to say something to her. Looking at him, Harley says, "What's wrong with you? And Bowen, let go of Deveraux and stop being a jerk."

Moving in closer, Marcus says, "Harley, we're not jerks if we give dwarves like you a ride." He wrapped his arms around her. Before she could blink, Marcus picked her up and ran down the hall. Totally thinking it was a joke, Bowen laughed and held off the boys. Anthony tried to reach out and grab her hand, but he franticly hit her head with her dress instead.

Screaming and kicking as he was running away, Harley bit Marcus on the hand. Letting go of her, he said. "Jeez, it was just a joke. I wanted to get you alone, so I could ask you out to prom."

Harley stared at him in disbelief, thinking it was a joke. There was no way she would go to prom with Marcus, even if he was the last man on earth. Instead of laughing in his face, she just looked at him and said, "Sorry, but no. I will not go with you." Marcus looked at her with sad eyes, but tried to play it off. "If you really liked me, you should've been able to ask me in front of Bowen and not ask me behind his back."

With a shrug, he seemed to stare right through her and walked off with as much swag as he could manage. Harley stood proudly, knowing she had stood up for herself and avoided breaking Bowen's bromance. Although a thought came to her. Maybe she should've just said yes to the only guy she knew liked her. What if she didn't get another chance? Guys weren't exactly making prom proposals to her.

Huffing down the hall to catch up to her, Anthony and Dev asked, "What was that?" Looking at them in confusion, she said, "He tried to ask me to prom while Bowen wasn't around." Anthony and Dev stared at her in shock. "I turned him down because he's Bowen's best friend, and he creeps me out." Looking at Anthony, she asked, "Why did you pull my hair? That hurt."

Anthony handed her dress back to her and said, "If I did, I'm sorry. I wasn't aiming for your hair. I just panicked." She looked at Marcus and Bowen, who was standing next to each other, pretending it was the funniest thing they had ever done to her. Marcus looked back and stared firmly at Anthony and Dev, ready to defend himself if they decided to run back at them.

"Unfortunately, guys. I have to go home with them. My mom didn't want us out late, and she's got me babysitting these boneheads all day. Thanks for helping me find a dress. I'll call you later," said Harley.

"You sure you don't want us to throw a bouncy ball at them and run? I've been working on my workout skills," said Anthony as he stood in his karate position. Harley shook her head, and Dev put his hand on Anthony's shoulder.

Chuckling, Dev said, "Harley, trust me. You don't wanna see that. Anthony, if you want me to, I can show Harley your moves on camera."

Anthony straightened up with an alarmed look on his face and said, "Harley's a smart girl. She looks like she can handle it just fine on her own."

Standing there, stunned by their inside joke, she pulled her shirt down and fixed the puppy ears headband that was on her head. "I'll call you guys later. I still have to remind Bowen to grab some broccoli and noodles for mom's stir fry." Waving goodbye, she headed down the hall after the boys, shouting at them to wait up.

Dev found himself looking at Harley as she walked down the hall to go meet up with her brother. They had been friends with her for so many years yet; he realized they had never met anyone else related to her. He knew she had a mom and a grandfather, because of the rumors about her dad leaving them, he never asked her for the details. She never invited them over, but then again, neither did he. They always played at the treehouse or Anthony's house, where his foster family would make snacks.

Looking at his watch, he saw that they had two hours to kill before he had to check in back home, so they continued window shopping. Walking around another kid play area, they landed by the bean bag store when Anthony's phone rang. When he looked at who was calling him, he immediately got excited and pointed at his phone. It was a senior girl named Katrina that he had been talking about. She was from a different school, and she oddly took a liking to him. It was odd because he was a sophomore.

Chiming in, Dagon said to Dev, *"You know what I think? I think he makes these girls up just to not look like he's in love with you."*

Rolling his eyes, Dev messaged, *"Pipe down, you're just jealous the ladies don't want you."*

"Me?" Dagon questioned. *"Maybe, but you know I'm half your inner conscience, so I'm pretty sure you're the one who's jealous."*

After noticing Anthony getting off the phone, Dev asked him. "So, when do I get to meet this lovely lady who likes to hang out in pet shops and also has a pet snake?"

Anthony shrugged, "Maybe I'll bring her to prom. She has mentioned that hers is right after mine, and I mean, it will save me the trouble of asking one of the girls from school." Looking at his watch again, he noticed they only had thirty minutes left. "Hey man, is that bear statue in the play area looking at us? Gabby has got to stop sending Mable after us. It's still never going to stop being creepy." Waving at Mable, Anthony and Dev head to the bathroom so they could quietly teleport back home.

Ready to hurl again, Anthony looked up and noticed they had landed at the treehouse and not in his room. The treehouse was nestled at the top of an oak tree that was easily fifty feet high. On the outside, it looked like a regular treehouse made from red cherry wood. When you stepped through the door, however, it was much, much more significant inside. Dev and his father had used a few magical spells to alter the space on the inside. From what Anthony had seen, the house had a full kitchen with a dining room and a bathroom with a working toilet and tub.

He always meant to ask how they made it work. There were multiple rooms that had different functions. One allowed the ceiling to open up so you could view the stars. Another was a massive library, complete with a side computer room. A third was a full entertainment center that they could watch movies and play video games in. Somehow, there was even a staircase that led to a second and third story full of bedrooms. Even Harley had came to hang out here, but she never saw it to this extent. Whenever she was around, the treehouse was at the base of the tree and was only one room with a few bean bag chairs and a hammock. Anthony could remember all the fun times they had here just hanging out.

"Hey man, I thought you had to be home to teach the twins how to do voodoo magic and stuff. Won't Mable be looking for you?" Said Anthony.

Trying to help him stand up. Dev said, "Maybe, but I wanted to just hang out for a little bit before I had to be locked indoors for the next thirty years till this warning is over."

Walking over to the hammock they made when they were in the sixth grade, they stared into the clouds. They talked about what it was going to be like to have real girlfriends and real adventures. Dev always wanted to bring Anthony to Zortega, but he knew that wasn't allowed, and his dad would never break any more rules for him.

Unbeknownst to them, in the shadow of a tree, was a mysterious figure. He stood and watched his most hated enemy sit back and relax with his friend, unaware he looked at the boy with him, feeling a pang of regret at the fact that he may have to destroy him too. He was innocent in all this and deserved to live his life. With one last look, he turned and walked off with his familiar padding next to him.

After a while, Dev took a look at his watch and shot up when he saw the time. "Aw, crap! Anthony, I gotta get home. You want to come?" He asked as he gathered his stuff together.

"Sure. Why not?" He grabbed ahold of Dev's arm as they flashed from the treehouse to the front door.

CHAPTER 8

Walking into the house foyer, Dev turned to his left and hung up his backpack and coat in the nook on the wall. Dev reminded Anthony to take off his stuff and hang it up. In the foyer were the beige color walls filled with family photos and clean and modern lines of different wallpaper in some rooms. With Anthony behind him, Dev noticed his mom was pacing with her coffee in hand. Dev knew that the only time she did that was when she was upset about something. She was walking from her prized gray marbled ten-seater table and spacious amber and black décor dining room, to the kitchen that was filled with the smell of coffee brewing.

With the twins throwing sparkle bombs at each other in the family room, Dev decided to go see what she was so upset about. After taking off his shoes and hanging his jacket up in the front hall, he quickly ducked as a rogue sparkle bomb ball was hurled towards his head. He grabbed Anthony and threw him in front of him, screaming. "Anthony! Protect!" He heard Anthony scream as he took the bomb straight to the face. He fell to the ground, wiping the glitter away from his face, as he wanted to call Dev a few foul names.

Laughing at them, Dev remembered how he loved doing that spell when his mom taught him. So, what else would a big brother do but join in the fun? Drawing some water out of the hallway plant, Dev stepped in front of Anthony, holding the water in his palm until it glowed. The light began to sparkle like a prism disco ball. After growing it as big as he could, he hurled it at them with no remorse, with a sinister smile on his face. Trying to block it, Ezekiel materialized a shield, yelling, "I got this!" Eland grabbed a blanket and jumped behind the couch before it hit them.

With loud roars and bangs of sparkles blasting all around the house, Aunt Lesley came out of the kitchen to holler at them. "Selena, your kids are acting like farm animals again!" The twins chose that moment to jump up and send a shower of sparkle bombs in every direction. Unprotected, Lesley took the full force of it and fell to the ground with a scream and a curse. Dev blocked with his own shield and ducked into the hall closet for protection, dragging Anthony with him.

Forming two bombs in his hands, he placed images of each twin in one and sent them off after them. No matter where they were, they would find them and shoot sparks as they chased them around the room. Peeking out from the closet, he watched as the twins ducked for cover from the hot flashes raining from above as they shrieked with laughter. He watched as his Aunt Lesley pick herself up off the ground, looking like a glittering mannequin, running out of the room, screaming for her sister. Adding more to the chaos, Dev manifested a giant bomb in the middle of the room and made it explode in a rainbow of colors, covering every inch of the family room.

Storming out of the dining room, Selena calls for Rodney to get the twins. "Deveraux Andreas Vanseal! I said, come home and help the kids get ready for their test, not start a sparkle war!" With a wave of her hands, the entire room was spotless. "Get your teenage butt in here and let me see what you bought for your Sophomore prom!" Grumbled Selena.

Stopping in his tracks, Dev knew that voice anywhere. Any time his mom used his full name, he knew he was in trouble and should come quick. Hearing the office door slowly open, the twins looked at each other and cloaked themselves while Dev dashed for the dining room. Looking around the dining room, he realized why his mom was so stressed. Sitting at the head of the oak wood table, Dev looked at his mom, worrying over party favors. She stood up and pulled out one of the eight seats in the center of the room. There laid the plans for the big Vanseal family spectacle birthday/Kaloke party all over the table. It worried Dev that because there were two kids this time, his mom would have to make it twice as big to impress the Gemini leader. It honestly relieved him that no one had witnessed his ceremony, because his dad was the leader of the month he was predicted for. Dev always felt bad for his mom though, because she had to carry him for three extra months just to give his line an heir. Supposedly there is an elixir the new wife has to take the night before the wedding to ensure one of her offspring was an heir, but she would never know which child the spell chose.

After staring at the bell-shaped bottle in the curio cabinet in the corner, Dev snapped out of it and handed his mom the suit and stuff he had gotten from the mall. "Take it out and let me see it on you," said Selena as she looked up for a minute from her invite list. Holding the tux up, Dev walked right through it and switched his clothes with the tux on the floating hanger. "So, what do you think, Mom? Superhero in disguise," said Dev. Letting go of her pen, as it continued to write invitations, Selena walked over to inspect him. "You're not a superhero in disguise. You're my little Cap, a born leader and gentleman," she said as she smoothed his collar. "Now go take it off, hang it up, go check the wards, and get ready for training. I got too much to put together, and your aunt and dad are no help," said Selena.

Before turning around to walk through the hanger again, he grabbed his mom and asked for a dance. Spinning her around, he swayed back and forth like they were at a real formal party. Smiling in her arms, Dev looked over his shoulder and seen his dad standing in the doorway, asking him to spin her once more. Casting smoke all around her while she spun, her outfit changed into a subtle white dress just like the one from her wedding pictures on the wall. Taking her hand, Rodney asked him to step aside and let a seasoned vet show him how to sweep a woman off her feet. Walking through the hanger, Dev changed back and left the dining room before they decided to have a fourth child in front of him.

"Hey Dagon, can you help me check the wards while I go hang up my tux," messaged Dev.

"Sure, but I want my fur brushed later," messaged Dagon back at Dev.

"I don't know who you are trying to look cute for. There's not another familiar for miles, for all we know."

"So. You know it's for when I howl at the full moon. I like my fur to blow in the wind if that's okay with you."

Hopping out of his chain, Dagon began to walk to the front door to go check the wards. Standing outside, he took a moment to just shake and stretch in the sun as he watched the joggers run by. The sun made him want to just lay in the grass and waste the day away, but he knew he was supposed to be on watch. The grass felt so good in his paws as he rolled in the dew of the newly grown blades. The warmth covered him like a blanket and almost lulled him to sleep as he nuzzled by the root of the tree. What seemed like a few minutes turned into an hour of peaceful dreaming when Eve's watchful cry alerted the home in screeches of owl fear.

Jumping to his feet in a daze, Dagon ran to help with any attack that Eve had sensed. Running towards the front gate, he sensed an immense power and saw a dark figure standing there. Mable was already standing there, seeming to be talking to the stranger. Without warning, the gates began to open, and the stranger walked in.

Dagon couldn't believe what he was seeing and sped up to intercept him. He leapt and bared his fangs, ready to attack when Mable leapt over and threw him off to the side. "Have you lost all sense, boy?" She growled at him as she

pressed him into the ground with her paw. "Take a close look at the man you are about to attack."

Dagon turned his head and looked at him, not really understanding what she was saying. All he saw was a regular man dressed in a three-piece suit with a short mohawk haircut and dark sunglasses covering his eyes. On his shoulder scuttled a small scorpion familiar. Wait, what? A scorpion, he thought. His eyes locked on the small creature that was crawling over the man's shoulders. It couldn't be. There was no way he could be here.

"That's right," a small feminine voice whispered to him. "The man you see before you is my Niyor and the head of the Scorpio line, Sir Nikolai." The scorpion smiled as she stared down at Dagon.

"Celeste, be nice, will you," he said with a chuckle as he looked down at the young wolf. "I'm sorry to have disturbed you. I only stopped by to have a meeting with Rodney. I didn't mean to intrude on a family evening." At that moment, Dev ran up and seen Mable standing over Dagon, pushing him into the ground. He screamed at her to release him. When she released Dagon from her paw, he ran to Dev's side and turned back to look at the man who was one of the twelve rulers. Nikolai saw Dev and smiled. "You must be Deveraux. Pleasure to meet you."

Dev stood there with his mouth open, staring at Nikolai. Then he bowed and stammered out, "Pa pp-pleasure t-too meet you, sir."

Nikolai stared at him with a curious expression then bursts out laughing. He had a deep booming laugh that seemed to fill the air. Nikolai doubled over and held his sides. Wiping away tears from his eyes, he looked at Dev, who still had his head bowed. "Dude, you really need to chill out and relax. It's not that serious. We're on earth, I'm just like you here. Please pick your head up." Dev looked up at him in shock and saw he was just standing there with a hand in his pocket, smiling at him. "You don't have to be so formal with me when it's just us, but keep those manners around others. Be careful how you address yourself, though. Anyway, I'm just here to see your dad. Is he here?"

Dev looked back at the house. "He's in the house dancing with my mom."

Slowly walking up the driveway, Nikolai asked him to fetch someone before he reached the door. It was rude to enter one's home without being invited in by the owners. Dashing to the door with Dagon in his arms, he ran up the driveway where Gabby stood waiting to greet the unexpected guest.

After exchanging a hugging embrace with her, he greeted everyone at the door. "Good evening, Selena, how have you been, my lovely horned mermaid empress? Your home is very warming, but I must bring worrisome news to your family. Is there any way to talk to your husband privately?"

After receiving a kiss on the hand, she smiled back at him and said, "You'll always be a flirt, won't you, Nikolai? Is that maybe why you have no one to rest your head with?" Shocked at her quick response, he gasped with his hand against his chest, pretending to be hurt.

"Oh, that's because Scorpio wants a seasoned lady to bare him an heir." Said Lesley as she twirled out of the dining room while pretending to fall into his arms. Stepping aside, Nikolai watched as Lesley stumbled into the chair next to him. Laughing in complete hysterics, Anthony choked on the glass of water he was drinking. Dev gasped for air when they saw her face after Nikolai didn't catch her.

"Hello again, Lesley. I figured you'd be here, so I come bearing the finest rum from one of my house warmings. I hoped you wouldn't have started without me, but why don't you help make everyone a stiff drink? Oh, and how is lady Autumn?" Asked Nikolai.

Glaring at him for not catching her, she puts on a saucy smile. She then replied. "Not old enough for you!" She snatched the bottle and headed for the bar to

pour herself a double. Walking out of the study stood Rodney, to greet his friend and companion leader.

"Rodney, I have news from the council. Well, not really the council. I've been doing some digging, and they talked to the python about some prophecy that was created." Looking at the extra kid in the room, Nikolai asked, "Should he be here? Who is he? This is a no outsiders conversation. Can we take this in your study?" Dev reached over and said, "This is the part where you have to leave, bro. I'll fill you in at school."

As Gabby walked Anthony out, the adults gathered in the study. The kids finished working on their school project while also trying to eavesdrop.

"You're not doing it right!"

"No, you're not doing it right!"

Grabbing the glass from the twins, Dev knew the spell they were trying to do, and honestly figured he'd do it himself. "Rogoca Enel," said Dev. Suddenly the air filled with the conversation they were having in the other room, as loud as a megaphone spilling through the empty glass.

"I have been laying low in Zortega, and they already had someone meeting with the python. Come to find out when I talked to Aries, she told me that Cancer's son, the one she's planning the wedding for, overheard his dad talking. The snake has an old score that the Ophiuchus line had waged before being erased and stripped from existence. The python said that it was a matter of weeks before he would slither with his master once more," said Nikolai.

"Nikolai, you lie. I have never heard of such a thing, and don't you think we would know of some hidden story?" Said Rodney.

"Honey, you don't think there is an Ophiuchan out there ready to wage war?" Muttered Selena.

"Who knows, honey. What else did Aries tell you?" Commanded Rodney.

"All she could get out of him was that, "My heir would rise to kill all twelve lives by the hand of the black bloodline. With four barons and countesses hidden away, it came in handy. That they will rise when the power matured into plenty." Unquote, and that's all he could remember," said Nikolai.

"I told the people they should've killed the damn thing when they had the chance," stated Lesley.

Rodney rolled his eyes at her outburst and turned back to Nikolai. "Was there anything else that was said?"

Nikolai looked around the room with a worried expression. "How secure is your home and your wards?"

Rodney seemed taken aback by the question. "My son was checking them when you arrived. Why?"

Nikolai continued to scan the room like he was looking for weaknesses in the defenses. Seeming relieved at finding none, he took in a deep sigh. "Aries told me two more things that really troubled her. She made me swear not to spread it around, or else it will cause panic." Rodney could see that whatever it was, truly troubled him. He sat back and waited for him to collect himself.

Taking another breath to express himself, Nikolai looked up and stated. "The cage around the python is weakening. Somehow, over time, the magic placed around it was fading around him. Soon, he will be strong enough to escape." The others in the room stared in shock at this news. There is no way they could allow him to escape, they thought. If the snake had managed to locate this royal heir, they knew there would be nothing but chaos and destruction. They knew it wouldn't stop at just Zortega, that he would come to earth too. He would destroy everything around him until there was nothing left.

"Is there anything we can do to stop this?" Sitting forward in his chair, Rodney's eyes began to glow in anger.

"Aries is getting ready to call an emergency meeting to see if we can find a way to strengthen the cage," Nikolai replied. "So be ready for when she calls so that we can all go and do what we can to fix this." He gets up, ready to leave.

"Wait!" Selena cried. Nikolai turned back to her. "What was the other thing that Aries found out? You said there was two things she learned." A look of pure fear flashed in Nikolai's eyes as he recalled the second thing that he was told.

He wiped a hand over his eyes and said in a small voice, "We may already be too late. The python said that before we imprisoned him, he had released parts of his spirit into four eggs and sent them to earth. They have hatched, and from what he said, they are giving him power and strength."

Selena and Lesley both put their hands over their mouths in shock, gasping, and Rodney just stood there. "How did we miss this? How did this slip past us? They are probably teaching these four people black magic right now!" Rodney yelled to no one in particular in the room.

"We were so caught up in our victory and ending the war," Nikolai said, "We locked him away and thought that was the end of it." He shook his head slightly, "We will fix this, no matter what. Be ready for the call, Rodney. All of us need to stand together, and as one of our strongest, we need you there."

Rodney stood tall. "I will be there and ready to do what is necessary." Nikolai nodded slightly, then walked out of the room towards the door. He walked into the family room and almost bumped into Dev sitting in the chair. Then he noticed the twins were still listening to the glass on the table as his voice echoed the two rooms. They fell back with a shout, thinking they would be in trouble for ease dropping.

Instead, Nikolai held out his hand to help Dev up. "Walk with me to the door kid." He said. Dev followed him across the room to the front door. Nikolai put his hand on the knob and began to turn it, then stopped. He looked at Dev, and his eyes glowed a deep emerald color as Dev stared into his eyes. "So, you heard all that, did you?" He asked quietly.

Dev just nodded his head, thinking he was still in trouble. Nikolai gave him a small smile, "Relax, kid. You're not in trouble, all right? Honestly, I'm glad you heard what I said. We will need all the help we can get with this threat that is coming. If there are others out there who have familiars that have part of Ophiuchus in them, then they will come for you. This way, you won't be caught off guard." Nikolai walked out the door but turned back to Dev. "Be on the lookout kid, the enemy is a lot closer than you think. Also, if you ever need help, give me a call, and I will do what I can."

As he walked away, Dev saw his familiar crawl back onto his shoulder as she turned to look at him. In Dev's head, he heard Nikolai's familiar speak. *"My Niyor has the ability to see parts of the future. The path laid before you is a hard one but can be overcome. It will be filled with trials, pain, and betrayal of the harshest kind, but you can fight through it. Be strong, Deveraux Vanseal, and you may yet save us all."*

With that parting statement, Celeste disappeared into Nikolai's watch as he reached the edge of the wards. As Gabby stood there, she removed the prism crystal that was shaped like a garden light and allowed him to pass. Then, with a wave, he flashed himself away. Walking inside, Dev saw Gabby standing at the door. "Did you get enough information ear-hustling? If you want to be an adult, young Cap, be ready for very dangerous adult responsibilities, but for now, go upstairs and shower and prepare for dinner in an hour," said Gabby. Nodding, Dev did as he was told and headed upstairs to go shower because he smelled like outside. Walking in the family room, he was greeted very hastily by his dad.

Rodney grabbed Dev by the arm. "No more games. You need to learn all you can before I go. Someone must protect this family. Even though your mom is royal now, she doesn't have the same gifts as you and I. This also means we're going to have to push their ceremony up so the twins can protect themselves." Staring intensely at him, Dev nodded and tried to head upstairs like Gabby said, but before he could, Rodney grabbed him for a hug. "Forgive me, but you must be ready, so meet me out back." After looking over his dad once more, Dev headed out back to do his daily training.

Sweating after a long and painful training session, Dev could smell himself from Mars. So, he decided to skip dinner and walked upstairs to wash up, but he soon realized how tired he was. Slowly stumbling around his room, Dev fell to the ground next to his bed.

CAPRICORN

CHAPTER 9

When Dev woke the next morning still on the floor. He rose and shook his head, not really understanding why he wasn't in his bed. Struggling to get up, he stumbled towards the bathroom to shower and get ready for the day. There was no way he was going to be any good for the track meet or training at this pace. After finishing up, Dev picked up his phone to check to see if he had any messages. There was a brief text from Coach Hunter explaining that they had canceled the track meet for today because of a string of storms.

"Yes!" He shouted in joy.

This meant he would have an entire day to just relax and enjoy himself. Smiling at that thought, he sat back in his oversized bean bag chair, closed his eyes, and relaxed. When he opened them, he was no longer in his room, but somewhere in the middle of a tropical jungle.

"What the hell?" He said, looking around. "How did I get here?" Everywhere he turned, thick and luscious vegetation surrounded him. The air was hot and humid. To him, it felt as if he was breathing in water. The jungle was alive with the cries of the animals that called it home.

"Hello, son."

Turning around, Dev saw his father standing there with a smile. He was wearing a three-piece suit, looking very out of place in the jungle.

"Dad?" He said, "What is going on? Where are we? Why am I here?"

His dad continued to smile as he rattled off questions. When Dev was finally out of breath, he just stopped and stared at his father, who was absently studying a small lizard as it slithered up a tree.

"Are you finally done?" Rodney asked. "Good," stated Rodney before Dev could reply. "The reason you are here Deveraux is because of the dangers facing us at this moment. I told you that you had to be ready, and this training will help." Hearing the word training made Dev groaned out loud, "So much for a relaxing day." He knew no amount of grumbling or complaining would get him out of this, so he took a second to get his head right. Closing his eyes, he took a deep inhale in and slowly released it. It was slightly more challenging to do this here than at home due to the humidity, but Dev pushed through it. Doing this two more times, he succeeded in calming his thoughts but also his racing heart. When he opened his eyes, he had a much more determined air about him. His father noticed this and nodded proudly.

"Good. Now that you have calmed yourself, this is your task." Rodney spread his arms and spun in a slow circle. "As you can see, you are in a vast jungle. Don't worry, you're still on earth. This is a paralleled domain of earth and Zortega, so don't be afraid you're not on any other remote world." As he dropped his arms and looked back at Dev. "However, keep in mind that there are still dangers that lurk here, and you must be cautious of them all." He

pointed his finger behind him and shot a blast of energy towards Dev. Before he could react, it flew past his shoulder and hit a tree with a thud.

Dev turned to look and was shocked to see the head of an enormous boa constrictor that had been slowly sneaking up on him. His head was easily the same size as Dev's, and its body was as thick as one of his legs. It was a dark brown color with green dots spotted over its scales. The sight of the massive snake caused his heart rate to start to rise. Before it overcame him with fear, he took a few exhales to steady himself. Rodney watched in silence as his son controlled his anxiety about the situation. Although he never said anything, he was still proud of the leaps and bounds Dev made during training. Instead of complaining or running away, Dev faced each challenge head-on and bested them all. When his time came, Rodney knew he would make an influential leader one day. Clearing his throat to get his son's attention, he continued to explain the situation to him.

"If you haven't noticed by now, Dagon is nowhere around you, and neither is your charm." With a look of alarm, Dev's hand shot to his throat where his charm usually rested. His charm was missing. He immediately dropped to his knees and began searching the ground. He panicked and called out to Dagon with his mind.

"Dagon! Dagon! Can you hear me? Answer me buddy."

When Dev heard no response, he stared at his father in disbelief. It took all his self-control to not launch himself at his father. The feeling of betrayal raged in him as he tried to control his emotions. Since the day of his Kaloke Ceremony, Dev had never been without Dagon, and it literally felt as if he was missing a limb. He felt a cold disconnect to Dagon, and it left him feeling alone and lost.

"I know what it feels like to be without your partner." Dev heard his father say. "I know because my father did the same to me when I was your age, so I understand your pain and feeling of loss. I know them very well, and it was the hardest thing to try and overcome. I felt as if I was missing my arm, but on a much deeper level. It feels as if you have lost a part of your soul." Dev watched his father, who stared at him with a look of pain in his eyes. It was a look so profound he knew his father had indeed gone through the same experience. Knowing that helped him steel himself against the pain. If his father could handle the pain and overcome it, so could he. Dev rose from the ground and with his fists clenched. He squared his shoulders and stared his father straight in the eye.

"Whatever this training is, I will beat it," said Dev with conviction.

His dad gave a brief nod. "For you to get home, you need to find your charm, secure Dagon, and teleport back." He said. "Until you find him, you will be unable to get yourself home. For the time being, you will be able to do minor spells to protect yourself from the elements as well as gather food and water. Also, you will retain your physical abilities and your ability to heal yourself. You will remain here until you have completed your task. Do you understand?" Dev nodded and looked around the dense jungle, trying to figure out which way to start. He looked back to his dad to see that he had disappeared. Dev turned in a full circle and found no trace of his father.

Walking through the brush of leaves and trees, Dev decided to find high ground first, just to see how big the place was set up for him. He found multiple slopes but couldn't get high enough to see anything different but more leaves and trees. Dev knew the only way he would get anywhere was to climb a tree for a proper vantage point. Thirsty and desperate, he spotted the tallest tree he could find and started to climb his way to the top. The bark was so sticky it kept ripping off the trunk with every other advance he made up the tree. Feeling the strain in his muscles, Dev decided to jump and swing himself up the tree to get up to the top faster.

Dev was still worried about his familiar and tried not to picture the worst of him being swallowed by an animal. I'ma save you buddy hold on; He thought. Finally, to the top, Dev was met with the most peaceful landscape of trees and plants. He scanned the area and seen that his dad had laid out a barrier

around the area, which meant he only had a few miles in all directions to look for Dagon.

Trying to think like his dad, he wondered where he could have placed his charm. It had to be somewhere remote, but not easy to get to without a challenge. Launching himself off the tree and down to the ground in an aerial backflip. Dev was unaware of the danger he had landed himself in. Underneath the tree was a field of covered up bear traps. When Dev landed, he carelessly knocked one of the chains over when he stepped forward. Snapping and clicking underneath his feet, Dev ran as fast as he could for the river he had seen at the top of the tree. Hopping and jumping through the trees, trying not to get his foot or leg snapped in one of the traps. Dev did his best to look around for anything shiny or encased as he ran.

Unnoticeable to him was an unlikely visitor that stalked him from close behind. Pouncing from tree to tree was a large animal. He had been watching the boy since he had arrived and feared for the direction he was heading. He wrestled with himself on if he should let him face the danger ahead like his dad wanted or help the kid, but his decision grew too late.

Falling over his own feet, Dev rolled into a small pit of sand. Laying there to take a second on why his dad couldn't have challenged him to play a board game. Rolling over, Dev stood up and heard the flowing water of the river close by. Unfortunately, the beauty of the wildflowers and freshwater smell was short-lived with the horde of attacking mosquitos.

"Dagon, Dagon, can you hear me, buddy?"

Stomping through the mud of the river trail, Dev noticed footprints that looked like his fathers, so he followed them. However, he followed them right into danger. Taking a minute to catch his breath, Dev noticed that he began to get shorter, and the mud from his shoes wouldn't let him go. Looking around, he realized that what he had mistaken for mud was quicksand. With his powers limited, he knew he wouldn't be able to get out using magic. He tried to stay as still as possible as he searched for a vine or low-hanging branch. While he looked, he felt his body slowly sink deeper into the thick sand.

Out of the corner of his eye, he noticed a dark shadow leaping through the trees. He began to panic as the shadow came closer. The mystery creature cleared the trees and came charging towards Dev, and he finally got a good look at it. It looked like the most massive panther he had ever seen. It had thick glossy black fur, razor-sharp fangs and claws, and burning purple eyes. It charged towards him and leapt with its jaws wide open.

Dev aimed at the panther and fired a few shots, but was unable to land a hit. Moving and wiggling too much made him sink faster, and it left only his top half. Panicking, he cried out for his dad. "Dad help! I'm about to die. Aaauuggghhhh," Dev screamed as he raised his hands to protect his face.

Leaping forward, the panther snagged him by the back of this shirt and pulled him out of the quicksand. He dropped him next to a tree and loped off into the dense jungle in a flash. Dev leaned against the tree and took a few deep breaths. He couldn't believe that he was still alive, and that the panther hadn't just eaten him. He looked around, making sure that he was entirely alone, but he could hear the beast breathing close by. There was no physical sign of the panther, so he picked himself up and continued searching for Dagon. This time, he kept a close eye out for quicksand and his new companion to come finish the job.

The panther was impressed with his relentlessness to finish the task his father set. The panther gave Dev a bread crumb to follow. Flashing out of the side of Dev's eye was a blue light that seemed to be some kind of homing beacon. Dev thought it would be best not to steer towards it because of his first attempt to follow something and how it ended so horribly. Watching the monkeys swing from the trees, he saw the sun lose its brightness as it began to set. The wind blew a colder mist then the hot humidity it had earlier. Wet and cold, Dev decided against it and aimed for some way to dry off or find shelter.

104

With crumbling leaves getting closer to him, Dev was met with a roar that scared the soul from his body. The panther was back, and he didn't want to find out if he was hungry, so Dev ran as fast as possible. The panther's roar sounded like he was closing in on him, so he changed directions. Crushing twigs and blasting bushes out of his way, Dev saw the blue light again. Did the panther want him to go this way, he thought? Going with that thought, he charged towards the blue light. As soon as he reached it, it blinked out. He stopped, panting hard, and looked around in the gloom. Off in the distance, he saw another flashing blue light and another farther down. Dev turned around and ran, following the trail of light deeper and deeper into the jungle. Soon there was nothing but darkness all around him.

He stopped for a moment to rest and catch his breath. In front of him was a trail of blue lights that zigzagged further into the jungle. The lights illuminated a small radius around them. Everywhere else, there was nothing but pitch black. Now that he was no longer running, Dev could hear the sounds of the jungle. The darkness of the jungle was alive with the sounds of nocturnal creatures out on the hunt. The screeches and roars were deafening. Picking himself up, he shivered in the icy breeze that began to chill his sweat. Closing his eyes, he focused and made his clothes more durable against the chill and dried his body. As his temperature began to rise, he set his sight on the trail of lights again. He set off at a slow pace, making sure to test the ground so as not to trip or fall.

In the darkness, he heard a soft growl off to his left. He looked in that direction and saw a pair of purple eyes flashing in the distance. At the sight of those burning eyes, he took off like a shot and continued to follow the lights. Off to his right, he heard a loud hissing sound, so he ducked just in time before the anaconda lunged to coil itself around Dev. With a ferocious roar, the panther jumped out and attacked the snake. They twisted and writhed together in a huddled mass vying for dominance. Not waiting around to see who would win, Dev took off again. The lights were pulsing faster and faster, and he felt he might be getting closer to his familiar. Up ahead, he saw a blazing golden light shining through the trees. They glowed brightly and turned the dark into day.

Behind him, he heard a loud roar and assumed the panther had been victorious in its fight. Bursting through the trees, Dev was met with an unbelievable sight.

He was in a large clearing ringed with twelve giant statues. Up in the sky was a full moon that shined brightly down on the clearing surrounded by thousands of stars. Taking a moment to catch his breath, he studied each one and realized they each represented an original line. They were set in a circle around the pedestal. Dev noticed one statue was destroyed. There was nothing left but the plinth the statue stood on. In the center of the clearing was a pedestal that came up to his chest, and on it laid his totem. Happiness bloomed in his chest as he saw the golden wolf head that housed his familiar. He walked towards the pedestal and reached towards his totem.

A growl from behind had stopped his advance towards grabbing it. As he turned, he expected to see the panther, but the sight that met him made his blood run cold. Slinking towards him was a shadow of jaguars. Their golden eyes glowed in the moonlight. They locked their faces in a vicious snarl as they stalked closer to Dev, which made anger rise in his face as they spread out to surround him. Dev decided he didn't come this far in the heat and cold to almost get lost in the darkness, and drown in murky quicksand to be eaten. Dev was so close to triumph, and they were not going to stop him. Before he could make a move, the lead jaguar leapt out of the jungle like a shadowy blur. The panther jumped over and knocked the jaguar to ground. They tussled and rolled in the dirt, spitting and snarling as they raked each other with their claws. The rest of the shadow chased after the dueling animals and jumped into the fray, trying to defend their leader.

Seeing this only caused Dev's anger to rise even more, but he had to help the panther. He looked around for a weapon and found a staff with a rounded top. He picked it up and with a loud yell charged towards the wrestling wild cats. He swung towards the first cat and brought the staff down on its head. It yelped and turned towards Dev in a crouch, hate burning in its eyes. The jaguar began to pounce on Dev as he met the attack head-on. He sidestepped the lunge and swung the staff with all his might. It connected and sent the jaguar flying into

another. Turning back to the others, he saw that a few had noticed his arrival and began to move towards him. Charging forward, Dev braced himself while throwing caution to the wind.

For the next gruesome minutes, Dev was lost in the intense battle. He swung his staff in every direction, beating back each cat that engaged him. He ducked and dodged many glistening claws and jagged fangs. His hands were bloody from gripping the staff. His sides burned from the few attacks he didn't fend off. While blood leaked out, he could feel his strength waning, but he refused to give up. After what felt like an eternity of fighting, Dev looked around and realized the last of the jaguars had run off.

He gave a sigh of relief and fell to his knees in exhaustion. He looked over at the sound of a whimper and saw the panther that had run to his defense. He was laying on the ground, licking his wound. Dev tried to move over to him but could barely get his legs to move. The panther looked over to him with a grunt, stood up and padded over to him. He picked Dev up by the back of his shirt and began to drag him over to the pedestal. Dev could feel himself fading in and out as the panther dragged him towards it. He tried to hang on as long as he could. He was so close he could feel the connection to his totem growing stronger.

A voice in the back of his head began to call him. *"Dev! Is that you? Come on buddy, don't fade on me now. WAKE UP!!!"*

Dev woke with a start and sat straight up while breathing in heavily. The panther released his shirt and sat back on his haunches, relieved to see the boy alert. Dev groaned from the pain of his wounds and took a second to heal the worst of them. He plucked a feather from one of his wings and pressed it on his chest. The feather began to glow and spread throughout his body. There was a two-inch-long cut on his leg that was leaking a lot of blood and bruises covering all over. The light slowly spread across his body and healed them all. Once the pain was gone Dev breathed in and sighed from the relief.

He turned to stare at the panther that had saved him multiple times. He didn't know where he came from, but he was glad to have had him watching over him. Now that he had a closer look, he saw that it had a strange looking scar. It looked like someone had tried to carve half a star in his forehead. It seemed relatively painful because it was still leaking drops of blood.

Dev stood on shaky legs and almost fell over from exhaustion. Dev took a moment to regain his balance and stood straight. The panther rose and padded over to him and stood at his side. Dev realized he still had the staff in his hand and used it as a crutch to shuffle over to the pedestal. The glow from his totem grew stronger as he approached, and Dev could feel his strength returning. He reached out to grab his totem so that he could be reunited with his partner and finally go home. Just as he was about to close his hand around it, the ground began to rumble and shake. Dev was thrown back on the ground. He watched in disbelief as the pedestal began to rise. He could hear Dagon howling and calling out to him. The zodiac statues rose until they floated at different levels around the pedestal.

"How am I supposed to get all the way up there?" He asked himself in disbelief. A square stone rose out of the ground at his feet. It stopped at mid-height, and Dev could see writing across the flat surface. It read:

To find your way to the top. You must follow the path that doesn't stop. To find your answer, look to the past. Follow it quickly from first to last.

Dev read it over and over again, trying to understand. He stared up at the statues as they floated overhead. He caught sight of the Capricorn's statue and watched it as it passed over him. Next, he saw Scorpio's and then Taurus. As he watched, he realized that the statues were out of order. Following their rotation, he saw that not one statue was in its correct order.

Then a thought occurred to him. Maybe that was the path he had to take. He had to find the correct order they were supposed to be in, but he just couldn't figure out which order it could be. Was it the strongest to the weakest? Or was

it the first to the la.... Wait, that was it. It was right there in the riddle. He had to figure out which one was the very first zodiac and then leap to the next one in that order.

Dev focused and tried to remember the lessons he was taught when he was younger. It was kind of hard. He had always tuned his dad out when history was being taught. He closed his eyes and focused. The images for each sign swirled around in his mind in a mass jumble. He stopped their movement and began to move them around. Placing them in a different order, but each one he tried seemed wrong. After a while, he noticed that while the combination wasn't correct, some signs were in the correct order. Instead of rearranging the entire line, he moved the ones that were out of place. This felt like one gigantic puzzle, and he had never really been great at them to begin with. Dev wasn't about to give up, because he knew he wouldn't get to Dagon without the correct combination. He continued to focus and rearrange the signs until finally; they were in the correct order.

He opened his eyes and stared up at the statues, focusing on the path laid out in his mind. He caught sight of the first statue he needed, and taking a deep breath, he leaped for it. He landed atop the statue and waited for a second. When nothing happened, and he wasn't blown off, he locked on to the next statue and jumped for it. While he was in the air, he tracked the other statues' locations and continued on his path. Leaping from one statue to the next, he made his way to the top. After reaching the final one, he took a moment to rest while looking at the pedestal that held his totem. Taking one more giant plunge, he flew through the air and landed lightly at the top. He was bathed in a warm golden light, and his totem appeared around his neck where it belonged. With his totem in place, he felt all of his powers return to him. When Dagon materialized next to him, Dev shouted with joy as he wrapped his arms around him.

"Good to see you again, buddy. I knew you could do it." Dagon said to him as he licked his face.

"Dagon. I'm so happy to see you. It was so miserable to be without you," replied Dev.

Dev stood up and looked out over the jungle that he had traveled from to get to this point. He looked down towards the clearing, marveling at how high up he was. He noticed a dark shadow moving and saw the panther slinking back into the jungle. It turned once to look up at him, and Dev raised a hand in farewell. He was surprised to find that he would miss him and was grateful for his help. He was proud of his accomplishments and felt stronger in mind and spirit. He closed his eyes and held his totem tight, and then when he opened them; he was back in his room.

"Oh, man. So glad to finally be back in my room. After all that, I need a nap," said Dev.

Looking out the window, he saw the sun had started going down. "Or, I guess I will just go to bed." He thought to himself.

"Well done, son, I knew you could do it. Weird though, you seemed to have found him faster than I thought. Did you run into any trouble?" Dev turned around and saw his father standing in his room, waiting for his return, but he was too tired to respond or give him a piece of his mind. Walking forward, Rodney raised one of his hands while also apologizing. "Unfortunately, I'm sorry, but I have one more test for you." His father placed his hand on Dev's forehead and made him fade into darkness.

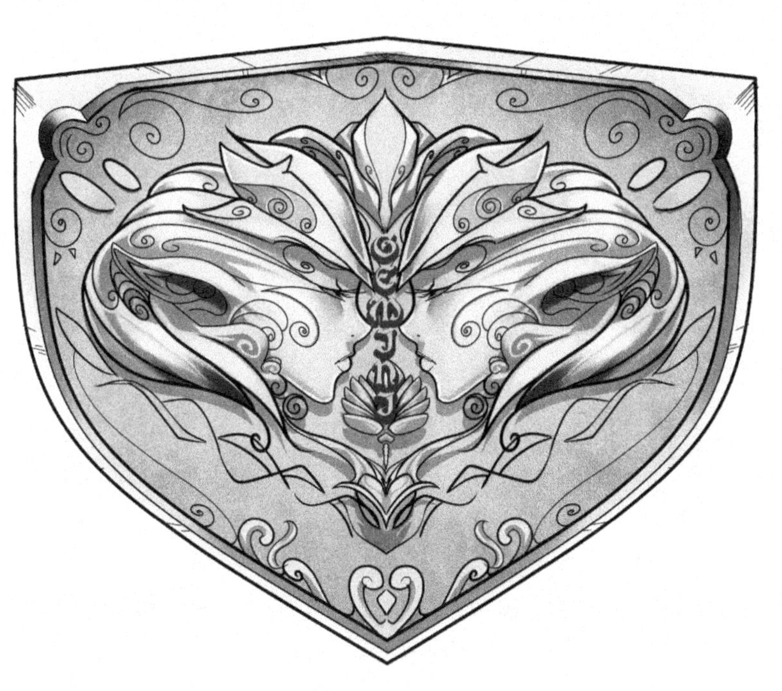

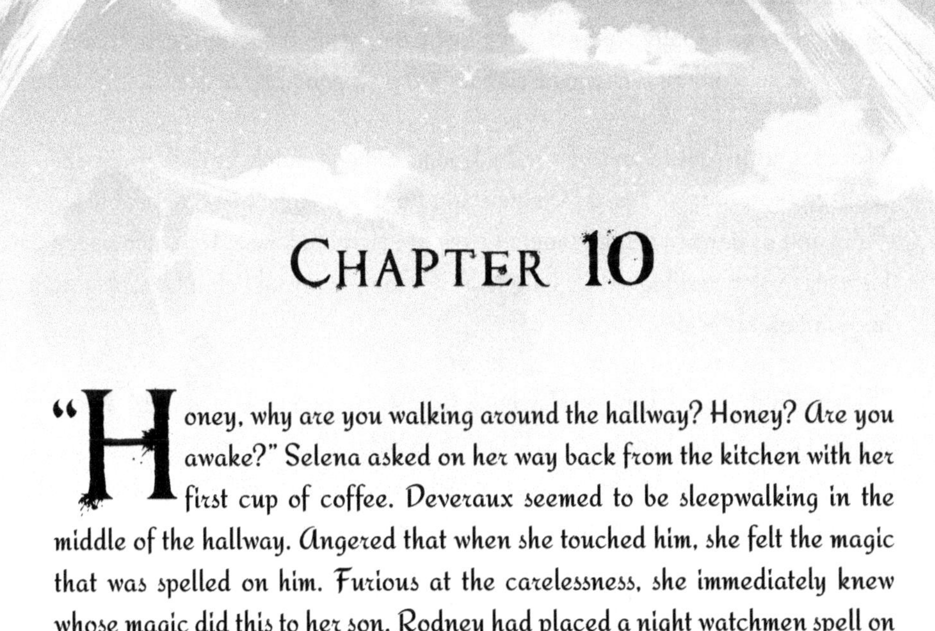

CHAPTER 10

"Honey, why are you walking around the hallway? Honey? Are you awake?" Selena asked on her way back from the kitchen with her first cup of coffee. Deveraux seemed to be sleepwalking in the middle of the hallway. Angered that when she touched him, she felt the magic that was spelled on him. Furious at the carelessness, she immediately knew whose magic did this to her son. Rodney had placed a night watchmen spell on him. "Rodney Lee Aubrey Vanseal!!! Leave my son alone!!!" She yelled as she blazed past him and busted through the master bedroom door. "You will not have him training this late on a school night. He needs his rest, and you know he was raised here, not back home. The night watchmen spell is for the soldiers to push past long nights of war, not long nights of book reports and math packets. If you don't want to sleep on the couch for the next week, go down that hall and take that spell off him!" Thundered Selena.

Rolling out of bed, Rodney reached for his robe and then headed down the hallway to where Dev was hunkered down like he was in anticipation of something. Looking at his son, he chose to try one last test before he took the

spell off. Stomping as soft as he could, he watched as Dev instantly turned around in a battle stance and raised the ground beneath the house. Dev thought he was protecting his loved ones, so he removed the house from the hallway where he and his dad stood.

"Oh shit!" Moving lightning fast, Rodney snuck up behind Dev, only to be met with a counter kick. Defending himself with an arm block, Rodney took a step back and thought of the best way to wake Dev up without him setting the house on fire. Dev was really trying to keep him from lifting the spell. So, a thought came to him. Rodney messaged Selena, *"tell your son to go to bed!"*

She curiously walked out of the bedroom, only to catch herself when she realized there was no floor. "Rodney, what did you make him do now? Dev? Baby, put us down!" Selena shouted from her floating house. Dev recognized his mom's voice and looked up only to have Rodney portal behind him, laying his hand on his back.

"Sleep, child, sleep." Laying Dev back to rest. He picked him up and waited for the house to float back down, listening to Selena's comment the whole way. After the house was safely back on the ground, Rodney made sure that Dev was safely back in bed before he headed back to his room to sleep.

However, when he reached the room, he saw his wife glaring at him from the doorway. He tried to smile sweetly and slip by her so that he could return to bed. She blocked him completely and pointed back down the hall towards the living room, "Couch," she said. Rodney thought she was joking and chuckled to himself as he tried to slide past her again. One more time, she pointed down the hall and said, "Couch." Then she turned around and closed the door in Rodney's face, locking it behind her.

Not believing what was happening, he tried to open the door, only to find that he couldn't make it budge. Using a little magic, he tried once more and found that the door still would not open for him. Realizing he was pretty much

screwed, with his head down and his tail tucked between his legs, he headed towards the couch to sleep.

The next morning Dev came downstairs and was greeted by his father sleeping on the couch. Slapping his dad on the shoulder, Dev walked past him towards the kitchen to grab some oatmeal before Anthony showed up.

"Why are you on the couch dad?" He asked. "I had the weirdest magical dream last night. I swear this training has me breathing magic. Do you think since things have been quiet and nothing has happened for the last week or so that I could get a break for one or two days? Prom is coming up, and I wanna be a teen for a bit," asked Dev.

Rodney looked up over the couch and said, "Sure, I'm going to have to use those few days for damage control to take your mom out anyway."

"Mr. Vanseal, would you like some coffee, dear?" Gabby asked as she made the kids sit down and eat their food before their mom took them to school. Dev just looked at his dad, wondering what he meant by that. He then grabbed his backpack and headed to the car where Anthony was standing. With him trying to audition every girl on the dance team, cheerleading team, and even debate team to go with him to prom, Dev never knew who he was talking to on the phone. He was that guy in school that knew everyone.

After moving the ward so they could leave, they headed to school. "So, Dev. Who are you taking? Remy is already thinking she has like four guys willing to ask her, and you're one of them," said Anthony.

Dev realized that going with Remy probably wasn't the best idea after that scene in the mall. "Man, I was thinking about it. I mean, it is something I've wanted to do since the fourth grade, but after how she acted in the mall, I don't know. I might just go by myself or just work on some more training with dad. Prom is not the end of the world, but battling these Kantors is. They've been super quiet, and I can feel something coming," said Dev.

"Save the world another day. You only get two proms and who knows a first time, wink, wink. Just pick your lady wisely because I heard there's an after-party at Grace's house. Only her older brother is home. Her parents are going to be celebrating their honeymoon in Aspen," stated Anthony.

Hopping out of the car, the boys saw trucks pulling up with all the decorations and food for this weekend. Rochelle City wasn't the biggest place to live. It had everything most big cities had, but what the city loved to do was make every party a thing to talk about. Since there were three high schools, everyone always tried to outdo the other.

After Dev said goodbye to Anthony, he looked around the hallway at all the couples that weren't couples two weeks ago and just laughed. It was crazy how it took things like a social party out of a movie for people to get the courage to just say hi. He knew he couldn't say anything because Anthony had to make a bet just to get him out on his first date with Remy, but hey whatever. Walking to second period, he looked around, wondering who he could ask. It wasn't like he had girls lining up to date the track star. Everyone wanted the football star or the basketball star. Dev knew that after his botched date with Remy, she wasn't an option. He knew she would just take over and make his prom miserable by trying to beat Simone MacAroy for prom queen. Shaking his head, he headed towards his class. As he sat in class, his mind wandered over the possibilities he had for a date. Sadly, there was not a lot to choose from. Before he knew it, he heard the bell signal the end of class.

"Please turn your homework up to the front so it can be graded," said the teacher in the background. Sitting in the chair, Dev felt a thump on his back.

"I can take it up there," said a voice.

Looking up, he saw Harley. "The bell means it's time to go, space cadet... you know you have been very quiet today. What's up?"

"Nothing. It was something Anthony was saying. Supposedly there's a party after prom, and I'm just trying to figure out what to tell my parents." Dev said as he grabbed his bag for the next class.

"There's a party?" Asked Harley.

"Yes. Has anyone came and asked you yet?" Asked Dev.

"Nope. I'm the weird girl with the crazy family, remember?" Said Harley as they walked.

Heading to class, he noticed the posters that had been placed all over the school, promoting the end of the year prom. A crazy idea struck him out of nowhere. Turning to face Harley, he stopped right in front of her and dropped to one knee with his hands behind his back. Using a small bit of magic, he produced her favorite carnation, which was an enormous sunflower, and he pulled it out for her to see.

She gasped at the beautiful flower and took it from him. "Well, well, what is this for my good sir?" She asked as she pressed the flower to her nose, inhaling the sweet scent.

He smiled at her, and, with a twinkle in his eye, he asked, "Ms. Braymark, would you do me the honor of being my date for prom?" The other girls in the hall began giggling at the display while the other boys rolled their eyes at the fancy prom proposal.

Harley looked at Dev in disbelief and thought, where did that flower come from? Shaking her head, she smiled at him because, for the moment, she didn't care. "Yes. Of course, I will, Mr. Vanseal, it would be my pleasure to be your date." Laughing in relief, Dev grabbed his stuff from the floor, and they continued on to class.

Anthony chose that moment to show up. "So. I see you finally proposed to her." He laughed, "So will you guys be having a fall wedding or something in the

118

spring?" He wiggled his eyebrows at both of them as they walked down the hall. Dev just laughed and smiled at his best friend and then looked at Harley, who was blushing from embarrassment.

"You're okay with going to prom with me, right?" He asked.

She rolled her eyes at his question while everyone else was watching. "Yes, I would love to go to prom with you, Dev. So, don't worry about anyone else, okay?" With that said, she clutched her flower and headed off to her science class. Dev smiled as he turned the corner and walked towards his history class, wondering how the rest of the day would go.

Walking into Mr. Houston's class, Dev saw Remy sitting in the front row. When she saw him, she glared as he walked to his desk. Not really bothered by her attitude, he sat down and pulled out his books to get ready for class. While he looked around the classroom, waiting for Mr. Houston to start, a folded piece of paper fell onto his desk. Curious, Dev opened it and read the note scribbled on it.

So, I heard you asked Harley Braymark to prom. What about me? Didn't our date mean anything to you at all? I can't believe you would do this to me. I thought you were different, but I guess you guys are all the same. Thanks for nothing. Never speak to me again.

The note was signed at the bottom by Remy. Dev looked up at her in surprise and saw her glaring at him from her desk. When she saw him looking at her, she raised her hand and flipped up her middle finger, mouthing the word asshole. Dev took a look at the note, then back at her, and did the only thing that crossed his mind. He laughed. He laughed so hard that he had to put his head down and bang the top of his desk.

"Mr. Vanseal, are you okay?" Mr. Houston asked from his desk.

Dev raised his head, "Yes, sir. I'm fine. It's just that Remy wrote me a hilarious joke, and I just couldn't hold it in." Remy looked even more outraged at the statement, which made Dev laugh even harder.

Mr. Houston looked between the two of them and said, "Well, Ms. Phillips, what's this joke? Why don't you share with the class?"

Remy stared back in shock at the question, trying to figure out how to respond. As Remy tried to come up with a knock, knock joke off the top of her head, she noticed all the kids in the class looking at her, waiting to hear the punch line.

The school bell rang to start the third period, and as everybody waited, Mr. Houston interrupted her to start the class. He was excited because they were working on Ancient Egyptian hieroglyphics. Very annoyed with him, Remy looked back at Dev as he sat at his desk and laughed. He even took the time to princess wave at her when she periodically stared at him every ten minutes.

"Wow, I can't believe she was so upset with you asking Harley to prom." Dev heard Dagon say in his head as he tried to concentrate on the lesson.

Chuckling to himself once more, he replied, "Yeah, I know it's crazy. Remy complained to everyone about our date, calling me weird, and now she wants another one."

"So, since you have a date, you know you need a corsage and a limo? Oh, by the way, does this make you and Harley an item now? Are you guys going to go steady with each other?" Dev could hear his familiar chuckling in the back of his head as he pondered those questions. He hadn't thought about needing a corsage or a way to get to prom with her without looking dumb. His car wasn't the best model out there and not the newest. Also, he hadn't thought about what it would mean if they did go to prom together. Would she expect more from him after, or would they still be friends? Still thinking over these questions, he felt the unmistakable feeling of someone using magic, but this had a dark and evil feel to it.

Lifting his head, he noticed something out the corner of his eye and looked out the window. He saw flames leaping across the outside commons area of the school. Flames were popping up one by one, consuming the bushes and plants from the school's garden. He couldn't believe his eyes and stood up, slamming his hands on his desk. The loud noise startled everyone, and they turned to him in shock.

"Mr. Vanseal? What is the meaning of this interruption?" Mr. Houston shouted.

Before he could answer, someone pointed at the window and screamed. "Fire!!!" The other students looked out the window and began to scream as they tried to grab their things and rush out of the room. Mr. Houston tried to gain control of the room to tell everyone not to panic and to head for the doors in an orderly fashion. Soon, the fire alarm began to wail and caused the students to panic even more.

Dev, along with the rest of the class, rushed towards the nearest fire exit. He looked around and saw other students from different classes heading in the same direction, all asking what could have caused this to happen. He reached for his backpack to grab his phone to call either his parents, Harley or Anthony, but realized he left it. Dev sprung out of the crowd and rushed back to the class before the teacher could stop him. He wasn't too worried about the fire or his safety because if it was absolutely necessary, he could flash himself out of danger. Feeling the heat, he reached the classroom; he was surprised to find that the fire had spread across the common area to the window. Thick black smoke was coming in through the cracks of the window. It stung his eyes and made it hard to see and breathe through the inky blackness.

"What the hell are you doing, you moron?" Dagon roared at him as he flashed himself to his side. *"That phone and bag are nowhere near as important as your life! Now let's get out of here before you get fried to a crisp!"*

Dev felt himself becoming lightheaded from inhaling the smoke and started coughing. He tried to use his magic to create a gust of wind to blow the smoke away, but nothing happened, and the smoke continued to surround him. He felt the dark evil presence when the fire first appeared, surrounding him, and it drove him to his knees. He could hear an evil laugh and what sounded like the hiss of a snake come out of the darkness.

"I don't know what is going on here, but we need to get out now!" Dagon cried as he tried to push him back towards the door. The heat and the smoke from the flames were making Dev disoriented, and he could barely focus as he crawled towards the hallway. With Dagon guiding him as best he could, he continued until he felt a pair of hands drag him out of the smoke. The figure helped him walk towards the fire exit and out into the fresh air.

They continued to walk away from the school, across the safety line behind the firefighters working on putting out the fire. A voice whispered, *"Good luck putting out that fire boys."* Startled by the voice, Dev tried to look at where it was coming from but couldn't see who it was in all the chaos.

Gulping for air, Dev wiped the soot from his eyes. "You are a complete idiot, you dweeb!" Looking to his left, he saw Marcus with soot on his face, slightly coughing as well. Dev couldn't believe that Marcus, of all people, had saved him. "I saw you run in and ran after you. Then I saw your butt getting ready to pass out, so I just slithered you out of there. The fire drills say stay low and close to the floor when there's that much smoke." He said as he wiped his face. "What the hell is the matter with you? Were you trying to fry yourself?"

Dev stood in shock, trying to process what had happened. Next thing he knew, he was tackled in a bear hug. Looking up, he saw Harley gripping him tightly, tears in her eyes. "Harley, I'm okay. Please let me go before you crush my lungs." Dev said through her vise grip. Harley released him with a slight squeak, and an embarrassed look as Anthony ran up to them.

"Dude, what happened to you?" Asked Anthony.

Harley answered for him, "Genius here decided to run into a burning building for some dumb reason." She glared at Dev as she wiped her face.

"You're not serious?" Anthony said with a look of disbelief.

"Yep," Harley said.

They shared a look and then both punched Dev in the stomach as hard as they could. Dev doubled over and held himself as Marcus laughed from where he was standing.

"If you ever pull another stupid stunt like that, I will do a lot worse than punch you, Deveraux Vanseal!" Harley growled.

"Yeah. What she said," said Anthony.

Harley walked over to Marcus and smiled up at him. "Thank you for running in after him. It was courageous of you."

Marcus smiled back. "Yea, it was, wasn't it? Maybe now you will consider going to prom with me?" He asked. Harley looked slightly embarrassed again as she looked at Dev, then back at Marcus. "I'm sorry, but I can't. I told Dev I would go with him."

Marcus blinked and then glared at Dev. "I guess I should have left you to fry, dweeb." He walked off, grumbling to himself.

"I need all kids to separate to their classrooms for a headcount," said Mr. Houston. The firefighter had given him a ladder, so all the teachers could count the number of kids outside. One by one, the principal allowed the students to call their parents to come get them for the day. The flames almost acted like a wildfire, but it had been raining just that morning with dew still left on the car windows, which was weird. "Okay, children, school is cancelled, and classes have been dismissed. Please look on the school website for when school will be reopening," said Mr. Houston.

"Is prom still in a few weeks?" One of the kids shouted.

"The gym was unaffected since it was on the other side of the school, so I don't see why not." Mr. Houston replied as he got down to talk to the rest of the teachers. This statement caused the students' spirits to lift slightly.

While most of the teachers gathered to find out what had happened to their classrooms, Harley's mom, Elizabeth, Mr. Weber, and Mrs. Jones all huddled in the corner of the crowd.

"Levi, I know you felt that energy. This was no normal fire." Mrs. Jones said to the principal.

"It's almost like the presence is still here, but very mute. I will not have the kids in danger," said Elizabeth, "I'm sending Uni to walk my kids' home. This is an attack!"

"Ladies calm down and have your familiars help. I want you two to fan out and see if you see anything or sense anything. This might be connected to our home problem or some punk kid lighting school fires. Libra send Uni with your kids back home and Gemini, you have Myuka blend in with the trees to keep a close eye on the other kids. I'll have Tyson go find Cancer, just in case if this is something more than a rogue student." Mr. Weber said to Mrs. Jones and Mrs. Braymark, also known as Gemini and Libra. Before taking off in different directions, both ladies nodded at Taurus.

"Tyson, I need you to go find Detective Erickson in Oklahoma at the Prickson City Police Department. Tell him I need him to come look at the fire to rule out Zortegan magic," messaged Mr. Weber to his familiar as he stood stunned over what had happened. Pulling out his Celestial item, he spoke into it. "I'm calling an emergency meeting immediately for everyone to assemble in Zortega within the next hour."

Chapter 11

Flashing in front of the police department, Tyson remembered to think small and stay invisible. Walking past all the police officers, Tyson walked around the desk and to the office door that said, Detective Daymon Erickson. He was the best detective they had on the force with the most collars on the police force. He was a tall, stocky guy with a black fade haircut and a nicely groomed goatee. His stature was one of confidence and curiosity of knowledge. He was sitting at his desk, determined to figure out the link between a few homicide cases. Fazing through the door, Tyson looked around the office as he headed towards the desk. He looked around the cluttered space full of bookshelves covered in case files. On one side of the room sat Detective Erickson at his desk. On the other side, there was a whiteboard with copies of photos and other information pertaining to a case. He walked over to a photo on the desk and greeted the sand crab in a seashell. The bull blew smoke out of his nose to get the crab's attention. The three-foot invisible bull with a lot on his mind startled Chandler the crab, from his slumber.

"Well, hello, how may I help you?" Said Daymon. Tyson was surprised that he noticed him from the flow of papers scattered on his desk. Asking once more, not even turning from his work. "Hey there, Scout, it looks like we have a visitor. I haven't seen too many of our kind in Prickson, Oklahoma. What brings you all the way this direction?" Said Daymon. Chandler scuttled over to his Niyor's desk.

"I've come with urgent news. My Niyor has asked that I come to find you. There has been what could be a magical attack on the school that hosts three of our royal lines' children. After the other magical attacks lately, he wants you to come and do an investigation on the school immediately so you can rule out a random student. So, please come, we need your help right away," requested Tyson.

Looking up from his work, he began to pet Tyson on the head, and then he grabbed his coat and keys. His concentration never broke as he changed his attention from his work to what Tyson just told him. Walking out of his office, he yelled out the door, "Captain, I think I might have found a lead, but it's outta town! Don't wait up for me!" Creeping over his arm, Chandler fazed back into his tie clip as Tyson followed Daymon out to his car.

Hopping in, Cancer asked, "So, where is Taurus now? Is he still back at the school?" Tyson nodded his head yes at Cancer. Putting the car in gear, Cancer said, "Hold on, it's much harder transporting vehicles across lands." Flashing through the portal in his rear-view mirror, he headed to Rochelle City.

Driving to the parking lot, Cancer pulled up in the back of the school only to witness the damage the fire had done. Tyson hopped out of the car and back to his Niyor in a friendly embrace.

"Hello, old friend. We meet again under what looks like more dangerous circumstances," said Mr. Weber to Mr. Erickson.

Looking around, he noticed all the teachers and firefighters." It looks like the science class got a little careless with the Bunsen burners, I see." Laughing

at his own pun, Daymon quickly could see how serious Weber was being, especially with all the teachers around.

"I'll pose as a fire and arson detective so I can get close to the commons area. Do you mind keeping people at bay so I can do a proper investigation for the council? I would hate to hear Virgo complain about how I didn't do it right." Patting his old mentor on his back, he walked over to the affected area.

After changing his appearance, he waved his badge to the fire chief and looked around. Weber then asked everyone to reframe from the courtyard until the arson detective deemed it okay to get their belongings. Cancer then emerged himself into the area once it was cleared out. It saddened him to have to tell Weber that it wasn't just a rogue kid, but completely magic-related.

He didn't know if it was Zortegan. It gave off the coldest energy he'd ever seen outside of the projection tests. Casting his hand over the plants, he felt an overwhelming signature coming from the cinders.

Standing behind him in the shadow of the tree was a figure that started whispering to Cancer, "The Qualum. I need the Qualum. It's the only thing that can save all of us."

It held out its shadow to touch him. Startled by it, Cancer jumped back. "Who's there?"

Looking around in a fighting stance, Daymon scanned the courtyard for whoever was talking to him about Zortegan knowledge. "Who's there?" Said Daymon. Standing behind the burnt tree, the figure just pointed to where the ashes started.

Clapping his hands to transform into his combat outfit, he manifested his weapons. A pair of double-bladed black and brass knuckles appeared in each hand. Each one had a six-inch blade on either side of his fist with sharpened barbs going across the front. Standing there with his magic expelled, he questioned the shadow's intention. Daymon then hesitantly crept towards the place the figure had pointed to.

His detective spirit always got the best of him, and he placed his hand over the spot. He instantly became overwhelmed with magical energy. The powerful magic was black as night and nearly engulfed him in negativity and hate. The fear Cancer felt made him cry out for help to his friend. Chandler did the one thing he knew he could do and encased Cancer in his crab shell. Chandler's love for him soothed his mind as the magical energy couldn't affect him any more inside the shell.

"Chandler, you must get me to Zortega at once. I need to tell Taurus what happened and what I found. Please, old friend," said Daymon before he passed out. Dashing as fast as he could moving through the portals, Chandler delivered his Niyor to the doors of the Nova Castle, where the meeting was being held.

"Help!" Chandler cried out, but the commotion of the many voices in the room couldn't hear him.

Standing at the hallway entrance was the General guard, where Avi Erwin was making his rounds. He rushed forward with his familiar at his side. A large cheetah-like creature with blue fur and green feathers in its mane. He had black spots traveling all the way down his body, ending in a tail with matching green and blue feathers. He wore an ornate black chest plate with the crest of the Paratar emblazoned on it.

He gripped his sword in his hand, ready to defend the hall if necessary. As he moved closer, he realized it was Chandler and his Niyor, Cancer. Sheathing his blade, he reached down to lend a hand to the unconscious leader. Cancer awoke with a gasp and sat up, panting hard. He looked around and saw that he was in Zortega outside the hall on the street. He looked at Avi, who was staring at him with concern as he reached to help him onto his feet.

"Are you all right, sir?" The guard asked as he stepped back to his post.

Taking a deep breath in while running his hand over his face, he replied, "Yes. Just a little shaken up, but I'm okay. Thank you for your help, General Erwin."

Unaware of what was happening outside, Taurus asked everyone that had materialized quickly to his meeting to join the table. Taurus stood at the head of the table, watching the assembled leaders argue back and forth over this latest incident. Although no one had been harmed, they knew this was a direct attack on them. Now everyone wanted revenge on this mysterious enemy, but no one knew who they needed to attack. This lack of information began to sow fear among the council. Banging his fist on the table to call the members to attention. "Everyone, please, we must not panic!" He shouted over the din of everyone screaming. They all stopped and stared at him, begging for answers from this newest attack.

"Someone, please tell us what is going on and why this is happening!" Pisces cried out from his seat.

Taurus bowed his head and exhaled before addressing the others. "I know that these are trying times, but we must remain calm and stand together. Now I have Cancer currently on the scene investigating the attack. He will give us a full report when he arrives, which should be any minute now."

Everyone sat around, looking at each other with fearful looks in their eyes. Rodney stood and addressed the table in a quiet voice. "I think I speak for everyone, especially myself, Leo, and Libra, when I say we need answers. This was a deliberate attack on not only us, but our children as well. This has gone on long enough!" He exclaimed as his powers exploded around him. Lightning flowed all over his body, flashing through the room. The other members threw up shields and ducked under the table to protect themselves. His eyes flashed with white-ish blue lightning as he raised his fist, shouting. "I say we go and question the python again! This time we demand he give us the answers we want, or we torture him!" Rodney looked around the table at the other members gathered there.

"So, who is with me?" Rodney asked.

The others stared at him in shock at his declaration and jumped when the doors to the hall burst open. Cancer rushed in, looking shaken and pale, after slumping down in his seat. The others stared at him as he put his head in his hands and took a few shuddering breaths. As Rodney watched Cancer collect himself, his anger slowly began to fade, and his powers dissipated as he sat down and waited to hear what Cancer had to say.

After Cancer had calmed himself, he stood and faced everyone. "Leaders of the council, I have finished my investigation, and Taurus was right to hold this meeting. There was black energy left at the school. It was Zortegan magic, but none I've ever seen before outside of the stories my predecessor used to tell me. A figure also visited me, asking for the Qualum. Whoever it was knew of our sacred book of magic and clearly wanted it. After this attack, I'm definitely sure that what the python says is true. The Ophiuchan line has plotted a return, but now the question is, what do we do? From what I could tell, that fire was lit using the darkest of magic. I could still feel the dark presence lingering over the damaged site. It was so strong that even after they put the fire out, I could still feel negative energy radiating from it. If it wasn't for Chandler, I would have been hypnotized into a completely dark and negative state."

He sat back up and exhaled a deep breath. Waving his hand in the air, Cancer made a pack of cigarettes appear in front of him. He pulled one out and used his magic to light it before taking a deep drag and exhaling the smoke from his lungs.

Taurus stood, and all eyes turned to him. With a grim look, he stated, "This is indeed troubling news. That spot must be purified, and all excess negative energy expelled from the school." The others nodded in agreement to the statement.

"Well, man, it looks like we need to go talk to the damn snake then. Something is happening, and I for one, need to be in the damn loop to better prepare

myself for what looks like an unstoppable attack," said Leo as he looked over the group.

"Yeah!"

"I wanna know as well!"

"Let's go right now!" Shouted the group.

Leading up to the head of the table. Sagittarius's light glowed around her in a warming embrace, one by one, the council took notice. She usually wasn't one to involve herself unless it was about resolving peace, so this action was a humbling gesture.

"I am all about getting answers, but I feel we should all calm down and head to the cell as the leaders we were all meant to be. Taurus, if you would be so kind, it is obvious that we need to be present in front of the snake to see and hear with our own eyes and ears." Said Renee. Glancing at the group, as they stared back at him, Taurus decided to just nod his head in agreement with Sagittarius.

"I will have the guards prepare our arrival because, for all anyone knows, this is just what the snake wants. He plans for all of us to be in one room with him," grunted Taurus as he sat back in his chair. He waved one of the Epsis over and told it to summon General Avi. When Avi entered the room, he dropped to one knee and bowed his head. "How may I serve the council?" He said.

"Avi, please escort the council to the Gravite Caverns so we can all get the questions that we seek," said Taurus. One by one, the members began to descend to the hallway and out the castle doors.

Avi rounded up some of his finest men to watch over and protect each member. Two in front and a council member in back, they strolled down the street for all the townspeople to see. Assembled down at the edge of the road by the moonlight river was the crescent turtles, all ready for them to ride to the Gravite Caverns. The seven-foot-tall and thirty feet long midnight blue turtles with coal-black shells were magnificent. As they breathed, their veins glowed an electrified white color was as piercing as their halo white eyes. Dressed in the most beautiful, majestic geode armor of Zortegan design, the leader kneeled to General Ervin. Holding out his hand to help the ladies on the back of the two-seater saddles, the council members hopped on the six turtles.

"Yah!"

Standing grand and strong, the turtles stomped in running formation. Building up momentum, the turtles began to expel their fins to fly. Gusting their fins in the wind, they traveled to the former brother land, which was now the forbidden home to the Kantors, the jailed, and Raymyth the Python. The canyons were the equivalent of a dead moon. It was made up of caves and craters, and nothing grew anywhere in this wasteland. They looked down in sadness at the way that this once beautiful land had decayed. The evil that radiated from the python had sapped the life from the land and left it an empty shell. Not only that, but it had also warped all that lived there into evil twisted forms. They could see dark shapes and shadows darting from cave to cave, emitting shrieks and growls as they fought and battled each other.

In the distance, they could see a mountain that looked like a jagged spire rising out of the ground. There was no safe way to climb it from the bottom to the top because of the sharp, jagged rocks that jutted out in all directions. At the very top was a cage that had bars that glowed with celestial magic that shined brightly. Even with the pillars in place, the evil power of Raymyth could be felt as it leaked out and continued to poison the region. What most were unaware of was that the mountain was a farce. Below the mountain was a swamp-like meadow that was truly breathtaking in size and ominous magic power. The meadow gave off an image of portrayal, so its emotions turned the area sad and gloomy once it lost its people. It now became a place of enslavement when the mountain was formed. The zodiac members all agreed that it was the perfect place to hide a jail in plain sight since the Lex Meadow protected the Gravite Caverns.

Holding on tight, the turtles began to dive in a Y-shape formation to the cavern entrance, which was once a geyser, but now it was a steam hole. Now, with Taurus being the Qualum's protector for this period, Taurus wondered if bring the book was a good idea. But it was the only thing that was strong enough to protect everyone. Weary of the snake's actions, he unpacked the bag that he carried on his shoulder and placed a small twelve-sided crystal with a Xlatherus key on the book. The Qualum was large in nature, its front cover held universal magic that was given to the Legions long before the Zortegan's came to be. Once opened, he started to read a passage out of the book to protect all the members. He then casted a barrier around the whole meadow to ensure nothing came in or out.

Landing the turtles on the outside of the steam hole, the captain made sure everyone was alright after giving the General the okay to open the entrance to the caverns. Standing in the center of the door, Avi took both silver nightsticks off his back and snapped them together. Kneeling, he pulled a celestial flower out of his pocket and placed it on the ground for the meadow to eat. Banging his staff three times, he shouted, "Alocknic!"

After a few silent moments, streams of purple and blue magic shot out of the ground and into the air, surrounding the circle. The zodiac members held on to each other as the floor began to drop away slowly. Surly enough in one corner a doorway was created, most of the new council members had never seen this before the Python was imprisoned.

"Do you really expect us ladies to walk down some secret hole of death just because Cancer can't interrogate a snake, right?" Aquarius shouted as she tried to act as if she was too proud to get dirty.

Looking at her, Leo turned and replied, "Woman, if you want the questions you need to be answered, you're gonna walk your butt down the corridor like the rest of us because no one is going to stay here or carry you."

Walking up to him, she shoved him out of the way with her shoulder. "You'd be wise not to piss me off, you're not the only one that knows how to make someone disappear. You young ones have a lot to learn about respect because if it wasn't for us paving the way for you to be here, you wouldn't be holding that leadership seat." Bossed Aquarius as she walked behind Avi down the dimly lit path. As they all walked through the hollow tunnels, they realized they had to keep close because every tunnel mapped a different jailed prison. The only ones that knew the true location were the Paratar guards, which happened to be the ones escorting them.

Marked by a steel-carved door and two guards was the cage of Raymyth, the familiar and soul spirit of the banished line of the Ophiuchan's. As they walked down into the cavern, they heard a soft hiss that seemed to come from the very walls of the cave. A deep chill seeped into their bones and made their hair on their skin stand on end. Out of the dark, they heard a deep chuckle that made the wall tremble from the echo.

"Well, well, well. If it isssn't the twelve leadersss of the Zodiac," a dark voice said from the deep inside the cavern. "My, my, I'm ssso ssstar ssstruck, I've got chillsss. If I'd known I wasss entertaining royalty, I would have cleaned up a bit." The group looked around at the walls as the voice continued to chuckle at their obvious discomfort. "I apologize for the messss, but asss you all probably know, I don't have many visitorsss."

They continued to walk towards the cage that was located at the back of the cavern. The closer they got, the more oppressive the feeling of his power was as it washed over them. Even behind bars, it made them feel violated and unclean, as if they had been dunked in a tank of toxic waste.

Rodney, walking with the group, could feel the darkness and raw power of Raymyth. He looked at the others and could see they were having a hard time standing against it. He manifested a shield around them and saw the immediate relief on the faces of the others.

"Well, look who hasss a boossst in power," Raymyth mocked. *"I don't remember the leader of the Capricorn line who imprisssoned me being thisss powerful."*

Rodney gritted his teeth at the remark but kept his emotions in check to keep the shield stable. He knew if he let his anger get the best of him, it would be hard to focus. In the distance, they could see a dim spark glowing. The closer they got, the more details came to focus. The glow was the light from the celestial bars. The only issue was they were a lot dimmer than they were supposed to be. It alarmed them at how dark they had grown from the lack of celestial magic.

Rodney boosted his shield's power because he knew without it, they would be at the mercy of his aura. The hissing grew louder as they reached the cage. They stared into the darkness, trying to get a glimpse of him. *"I profusssely apologize for not being where you can ssssee me. One moment, pleassse,"* the voice stated. Soon they heard a scraping sound against the stone floor coming towards them. *"Pleassse don't be ssso afraid of me. I can't break out of thisss cage... yet,"* said Raymyth with a chuckle. Out of the darkness came a head the size of a garbage truck. Its scales seemed to sneak out like flower petals. They were a bright blood red with black tips. His shiny blue opaque eyes were the size of battle shields that slowly blinked as he watched them from beyond the bars. A large black tongue flicked out of his mouth, back and forth, tasting the air as he slid closer and hissed softly. The twelve leaders looked up in horror and amazement at the sight of their enemy's authentic form.

They stood back behind Rodney's barrier, grateful for the protection from the worst of this creature's malevolent power. *"Ssso many visssitsss in sssuch a ssshort amount of time. It almossst ssseems like you guysss missss me all of a sssudden."* Raymyth said with a chuckle. *"Ssso, to what do I owe the pleasssure of your company thisss time? It mussst be dire to warrant the full council to come ssssee me."*

With much hesitation, Pisces, the eldest of the twelve, stepped forward to speak for the council. "We have come here for the safety of our people and our families to stop the rumors that you've had anything to do with the recent attacks," said Pisces.

"Attackssss, you sssay? Pleasssssee do tell a lonely sssnake who doesssn't get much contact with the outssside worldsss."

Looking back at the group for a moment, Pisces' eyes started glowing as he spat out. "I might be an old man, but don't make me find a way to make spirit sushi." Staring at the creature, they almost saw an evil grin come across his face as Pisces began to speak for him.

"What Once Was A Vision Of Complete Domination Turned Into A Travesty. Only Two That Can Derail My Long Casted Prophecy. Royal Legacies Demanded One Unfit To Exist But Into The History Books, Their Will Be A Twist. Two Lines Remain Angry, But They Don't Know Their Worth. If Their Generations Remain Angry, It Will Be Our Rebirth. My Heir Will Rise To Kill All twelve Lives By The Hand Of The Black Bloodline. They Will Rise When The Power Matured Into Plenty. With Four Barons And Countesses Hidden Away, It Came In Handy..."

Rodney stepped forward, shouting, "Enough of this! Tell us what you have done to cause us so much strife!"

Raymyth stared at him, continuing to flick his tongue in the air. Suddenly, his eyes grew even more significant, and he jerked straight up. *"What a pleasssant sssurprise. I may not have to break out to get what I want."* Ignoring Rodney, he stared straight ahead at Taurus, who was clutching the bag containing the Qualum to his chest. Raymyth could smell the leather binding with the Jalacken snake buckles. He remembered how beautiful its Vewanic armor was. It was soft, but without the key it was utterly impossible to penetrate because of the blood seal of the twelve original Legacies. Suddenly, Taurus started to slide forward, as if he were being pulled by some unseen force.

"What's happening? Help me!" Cried out Taurus.

"Grab him and pull him back!"

Everyone jumped forward to grab Taurus and yank him back before he was dragged in front of the cage. Raymyth continued to stare at the Qualum that was slowly brought before him. Rodney stared in shock at the turn of events and did the only thing he could think of.

Using his power, he opened a portal and pushed Taurus back into the council room. Immediately enraged, the snake through his head back and roared, a deafening din full of rage that threatened to bring the entire cave down. He began to thrash around and slam his head against the bars. Without a second thought, Rodney ushered everyone through the portal. While he was doing that, Aries and Scorpio began shooting celestial power at the cage to reinforce it. Under no circumstances could they allow the snake to escape.

"THE TIME ISSS AT HAND!" Raymyth roared. *"I WILL BE FREED, AND I WILL EXACT MY REVENGE ON THE TWELVE HOUSESSS."* He continued to try to free himself from the cage, but the bars were still holding strong thanks to the extra energy. Rodney felt a chill run down his spine as he heard those words. He turned to look at the snake who was glaring at him while still trying to slither around. He checked to make sure everyone had gone through the portal, and then he followed the others and closed it shut behind him.

LEO

CHAPTER 12

"Do not be alarmed. I will alert everyone shortly on a plan to find these so-called four Ophiuchus members." Taurus shouted. All the council members rushed home to their loved ones in a full-blown panic.

Grabbing Libra's arm and turning her around, Rodney said, "I know that we have had our differences, and I know you blame my family for going rogue in the war, but we have to come together if this attack is real. Me, you, Aries, and Scorpio are the strongest at combat, and we're going to need to be the four directional leaders. We're already going to be outnumbered if there is five of them. They have had over a thousand years to prepare and train, and they could be even stronger than the leader of that time. Please let's get the kids together and train, so we have a second line of defense. They need to be taught like we did."

Stopping and thinking for a minute, Libra snatched her arm away. "I need to go check on my kids. My line has been tricked by yours once before and so help me if something happens to my babies, I will not care about the balance of our lines. This plan has been in motion for years, Capricorn. I know firsthand because my husband didn't leave me. He was taken when I was attacked for the book that year. He died trying to protect the book while I cowered and went to protect my kids. I almost lost the book, and to ensure there wouldn't be chaos, I lied and said he left the kids and me. We looked everywhere for clues on what happened and who attacked, but we found nothing, so I left it as nothing. Maybe I should have said something to the council, but I didn't, and we could have been more prepared. I just want to protect my family, and that's what I'm going home to do until I decide to relive this fight." Waving her hand and throwing her compact into the portal, she vanished.

Stunned, he shouted back at her, "Get back here and tell the members this! You're being a coward!" Punching the air, Rodney took a minute to breathe. After thinking it over, he thought about the prophecy and decided to go to the royal library to look up anything that could add merit to his words.

Flashing back to the house after taking a detour to her and Johnathan's favorite place on Zortega's Rockbelly Bellows, it was on the sun's moon. She entered the kitchen, her cries echoing through the house. "Ambrose? Dominic? Keith? Kids? Where is everybody?" Becoming angered even more, the house began to shake.

"Looks like my little sister is home. Keith, should I go get a tranquilizer dart? She sounds like she's going to be hard to put down. I'll bet you two hundred Nupqrawls that, that Vanseal guy got under her skin again. I'm thinking she might be more in love then angered. What do you think?" Ambrose said lightly, laughing while sitting in his reading chair.

Rolling his eyes, Keith wiggled from his chair to stand. Annoyed at being interrupted during his basketball game, he went to go greet Elizabeth. "That crazy girl loved my son, and if she ain't changed on him in the last ten years, she's not going to. Axer, go get the kids and tell them to hurry home and don't doddle like you always do. It looks like she means business." Keith said as he tapped the head on his fox cane that he held in his hand.

Dominic was in the dining room, cleaning silver when he felt Mrs. Braymark's energy breaking up the house and everything around her. Before Keith had enough time to leave the parlor, Dominic had casted a very powerful spell. Spinning two fingers on the table, he twirled Elizabeth and her energy to a small town in Kansas to live out her tornado dreams until she calmed down. Content with his actions, he went back to cleaning after cloaking the house so that it could repair itself. Dominic had spent many hours tending to the safety of the home since the break-in ten years ago.

Standing in the doorway, Keith watched Dominic not even break a sweat or lose his rhythm for polishing his silver. He shook his head at what he had just saw. "I'll never get used to you Legions. It's like you have all this rule and power and refuse to use it other than to serve and discipline the royals. But hey when you're done placing her in time out for us, please let her know I sent Axer to get the kids home. Also, would you mind bringing me a beer to the parlor? Thanks, old chap." Turning around after making his request, he walked back to his chair and the game. Not wanting to raise any alarm, he looked at Ambrose with concern on his face. Seeing the worry on Keith's face made Ambrose now worried about his little sister. Ambrose tried sensing for her, and even though he thought it was funny, she was being grounded for literally throwing a tantrum in the house. He wanted to make sure she was okay. So, after twenty minutes or so, he picked up on her energy and made a portal to go retrieve his past-out sister.

Meanwhile.

"Wow. That was crazy. I never thought I would be in a school fire," said Bowen.

"Bowen, I don't think it was just a normal fire. I saw someone on the roof right before the firefighters showed up. They looked like they weren't putting out the fire, but also trying to make it grow. I don't know, but it looked weird and felt weird too." Said Harley, looking back in the school's direction.

"Harley, I think you've gotten paranoid, little sis. There was nothing but clouds of smoke in the sky. Maybe one was shaped like a person. I think you just want to see something because all these crazy council members wanna stir the pot. What are we supposed to be afraid of? Really, they have been at peace with everyone since the war. Sis, it was a real fire some dumb kid started, and this lockdown thing will soon be over, watch. I mean, how can you put us royals on lockdown? Don't they know we could squash them in minutes?"

"False alarm or not, I wish Dad was here. He would know what to do, and he would be keeping Mom from spazzing out over everything. Just because the royals are powerful doesn't mean that we shouldn't protect the order of things. I know you're not next in line for the Libra line, but what if Leo's line is wiped out all the way down to you? You know you would have to take over and sorry brother, but you're nowhere near prepared, and that's what they're trying to protect." She said as she looked at her brother. Walking in silence, Harley noticed her backpack moving around. Startled and confused, she dropped it, and her duel Scythes appeared in her hands, ready to defeat the intruder. Axer peeked his head out, confident that she wasn't going to hurt him. Axer said, *"You know, you really should be more careful leaving your tuna sandwich in your lunch box. A fox could really get love handles from all the leftovers."*

"Oh. God, why are you here? I don't need help from you to watch the kids walk home Axer," said Uni. Stopping in mid-stride to turn around, they had realized they had been followed. Bowen shakes his head at his mom's anxiety to send her familiar after them. *"Oh, don't get your fur colors mixed up. I'm here on full report duties by the boss man."* Harley shrieked at the sudden appearance of the familiar. *"Plus, while you watched the kids, your Niyor was being put in time out. I bet Dexter a week's worth of lagesses candy if she destroyed an entire city,"* giggled Axer. Looking at him with total confusion, Uni decided to call over to his Niyor but was met with no response. *"What happened, and what are you talking about? You know what, finish walking the kids home Axer, I need to go check on Elizabeth. I felt her emotions, but I couldn't go to her because I was ordered to stay with the kids."* Uni cried as he appeared in front of the children on the sidewalk. Then, just as fast, he was gone in search of his Niyor. Harley just looked at the spot he was standing on as Axer still chewed on the remains of her lunch.

Licking his lips, he hopped out of the bag and stood up on his hind legs to walk next to them. "Hey, what's up, bro? You're going to give our little Harls an anxiety attack, popping up like that." Bowen said as he dragged a stick across the gate.

"That just means that your Uncle's training is working. It seems to me you're on your toes." Axer replied as he noticed kids playing at the park.

"What do you want, you little pain in my ass!" Shouted Harley.

"Your grandpa wanted me to tell you something...." Axer said as he dashed off on his hind legs towards the kids at the park. Snapping her scythes back in place before anyone could see them. She slapped her hand on her face as she saw Axer playing hopscotch behind the kids that couldn't see him. "Get over here, you!"

Some of the kids at the park stopped and stared at her in surprise. Watching her face drop as the moms called their kids to their sides, she could hear Axer singing.

"Hop, hop, and don't stop. Throw out the rock and race to the top. Step on a line, and you'll be fine, only cause your score won't be better than mine."

As Bowen walked away, Harley began to holler at him when she picked up her bag. She had now noticed Sidney, Bowen's familiar, was in her bag like the little raccoon he was. Scurrying back over to them, Axer remembered what he was supposed to be doing instead of beating the kids in hopscotch. *"Bowen... Harley.... I remember now. I was sent to tell you to get home. Your mom started a tornado, and she's in love with another man, and Dominic banished her away to someplace called Kanasis. I mean, Kansas."* Axer said as he vanished from sight, giggling.

Completely confused and baffled by the message Axer gave, they looked at each other puzzled. "Bowen, we need to get home. Something's wrong. I can feel it. Why would Grandpa send the fox if we are only fifteen minutes away?" Harley asked, and Bowen just nodded and agreed that maybe she was right. So, without any hesitation, they ducked behind a bush to make a quick trip home.

In a valley in the small city of Manhattan, a very exhausted Elizabeth turned. Drained from expending so much energy, she lay in the grass with tears streaming down her face. Saddened by her look, Ambrose took off his jacket and gave it to her to keep her warm. "Thank you. You've always been a great big brother. When I get home, I'm firing that..."

"Shush now. You know you can't fire him, and he did this for your own good. You're so powerful, and your emotions have amplified them for so long. Especially being trapped behind staying strong for your kids. I'm surprised you haven't exploded long before now." Ambrose said as he sat down beside her and admired the small city below them.

"Am? Do you still know a guy that could grow some powerful Stone clovers?" Asked Liz.

"Stone clovers? What's going on that we would need stone clovers? They were burned from the land years ago to not be used against us in battle ever again. Why on earth would I risk jail for two hundred years to get you those? Liz, explain yourself." Ambrose said as he looked at his sister with deep concern.

"Ambrose. It's all my fault. The Ophiuchan line is making a move to come back. I knew something about it and didn't tell the council. I still can't tell them. What if they disrobe me? Harley's not ready to lead an entire line herself."

"What are you talking about? You knew about it?" Asked Ambrose.

"Ten years ago, I believe it was their first attack on the royal that had the Qualum, which happened to be me. I was upstairs, and it happened so fast. Johnathan tried to protect the book while I protected the kids. Even Keith only saw a few minutes of the fight over the book. It was well hidden, but I guess the intruder managed to find it. Keith tried to save him, but the intruder snatched Johnathan and disappeared into a portal seconds after Axer grabbed the book back. See, he didn't leave me. That's just what we told everyone while we searched for him. Years went by, and there was no sign of anything until now. What if they're using Kantors to steal magic powers to release this guy? He could be the heir the snake is prophesying about. How do I tell my people that their leader knew that there was a threat, and we should have been ready to fight? I didn't want to put my kids through war training. I wanted them and the rest to live peaceful lives away from the things we protect them from."

Stunned at her words, Ambrose just sat there, wanting to smack her in the back of the head for her idiot mistake. "Elizabeth, you have got to be kidding me! How could you just not tell them? This is not just some secret you and Keith just willingly keep from everyone. You're not protecting anybody and so help me, if you don't get up and go tell them what you know, you won't be happy with me. I know you're the leader and I know you're stronger than me, but I will put my foot so far up your ass, Johnathan might have to show up to pull it out! You did that for you and your marriage to by time to find him. You knew they would have abandoned him just to keep the threat away from Zortega. Elizabeth, I'm so disappointed in you! You need to fix this now! Get up and let's go!" Said Ambrose as he picked her up and flashed them a portal home so he could pick a fight with Keith.

Harley and Bowen walked into the house. "Hey, Grandpa, we're home. What's the big rush? We were just down the street!" They shouted as they put their school backpacks on the wall. "Welcome home, young Harley. I advise you to get in your training gear and young Bowen, it wouldn't hurt for you to get ready to play bouncer for your dear grandpa. He's been enjoying his spiked ginger ale." Dominic said as he cloaked the living room before vanishing.

Wondering what he meant, Harley sat on the couch to watch tv. "Sage? Sometimes I wish I had you as a sister. Bowen is such a pain. He always has it

so easy since I'm next in line to be the leader. I know that until I go to Zortega, I won't have any royal duties, and we both just get to blow off as teens, but I ..."

"Girl, I pretty much am your sister," responded Sage. "The sister of your soul. I always have your back, no matter what. If anything happens to you, I'm right there with you." Sage materialized and settled on the couch next to Harley. "Your fight is my fight. All I care about is your safety and wellbeing." She hopped over to her and nuzzled her cheek softly. Harley felt better and smiled, she was grateful for her familiar, always knowing how to make her feel better.

"Sage, I don't know what I would do without you being here. You really are my greatest friend." Sage flew into the air and hovered in front of Harley's face. There was a mischievous glint in her eyes as she stared at her.

"Is that so?" Sage asked, "So, what about young Deveraux Vanseal?"

Harley blushed slightly at the question and turned away. "What about him?"

Sage chuckled softly at Harley's squirming, "I see how you sometimes just watch him with a small smile. Wishing you could just admit how you feel about him."

Harley felt her face getting redder as Sage continued to talk. "I don't know what you are talking about. Dev and I are just friends, that's it. Besides, he likes girls like Remy Phillips. Girls with all beauty and short fuses."

Sage sighed softly to herself at her friend's denial, but she decided to leave it at that. She knew one day she would work up the courage to admit her feelings. Flying overhead, Sage decided to go get Harley something to eat in the kitchen. She spotted Sidney munching on a chocolate chip muffin while being all cozy in the cat's climbing tree. Perched on top of the door, Sage scanned her prey when she heard...

"Oh man, the Zortegan is coming! The Zortegan is coming! Battle stations! Hide all the knives and the foxes and head for the safety of the nearest panda bear." Axer screamed as he ran through the house with a stuffed unicorn.

"Braymark! How dare you help cloud my sister's judgment to the council!" Exclaimed Ambrose, dragging his sister in behind him like a battering ram. With his adrenaline pumping and his intentions clear, everyone in the room knew this wouldn't be good. Flashing immediately into his training clothes, Bowen dashed out of the garage where he had been working on the car he and his dad had promised to repair together. He went to stop Ambrose from destroying the house, or worse. "Keith, you get out here, you old dusty fart, and your story better match hers!" Ambrose shouted, his eyes glowing in full fury.

"Now boy, I know you didn't just summon me like I belong to you," Keith growled, walking into the living room from the study down the hall. "What are you referring to?" Although he walked and spoke calmly, there was a fire burning in his eyes as he stared down Ambrose.

"I'm referring to what really happened ten years ago," Ambrose said, looking at Elizabeth.

She looked back at him and nodded in shame. "It's okay, Keith. I couldn't keep it in anymore. The situation in Zortega is getting worse. We even spoke to the snake today. I had to tell someone what I know before I tell the council." Sparking up his magic, Bowen knew this was going to be a fight.

"Guys, cut it out!" Harley said as she tried to run over to her grandpa.

Whoosh! A swirl of wind whistled as Bowen blasted her out of the way to protect her. "Sage, get her out of here! I don't need my little sister hurt." Bowen shouted as he prepared himself for the first hit thrown.

"I'm not going to ask you again, old man! You know it's her duty to report all attacks on that damn book!" Ambrose growled again as he built up his magic. Keith stepped back into a fighting stance.

"Boy, I like you, and I wouldn't want to embarrass your ass in front of this whole family. Remember, that was my son, and I loved him as they ripped him from my world. Plus, it was her idea."

Shaking his head, Ambrose shouted, "Liar!" and charged at Keith. He soon realized that something was wrong. Bowen was holding them separate pretty easily. Keith looked at Ambrose in the same manner as he tried to activate his staff. Barging back into the living room, Harley saw a pitiful sight. Grandpa Keith was trying to manifest his staff while Uncle Am was staring at his hands, wondering why he couldn't throw anything. Laughing in full hysteria was Axer on the couch. *"Dominic left you guys with a little, "Handle this like gentleman, surprise, I see."* He floated into the air and began speaking in an announcer like voice. *"Well, in this corner. My main man, my partner, my Po-Po-Ge-Jo, Keith, 'old fart' Braymark."* Axer jumped up and down, clapping his hands. *"Yay! Yay! Now, in this corner, we have that one guy that actually thinks he stands a chance... What's your name again? Oh yeah, not gonna win."*

Getting angry, Elizabeth shouted, *"Shut up already, Axer."* Uni found a scarf on the back of the couch and hogtied him with it. Ambrose and Keith began throwing punches and tussling on the floor. Harley couldn't take it anymore and ran to break them up before they hurt each other.

She decided enough was enough and hoped that maybe the magic blocker only worked on the adults. Sparking her fingers with electricity, she believed her thought to be true. "Stop! Don't you guys care that we might have been attacked today at school? You came storming in here and barking at each other about something ten years ago! Now explain to all the people in the room and act like we're not a crazy messed up family for once!"

Ignoring her for a moment, Keith got one more good stomach punch in. Bowen pulled them apart before his sister's bolt hit the marble floor. Keith closed his eyes and bowed his head in shame at the secret he had been holding in for so long.

"So, tell me what really happened that night," growled Ambrose.

Keith sighed as he gripped his cane. Walking further into the room, he sat down in an armchair. He stared into the fire in the fireplace and seemed to be a million miles away. The creases in his face seemed more profound, and his hair was almost white. When Axer appeared in front of him with a glass of brandy, he settled on the head of the armchair, uncharacteristically quiet. "Kids, I'm so sorry that you have to hear such a terrible story, but it was the day I lost my only son and its one of my most horrible memories. I had sent Dominic to go get some truffle smears for your grandpa's bad knees. Your dad and I were sparring right after we had sent ya'll to bed and decided to take a breakout on the porch for a drink. Good thing your dad cut the night short, or we would all have been in great danger. When Dominic left for the night to spend time with your mother, an intruder had snuck in our wards. In all the distractions, I was down by the garage when Axer heard the house rocking. To my surprise, a Kantor was waiting for me outside the house when I ran back up, so I had to get past him first." Keith said as tears filled his eyes.

Hugging Uni and walking over to Bowen, Elizabeth chimed in. "Do you kids remember the night dad left? Well, the intruder fought your dad and then took him with him through a portal, trying to recover the Qualum. I'm so sorry we lied to you. We said that your dad left, but the truth is, he just disappeared, and we weren't able to find him. We couldn't let the members know because they would have forbade us from going out to look for him. Your grandpa and I couldn't just sit back and not look for our loved one. Uncle Ambrose is right. I have to go report what we know because your grandpa actually got a look at him, and he won't even completely tell me who he is."

Angered by their confession, Harley stormed upstairs, but not before shouting. "My dad could be alive, and you lied about it!" Saddened by her reaction, Elizabeth looked at Keith. Bowen looked to his mother and said, "Go after her mom. You need to talk to her." She looked towards the stairs and sighed as she headed up after her daughter. Ambrose continues to glare at Keith, wishing he could throw another punch at him. He stood there, fuming over the hopeless situation that his sister had put herself in.

Although he could understand why she did it, he knew all too well how cold and cruel the council could be. In that regard, he sympathized with his sister

and her dilemma. However, that does not excuse keeping secrets that could have possibly endangered their entire world. Had the council known about this attack when it happened, they may have been able to emplace countermeasures to stop this. Now they were caught trying to chase after a threat that had been around for years. If it was the last thing he did, he would make them come clean to the council so they could hopefully put an end to all this.

Waiting in the room was Dominic standing at attention, ready to take down the barrier as long as the gentlemen were on their best behavior. "I have prepared dinner in the dining room for anyone that is hungry. Young Bowen, thank you for keeping these hot heads in line while I prepared the meal. Also, if you would be so kind as to go to the training area, I have set up some obstacles for you and your uncle to take your anger out on." After he removed the barrier, the room fell silent of all the news they had just absorbed, but Dominic was right. Taking the higher road to the issue at hand, Ambrose grabbed Bowen around the shoulder and lead him out to the training field for a little target practice. Passing up dinner, Keith headed to his room, with mementos of his son covering his shelves, a nice solid bed in the corner, and a computer desk next to his sleeping chair. Keith pulled out a book that had a photo from his desk and sat down. "I know it was you that day, how could you do this old friend you were like a big brother to him."

CHAPTER 13

The rest of the week passed with a tense atmosphere. Thankfully, it was uneventful for both families as they stayed on high alert. Days turned into night, and nights turned into days as a few weeks had laps by. Due to the fire, the school was closed while the city mounted an investigation. Dev spent his day's training with his father, while Harley stayed locked in her room, not speaking to anyone. Without his friends around, Anthony began to spend his time with Katrina. Even though she was supposed to be in school, she would skip so they could go for walks or grab a bite to eat. He enjoyed her company and found himself wanting to spend more and more time with her. When the days passed, Dev's family decided to move his sibling ceremony up just to be safe. As Friday drew bright, Dev laid in his bed, staring at the ceiling as he relaxed for a few minutes. The silence was suddenly shattered by the scream of his mother.

"Rodney, did you send out all the invitations?! Gabby, does the potion have all the ingredients needed for the family members to pass through the spiritual galaxy? Why isn't anyone answering me?" Said Selena as she held her list of things to do in her hand.

"Sister, why do you worry so much? If they have seen one ceremony, they've seen them all. Tomorrow is going to be one big family reunion where they tell me how I'm wasting my life, and how you married the golden boy and bonded our families like some winning prize horse. Did I really shame everyone that bad for the man I loved? Lesley this and Lesley that, look at your sister's royal kids' blah blah blah. You know what? I'ma go to the Bermuda triangle and wait out there until the kinfolk have gone back to the grave, especially Mom." Said Lesley as she banged her head on the table in remorse of her hurt memories of her family's constant pressure.

"Oh, Lesley, knock it off. You gave yourself half of that hurt and pain by always being the look at me child of the family. You chose to steal, you chose to fight, and you chose to do the things that you did. All for attention and because it wasn't what you wanted; you blame everyone around you; that you don't like for your lifestyle choices. Do yourself a favor and don't get so drunk and cry about how Dad took Autumn from you because you broke the rules. You're here to celebrate, not make a scene, and honestly thinking about it, I wouldn't want you two in the same room after so many years anyway. I have enough of a headache coming on with Rodney's mom. Now shoulders up, pinch them rosy cheeks, and give your sister a hug," said Selena while walking over to Lesley to give her a halfhearted hug. She then held Lesley's hands out and filled them with decorations so she could go put them up in the next room.

"Wow, I felt the love, sissy. You're just as cold as Dad. How would you feel if you couldn't be celebrating your twins' special day?" Snapped Lesley.

"That's the thing sister, I wouldn't know how that felt because I didn't disobey my parents," snubbed Selena.

Angered by her lack of emotion and sisterhood, Lesley began to power up a spell and aim it at her. But as much as she hated it, everything she said was

right. She knew it was her fault for falling in love instead of just listening. It was silly to have thought they could run away together and live happily with a baby on the way. She remembered the day her daughter Autumn was born and how when Autumn father came to see his new baby, Lesley father had him beat and chased away. No one else in the family knew who he was except her parents. Shortly after, her mom and dad decided to split up, and her father took Autumn to some hidden place called Tallulah, a few weeks after she was born. Displacing her anger into sadness, she walked away to go have a cry before everyone arrived tomorrow.

Knocking on the door, Selena tried to get Rodney, who she thought was hiding in his office, to help her set up, only to realize he wasn't there.

Skipping out the door this morning, he and the twins had gone out for their final day of innocence. One of Rodney's favorite things to do was take the kids out to the beach and ride the summer clouds where no one could see them. The day was perfect because a rainbow was out. The colors were so beautiful; it was like touching a prism in real life. The twins needed a day of fun. It would help them relax some before their big day.

Sitting in the cloud, Rodney looked up to the moon and held them both tight. "Kids, I want you to know that tomorrow is a day that is going to change your life's and drive your mom to a waterfall full of tears. Either way, it goes, we will be proud of you. Familiar or no familiar. I want you to do your best and really try not to let the judgmental eyes of tomorrow night affect you during your concentration. I love you, and I always will, regardless." Said Rodney as he hugged each one, then drew cloud animals in the sky. Eland loved it when her dad did that. It reminded her of when they would fly in the sky right before it rained.

Pulling two boxes out of his satchel, Rodney handed them an early birthday present. Eager to open it, they revealed what looked like a donut hole with V-like edges. "Dad, what is it?" Asked Eland.

"That, my daughter, is a Holju. It is a healing star that can revive a life. It is very rare and valuable, but it can only be used when the two halves are placed together. This is why I'm giving you the yellow side and Ezekiel the blue side. I've concealed them to look like necklaces, but you have to promise me you'll never lose them."

Looking at him in confusion on why they would need it, Ezekiel said, "We won't let you down, Dad!" Laughing in joy of his own son's encouragement for his own worry. Rodney stared at his twins as he realized they soon wouldn't need his constant protection. Thinking to himself while they went back to drawing in the clouds. What if one doesn't make it? But if both make it with this new threat, he would unfortunately have to let Gemini train them fast, but he cringed at the thought of having to strike his only princess. Snapping out of it, he saw Ezekiel riding the dragon Eland had made in the sky. With a hark cry ringing around his head, he knew that he was busted for sneaking out.

"Rodney Lee Aubrey Vanseal, I've got forty family members, friends, and royalty coming to my home in the next two days! How dare you leave me here with my self-medicating sister and a laundry list full of things to do! I still need two cakes, and I need you to contact all of the family on the royal line side, so they'll be ready to pass through the door! Now with everything going on, I don't want any surprises with what you told me about Libra's missing husband!" Shouted Selena in Rodney's ear from across the states. Startled by all the chatter, Rodney knew it was time to get back home before his wife went on the warpath trying to find them so they could help.

Selena felt so overwhelmed at home. It was always a feeling of being judged because she wasn't royal herself. Rodney always told her that it never mattered, but every commoner wanted the glory of what the royals had. However, unless you were fortunate to marry one, you were just a normal Zortegan with commonwealth and no chance to see the outside universe. She always wanted to prove that she was worthy of the life Rodney gave her. So, hosting a great party with royal traditions in honor of the council and the royal lines was how she proved it.

Portaling in on a cloud that looked like a *Faux Loc*, also known as a snake dragon. Ezekiel stood tall as if he were a *Faux Loc* sky warrior like his early cousins who had chosen the military path. Sliding off the cloud behind them, Rodney blew the dragon cloud away, only to have Ezekiel standing on the coffee table. As fast as whiplash Selena was ready to rip him a new one for standing on her table instead of finalizing their totem for the ceremony.

"I need you kids to go upstairs and pull out your robes and grab your stuff to go with Gabby. You know we can't see you the night before the event and since there are two of you, Gabby had to call in her friend to take the other." Grabbing them in for a nice hug, she turned and looked at Rodney, mad at him for not asking her if she needed any help before ditching for the whole day. "Now, before you go tiptoeing off, Sir, did you contact Gemini and ask her for her requests for tomorrow? Every member likes their stuff a certain way, even you. I will not be embarrassed by not knowing how she likes things."

Stopping in his tracks, he stood there, looking at the ceiling as he got caught trying to slide away. "Yes Hunny, I'm going to the store to get the stuff right now just for you." Said Rodney as he made a face at her behind her back.

Meanwhile.

"Hey, you nervous?" Asked Eland, walking up the stairs into their half sports team and half glittery purple room.

"No, are you?" Replied Ezekiel as he grabbed the things his mom had told them to get out of the drawer.

"Not really brother, but you know I don't like the fact that all eyes are on us tomorrow." Said Eland as she plopped onto the bed, looking at the robe she had to wear.

"I know it's pretty weird. I hope that we don't have to have a lot of royal duties. It's hard to be prepared to change lines when you can't know the rules until you pass this thing." Said Ezekiel, shaking his head.

"We are going to pass, and then we are going to have cake. So just think of the party at the end of the ceremony because that's what I'm going to do. Looking at everyone staring at me is going to make me nervous, and I don't want to mess up. I want to see what my inner self looks like. I hope he or she is cool like us and likes to have fun." Said Eland grabbing her red sparkly bag so they could go back downstairs.

"Hey, Bonnie and Clyde," said Dev as he entered their room. "You guys ready for tomorrow? It's your big day and, trust me, if you're scared don't worry, everyone will be there to witness it. I swear, I was sweating a river standing up there with all eyes on me breathing down my neck," grinned Dev as he toyed with them for a second. Happy with doing his big brother deed, Dev then ghostly walked out of the room. Turning to look at each other in slight fear, Eland headed for the hallway, but Ezekiel stopped her. "Hey Eland, don't forget your dream catcher. We are supposed to place it over our heads before we go to bed. It's supposed to help clear our minds before the ceremony. By the way, you're right, we are going to pass this thing. It's always been me and you for a long time, and now were going to be a foursome. I bet mine is cooler than yours, though, because I'm cooler than you," giggled Ezekiel. Throwing the nearest pillow at her brother, Eland said, "Take that back!" After about five minutes of hitting him with it, he rolled his eyes and shouted, "Never!!!" Forced to give up, she went to her dresser for her totem and her dream catcher as he did the same.

"Kids, they're waiting on you! Hurry up!" Shouted Selena up the stairs.

Standing in the room, Eland said, "After you," as she waved her arm and hand out the doorway gesturing, he go first. While he walked out the door, Eland had a dirty trick up her sleeve for what he said. She took one foot and placed it on the back of his knee. Simultaneously Ezekiel began to fall face-first on to the hardwood floor as she ran past him and down the stairs so he couldn't get up in enough time to retaliate. Dashing down the stairs after her, Ezekiel tried to catch her before she could get behind Mable for protection. "Okay kids, be on your best behavior and give your momma one more hug for the road," said Selena as she choked up slightly in attempts to wait for them to leave before she

shed tears of worry and joy. Scampering out the room, she went to go check the yard where the ceremony was going to be held.

While Dev watched his mom dash to the kitchen to go cry for the third time, he was struck by an overwhelming sense of connection. Someone was calling to him, almost like they needed help of some kind. This connection was different than a simple message through telepathy. It had an out of body feel to it. It slithered all over his body, showing him images of a room and a twelve-sided stone. Dev was holding his head like he was having the worst headache in the world. Falling to his knees as another image floated through his head. This time it was an image of a great battle somewhere he had never seen before. He could make out that some of the dead soldiers were royals because their eyes were pure white. He was sure of it because that is what happens to royals when they are wrongly laid to rest.

Dev screamed in pain. Whoever was doing this made him feel every dying breath. Laying on the floor, Dagon repeatedly tried to escape his totem necklace. He was confused because it wasn't working with every attempt he made. "Get out of my head! Mom help! Dagon help!" Yelled Dev.

Rushing in the family room, Lesley placed a shield around Dev, casting a blocking spell on him she had learned from her travels. Transforming into her fighting stance and outfit. Clicking her lipstick container had made it transform into a two-stranded pink whip that was covered in black electrified auras. Pulling the whip apart, she was ready to fight and waited for her first opponent. Dev felt a bit of comfort being placed in the bulb. The pain was gone, and the image slowly dissipated. The connection was lost, and Dagon could now escape his totem. He then pawed at Dev's shoulder to try and look him over.

"If you can get out, go get Mom. Aunt Lesley will need help if someone is really attacking us." Said Dev. Howling at Lesley to let him out, she moved back to create a dime-sized hole in the bulb. Shrinking down, Dagon ran for the backyard where Selena was riding the lawnmower to cut the grass. Barking and howling at her did no good, so he did the one thing he could think of, which was to jump in front of the mower. She wouldn't mow me over, would she? He thought. Running with high hopes of not killing him and Dev, Dagon jumped in front of the mower about five feet from her direct path. Startled, Selena hopped off the acceleration and shut the noisy mower off to yell at him for the stupid choice he made.

"Mrs. Mom, there's no time! I'm so sorry! Dev is in trouble. Someone was attacking him inside," said Dagon as he ran back up to the house after his Niyor. Angered that someone would even be brave enough to attack a royal's home the day before her babies became official put her in momma bear mode. Grabbing her earrings, she revealed her signature weapons, hematite, and diamond-encrusted short-armed staffs. Each tip was a sharp, poison-dipped arrow. She ran up the lawn into the house, only to not see a fight or enemy but Dev laying on the couch with Lesley hovering around him.

"What happened to my baby? Lesley, what did you do now?" Shouted Selena at her as she shoved her way over to her son.

"I didn't do anything! I found him crying in pain, but I thought I'd be the one to come to your son's rescue since keeping up appearances is more important than hearing your son cry out for you in pain." Growled Lesley as she put her whips away and headed back up to her room. "Mom, call Dad. Someone kind of took over my body. I saw things and felt things, and it hurt so bad!" Said Dev as he stroked Dagon's head. Dagon was nuzzling his arm, after looking him over one more time. Selena nodded her head in acceptance that this was a situation only her husband could give him answers to. Kissing him on the forehead, she messaged his dad to return home because there might have been an attack on their son.

Standing up, he messaged his aunt to say, *"thank you for all her help."* He thought to himself. What did this mean? Was he developing a power he had no control over? Who else had the power to control a person's mind? Dev walked up to his room to grab a notebook out of his backpack. Staring at the paper, he tried hard to remember the images and all the details of the memory. Sitting on

his bed, Dev could hear his mom breathing down the doorknob as she waited for his Dad to arrive.

However, when Rodney arrived and before he could enter Selena asked him a troubling question, "Rodney it can't be him can it?" Looking puzzled Rodney went to investigate what happened to his son.

Knock, knock.

"Can I come in, son?" Asked Rodney. Over his shoulder he could see his wife hovering over Dev's bedroom, so he shooed her away from the door.

"Dad? Something took over my body and forced me to see something. It's like it was the future, but it felt like a dream too. I felt everyone's mental pain as they were dying. Most of them cried out for their kids to just say goodbye one more time. I could feel a person almost inside of me. I saw this girl in one of the images, and it was like I was being pulled towards her." Dev paced around his room as he talked. "I know I'm not making sense, but it was so scary until I felt her. Who was I connected to? Have you heard of such a power?" Dev rambled on as he looked at his dad, hoping to see if he understood. Still waiting for his father to answer him, Dev stopped pacing and sat down on his giant bean bag chair. Pressing a pillow against his face, Dev was left with silence as Rodney just stared at his son, wondering more.

Clearing his throat before he spoke after hearing his son's vision, Rodney asked, "How much have we taught you about your heritage, son? Years ago, your great Grandpa Corleejus used to talk about this story of three people that shared a bond called a Triquetra Vinculum. They are very rare and are extremely dangerous. Legend has it that our powers come from these three people over centuries ago. When they die, they are reborn every couple of thousands of years in secret to any one of our lines. They ended the war using their combined elemental powers to eliminate a whole bloodline, but word has it they died doing it. That's why we're represented by the four elements earth, fire, wind, and water. Their powers were unimaginable on their own, but when placed together, it was an unbeatable weapon. One controlled the earth, but he also was the vessel for the body being strong and grounded. One controlled the air that takes your soul to the heavens after you die, and she could invoke anyone's soul. The last one was always considered the manipulator of the mind. He controls water, and just like how water flows, it can also never be tamed, just like him. During the Zodiac wars, the council lied to the people. They found out the three had been reborn, so they used them to end the suffering the thirteen line were causing with all death and destruction. The council tracked them down and after every attempt to overthrow the Ophiuchans; they came up with a solution. They sacrificed the three by combining them into one line. It forged the only weapon strong enough to defeat the Ophiuchan line."

Looking confused on how this could be true, Dev asked, "Are there any alive today? Is one after me?"

Standing up, Rodney smoothed out his shirt and said, "Tomorrow is going to be a long day, and I will tell you more when the time is right. I think you need to get some rest. Go relax and read a book, I need you on your toes for the ceremony tomorrow. Also, you have your track meet the next day. I don't want you thinking about these visions while you run your four-by-four relay hurdles. Now I'ma go and calm your mother down before she places this family into cryostasis because you got hurt and her children are growing up. Hell, I might need a pace-maker with the way she worries me to death but gotta love them curves and those...." Interrupting him as quickly as he could, Dagon began to howl in Rodney's ears. Rodney clearly took the message and walked out of Dev's room, chuckling to himself, while shutting the door behind him.

Rodney went downstairs to go hug his beautiful, Hunny bunches of sugar Wheaties, he called her, when he was met by his Aunt Delila. "Well, well, well, little Rodney Vanseal," said a glowing orb that bobbed up and down at eye level. Rodney wore a wide grin that the first person to arrive was his favorite aunt in the whole world. "Well, well, well, if it isn't old lady Dee. Glad to know you won't take up so much room in that form. So thoughtful of you," he replied with a mock bow and a laugh. She cackled at his response and transformed into a middle-aged Zortegan woman with glowing green eyes and a bright smile. "Still a little smart aleck, I see. Don't forget, I can still take you, even if I am dead." Rodney smiled wider and kissed both of her cheeks since he couldn't give her a real hug. Delila was a lady that loved to live in the era of the 1920s with the feathers and crimped to perfection hair even though she was born way earlier. "I have a present for the boy. Is he up?" said Delila.

"Yes, but we had an accident today, and I wanna give him some rest. He'll come out later to do his chores," replied Rodney. Strolling down the hallway, Rodney went to the hall closet to grab sheets and things for the guest house since people were starting to arrive. Left alone in his room, Dev wondered, who was that girl? She was so powerful, and why didn't she scare me like the other connection I felt?

Relaxed but still full of adrenalin, Dev felt someone sneaking up on him, and in a flash, he hopped up and trapped the figure in a ring of fire about as high as their knees. "Relax cousin, it's me, Makayla. Why you so jumpy? I wasn't going to hurt you." Relieved it was her, he smothered the flames. "When did you get here? The little kids aren't supposed to be here until tomorrow," said Dev to his little cousin. "I know, but I was bored. Traveling is no fun. Hey, you wanna see the cool new trick I learned? Hey, how come you guys don't come and visit? Can I sleep with you? The dead gives me the creeps." While Dev's ten-year-old cousin rambled on and on with thirty questions, he hadn't answered one too. Dev decided to take a minute to look up what his dad had told him on the internet.

Triquetra Vinculum: Meaning a magical triangle bond between three people.

Finding very little information, Dev texted Anthony:

> Hey dude, I know it's late, but can you find anything on this
> phrase for me? It's urgent. (Triquetra Vinculum) Thanks. Hey,
> bring my lucky socks I let you borrow so that I can have them
> for the track meet on Saturday. Running man emoji.

After sending his text, Dev decided to take his dads advise and just relax. But he knew before he did, he needed to do his evening chores and get away from Makayla. As the night soon fell over the house, Dev checked the wards one more time. He had a lot going on in the next few days and didn't want to be worried about anything else. He had to be ready for the ceremony tomorrow. With a slight smile, he began thinking of ways to sneak an extra piece of cake. Then the day after, he had the track meet for the state championship.

He was thrilled he was going to see his cool family members once more. His Uncle Pat was hilarious, and it was too bad he had died during a bike ride to the Grand Canyon, or he would have shown him how to ride. He laughed to himself at which family members were bound to fight, because royals and non-royals always had a different way of living. All Dev knew was that he was looking forward to being a proud big brother of two junior royals.

LIBRA

CHAPTER 14

"Good morning, my young, sweet grandson. How are you this morning?" Asked Lady Julia as she petted her grandson's hair and face. Opening his eyes, he glanced at his alarm clock and was annoyed at the early hour. Grumbling, he thought, why is it that at every family gathering, I can't ever sleep in?

"Hi, Grandma. How are you doing, and why are you in my room?" Said Dev as he rolled over, trying to keep himself covered.

"Sweetie, I came to see you, of course. Now get up, put some lead in your step. You're going to be an old lady's big helper, and I'll give you five dollars. How does that sound?" Asked Lady Julia as she fixed her lipstick in his bathroom mirror. Her familiar, Lord Websly, a large black tarantula, was scuttling gracefully around her shoulders, watching everything with his beady eyes. He was rather hairy but well-groomed, and his fur also had a slight sheen to it. There was a bright red mark on his back that made many people mistake him for a black widow. He looked every bit as pompous as his Niyor. He even had a small monocle over his eye and a black and red top hat.

"Grandma, as great as that sounds, I have to help Mom get the party ready," said Dev as he called for some shorts and a shirt out of the closet. Walking out of the bathroom, Lady Julia saw the clothes he was about to put on and changed them with a snap of a finger.

"Royals shouldn't wear such ghastly clothes like that, especially on a day like today. I blame your mother for not teaching you how to dress like a proper royal," said Lady Julia. She kissed him on the cheek and told him to get dressed, because being in your skivvies in front of a lady is not respectable. Griping softly, he waited for his grandmother to leave the room. Once she walked out, he closed the door and locked it with three different enchantments, then dove back into bed and pulled the cover over his eyes. Just as he was closing his eyes, a voice called his name.

"Dev! Come downstairs and say hello to your grandmother," his mother called. So, upset over being unable to close his eyes again, Dev flailed out of bed like an angry toddler. Dev stood up and saw a note that was left for him with a little gift. His grandma refused to unlock his closet until he put it on. He groaned and moaned down the stairs with his grandma's outfit. It was a scorpion, high collared tail wrapped around his neck. The royal lines, colors of silk made into a long-tailed coat jacket with a peplum and his weapons belt. However, Dev had a surprise for his grandma. He didn't wear all of the outfit but decided to mix it up with a billed hat and jeans he took off yesterday. Dev wore the outfit wrong just to make her as annoyed as he was about the fact, he was forced to wear the garments. Laughing hysterically in the corner was Rodney, Dagon, Stover, and Chase as they turned their heads and saw what he was wearing.

"Hunny, why on earth do you have that ridiculous get up on?" Giggled Selena as she pinched her lips together, trying not to bust out in a smile or laughter.

"Grandma came into my room and said I had to wear it. That I need to represent as a royal, not a normal boy. I just wanted to sleep in and pick my own clothes," said Dev as he pulled his scorpion tail collar off his neck.

Walking out of the study was Delila, "Oh my! What is that ghastly three-thousand-year-old thing doing here?" Rodney got up from his place in the corner after his good laugh to join her.

"My mother-in-law always feels like she should poke her royal little nose in things and tell me how to raise our..." Grumbled Selena under her breath so only Rodney and Delila could hear clearly.

"What the love of my life was saying is that my mom and your sister went overboard and brought one of Grandpa's old royal ceremony outfits for Dev to wear today. Hunny, why don't you go greet the rest of the family, and we will formally laugh at your son for you," said Rodney as he felt a scalding hot sensation on his back. His mom was trying to set Yendor on fire for trying to eat the collar. "Mom! Leave Yendor alone." Rodney yelled as he extinguished the fire around his familiar. Walking in the door and overhearing the conversation was the most unlikely guest. "If you speak to your relatives with that much disrespect. I'm aghast at the thought of how you speak to someone outside the family," said a cold, deep voice from the doorway. Both Rodney and Delila froze, stopping their affectionate banter, and turned to stare at the speaker, with slight anger in their eyes.

Standing there was a large man with a deep bronze skin tone and cold piercing eyes with purple irises. He had what looked like a permanent sneer on his face as he looked around the room. He had an air of power about him that seemed to fill whatever room he just happened to be in. He wore a crisp black pinstripe suit, a white shirt, and a deep purple tie that matched his eyes. Gabriel Dumont was Selena's and Lesley's father and Rodney's least favorite person on the planet. Next to him stood a young woman who was the spitting image of Lesley in every way. However, instead of a sneer, she had a bright smile plastered on her face as she saw her favorite uncle. Rodney smiled at his niece, Autumn, and moved forward to say hello. Before he could reach out, Gabriel cleared his throat and stepped slightly in front of her stopping his approach.

"I believe you should address me first, Mr. Vanseal." The hulking man stated as he continued to stare down at him with barely veiled contempt. It was no secret that Gabriel never believed that Rodney truly loved his daughter. He thought that he only married her as a political stunt to gain the council's approval.

Rodney sighed inwardly, but stared his father-in-law full in the face, refusing to be intimidated in his own home. He stuck his hand out for a greeting and stated, "So glad that you could make it, Mr. Dumont." Neither of them ever called the other anything than their last names, no matter what the occasion. Although they never openly fought, they refused to accept the other person.

Pained with an oncoming headache, he heard Gabby shouting up the stairs in full distress for him and Selena. She was in the kitchen being smothered with undying molestation and affection from Selena's Cousin Chase. Telling his company to, "Hold that thought," Rodney went downstairs to go place his wife's family in check and remind them of the rule of keeping his hands off of Gabby. Cousin Chase always had a thing for older women. Tragically when he died, he was only thirty-five. Chase was one of Selena's favorite cousins and the twin's prank partner in crime at all the family events. He was about five foot four and had really short curly hair. He had his totem tattoo up his arm, and he walked with a little limp from a severe burn he got before he passed away. He always liked to tell Dev it was from running across lava when volcanos erupted. Unfortunately, one day he tried running across one, slipped, and didn't make it out. When he came back as a spirit, Rodney and Selena had gotten married, and he swore he was going to chip that icy heart of Gabby's.

Barging into the kitchen. Rodney saw Selena greeting her older cousin with open arms and a smile. "How have you been?" Said Selena as she passed Rodney a very stiff drink to calm him down.

"I've been good, sweetie, age has served you well. Come, give your cousin one more big hug! You have to throw more parties so I can visit more often. The underworld waiting in line to be reborn stuff is so time consuming and a total drag," said Chase as he hugged her just a little too tight and too long for Rodney's blood pressure.

"Bun cakes, Ma'am," said Gabby as she pulled eight delicious smelling cinnamon bun cakes out of the oven.

"I'll take any buns you wanna serve me," gestured Chase with a wink at Gabby.

"Okay, that's it! Boy, if you weren't dead already, I'd throw you into the sun. I have already banished you to the tides of Helldes." Shouted Gabby with a blushed look on her face.

"Baby, I'd drown all over again to make you my sea wench in my next life, which shockingly comes up in three thousand years. So, do me a favor, and when I'm born, give me chest-to-chest action," said Chase as he pretended to imaginarily hug her by himself. Rolling her eyes at him as he talked to himself about their life that was never going to happen in any century, she went about her daily chores. Afterwards, she heard more guests arrive and left Chase to his kissing.

Addressing him, she spoke, "Sir Rodney, Lady Caroline, and Sir Stover have arrived. Damn near gave me a fright when I was putting fresh lemonade out on the patio. In my day, you at least belled before you portaled into someone's home. Also, young Myler is with young Autumn, and the twins will be arriving shortly. I will excuse myself to retrieve Miss Eland, and tonight, I will be preparing grilled and stuffed broccoli seafood salmon."

Nodding to Gabby at how wonderful that sounded, a long-remembered face walked into the kitchen to greet everyone. It was Caroline, his overzealous little sister. She didn't want to be away from her post for very long because of the danger lurking around, but she wanted to fly into say hi. She was one of the first female warriors to become captain of a region. She was very fierce and played only by the Zortegan way. When no one was looking, she was a softy to the kids. She stood a statuesque five-foot-ten in all her armored glory. The armor shined a white pearl metal with the Zortegan Paratar's army symbols carved into it. Caroline was a complicated one, because despite being by the book most of the time; her hair had the coolest two-layered mohawk hairstyle that looked like dragon spikes when she put her helmet on. Her beauty won her many yolwery offers for her hand, but no one was ever able to best her. Caroline hated changing herself for anyone, so she didn't transform, but she did tuck her wings into her sides a little more than she liked. Walking over to greet her brother, she stood like she would with any royal in front of her. Shortly after pretending they cared, Caroline punched Rodney in the shoulder.

"Hey brother, how are my niece and nephew? How's Dev? I have some marvelous stories to share with them of me going to the Mirrored Dundee Desert Islands." Said Caroline. Watching Stover pillage through the drawer made her throw a knife behind her back at him. It flew right in front of Gabriel's face, cutting the air in front of his nose. When the knife hit the shelves of her target, Caroline said, "Put Lady Gabby's sea glass back, you heathen of a thief."

Pouring himself a double shot this time, Rodney wrapped his arm around his younger sister with fearsome joy. "Hey, little sister, how have you been? How's home? And can you not throw knives? Last time you were here teaching the kids how to throw, they used the spots on Tiye as a bullseye for practice."

"Sir, I have retrieved young Eland, and we are awaiting Sir Ezekiel as we speak. They will reside in the parlor for now," announced Gabby on her way back in.

"Gabby, please stop sounding like a British nanny because my mother is here. This is my house, and it already sounds like it done went to the crazy land. Stover stop stealing Gabby's sea glass we know you're trying to sell it for information on Vamperous and Emphanalt stones. Mom come watch your brother! He hasn't even been here twenty minutes, and he's trying to steal stuff to take back home."

Stover was a short man that was skinny as a pole and just as slippery with his fingers. He was well-dressed and well-off, but Stover had a problem. He loved

the thrill of not getting caught, even though he was a horrible thief. Stover started stealing more after he stole a healing stone that everyone thought had been destroyed. However, Rodney's Mom knew what it was. She sent it to Rodney and asked for it to be given to the twins for a special birthday present.

Dev watched his grandma move things around in the house, and his dad get short of wanting to put everyone out that annoyed him. He saw Rodney grab Stover and escort him to the family room to be watched by his sister. "Come on Nephew, you know I'm good for it," said Stover as Rodney manhandled him out of the kitchen.

Dev could hear them talking: "All you're good for, Uncle, is the authorities showing up at my house asking about contraband!" Replied Rodney. He shoved Stover into the living room and started to walk out. Unfortunately, Rodney noticed him rifling through the drawers of the cabinets in that room too. Shaking his head and wishing he could just go back to yesterday, he snapped his fingers and placed a shock spell on everything with a lock. Pleased with himself, he turned away with a small smile as he heard a loud yelp come from the living room.

"Nephew, that was uncalled for!"

Waiting with curiosity on who was going to show up next, Dev walked over to Myler and Autumn. They were the only ones roughly his age that he actually got along with. Myler was showing Autumn his Zortegan War hammers, and she was showing him her bow and arrow. They were both pretty cool. Autumn's bow was almost invisible, and it was electrified, just like her mom's whips. The silver arrow tips on the bow were just as deadly. Honestly, they both forged weapons that had some unresolved anger surrounding them. Myler's hammers were so cool to Dev, they were an antique charcoal bronze with white handles. The heads were shaped like a five-sided rectangle. Dev heard when he used them, they shocked the ground like an earthquake.

As Dev was about to say hi and join in the 'whose weapon is cooler' club, he heard Gabby say, "Refreshments are on the porch. Please make your way outside, and I will have dinner ready in an hour." His cousins looked up at the announcement and saw Dev standing there.

Autumn smiled and greeted him warmly. "Hi, Dev. How have you been? It's been way too long since we've seen each other."

Myler smiled as he rose, and with a flick of his wrists, he spun his hammers until they shrank into small cufflinks that he placed on his sleeves. He reached out to shake hands with Dev. "Good to see you, cousin. How's school goin' on this side of the country?"

Dev shook his hand, and then they all headed outside to grab some snacks. "School's going pretty well right now. Just doing homework and running track. We have a meet tomorrow that I'm really excited about."

Myler laughed. "I've watched you run at a few of your races. I don't know how you manage to keep your powers in check when you run. If it was me, I would have boosted myself every time just to make sure I won the race."

Autumn shook her head at that statement and started to scold him. "That's cheating, Myler, and you know it! We live by a strict code of honor, and it wouldn't be good to abuse our abilities in such a way."

Dev nodded in agreement while he grabbed a few cookies and a glass of lemonade from the table. "I know that if I used my powers, I would win hands down, but I don't want to win like that. I like the rush of just using my body and my training when I run. It proves who is the better racer in the end. If I used my powers to make myself faster, there would be no point to the race."

Myler snorted at that statement saying, "Still, it would be so easy for you to be the best runner there is. Plus, technically you would still use your natural abilities. It's not your fault that the humans you run against don't have the strength."

Dev just shook his head at his cousin's thinking, knowing he would never convince him. Instead, he turned to Autumn and asked her how school was.

"It's going well, I'm getting ready to graduate soon and head off to college." She seemed sad about the new adventure though, instead of excited.

"What's wrong, cuz?" Myler asked. Autumn looked up at the house where Gabriel was standing with a drink in his hand and staring off into the sunset.

"Grandfather wants me to go to a college far away. He says it's because it's an amazing school, but I know he just wants to keep me from my mother." A single tear ran down her face and dropped into her lap. Looking sad now that she had to think about it, Dev and Myler looked at each other. Sparking up an idea, Myler and Dev seemed to have had a silent conversation.

Ever since they were kids, they never understood the reason for the separation between their aunt and cousin, but they both thought it was wrong. All they had ever been told was it was forbidden for them to be together. So, every time there was a family gathering, they had to sit back and watch the two be miserable in the same room but unable to interact with each other.

Myler sent a quiet message to Dev. "You thinkin' what I'm thinking?"

Dev gave a nod, and they started to formulate a plan to get Mother and Daughter reunited. Dev placed his hand on Autumn's shoulder. "What if we could get you a few minutes to speak with your mother?"

Autumn looked up in shock at her cousins, not daring to believe it was possible. "Would you really do it? Grandfather would be furious."

Myler waved away her concerns. "Who cares what he thinks? The old man needs to get over himself and stop being such an ass!"

Dev laughed at his comment and said, "Yeah, you two deserve some time together. So, we're going to give it to you."

Autumn sprung up and hugged both of them close before giving them each a kiss on the cheek. "Oh, thank you, thank you, thank you! You two are the best cousins ever! So, how are we going to do this?" She asked.

Myler spoke up first. "I'm going to go and distract the old man with a bunch of questions about our history. While I'm doing that, Dev is going to grab your mom and bring her to his treehouse, right?"

Dev nodded. "It's not that far away, just about a short walk down that path, remember? We used to play in it when we were younger."

Autumn remembered the treehouse that he made. She couldn't believe it was still standing. "Is it still standing? Never mind that. What if we get caught? What if Grandfather finds us?" Autumn asked. "We'll have our familiars keep an eye on him. They will be able to tell us if he starts to look for you, okay?" Said Dev.

Although Autumn was excited at the prospect of having time with her mom, she was still slightly worried about making her grandfather mad. Whenever she asked to be with her mother, he would become furious and tell her that it was forbidden for them to ever be together. In the end, it was Cadence, her familiar, who gave her the push she needed. He was a majestic parrot with vibrant colors. He flew down from the top of the house and settled on the table. He stared at her with his dark beady eyes that were full of compassion and love.

"You have dreamed about this moment your entire life. I've sat back and watched you cry and beg for a moment with your mother. I hated myself that I could do nothing to give you what you wanted. Your cousins are here ready and willing to give you that, so I say take it. I will help them keep your grandfather distracted." Assured Cadence.

She felt tears of joy fall down her face as she stared at her family. Finally, she nodded and smiled as she wiped her eyes. "Okay, let's do it!" She got up and headed towards the path that led to the treehouse. Cadence took off and flew towards the back of the house where Gabriel was standing. Dev bumped knuckles with Myler as they set off to complete their own parts of the mission. Myler headed straight for Gabriel and began to engage in a conversation with him. While Dev headed towards the house to search for his aunt.

CHAPTER 15

The first person he ran into when he walked inside was Gabby, who was still trying to escape Chase's amorous advances. She bumped into Dev just as Chase pounced over to wrap her in a tight bear hug. Quick as a flash, Dev threw up his hand and halted his cousin in midair. Then he slowly directed him out the door and quickly shut it as he dropped him on his head. "Thank you, Hun," Gabby said, giving him a peck on the cheek.

"Anytime Gabby, but quick. Do you know where Aunt Lesley is? I need to find her."

Gabby looked around the room. "She was just here a while ago, and I think she may have gone up to her room. You can check there." After giving her a quick kiss on the cheek, Dev flashed himself upstairs outside of Lesley's room. He went to knock and heard a muffled sob on the other side of the door. He pressed his ear to it and heard the unmistakable sound of someone crying. It broke his heart to hear her like this. He was happy that he and Myler had come up with this plan.

Dev knocked on the door. "Aunt Lesley, are you in there?" He could hear a shuffling and then the sound of someone blowing their nose.

"One-sec Nephew. Be right there," replied Lesley.

While he waited, he called Dagon to his side. The wolf appeared next to him, cocking his head to the side, looking curious. "I need you to do me a favor and keep an eye on Gabriel for a little while. Autumn's familiar is downstairs now, watching him from behind a tree. Go give him a hand."

Dagon gave him a nod, but he had to ask, *"Why am I stalking the old man exactly?"*

Dev looked around to make sure no one was around. "We are trying to give Autumn and Lesley some time together, that's all. You in partner?" Dagon was all too proud to help out with this super-secret mission.

Dagon headed off to help Cadence as Lesley opened the door. Although she tried to hide it. It was easy to see that she had been crying. "What did you need Nephew?" She asked. "Is everything okay?" Dev didn't answer. He just took her hand and flashed them both to his treehouse. "Dev? What are we doing here, sweetie?" He let go of her hand and stepped back, looking into the window. Autumn was sitting in one chair with a small smile on her face as she read a book.

Turning back to his aunt, he said, "I know how upset you've been since Gabriel and Autumn came. I wanted to give you something to smile about." Saying that, he opened the door so Lesley could see Autumn. Her daughter looked up, and tears welled in her eyes as she saw her mother standing there. Lesley gasped and ran forward to hold her daughter, who rushed at her at the same time. The two women clung to each other and collapsed to the ground.

Dev smiled at the two of them, happy that he could do something for them both. He started to back out of the room to give them privacy. "Wait!" He heard his aunt call to him. Dev turned back to her as she walked forward and gave him

a giant hug. He hugged her back and winked at Autumn over her shoulder. Lesley pulled back and looked at him. "How did you manage this Nephew?" She asked. Dev smiled and explained.

"Myler and I were tired of seeing you two so close but so upset that you couldn't be with each other. So Myler is currently keeping our grandfather busy with conversation. Our familiars are keeping an eye on him in case he moves."

Lesley laughed at them and gave Dev another hug. "Remind me to give Myler a hug when we get back, and thank you again Dev. This is the best gift ever." With that, she turned and walked back into the treehouse with Autumn, where they sat down on the couch and began to whisper to each other.

Dev turned and closed the door to give them some privacy, but he stayed close so that he could give them fair warning just in case Gabriel came looking for Autumn. While he stood there, he tried to block out what they were saying, but it was hard not to hear them as they laughed and giggled with each other.

"Oh my god, Autumn, look at you. You are all grown up and so beautiful." He heard Lesley say.

"Thank you, Mom. I'm told I look just like you. This is so surreal. I don't know what to say, but I have so much to say," Autumn mumbled, as tears began to crawl up into her eyes.

Lesley just looked at her with such a proud feeling, "Yes baby, you do look a lot like me. However, you have your father's personality and eyes. They are alive with the same defiant fire that he has." There was a tinge of sadness in her voice as she spoke about Autumn's father. "Relax Hunny, and I'll tell you as much as I can, and maybe you can tell me something exciting about your life."

Wanting them to feel more comfortable, Dev decided to change the cramped outdoor space to something they might feel better in. Making the room change, Dev presented them with a yoga lounge-like room, with oversized ottomans and a fuzzy blanket to share. He even went as far as to add a nice steamer that smelled like lavender. He hated the smell and knew it would take weeks to get it out, but for this, it was worth it.

"Thank you, Dev!!!" They cried out together. He laughed in response to himself.

"Mom, I don't know anything about my father. Grandpa won't tell me about him. What is his name? Why can't I see him? I barely get to see you because of some rule you broke. It's not fair that I'm punished because..." Hugging her close, Lesley could feel her pain. "Mom, you left me. Please, I wanna be with you and dad, I don't wanna live like this anymore. Take me home with you, please. Mom, please." Autumn said as she peered over Lesley's arm up at her.

"Hunny, I've tried many nights to take you home with me. I almost got away when you were two, but..." Lifting Autumn's head, "Your Grandfather has always stopped me from protecting not just you but also me. Your father and I have always had a Romeo and Juliet kind of story, but without the death ending." Said Lesley with a sigh and a small kiss on Autumn's forehead as she wiped a tear from her face.

Trying not to be the eavesdropping cousin, Dev couldn't believe what he was hearing. His grandfather was very powerful, but when it came to Autumn, no one got the best of him. Even with this little escapade, Dev fully expected him to come down the path and bust all of them. Dev remembered a time he tried to sneak Autumn over to his house for a party, and Gabriel had all but blasted him back to his house. He didn't want to relive that experience. So, it baffled him that someone managed to sneak past any of Gabriel's wards with any kind of ease.

"I love you so much, Autumn, and I wish I was there to watch you grow up every day, but I was at every softball game you've had. Whenever you wished for me at night, I heard your prayers," said Lesley as she mustered up the stubbornness to hold in her tears. Autumn explained, "I want you to know that I don't blame you or him for what happened. I know that if you both could be together, you would be, and we would all be one big family." Lesley sniffled as she heard

this. All she wanted was to be with the man she loved and raise their daughter together. However, family ties and politics made that impossible, so they were stuck with this horrible situation.

"You have to tell me everything. I don't know how much time we have, but I want to make the most of it and just hold my baby," said Lesley. For a few more minutes, Dev stood outside his treehouse listening to mother and daughter reconnect after so many years being apart. He smiled again to himself that he was able to bring them together, even if it was for a few minutes. Out of nowhere, he heard a howl come from the house. He knew who it was and sent Dagon a message.

"What's going on buddy? Is everything okay?" Dagon sent back a quick message, "Gabriel is walking around the house looking for either Lesley or Autumn. From the way he's looking, he's getting suspicious. Cousin Chase just said he saw Autumn heading down the path towards the treehouse, and he's headed that way!"

Dev cursed to himself silently as he heard this news. He could still hear Lesley and Autumn inside having their bonding moment, oblivious to the world. He lightly knocked before entering and walked in the door. "I'm sorry to interrupt, but Gabriel is on his way here. Aunt Lesley, I'm sorry, but we have to get you back to your room."

They looked at each other and gave each other a big hug. "Autumn, I love you, and I promise that this won't be the last time we are together."

Autumn smiled up at her mother, wishing they had more time together, but she understood. "I love you too Mom, and one way or another, we will be together." Both women had tears in their eyes, Lesley stepped back next to Dev and took his hand. Even Dev's eyes felt slightly moist for a moment. Outside, he could hear approaching footsteps and a voice calling out for Autumn. She looked slightly alarmed and said, "Go on! Get her out of here now! I will handle grandfather!"

With that, Dev grabbed her and flashed Lesley back to her room before they were caught. When Dev landed in her room, he sent a message to Dagon to let him know they were in the clear and that the plan was a success. Out of the window, he heard another howl and a loud caw as Dagon, and Cadence celebrated together. Making her voice carry through the home, Dev heard his grandmother Julia say, "What is wrong with those familiars? They are almost rabid." Dev and Lesley laughed to themselves on knowing why they were so celebratory. After asking Dagon if they were followed, he poked his head out her window and then started to head out the room.

"Nephew?" Dev heard his name called and turned around and saw her smiling with tears in her eyes. "Thank you again for what you did. I will be sure to grab Myler and tell him thank you as well. You both gave me an amazing time with my daughter." Heading down-stairs, he pretended to see if his grandpa had caught on to where Autumn went. Seeing Myler sitting on the couch made Dev think he had run out of annoying things to talk to Gabriel about. There was only one way to find out, so he sat on the couch next to Myler and told him Lesley said, "thanks."

"Dinner is waiting in the dining room," said Makayla as she ran around the house telling everyone. Hoarding into the dining room, everyone's eyes sparkled as they saw a taste of home in the décor. Dev and his family gathered around the table. Some were already sitting, and all the ghost family went to go rest for the evening, preparing for tomorrow. A typical family would gather around a small ten-seater dining table and enjoy the food that had been given, but not the Vanseals.

Gabby and Selena had done the works and even transformed the whole dining room into a grand dining hall with the longest table they could float in. Walking in after changing clothes was Lady Julia, Rodney, and Selena. Being the ones that represented the line, Dev's grandma had made them change into clothes fit for royalty. Rodney mixed it up with a very classic suit coat and his tunic, looking and feeling very comfortable. While Selena groaned about her high-low dress with a corset peplum that Julia wouldn't let her customize. When

they entered the room, it was almost like the guest knew the events were about to begin.

"If you may all take your seats, we will begin to eat the meal that Gabby has prepared for us," said Rodney as he escorted his wife to the table. Placing his Mom right across from Selena and asking Gabriel to join the seat next to hers, everyone in the room began to sit. It was almost like a teardrop could be heard because other than the Zortegan music and chairs scraping across the floor, it was very silent.

Most of the family was closely watching which one of the grandparents was going to throw the first dart. Rodney had a plan to keep the dinner very peaceful. Then, to everyone's shock, Mable walked in and escorted both of their familiars out of the room and into the company of Gabby. Dev looked around the table and saw all the family members had gathered to eat. They stood up to show respect for the one that made the meal. But in Uncle Stover fashion, he had to make it the longest thanks speech ever.

"I know I speak for everyone here in giving a great thank you to the lovely Legion of the house. For making this beautiful spread that we all may sit and enjoy." He said as he raised his glass. "Also, big a thank you to Rodney and Selena for welcoming this family together again in honor of their wonderful twins coming of age. It has been many years since I have seen a bounty of food and wonderful cutlery as magnificent as this." As he said this, he tried to slip a gold jewel-encrusted fork into his pocket, but was smacked in the head by his sister. "Ouch. Julia, that was uncalled for!" He whined as he placed the fork back on the table. "As I was saying, this meal looks absolutely fabulous from the steaming platters of meat to the wonderful, sautéed vegetables."

As Dev and everyone's knees started to buckle from swaying back and forth from listening to how wonderful the broccoli looked on the plate. Dev noticed how happy Lesley was. Even though it hadn't been a long meeting, Dev was happy that he and Myler pulled it off for her and Autumn. Bored with his rant, she raised her wineglass and winked at the boys while also stopping Stover's never-ending speech.

"Okay, okay, we get it! The food is wonderful, compliments to the chef. Now eat before I lose my appetite listening to you slobber all over the food." Thankful for Lesley jumping in, they all sat down and began to eat their salmon.

Placing a napkin on his lap and pouring himself some juice, he began to eat while listening to everyone around the table. Everyone was having short, small conversations, but everyone was curious if the twins were going to complete the ceremony tomorrow. Dev was getting so bothered by the comments they made. He had so much faith in them, and everyone else seemed to think it was fifty-fifty with Ezekiel as the winner, like this was some sports game.

Tuning the table out before he got angry, Dev decided to add some entertainment to the dinner, so he focused his energy elsewhere. Someone dimmed the lights to magnificent sunset colors of oranges, yellows, and bluish reds. Then flowers, along with flower petals, appeared to be falling from the sky in different shapes and colors all in an amazing light show. All the younger cousins enjoyed every minute of the show, but he worried about his Cousin Ralston. He lit the petals on fire every time they touched his food. So, Dev did the one thing he knew would make the others laugh as well. He showered him in flowers until he looked like a mountain of rose petals.

While everyone was finishing their meal, Dev's show was coming to an end. Rodney stood and invited the adults out to the family room for a nice wind-down and drinks. "Kids, after you have finished your meal, clean up, and retire to your rooms. Tomorrow is a long day, and the twins will be preparing first thing in the morning, ready to embrace their new line. I just want to give them hope and love, just like we were shown on our special day." While making the decision to have dessert or finish for the evening, most lifted their glasses and agreed to his kind words. He walked over to Gabriel and asked him to join him, but he refused, so he proceeded to the family room while all the kids started to make their way upstairs.

"Thank you for this lovely dinner, but I need to take Autumn home for the evening. We will return for the ceremony, but I can't have anyone sneaking around in the middle of the night," said Gabriel. He pushed his chair back and walked over to Autumn. Waving him off, Rodney bit his tongue because he didn't want to be on that broken record again between him, her, and Lesley. Escorting Autumn up from the table, Gabriel flashed a portal in the room, and away they went.

Dev looked at Lesley's disappointment, and knew she was going to head straight for the bar now that Autumn was gone, so he decided to ask his Mom if she needed help cleaning up. "Thank you so much, but it's okay, baby, I got it. Go to bed. It's adult hour now. I need you to be up bright and early so you can greet the twins, because I know your dad is about to drink and play Baw Bas." Laughing at how competitive his dad could get, Dev hugged his mom goodnight and did as he was told.

CHAPTER 16

Sitting on the roof of the house, Dev thought about what this day meant for his siblings. He rose to make sure he greeted both of them back home. Gabby had taken Eland back to where she was, because the family was too rowdy for her to get a good night's rest. His dad promised him he didn't have to wear the old school get up today, which made him super happy. He liked the royal robe his mom brought back from Zortega. She had it made from the castle seamstress for his upcoming trip and special occasions. His coat jacket with tails was embroidered with silver crystals and the Capricorn colors, but it was a little big. The high collar neckline had tassels falling from the shoulders and three-quarter inch sleeves. Gabby pinned it up in the back, so it fit just right for now.

For right now, he just sat in his sweatpants as he looked out past the trees and admired the warm sunrise. The sun glowed with the brightest red, orange, and purple colors as the yellow filled the white clouds. He soon knew he would be leaving the twins for Zortega and hoped that their new line was kind to them.

When Dev looked behind the groves, he saw a cloud moving and thought it was odd because there was no wind. Afraid of a potential threat, he stood in his stance until he noticed it was a unique creature that one of his siblings was on top of. He thought maybe that was a Faux Loc his dad had told him about. His brother Ezekiel was doing his best to look like he was a Paratar warrior. Shockingly enough, Aunt Caroline was riding it for him as she brought them in for a landing. Riding in from the west was Eland on a Faux Loc as well, but she was holding on for dear life. She looked terrified because these were real and definitely not clouds. Guiding her in was another Paratar warrior. Before Dev could catch his breath at how amazing they were, Caroline was standing in front of him on the roof.

"So, Nephew, why do you look so speechless? Hasn't your father told you about these creatures? There are many different kinds of them in our land." Nodding his head up and down, Dev marveled at their beauty. They were as big as his house. The underbelly was silver with hard scaly armor, but the top was the smoothest fur you could pet. The Faux Loc was a snake by human standard, but its wings flapped with such glory. Its armor was gold on top, and it peeled out of its head and spine like a dragon's fury with fangs to match.

"I normally can't leave my post, and so far, I've done it twice this week because you guys are family. So, I decided to start the morning in style and bring Eria and Amina out for a field trip," stated Caroline.

Making the twins get off one by one, Caroline told Dev to take them inside as she fed her Loc a fish for the great deed it did before sending it home. Dev escorted them to their rooms and said, wait here, the fun was about to begin.

While the twins went into their rooms to practice more, Gabby passed Dev in the hallway with two plates of fresh eggs for breakfast. He could hear all the commotion and the crowd of ghosts that had shown back up, along with new family members. With ten hours to kill, the family chose to talk about the new threat and everything back in their day, but the kids and teens sharpened their skills outside.

It eventually got to the point where his dad even allowed Caroline to referee small power matches. Outback was some kid vs. kid battles with the adults

cheering on the sideline. They shouted Zortegan battle cries, and everyone could hear, and you could see how proud the Paratar in Caroline was watching them.

Dev watched from the sidelines as his cousins Makayla and Chelsea squared off against each other. Although they were unable to fully use their magic, they were trained in hand to hand combat. Instead of throwing spells, they threw punches and kicks. They darted back and forth across the field, trading blows and doing all they could to not fall out of the allotted rectangle.

The younger kids were not allowed to do as much as the older fighters. No one wanted them to get hurt or hurt the people around them, mishandling their magic. Dev was impressed with Chelsea's fighting style for a girl, because he thought her flips were really poetic. Makayla was having a really hard time landing any kind of a punch on her to end the fight. She knew if she hit her one good time, she would tap out, because Uncle Kilo's kids weren't the toughest.

"Point for Chelsea. One more and Makayla has to forfeit the kid's title," said Sraw as he flagged her for the point.

Standing closer to the kid's side, Dev saw how mad that made Makayla. She was the champ of the last two matches, and she hated to lose to anyone. She even said she could take Dev down one day, which always made him laugh, but his Dad always told him to watch his opponents close because you can always be bested. Screaming out in a fury, Makayla's anger proved more significant than her patience was to land a blow on Chelsea. So, she did the one thing she wasn't supposed to and powered up an attack at her.

"Foul, Foul! Stop her!" Said Lady Julia from her overhead view of both arenas. Seeing the upcoming spell aimed at Chelsea scared everyone to duck for some cover in hopes she casted it correctly. Dev decided to do the one thing he thought was best, and that was to grab Chelsea out of the way. Fortunately for him, Sraw, Rodney's best friend and right-hand man, beat him to the punch shielding her from it. After it dissipated, he stepped in front of her disqualifying her from the match and declaring Chelsea the winner.

Relieved with not having to be the hero, Dev looked over at the adult sparring match between Stover and Kilo. They each were both of the girl's fathers, and they were sparing just as hard. Safire, Lesley, and Rodney were all standing around cheering on Kilo while Selena, Ralston, and Gabriel cheered the loudest for Stover. Dev loved watching the adults play way more than the kids, because they could use weapons if they wanted. The magic that they displayed was unreal. The fighting arena changed randomly, and the crowd were allowed to throw in hazards to knock the other player off their game. The fight didn't end unless they were entirely knocked out the ring or if the ref called submission. Caroline loved a good fight, so it usually never got called.

"Vella, Vella!" Called out the family. "Come on, get him!"

Walking over to join the commotion, Dev was stopped by Myler. "Hey there cuz, I heard someone wants to challenge you." He said with a laugh. His interest piqued, and Dev asked, "Oh really? Who wants to challenge me?"

The look in Myler's eyes changed as he stepped back and flicked his right wrist for his war hammer to appear. The laughter faded from them and was replaced with the spark of a challenge. "I do, Deveraux Vanseal." He said as he pointed his war hammer at Dev. "I want to settle our feud once and for all. Which one of us is the strongest?"

Dev stared at his cousin in shock at the challenge. Before he could respond, a voice rang out. "Hold on there! If we are going to find out who is the strongest, you can't leave me out."

Stomping across the yard was Autumn, with Cadence fluttering around her head. She strode towards the two of them, glaring daggers as she drew closer. Her gaze was so intense that Dev and Myler both backed away from her a little bit. "I, too, will be a part of this battle, and I dare either of you to try and stop me," said Autumn, gearing herself up for a fight. Both boys stared at her in shock, then glanced at each other. With a quick shrug, they looked back and agreed to a three-way duel.

Together they turned and walked towards the field just as Kilo blasted Stover straight into the air. Everyone watched in anticipation as Stover seemed to float weightlessly before crashing back to earth. He landed in a crumpled heap and lay there unmoving. Rodney rushed forward to check and make sure his uncle was still alive. After a few moments of checking his vitals, he rose and addressed the crowd. "Uncle Stover will live; he just needs some time to rest. Which means that Kilo is victorious." The crowd jumped to their feet and cheered for Kilo, who then bowed to them and walked off the field, carrying Stover back into the house.

Shocked that Stover went down so quickly showed Lady Julia and the rest of the family that he was way too focused on stealing. Much to everyone's surprise of his defeat, the next event to follow paled in comparison to some's disappointment. After ringing the doorbell a few times, a surprise guest decided to come around back to hang out and check on his best friend.

Enthused at the sight, he saw before Stover landed; Anthony had never seen Dev's backyard look so transformed. It had slipped his mind that Dev had told him the twins' special party was today. Looking over at Dev, Anthony wondered if he could just sit and watch until all the real magic stuff started because then he knew he would have to go. Walking straight ahead to go say hi, Anthony was met with a blood-curdling scream. Anthony had accidentally glided through Sraw's dead mother, who had just popped over the plain to visit the celebrations. "I'm so sorry ma'am, I didn't mean to, I just thought you were a sun glare... I..." Said Anthony as he blocked himself from being blasted like the guy he just saw.

Amused by his mistake, Dev dashed over to protect him before his extended Grandma Kedra could use him to start a raving mob.

"Dude, what are you doing here? Most of my family doesn't know you know about me," said Dev as he rushed him over to where his mom was standing.

"I forgot about today, and I haven't heard from you since your vacation in the jungle. So, I thought I would stop by," replied Anthony.

"Well I never, is that a human, and what is he doing at one of our most cherished events? He walked right threw me and didn't even have the gall to look me in the face and apologize for that invasion of privacy," snorted Kedra.

"I can't see you, that's why. I can see only see familiars," said Anthony behind Dev and his Mom.

"Dude, not helping," said Dev as he almost tied a scarf around Anthony's mouth.

Floating down to the ground was Lady Julia, looking very sternly at her daughter-in-law and son. "Is this true, son? You know the council has a very strict policy about humans knowing people like us living among them. How do you know he's trustworthy?"

"Mom, he has been Dev's best friend since they were kids, and I trust him. Also, before you sound the alarm squad out on him, you're going to have to get through Gabby. So which side do you and Lady Kedra wanna be on? Mine and we keep having fun playing Jeuhra or Gabby's nasty side for messing with one of her adoptive children." Said Rodney as he looked at her for an answer in front of everyone.

Waving his hands at him, Rodney spelled Anthony so he could see everyone. Taking a deep breath in, Anthony opened his eyes and was shocked at the sight before him. All around him were ghosts and spirits of different ages. Some were in there Zortegan form, while others were just bright balls of light. As he took in the sight, his skin burned as a combined symbol of a backwards C, and L, had appeared on his neck.

"Grandma, can you please take that truth spell off him, he's kept all our secrets for years." Said Dev as he gestured between his dad and his grandma. His grandmother shook her head as she turned to walk away. "As long as he is here, he will tell the truth, and I will know where he is." Dev turned and stared at Anthony, who was rubbing his neck where the burn had appeared. His father walked over to examine it, then raised his hand to remove it, but was quickly stopped by Kilo.

"I wouldn't do that, Nephew." He said as he grabbed Rodney's hand. "The last person who tried to remove one of her spells from someone paid dearly." With that warning, he strolled off inside the house.

Rodney growled softly in the back of his throat, severely angered by his mother's actions, and looked at Dev and Anthony. They stared back with shock and anger on their faces. "I'm so sorry, boys. Don't worry, I will remove it." He raised his hand to place it on Anthony's neck one more time.

"Mr. Vanseal? What are you doing? Oh my, hello, Anthony. I didn't think you would be dropping..." Everyone turned to see Gabby standing near them with a tray full of snacks. Her face, however, was not set in her usual sweet smile. She was staring with a confused expression that slowly turned to shock and then anger. Dropping the tray, she rushed to Anthony's side to examine the mark on his neck. Dev and Rodney could feel the power radiating from her and knew this would not be good. They started to try to back away slowly to avoid her wrath. "Deveraux Vanseal," Gabby said in an ice-cold voice. She stood tall with her aura magnified around her, ice cold black eyes, and her tattooed Legion mark present. Looking at her, Rodney knew to not let the boys make any sudden moves.

Dev winced at the tone but still responded, "Yes, ma'am?"

Gabby slowly raised her hand and, with a slight tap, removed the mark from Anthony's neck. She then turned to look at Dev. Her eyes, which were usually soft brown, were now a deep, cold black. It felt like looking into a black hole. He feared he would be swallowed up by that bottomless gaze, but he couldn't look away. "Who did this? Who marked Anthony in such a way?" She asked, her voice barely a whisper.

Rodney stepped forward with his hands raised in a placating manner. "Gabby. Relax. Anthony came over unannounced, and no one else knew that he has known our secret. My mother overreacted, because of her views of humans and marked him just to make sure everyone felt safe," he said.

Gabby closed her eyes and took a deep breath. "I truly hate the way some of our kind see humans as beneath them. Anthony would never hurt anyone, and he has been nothing but loyal to us, Mr. Vanseal." Gabby replied. "Now, where is your mother?" She growled. She began to look around until she zeroed in on Lady Julia. Having her in her sights, Gabby marched in her direction. Dev, Anthony, and Rodney shared a glance and ran after her. Before they could catch up, Gabby grabbed Julia and knocked her straight into the sparring arena. "Lady Julia Vanseal, I challenge you to combat."

Julia rose to her feet and brushed her clothes off as she glared at Gabby. "You dare to challenge me?" She cried. "Have you forgotten? I'm a royal!!!" With that, she launched herself at Gabby only to be stopped in mid-air. Gabby had a hand raised and was holding Julia frozen ten feet off the ground. "You may be a royal, but I'm a Legion. My power will always trump yours," said Gabby, "I should punish you severely for what you did to Anthony, but this is a family event. It should be full of love and laughter." As she spoke, she slowly brought Julia down to the ground. Breathing a sigh of relief, Julia looked over at Dev, Rodney, and the human who were all on the sidelines watching this spectacle with the rest of the family. She gasped when she saw her brand had been removed from Anthony's neck. "Who removed my seal from that human's neck?" She cried in outrage. Gabby smirked at the angry look on her face. "I did," Gabby responded, "That boy, over there, is loyal to this family and is no danger to us in any way. He didn't deserve to be marked like that. While he is here, he will be treated with respect and never harmed, because he is under my protection. Now apologize!" Gabby wind blasting her over to where Anthony was standing. She then floated Julia in front of Anthony, so she could do it face to face.

Standing there, half terrified, Julia eat him, and half happy that she was being humiliated, Anthony stared her down as if he wasn't scared. "Now, apologize for your rudeness to your grandson's friend," said Gabby as she spelled a charm necklace around her wrist. "There that will keep you from using your magic until I feel you have earned it back."

"I will never apologize for doing what is right and for doing your job, and that is to protect our family." Screamed Julia as she squirmed around, trying to get free. She could feel the eyes of everyone on her. Waiting to see if she would vomit the words, I'm sorry. She finally decided to swallow her pride and save some of her respect. She knew her fellow believers weren't rushing in anytime to help save her. Whispering the coldest words to ever leave her mouth, "I was unaware that you were embraced by my family, human friend of my grandson. I admit, marking you was a little harsh before I understood the whole story."

Somewhat pleased with her apology, especially from her, Gabby flashed her to the chair she was sitting in and went back in to make more snacks.

"Alright!" Rodney cried, "That was certainly exciting. Who will be our next Jeuhra challengers?" As one, Dev, Myler, and Autumn shouted. "We will!" Everyone around them quieted in an instant. Rodney stared hard at the three teens and slowly approached them. "Three fighters is not really encouraged. Are you sure you want to continue?" In response, all three conjured their weapons. Dev's black Katana gleamed in the afternoon light, confident about the choice; they all walked past him and took their place on the field.

The crowd was shocked by this turn of events, but soon bets were being placed on who would come out on top. No one had ever seen a teen every man for himself kind of battle and couldn't wait to see who would win. The three cousins stood tall and stared each other down. They reached within themselves and released their power. The force of it drove the onlookers back and forced Rodney to place a shield around the field.

Everyone watched in awe as the power of these three teens raged around them in a chaotic storm. Dev was in his corner, surrounded by bright red flames. His eyes seemed to be two bright fireballs. Autumn was engulfed in streaks of black lighting that trailed all over her body. Myler, who seemed to be encased in an armor made of pure earth with small boulders flying around. Rodney watched from the sidelines as their powers struck each other inside the shield, fighting for dominance. He knew that Dev was powerful, but was surprised at how far his niece and little cousin had grown since he last saw them.

"They look pretty awesome, don't they, sir?" Rodney turned to look at Anthony. Anthony watched them carefully as the maelstrom of power raged behind the shield. There was a hungry gleam in Anthony eyes. "Anthony, are you alright?" Rodney asked. "Yes, sir. I am fine. Just a little jealous is all. I sometimes wish I had abilities like yours. Anyway, enough about me. This looks like it's gonna be one hell of a fight." Raising his fist up to swing it into the air, Anthony started to cheer loud for Dev.

Rodney gave a small laugh and turned to look back at the field. The three teens still had not moved, yet their power was growing stronger. They seemed to be waiting for something. With a jolt, Rodney remembered he hadn't given the call to start the fight. He walked forward and called out. "This is a no holds barred fight. Every man or woman for themselves. Do you understand?" They nodded their heads as they continued to stare each other down. "Ok. On my signal. 3. 2. 1. Figh..."

"Hold it!!!" A shrill voice cried from the crowd. Everyone looked towards the back, and as one, the three teens inside the shield released their power. They too, turned to see who had spoken up; however, they seemed to recognize the speaker from the looks on their faces. Dev glanced at Myler.

"Dude, you said she wasn't going to be here." Myler said and shook his head in disbelief. "She told me she couldn't make it," Dev stammered.

Autumn groaned loudly. "This can't be happening. Why did it have to be her?" She cried.

They all watched in horror as a girl the same age as them stalked towards the field. She was about five foot eight, mocha-colored skin, and had dark freckles over her face. Her hair was done in long braids down her back, and her piercing green eyes glared at all of them. At her side trotted a small tiger cub. Its back was arched, and its orange eyes seemed to track everyone in the crowd. As she approached, a small figure darted from the crowd to leap on her back.

"Bailey!!!" Makayla cried as she latched on to her older sister. "I didn't know you were going to be here." Makayla tried to hug her sister, but the next thing she knew, she was being dropped onto the ground and left behind.

"I told you not to touch me, little girl." Bailey snarled as she walked off without even glancing at her little sister.

Makayla looked at the ground, and tears started to fall as her sister coldly dismissed her. Dev's anger slowly started to rise as he watched Bailey mistreat his cousin. And from the looks on Autumn's and Myler's faces, he wasn't the only one. Dev should have known that Bailey would find a way to ruin this day. Ever since they were kids, everything had to be about her or involve her. She always found a way to be the center of attention and try to show how she was the best of all of them. He was hoping that she wouldn't make an appearance, but here she was.

"If it isn't the royal brat herself, Bailey Vanseal."

She was the daughter of Dev's Uncle Kilo, and she believed that she should be the one to take over The Capricorn Line. Anytime she showed up, she tried her best to one-up Dev in everything they did. Whether it was hand to hand combat or baking cookies. She tried to show she was number one. Now, here she stood. Ready to try and prove herself better than everyone all over again. With her signature weapon in hand. A thin rapier sword made of Zortegan iron. Although it was blue, it gave off a faint glow in the broad daylight.

She stopped at the edge of the field and smiled a cold smile. "Well, if it isn't my favorite cousins." She said as she asked Rodney to step onto the field. "Y'all look so strong and getting ready to throw hands. I'm confused though, as to why nobody invited me." She pouted a little as she made that comment. "I mean, after all, I'm the strongest one of all of us. Without me, it wouldn't be much of

a show." She walked over and took her place at the fourth corner of the field and crouched down into a battle stance.

Dev tightened his grip on his sword, readying himself for what he knew would come next. In a flash, she sprang and thrusted her sword forward, intending to impale him through the chest. Dev took a calm step to the side and slightly clipped her foot as she passed. The force caused her to flip over and land on her back in a huff. She jumped to her feet and glared at Dev.

"That was a lucky shot, cousin." She said as she crouched again to attack. "It won't happen again."

She stood in her crouch, her eyes jumping from each of her opponents. In the blink of an eye, she was off. This time she darted towards Myler, who was a little late raising his hammers. The tip of her rapier slashed across his shoulder, giving him a shallow cut as she flew past. Myler ran a hand over the cut, wiping off the blood. Bailey cackled with glee as she jumped up and down for besting him in speed.

"See what I did there?" Bailey cried, "That's what's gonna happen to all of you." Dev groaned to himself and looked out at the crowd. In the back, he could see his uncle Kilo covering his face at his daughter's antics. He focused back on Bailey as she stood there, gloating over such a minor wound. She stopped hopping up and down and pointed her blade at Dev. In a flash, she was gone. Dev closed his eyes and used his energy to pinpoint her location. He could feel her closing in, and at the last second, he dropped to the ground to evade her blade. She landed lightly and bounced up again to attack.

However, instead of Dev, she charged for Autumn. In two steps, Autumn ran forward and jumped. As she sailed over Bailey's back, she grabbed Autumn's foot and yanked her towards the ground. However, Autumn pushed her foot off Bailey's chest, slamming Bailey down. Bailey's eyes bugged out as the air was pushed from her lungs. With a snort, Autumn glanced over to Myler, who smiled and stamped the ground, causing a pillar of earth to launch Bailey into the air. She screamed as she soared upward and then began to drop towards the earth. Autumn raised her bow and pulled back the drawstring. She took aim and let an arrow loose that sailed towards Bailey. It snagged the collar of her shirt, causing her to slam into a tree. She hit it so hard; she was knocked out and hung there limp and unconscious. Everyone was completely silent after watching that simple display of power. The three that were still on the field made it look so easy and so effortless.

Kilo signed inwardly and shrugged his shoulders at Makayla to go retrieve her sister from the tree. Dev stepped off the field and walked over to Makayla, who was still huddled on the ground. He picked her up and held her close, whispering to her that it was alright. He rocked her slightly, then set her down on the ground and wiped her tears. "She won't bother you now and you're the best little cousin in the world," he said with a smile. She smiled back and hugged Dev around his waist before she scampered off to play. Dev smiled after her and looked and saw his mother smiling at him with pride.

He walked back to the field and said, "Now that, that is taken care of. Shall we get back to the main event?" The crowd cheered as all three laughed at the crowd's excitement. Quick as a flash, Dev jumped back in and flew at Myler. He pulled his fist back and put as much force behind it. Before he could connect the blow, an arrow flew across his path, making him stop up short. Myler took advantage of the confusion and swung his hammer at Dev's face. Dev pulled back at the last second, but was still blown back from the wind created by the attack. He flew back and corrected himself and hovered in the air. He looked down just in time to see Autumn launch another arrow. This one aimed at his face. He slashed his sword through the air, cutting the arrow in half. Out of the corner of his eye, he saw something fly towards him. He tried to dodge it, but was unable to do so. He took a full sparkle bomb to the face, and he started to fall back to the ground.

He could hear his Aunt Lesley screaming from the crowd, "How you like them apples, nephew? Revenge is mine! Ha-ha!"

"Really, Aunt Lesley? This is how you do me?" He growled as he wiped the glitter from his face. He could hear the crowd laughing and knew he had to look ridiculous. He glared at Autumn, who was laughing herself. "I'm so gonna get your mom for this cuz." Dev said.

Autumn stopped laughing and glared back. She drew her bow and snarled, "I'd like to see you try." Dev gulped as she began to fire arrow after arrow at him. He jumped and flipped across the arena, dodging the arrows as they flew.

The crowd cheered as they watched the three teens fly and charge each other in combat. They had never seen a battle so fierce, especially not one fought by anyone so young. The sheer magnitude of their power was astonishing to behold and once again caused Rodney to place a shield over the field. As he watched, he thought back to the training fight he had with Dev awhile back. The power he displayed then was weak in comparison to now. It baffled him that his son's power had grown so fast in such a short period.

Rodney was brought back from his thoughts as he saw Myler fly through the air and hit the barrier. He crossed his hammers to block a slash from Dev's sword. Myler dropped to the ground in a crouch and brought his hammers down to strike the earth. Each time he hit the ground, a boulder rose and flew at Dev and Autumn. He continued to strike his hammers as if they were drumsticks, and the earth was his own personal drum. Dev and Autumn stood back to back, fending off the boulders as best they could. Dev's blade was nothing but a black blur as he slashed and cut at the boulders. Autumn was firing arrow after arrow in a never-ending barrage. As if giving the finale an epic drum solo, Myler brought both hammers down in a resounding crash. The boulders fell to the ground in a clatter, and a shadow fell across the sky. Dev and Autumn looked up to see a boulder the size of a mountain fall from above. The crowd watching screamed in terror and ran back towards the house for cover. The only ones who remained were Anthony and Rodney.

Dev and Autumn looked on in shock and then back at each other and started to laugh. "Really, Myler?" Dev asked. "You resort to this attack?" He looked over at Autumn, who was wiping a hysterical tear from her eye. "I guess we should stop playing around," Autumn said. With that, she released her maximum power and drew her bowstring back and aimed it straight into the air. An arrow made of black electricity flared to life. The power emanating from it flared around Autumn and made her hair rise around her. Dev released his power and made it flow into his sword. The blade was wreathed in black flame, and it heated the air to an almost unbearable level. Rodney's shield was the only thing blocking the power from scorching Anthony and the rest of the grounds. Dev launched himself into the air at the gigantic boulder bearing down on them. The arrow Autumn had been manifesting had grown to an unimaginable size, and she released it and watched as it flew alongside Dev into the sky. With a sound of a sonic boom, Dev and the arrow connected with the boulder and shattered it into nothing more than pebbles. The pebbles soon began to fall to the ground, creating a big dust cloud. Dev landed lightly on his feet and snapped his fingers, making the rest of the pebbles disappear. He sheathed his sword just as Autumn put her bow away. They looked over at Myler, who was sitting back enjoying the show with his hammers at his side. He stood with a grin and turned his hammers back into cufflinks. "Good show, cousins." He said with a laugh. "Shall we go ahead and call this one a draw?" The others laughed with him in agreement while wrapping their arms around each other's shoulders. Then they walked off the field towards Rodney and Anthony to admire the mess they made.

CHAPTER 17

While everyone was watching the matches, time passed by rather quickly into the evening. Soon, Dev noticed the house transforming for the night celebration. That made Dev happy but upset, because his mom shouted that it was time for everyone to clean up for the ceremony.

All dressed up and ready to embark on the most joyful moment of a Zortegan's life, Dev went downstairs to go find his spot. Standing in the family room, he saw Delila shimmy herself down the stairs in her royal shawl and gown. She met the twenty or so ghosts that gathered for today's event. At the front of the door to the patio entrance stood Lady Julia and Uncle Patrick. He was so honored to hear that the twins wanted him to introduce them.

Standing there, he felt his grandmother's eyes burn into the center of his forehead as she walked over to him. "Grandson, your dear old grandma, came a long way and worked very hard at getting the fit just right for tonight's events. Please, darling, tell me where the outfit I had brought for you is?" Said Julia in a soft tone.

"I asked Mom and Dad if I could wear mine tonight, and Mom said yes..."

"Well dear, good thing we still have a few minutes before the moon is ready. Go put it on for your dearest grandmother for the photos afterward."

"Um, I would, but I don't know where Mom took it. I think she said something about flying it to the nearest volcano or letting it slip out of her hand next to the fireplace." Dev slowly walked away from the rising anger on her face.

"Oh, she did, did she?"

Coming out of the dining room, Rodney was looking at his watch and knew the time had come. Dev thought it would be a good idea to let his dad know his mother was not happy with the wardrobe change, and to protect his mom. On that note, Rodney reached for his wife's hand and asked everyone to take their positions. Filled with pride and joy, both parents waited until all their family was out the back door.

Rodney looked around once more, then nodded at his great Uncle to go retrieve the twins so they could start. Uncle Pat closed the door right after them. He felt comforted by the midnight blue sky that surrounded this moment they were about to have. Today was going to be a great day, Dev thought. The night was bright with a multitude of stars and a magnificent blue moon as the Vanseal family members stood outside behind their house in the backyard. The clearing was ten acres of woodland, and in a small circle, they waited for the guests of honor to arrive.

Dev stood next to his father, who was clothed in the celestial robes of The House of Capricorn. On his face, he wore a mask in the shape of a goat, and in his hand, he held an enchanted mirror. Dev remembered that that mirror would show the person who stared into it, the authentic form of their familiar. It would act as a gateway for it to come to this world. The rest of the family was standing around in a large circle at a raised altar, waiting, partnered with their familiars floating around them. A path was made from the altar to the house with glowing crystals on both sides. It was meant to light the way for the new

initiates who were to partake in their Kaloke Ceremony. This ceremony was a means for each member of the zodiac houses to finally learn the true form of the spiritual familiar that came to be on the day they were born.

Tonight, it was the time for Eland and Ezekiel to take the next step in their training and meet the partners of their souls. Getting the signal that they were ready, Gabby told the twins and Pat it was time to go. Spelling them a small stone for luck, she kissed it and placed it in each of their pockets. "I did the same thing for your brother when he stood here. I'm so proud of you two. Now, go knock 'em dead," said Gabby as she stepped back out of the way.

When the doors to the house finally opened, both twins stepped out onto the path. They were wearing white robes that seemed to glow in the moonlight. His father raised his hand and beckoned the two to come towards the altar. As the twins began the slow walk from the house, Dev couldn't help but notice how nervous and terrified the two of them were. Eland was trying hard not to hyperventilate. While Ezekiel was trying to look calm, but Dev could tell by his jerky movements that it was taking all his willpower to keep moving forward. Dev remembered his own ceremony and how scared he was, but at the same time, he had been excited. He couldn't wait to reach the altar and finally see the true form of his familiar. He had also been scared that nothing would happen at all, and while that was rare, it was still something that happened from time to time. On those occasions, the person who didn't have a familiar had his powers stripped and was seen as a nub amongst the family. It was a sad and terrifying prospect to think that today was supposed to be the happiest moment of their lives could also lead to despair. Soon their own family would treat them as a pariah, an outsider. Someone who was family and yet at the same time was not.

Now, watching the twins make the walk, he could completely identify with the nervousness and fear they felt. When the twins finally reached the altar, they knelt and bowed their heads almost in prayer as they waited for their father to begin the Kaloke Ceremony. Rodney Vanseal looked down at his two youngest children through the mask on his face, feeling for them as he saw the way their bodies shook. He stepped forward towards the altar with his familiar walking close behind him. His eyes began to glow a bright light blue. "Rise and state your names so that the spirits may know who comes to this holiest moment in time." His voice rose loud and clear, and as he spoke, the moon seemed to shine brighter directly on the twins.

Each one rose, and all traces of fear and nervousness seemed to have melted away from them as they each shouted their names to the heavens.

"Eland Eliza Vanseal!" Shouted Dev's little sister with fiery determination blazed in her face.

"Ezekiel Joshua Vanseal!" Said her twin brother bright with a spark of power that was slowly building to a raging inferno. Behind his mask, Rodney Vanseal smiled at his children as they proudly proclaimed themselves to the realm of spirits. He turned his back to them and raised his hand with the mirror, shouting to the sky.

"I, the leader of The House of Capricorn, beseech the spirits to open the gates to their world and name these two initiates worthy of gaining their familiars!"

At this point, each family member, dead and alive, formed a circle surrounding the alter, raised their hands toward Rodney, and fired pure magic towards the mirror. As the magic combined with the celestial item, it began to glow and floated out of Rodney's hand. Soon, each member of the family's eyes began to glow the representative color of their line. They spread their arms out to their sides while continuing to let the magic flow, forming a protective bubble around the altar and the twins as they gazed in wonder at the spectacle before them. The white and blue lights shined bright as the violets and greens swirled overhead. A yellow strike of lightning shot out of the night skies.

Rodney turned back to the twins and pointed at Ezekiel.

"Do you, Ezekiel Vanseal, swear in front of family and spirit that you will obey the laws set down by our ancestors?"

210

In a clear voice, Ezekiel responded.

"I do."

"Do you also swear that you will do everything in your power to protect those around you in times of crisis and keep them from harm?" Again, Ezekiel stated.

"I do."

"Do you swear that even under torture or penalty of death, you will never reveal the secrets of the zodiacs to anyone other than those already properly initiated?"

Again, Ezekiel stated,

"I do."

"Then take the mirror and look upon the face of your familiar and know him well." The mirror slowly descended and stopped directly in front of Ezekiel, who stared into it. At first, all he saw was his own face, but shortly after, mist shrouded the face of the mirror. When it cleared, staring back at him was the face of his familiar.

"Now say your spell to retrieve your familiar. If you do it correctly, they shall be yours since your heart has proven to be pure of moonlight by the mirror," said Rodney.

Aunt Lesley, who was still somewhat drunk, decided to whisper to herself, "No pressure, kids." Due to it being very still and quiet around the alter, it sounded as if she was speaking loudly, so everyone heard it.

Rodney took one look in her direction and flicked his finger at her, shutting her mouth completely. "Lesley do be quiet," he stated before turning back to the children.

Ezekiel moved back, stepping up to the mirror. Holding it in his hand, he recited. "Chichen muileti da cend ta phecy." Slowly a mist began to pour out of the mirror, and through it floated a silver lemur. It inched closer to Ezekiel, who stared back, never breaking eye contact as it sniffed slightly at the boy. Ezekiel seemed lost in a trance as he stared at the lemur that was now entirely removed from the mirror. Everyone in attendance knew exactly what was going on. Ezekiel was mentally communicating with his familiar. He was learning his name was Semi and swearing to always be by his side until the void claimed them both. After what seemed to be an eternity, the boy and the lemur seemed to smile at each other, and the lemur floated forward, setting himself on Ezekiel's head.

Eland, who stared in rapt attention, wondered when her turn would come. She could feel herself getting impatient, but knew she had to keep her heart pure. She just always hated that because he was born four minutes before her, he always went first.

The mirror began to float towards Rodney, who then turned to Eland and once again stated the same questions to her as he did Ezekiel.

"Do you Eland Vanseal swear in front of family and spirit that you will obey the laws set down by our ancestors?" in a clear voice, Eland responded.

"I do."

"Do you also swear that you will do everything in your power to protect those around you in times of crisis and keep them from harm?" Again, Eland stated,

"I do."

"Do you swear that even under torture or penalty of death, you will never reveal the secrets of the zodiac to anyone other than those already properly initiated?"

Again, Eland stated,

"I do."

"Then take the mirror and look upon the face of your familiar and know them well."

The mirror slowly descended and stopped directly in front of Eland, who stared into it.

"Now say your spell to retrieve your familiar. If you do it correctly, they shall be yours since we have proven your heart and souls pure of moonlight by the mirror," said Rodney.

Eland moved back, stepping up to the mirror, holding it in her hands she recited, "Chichen muileti da cend ta phecy," This time as the mist began to clear, a white-and-gray husky appeared in the face of the mirror. It jumped out and floated towards Eland, eager to meet its new partner. Eland smiled brightly at the husky as she stared into its deep blue-black eyes. She made the same promises to it that Ezekiel had made to his familiar. The husky had settled at her feet and Eland dropped to her knees and wrapped her arms around it.

Smiling at both of his children, Rodney asked them both to rise. Selena was so proud, but also nervous because they had only finished one half. This part was where it could all go wrong. Just because they saw their familiar didn't mean the twins connected to them by bond. If they messed up, they would become Kantor's and their powers would reject them. She knew they were strong, and they had been studying and practicing hard. She sat back and watched anxiously, knowing her babies could do it.

"Now that you both have been granted your familiar, the time has come for you to choose your totems."

Both children placed their hands out in front of them and began to chant the spell they had been taught. The spell would change the rocks of silver magnetite they had both carried around into a special shape fit for them. It was hard to create, but the charmed item would act as a vessel for their familiars. Only royal kids got the rocks and anyone non royal would get the paint to create a vessel tattoo. Raising their other hand, they were to make a star that would morph into their totem. Once done, the spell would link them forever.

"Poe' lin Cambrtic Goursha Obeyo, Poe' lin Cambrtic Goursha Obeyo, Poe' lin Cambrtic Goursha Obeyo!"

A golden glow began to shine between their hands as the charms took shape. Eland's charm shot up and wrapped around her wrist, forming a gold bracelet with a charm in the shape of a husky on it. Ezekiel's totem stopped glowing, and everyone took notice, shocked and scared, but they told him to keep going.

"Poe' lin Cambrtic Goursha Obeyo!" He cried out in total agony that he wouldn't complete the ceremony. Seeing the look on his face, Dev decided he couldn't let him think he was alone. Doing the only thing he thought he could without jumping in there for him, he broke rank and began to help him chant.

He messaged him. *"Come on, Zeke. You got it. Believe he belongs to you. Trust yourself because I'm right here with you."*

As his faith began to dwindle, Eland placed her hand on his shoulder. "I'm not celebrating without you, so give it one more try."

Closing his eyes and taking a deep breath, he started the spell over. In amazement, a star shot into the air and wrapped around his pointer finger to form a ring with the imprint of a lemur on it.

When both children stopped chanting, Rodney stepped forward and stated, "Congratulations on finding your familiars. Now introduce them to the family."

Ezekiel stepped forward with the lemur on his arm and him raised him proudly.

"This is my familiar. His name is Semi." With that, Semi floated into the air and disappeared into the ring on Ezekiel's finger.

Next, Eland stepped forward with the husky right at her side and stated,

"This is my familiar. Her name is Simi." With a howl, Simi floated into the air and ran into the charm on her wrist.

Rodney addressed the twins, "You now have completed the Kaloke Ceremony and become full-fledged magical Zortegans. Now you have to pledge your loyalty to your new house line. In any event, pledging to your line means that you will save and protect your brethren from all harm, regardless of family lines." Turning to the mirror, Rodney called upon the infinity scroll. In the blink of an eye, the scroll came through the mirror.

"Now, with a heavy heart, I introduce your house line leader, Mrs. Adare Madison Jones of the Gemini line," said Rodney.

Entering the dome among the family members was a figure in a royal hooded robe. Shockingly enough, Dev's mouth dropped when she unveiled herself. It was Mrs. Jones, his math teacher. Taken back at the fact she was the Gemini leader, he finally realized why his mind spell didn't work on her in class. She was so majestic, but he wondered how come no one had told him she was the Gemini leader!

With Dev still staring at Lady Gemini, she approached the altar and took the scroll from Rodney to perform the spell that would unite the twins to her house.

As Gemini stood, her eyes glowed a deep emerald green as she asked Ezekiel, "Do you pledge your loyalty to your new house line? In any event, pledging that you will save and protect your brethren from all harm, regardless of family lines?"

Looking at his dad, he smiled and said,

"I do."

While saying his pledge, he took the vial of blood his mom set on the table that she kept since their birth and signed his name on the scroll.

"Fricdaraw, I now accept you, Gemini," said Ezekiel. Now Gemini turned towards Eland.

"Do you pledge your loyalty to your new house line? In any event, pledging that you will save and protect your brethren from all harm regardless of family lines." Looking at her mom as she cried a happy tear. She stood tall and said,

"I do." While saying her pledge, she took the vial of blood and signed her name on the scroll.

"Fricdaraw, I now accept you as Gemini," said Eland.

After looking at the scroll, Gemini rolled it up and placed it back in the mirror, and then proceeded to honor the twins with a welcome. As each child stepped down from the altar, their eyes began glowing a bright green color. The remaining members released the hold on their magic and let the protective dome fade. They then stepped forward to congratulate the twins.

As the ceremony came to an end, the moon seemed to lose some of its brightness, and it was almost like the stars began to wink out one by one. The family headed towards the house, happily laughing and hugging each other, ready to cut the cake. Not knowing that evil was lurking close by and waiting for the chance to strike. A shadow waited and lurked for a minute of peace in the excitement.

CHAPTER 18

As the party raged on inside, one by one, the familiars of the twelve leaders began to appear in the clearing. They all stood in a circle, much like the one for the twins' ceremony. The last to arrive was Yendor, followed by Semi and Simi. At the edge of the clearing stood Mable and Dagon, along with Tiye and everyone else. Eve was perched on a branch, and kept a lookout. The two newest familiars took their place in the center of the circle and faced Yendor and the chameleon Myuka.

Yendor stepped forward and spoke in a clear voice, addressing everyone. *"Please welcome our two newest members, Semi and Simi, to the fold."* The elders all dipped their heads in acknowledgment. *"As is our custom, the young must be aware of all current situations going on in our world. We all agree that right now is a perilous moment in time. The mighty python familiar of the Ophiuchus line is growing stronger, and his influence is being felt all over. We of the spirit realm feel it more intensely than our Niyors, because he is one of us."* Everyone tensed at these words, knowing them to be true. For quite some time, they had been feeling the presence of their great enemy, and overtime, it had grown stronger. They worry that soon he would be able to escape his prison. "We have to warn our partners of any new threat that comes our way. However, there is only so much they could do in this situation."

Myuka stepped forward and picked up where Yendor left off. "All of us know of the attack on the Braymark family so many years ago. That was the python's first attempt at freeing himself. He tried to gain control of the Qualum, and in doing so, we lost two very valuable members."

She paused as she looked around at the other spirits and revealed a great secret. A secret they had kept from everyone, except other familiars. As far as their Niyors knew, Jonathan Braymark and his familiar Ebon had died the night of the attack. What they didn't know was that after extensive searching, he had been found, and he was far worse than dead.

"Behold young ones, take heed at what you are about to hear, and remember that your Niyors can never know of this until the time is right," Yendor stated as all the others looked to the sky. They saw a portal that was forming, and it looked like a black hole spinning in reverse. It spewed out darkness as it rotated silently, and a significant presence could be felt radiating from it. Slowly a shape began to appear as a creature stepped out, made entirely of shadow. It's shaped condensed itself, and it slowly sank to the ground to stand in front of the familiars.

Dagon, who had been watching the entire scene, felt a twinge of pity coming from the pair of newbies. They trembled silently as the dark creature rose and walked towards them. Dagon remembered how he felt when he learned the truth and how shocked he was and what had indeed happened. The creature stopped in front of Semi and Simi and stared down at them with his soft purple eyes. They stared back, taking in his full form. The first thing they noticed was a surprising mark on his forehead. It looked like a star with a missing point. He let out a low purr as he settled in front of them, trying to calm their fear.

He spoke in a deep voice: *"Do not fear me, I mean you no harm."* The two familiars stood there in shock at the creature before them. He looked like a giant cat with a wild feral gleam in his eyes. He looked down at them and seemed to smile softly before beginning to speak. *"I know this must be hard for you to understand. After all, everyone believes that my Niyor and I died during that attack. That couldn't be farther from the truth."* He sighed and bowed his head. *"What happened that night was a complete accident that we both regret to this day."* There was a deep sadness in his eyes as he continued with his story. *"We were doing all we could to protect the Qualum from the intruder who broke in. Our powers together were nowhere near a match for his, but we still tried to hold him off. Jonathan's father came in and tried to help us by firing a spell. Unfortunately, it missed, but it caused the intruder to mess up the spell he was using with the book. A portal opened and sucked Jonathan and me inside it. The masked figure was drawn in as well, but he dropped the Qualum, so he lost his advantage over us. While in the portal, our battle continued as it transported us to an unknown location. Which turned out to be the future as we know it if we do not stop the snake from succeeding in getting the book. There is a spell inside it that would erase a line, but it would give all the power of that line to its caster. Since all twelve did it to cast him away, we're pretty sure from what we saw he wants to return the favor permanently. In our struggle, we soon learned that we were cursed by the spell and banished in opposite directions. Us towards the future, and we assumed the Ophiuchan to the past. Who knows what kind of plan he could be setting up right now, ten years in the past for our present?"* The two in the center stood and stared at Ebon with wide eyes as they heard this tale, barely able to believe it.

A thoughtful look passed over Semi's face, and the young lemur raised a small paw. *"Quick question."* He looked around and directed his question at Uni. *"Why does your Niyor not know that her husband is still alive?"*

Uni looked back at Semi and bowed his head sadly. *"When we found out what had truly happened, we chose to keep the information to ourselves. If she were to have found out what had happened, she would've neglected her duties as a council member, and we couldn't allow that to happen."* Soft tears rolled down

Uni's face as he continued to speak. *"We spent years trying to find ways to bring him back. Nothing we did worked in any way. Then one day, he managed to find his way back to us. However, he asked us to keep his return a secret for a while. Our only contact with him is through Ebon. Other than that, he only appears during Kaloke Ceremonies so that we can explain this dire situation to new familiars."* Uni stepped back to his spot as he finished speaking and sat with his head bowed, staring at the ground.

Yendor stepped forward and looked them both in the eye. *"You both now know and must swear to keep this information a secret until otherwise told. Do you both understand? Our Niyors can never know of this until the time is right."*

Simi and Semi looked back and then stared at each other. This was so much to take in, and it went against everything they knew and believed to hide something from their Niyor. They were a part of each other. They shared everything, memories, and pain. There was even a small period where they both would merge with their Niyors and see everything they had ever experienced so that there would be no secrets. To intentionally hide information felt wrong.

From outside the circle, Dagon sat back and watched the two new familiars deal with the same inner struggle he did when he had learned the truth. He stepped forward and cleared his throat and bowed his head respectfully as he addressed the group. *"Permission to enter the circle and speak. Sir?"*

They made a small opening to allow him to enter. He stepped forward, and before he spoke, he bowed to Ebon, who returned the gesture. He turned to the young familiars and stared at them as they looked back at him, their eyes begging him to help. Sighing softly, he spoke. *"I understand exactly how the two of you feel about this whole situation. I remember fighting an inner battle with myself to either tell the truth or follow my orders. When I took a moment to think about it, I realized they were right for the way they handled this."* Semi and Simi looked confused at what he was saying. *"Had our Niyors learned he was alive, they would have searched for him, and then due to his connection to the enemy, they would have captured him and locked him up."*

Ebon growled softly at this statement, swearing he would never have let that happen.

Dagon continued to speak. *"There will come a time when we can tell them, but for now, we need to keep this to ourselves and do all we can to help Ebon and Jonathan in their mission. Do you understand?"*

Simi and Semi remained quiet for a short amount of time. They looked straight at Dagon and stated together, *"We understand, and we swear to keep this secret."*

Yendor nodded back at them, accepting their responsibility. Stepping forward, he addressed the group as a whole. *"Now that our newest familiars have sworn their oath, it is time to conclude this meeting. Thank you for coming."* Bowing to the other familiars, he led Simi and Semi back to the house to continue the party. One by one, the other familiars bowed to each other and then returned to their homes for the night.

The only ones remaining were Ebon and Dagon. Ebon stared at the young wolf in front of him. He could feel the power emanating from him, and the sight gave him hope for the future. *"You should head inside and be with your Niyor. I'm sure he's looking for you,"* said Ebon.

Dagon looked back towards the house and then at Ebon. *"Things are going to get worse before they get better, aren't they?"* Asked Dagon.

Ebon nodded his head slowly. *"Yes,"* he replied softly.

"Can we truly stop what is going to come?" Ebon stared him straight in his eye.

"Only if we stand together, will we prevail." Dagon didn't seem satisfied with that answer, but he accepted it and headed inside, leaving Ebon alone in the clearing.

He sat quietly, watched the stars, and contemplated all that had happened. Ebon smiled slightly to himself as he thought of Dagon and the strength he had shown when he stepped forward to speak. He may not have noticed, but he had the entire council staring at him, hanging off his every word. They each took his words to heart, helping to quell their own uneasiness that they felt. That leadership and strength would be needed in the future. It was one of the reasons he was trying to rewrite what he and Jonathan had seen. In that future, Dagon and his Niyor, Deveraux Vanseal, were no longer of this world, and without them, this fight would be lost entirely.

Dagon returned to the living room and saw an entirely different scene than when he left. On one side was Gabriel and Rodney, who seemed ready to tear into each other. Lesley was standing at Rodney's shoulder, glaring daggers at her father, who was holding Autumn back from reaching her mother. Cadence was flapping around Gabriel's head and cawing at him. Yendor, who had also just returned to the house, rushed to Rodney's side, bleating in anger while Eve hovered in the air hooting loudly.

Gabriel's familiar, a large white gorilla named Kalyi, was pacing back and forth in front of his Niyor, growling and beating his chest at Rodney. On the other side, Selena stood in a similar stance, locked in what seemed to be a cage of silky strands with Lady Julia. At the top of the cage stood Websly, who continued to produce more webbing for the cage. Tiye could be seen pacing back and forth in front of the cage, trying to cut her way in. It was no use, however, with each swipe, Websly just made the cage stronger.

Cousin Chase was running around the room, talking with other family members who seemed to be taking bets from the sidelines. Every time he passed Gabby, he tried to rub her arm or pinch her behind. With each attempt, she smacked him so hard he crashed into the wall. From the few new dents on the wall, everyone could see that Chase had been slammed quite a few times. Dagon continued looking around for Dev to make sure he was ok. Dagon finally saw him seated in a chair a few feet away. He had a shield around himself, and the other kids were staring back and forth between the two separate groups.

There was a loud yell as Rodney and Lesley both went flying back through the air. They nearly crashed into the barrier around Selena, but thanks to Dev's quick thinking, they were caught mid-air and softly set down on the floor. Rodney gave his son a quick nod of thanks and then turned to fire back at his father-in-law, who was laughing at him.

"At least someone in this family knows how to think and act quickly. Honestly, who really taught him? Because there is no way, it was you, with your slow reflexes."

Rodney's teeth grinded as he growled. "I've had enough of your insults to my knowledge and character, old man! Since the day we met, and I asked for your daughter's hand, you have belittled me and tried to say I was unworthy! Not once have I ever done anything to dishonor you, her, or your family. I have loved her and protected her with every inch of my being and power! We have given you three beautiful grandchildren, and you come here during my youngest's Kaloke Ceremony and continue your disrespect towards me!"

The more Rodney screamed, the more his power began to build. The tension in the air was so thick you could wave your hand through it. Selena and Julia seemed to have forgotten their own disagreement and were staring in shock. One in anger at her son's treatment, the other at her husband's anger and pain. Seeing the raw power emanating from his son-in-law, Gabriel took a slight step back. He stared around at the faces of the other family members. Some looked scared, others were on the verge of tears, and some stared at him in complete outrage. With a slight cough and an embarrassed look, he glanced over to his daughter. She had her hand covering her mouth and was weeping softly. She ran to her husband and placed a gentle hand on his shoulder.

As soon as Rodney felt her hand, he calmed down and stared at her with all the love in the world. Selena smiled at him and placed a gentle kiss on his cheek, then whispered in his ear. He smiled and looked around the room at the family gathered there. "I apologize to everyone here for my outburst, but my wife is tired and wants to go to bed. Eland, Ezekiel, please come here." The twins stepped forward once Dev dropped his barrier and stared at their father. He smiled down at them. "I'm proud of you for making it through your ceremony. I know you will make your new line proud. Always remember we are here if you need us." He linked arms with his wife, then addressed the room one more time. "Thank you all for coming. I trust you can all find your way out when you're ready. Goodnight, everyone."

With that, he and Selena walked from the room and headed upstairs. The rest of the family continued to look around and whisper to each other about the turn of events. From the doorway, Gabriel gave a sniff of disdain and straightened the cuff of his suit. "Better he bow out gracefully than receive further humiliation from me beating him into the ground. I mean, how would it look for a royal to be beaten by a commoner?" He gave a weak chuckle at his own lame joke, trying to sound confident in himself. However, deep down, he knew if it had come to a fight, Rodney would have taken him down without breaking a sweat. Dev, who had been tending to the other kids this entire time, ensuring that they stayed calm, stiffened when he heard his grandfather's comment.

"Grandpa, I thank you for coming, but I think it's time you left," said Dev.

Gabriel looked at him. "Since when do you take that tone with me, boy?"

Dev just looked at him and repeated, "Thank you for coming, but I think it's time you left."

Gabriel's face contorted in rage. "I will not be ordered around by some brat barely out of his training diapers."

Dev merely stood there and slowly let his power rise. Soon everyone in the room could feel it, and some even backed away a little. Gabriel stared in shock at the power radiating from his grandson. Rodney was strong, but this child was becoming more powerful. A sense of pride flashed through him as he saw how powerful his grandson was. Although Gabriel never showed it, he was happy at the lessons that Rodney was giving Dev, and he could see the results from them. Once Dev truly came into his powers, he would be a force to be reckoned with.

Staring into his eyes, he saw the steely resolve that said he would fight him if he had to. Not wanting to be on the receiving end of his grandson's wrath, Gabriel turned and began to walk out the door, grabbing Autumn's arm to lead her out. A cry of anguish made him stop and turn back.

Lesley was in tears with one hand on her lipstick whip. The other was reaching out to her daughter, her eyes begging her father to let her see her. "Please let me be with my baby. Even if it's just for a few minutes."

Autumn tried to walk forward to her mother's outstretched arm, but Gabriel blocked her way. Although it hurt him to deny his daughter and granddaughter a reunion, they both deserved, he knew he couldn't. So, as always, he made himself out to be the bad guy and the black sheep of the family.

"You know the rules, Lesley!" He snarled at her with a contempt that he genuinely did not feel. "Neither of you are allowed any interaction with each other. Let's go, Autumn." With that, he grabbed her arm and marched her to the door. Autumn screamed for her mother the whole way. Lesley cried and begged for her to be brought back. With each cry, his heart broke over and over again. He knew what he was doing was painful, but it was better than the alternative. So, if he was hated, then hated he would be to keep his family safe.

Back in the living room, everyone was still standing around in shocked silence. Dagon walked up to Dev, who was trying to calm his younger cousins down. *"Are you alright?"*

Dev sighed and looked around at his remaining family. Most were still looking at him with slight fear at his display of power. He hated to have them look at him in that way, but he knew it couldn't be helped now. Dev smiled slightly at Dagon and reached down to rub his head. "Yeah, I'm fine. Don't worry. Where did you and Yendor disappear too?" He asked.

Dagon closed his thoughts off from Dev, afraid he may see what had transpired outside. "We were just showing our new guests around the house, that's all." He looked over to where the twins were chatting with their familiars, laughing and smiling. Dev smiled at the sight and was glad that his siblings were safe.

Gabby walked into the room and made a beeline straight for Dev. "I know it's a special occasion, but I think it's time for you to head to bed. You have a track meet in the morning, remember? Don't want you to be too tired."

Dev looked around the room at the remaining family, still lingering and talking. "I still have to see everyone out, Gabby." He said.

"Don't worry, Hun, I will see them out with plenty of birthday cake," Gabby said. "You head up to bed and get some rest for tomorrow." With that, she walked away.

Dev headed for the stairs with Dagon on his heels. The last thing he heard as he headed up to his room was a crash. Followed by Gabby yelling at Chase to keep his grubby paws to himself before she popped him like a ghost balloon. Dev chuckled to himself as he climbed the stairs and headed to his room to sleep.

CHAPTER 19

The day started bright and clear, not a cloud in the sky. The sun felt good on Dev's back as he stretched out his legs and got himself ready for his track meet. He was somewhat on edge because this was the day of the championship. Coming from a family of magic users, it became second nature to use magic in everyday life. However, when he was on the track racing against regular humans, he never used his abilities to get the upper hand. Whenever he ran, he prided himself on only using his body and his focus to keep himself going. He even went as far as to leave his wolf necklace with Dagon inside, tucked away in his locker. Every race he ran, Dev wanted to make sure he won fair and square and never cheat. Today was no different, even though this would be an important race. In these moments, he wanted to be just like his teammates and opponents. He looked at them, always pushing themselves beyond the brink to win the race. Dev felt he owed it to them to push himself just as hard.

Even with his necklace in his locker, he could still hear Dagon in his head, pumping him up. *"You got this boss! Put your head down, open your stride, and run like the wolf you are."*

Dev smiled at his message. Ever since he joined the track team, he ran as hard and as fast as possible, and whenever Dev won, he let out a loud howl at the end. It got to the point that the other students would join in and had even dubbed him "The Wolf." He found it extremely ironic that he was given this nickname. He even had "The Wolf" stitched on the back of his jersey.

Dev finished his stretches and took a second to get his breathing under control. He scanned the stadium; every seat was filled with family and students. Not that this was all that surprising. This was going to be the biggest race in what was a brutal rivalry between two separate schools. Mountainside High school was the only other school to beat them at any meet. He could see the other squad in their blue-white warm-up jerseys getting ready for the day on the other end of the track. Unfortunately, there was one person he was looking for in particular.

After scanning the team, he saw the one he was searching for. At six-foot-tall was Mr. lean and strong, James Avery was the star runner of the Mountainside High Mustangs. After Dev, he held the second-fastest speed in the state. People had begun to call him, "The Stallion," which made Dev laugh because he could outrun a horse any day. They had met last year, and it had been Dev's first and only lost since joining the team.

He walked around the track to where the coach had just finished drawing the line up for the race. Coach Hunter looked up as he approached the side where the starting blocks were laid stacked on top of each other. "Vanseal!" He yelled. "Tell your teammates I want a formation. NOW!!!"

"Yes, sir, coach!" Dev yelled back. He ran to the edge of the track and stood at the position of attention. "FALL IN!!!" He cried. Every member of the team within earshot ran towards him to gather in formation next to him. When everyone was standing at attention, Coach Hunter walked up behind Dev, who executed an about-face and saluted him. "All present and accounted for, Sarge, I mean, Coach." Hunter returned the salute, and Dev thunder clapped to the back of the formation.

With all the others laughing at Dev's display, Anthony decided to bring attention to the score clock. "Hey, Coach, before you go and make us do frog jumps for Dev's ballerina claps, we need to go warm up. Our races are next."

Bothered by the fact Anthony was right, Coach Hunter shouted, "All right, I want high knees, all at ninety-degree angles. I need you to jump like this day was your last, and if I see laziness, it just might be."

The team groaned in response and began to run through the warm-up routine set aside for them. James Avery ran up and burst out laughing. "Look at those guppies run."

Anthony stared at him and, in response, asked, "Hey, Avery, what do gay horses eat?"

As one, the entire team yelled out in a feminine voice, "HHHHAAAAAAYYYYYYY!!!"

As the kids busted out in laughter, the judge called out with the megaphone, "Now calling twenty-five, number twenty-five to the long jump!" Now with a smirk and a grin, Anthony hopped, skipped, and jumped over to his place in the lineup along with the other three jumpers. With the entire squad cheering him on, he waved at the ones that weren't busy with their races and events. Anthony pumped himself up, listening to the crowd while shaking his arms and legs out.

"Number twenty-five? Anthony Pike of Reda Miles Magnet?" Said the line judge.

"Yes, that's me," said Anthony as he did his final stretches before leaning on the line. Calling over to the sand volunteer to clear the sand and the measure judge to be ready, she told Anthony to get ready. Waving a flag, she signaled number twenty-five's first attempt after marking him off the board. "Okay son, you can go at any time. Just remember, feet together, or the back foot will be the score. Also, exit to the left of the lane." Said the nice lady as she signaled the flag down on Anthony.

Determined to crush his first jump, Anthony began to run. As he watched, Dev felt a source of power that was ever so faint behind him. A man was standing in what looked like Lincoln stars' colors of green and gold on the starting line of the shot-put event. It was hard to see his face behind the netting and the blistering sun, but he was definitely where the power was coming from.

"Foul!"

Dev quickly turned around to see his friend face first in the sand as he had tripped entirely over his own feet. That was very unusual for him since he was ranked first in the district. Dev used to joke with him that it was from him jumping and dodging when girls threw stuff at him. Dusting himself off, he got back in line to start his second attempt at the jump.

Dev looked back over to where the man was standing, but he noticed the man slipped out of sight amongst the crowd. Dev was confused. Why was that man staring at Anthony like that? Could he be a scout? He thought. If he was a scout, wouldn't he be closer to the sandpit to see his skills up close? And why did it seem like powers were coming from him? Snapping out of it, Dev looked around once more to see if he was still there, only to see a figure of the same frame standing in the bleachers.

"Foul! Jump two was unsuccessful!" Said the judge. "Pike, you're going to be doing drills till your feet bleed! What on earth are you doing?" Screamed Coach Hunter. He pulled himself away to watch the boys pole vault to make sure no one else was messing up.

"Hey, Dev, if you're messing with me, cut it out. I wanna win, and we need all the points we can get off my jump! You know Cramer can't jump farther than me," Said Anthony with disdain in his voice as he shouted over to Dev.

"Dude, it's not me, I promise! Someone else is here, and they're not trying to cover up their trail," Said Dev with conviction. "Don't shoot the messenger. Aunt Lesley is here. I'm going to see if she can find that man I just saw. I thought

he was a scout, but now I think he's casting on you." Said Dev as he scanned the crowd for his aunt.

While Anthony stood up for his third and last attempt at his jump, Dev sent out a message to Lesley asking if she had felt a strange presence around or if she had seen anything weird.

"To be honest, nephew, I have been feeling a slight surge of power every few minutes, but I never seem to be able to locate it. I've already messaged your parents to let them know to be on their guard when they get here. For now, just focus on your race and do great. Eve is flying around, keeping an eye on the area," Lesley said in response.

Dev looked towards the sky and could see the shape of an owl softly gliding overhead. "Hey Dagon, I want you to come out and help Eve protect the area while we do our races and events," messaged Dev.

In response, Dagon materialized next to him, looking slightly worried. "What's going on out here?" He asked. "I keep feeling waves of strange magic."

Dev explained the situation, and Dagon looked even more worried. He had an idea as to who was casting the magic, but he just couldn't figure out why he was targeting Anthony.

As Dagon checked the grounds, he noticed a chimpanzee hanging from the rafters, but she didn't look like an ordinary chimp. It had beige fur with gray stripes and white eyes. Dagon figured he'd check the chimp out while he used her vantage point. Climbing up into the rafters, the chimp seemed spooked by Dagon, so she darted to the other side of the rafters where she thought he would leave her in peace. Dagon knew he wasn't going to hurt her, but it was weird that she noticed him while he was invisible.

Walking up slowly, Dagon asked her in a soft voice, "Can you see me?"

The chimp glanced back at him and stared. After a few minutes of acknowledging that she could see him, she answered back to him, *"Now, what makes you think I can't, familiar?"*

Taken back by the fact that she could see him and also knowing what he was, shocked him and had Dagon in full attack mode. He raised his ears and displayed his fierce black fur and perfectly snarled fangs. *"Dev, I found his familiar, and I got her cornered,"* messaged Dagon as he continued growling at her.

"I wouldn't do that. Why is it every time a boy sees a lady, he acts all tough? I saw some stuff going on, and I came up here to look after my Niyor if you don't mind," said the lady chimp.

"Tell me who your Niyor is right now." Growled Dagon again.

"After you..." She said so coyly. Met at a stand-still, Dagon refused to say who his person was just in case she was up to no good. Not wanting to let her out of his sight, he sat and used the same vantage points she did for Eve and his covert operation. Dev looked up when he heard Dagon's message and almost skipped the race, but he heard his coach calling him.

"Vanseal! I need you to get your head out of the sky and warm-up for your race!" Shouted Coach Hunter as he shook his head. "Does no one want to win this championship today? I swear kids these days just want the win without the effort!" Snarled Hunter.

"Now calling for the one-hundred-meter dash." All the students in that event gathered to the starting line. The line judge proceeded to explain that there would be four heats of six, since there were so many schools, and the fastest times would place for the final.

Wondering if Dagon or Eve had seen the man lurking in the stadium, Dev began to get himself in the game for this race. "Number thirty-three, you are

234

in the second set along with... three... eight... twenty-seven... forty, and twelve," called out the judge.

Dev cringed as he heard the number twelve called out because that was James, "The Stallion," Avery's number. This meant they were racing them against each other before the final match. Tickled by the banter they shared earlier, Dev knew he was still no ordinary opponent.

With what felt like the eyes of the whole school on them, Dev could feel the pressure to not get bumble feet. Dev slowed his breathing and centered himself for the race. He pushed everything else out of his mind and looked straight ahead down his lane. He could hear the others trying to call out and psych each other out. He blocked them out and waited for the race to begin. As time slowed down around Dev, the male line judge called out over the speaker, "Practice blocking until we find number forty." Hearing that brought Dev out of his head for a moment. He looked to his right and noticed that one of the racers was indeed missing. He found that very odd because of how important the race was. He could never imagine anyone not wanting to be here. While the ref went in search of the missing racer, Dev tried again to center himself.

"Hey Vanseal!" He heard someone yell. He looked towards the voice and saw James walking over to him.

"What's up, Avery? Want my autograph for when I win the race?" Dev said with a laugh. James just rolled his eyes, "No thanks, just thought I should come over and say no hard feelings for when I make you eat my dust."

Dev laughed again. Although these two were rivals, Dev knew that James was a great guy and couldn't help but respect him. Before a race, they usually always bantered back and forth with each other. Then at the end, they congratulated each other on having a good race, no matter who came in first. They all came together to the starting line for the practice. This was mostly just for everyone to warm-up and get their blood pumping before the actual race.

Dev lined up with the other racers and stared down the track. "Get ready to eat my dust, Vanseal." He heard Avery say to him. Dev just chuckled slightly and got himself in the ready position. He had no intention of losing to Avery, even though this was just a warm-up. The judge raised the pistol and fired.

Dev took off with James a step behind him, trying to pull ahead. Neither of them was going all out at the moment, so they stayed pretty even with the other racers. Unsure if he was playing with him, Dev decided to take his focus off of him and aim for the lemon-lime green tape. So, Dev evened his breathing and got into a rhythm, opened his stride, and glided to give himself a little extra distance. James kept up with him stride for stride, but just when Dev thought he had out jogged him, they both ended up crossing the line at the same time.

Hunched over and confident in his time, Dev looked over as he realized Avery beat him by an elbow. Even though they were the top times' Dev felt like it should have been a piece of cake. "Dev, my man, if I knew you had gotten soft, I wouldn't have gone easy on you." Laughed Avery, "but it's okay, I'll let you hold my medal and pretend to be the champ this year."

Dev did the one thing he knew he could do without showing his true colors, and that was to grin and walk away. With the feeling, this might not be his school's year. Dev looked up at the leader board for all the schools in the district. Mountainside was in first place, then Lincoln Star was tied with his school, so it was like they were in third place out of the six schools. Dev knew they had to start winning some events, so he rallied the runners that weren't racing up for a pep talk.

Crowding around the thirty-yard line, Dev spoke, "Guys, I know we are so much better than this. It seems that we're off our game, and we need to pick it up for our school, for our seniors, for our pride, and bragging rights. I will not let another year go by and not take the win. Let's pick it up. I promise our luck is going to turn around. I'm going to give my all, just like I want you too." With all the girls and guys looking at him, they all nodded and agreed. After his speech, some of them went to go warm-up for their next races.

"Hey Dev, Anthony. Good luck!" It was a small voice they heard from the student section. Harley had been gone all day to do some shoe and jewelry shopping with her mom, but she made it a point to stop in and watch a run or two. They took a second to wave from the field, but Anthony was more concerned about how he couldn't make the jumps he had made a hundred times.

"Dev, did you find that guy?" Asked Anthony.

"Not yet. I'll ask Dagon to see if he's seen anything." Walking back over to the cool-down area, Dev messaged him. *"An update would be nice, Dagon?"*

Looking down from his spot, Dagon messaged him back. *"Nothing to update, just go race and beat his butt. I got a name out of the chimp. Her name is Delexi, and I hope she's not with him, she's kind of nice to talk to,"* said Dagon.

Shaking his head, Dev shook his limbs out, ready to hear the judge call the final six runners for the four by one hundred final.

"Calling all runners to the starting line!" Said the line Judge as he retrieved the pistol. "Blocks Ready?" Dev slowly began to hone in, and then he proceeded to back into the blocks. With his fingers touching the starting line ever so lightly, he made sure to have the best form possible.

"Ready!"

With the wind on his back and sun on his face, he knew he had to get the best time in the final race. At the sound of the pistol, Dev took off like a rocket. He could hear the other racers around him, but he had eyes only for the finish line ahead of him. He pumped his arms and legs as fast as possible, knowing that to the spectators, he was nothing more than a blur. Keeping count in his head, he reached the halfway point at two-and-a-half seconds. His heart was racing in his chest, and his breath came in shallow puffs from his lungs. He felt a presence behind him and knew that Avery was trying to close the gap between them.

Without looking back, he knew that he was gaining on him fast. Dev kept pushing to stay ahead. Soon, he felt his rival pull even with him and could hear him gasping for breath as they raced onward. He could see the finish line coming closer, and with every bead of sweat pouring out his muscles, he added a little more speed.

Dev rocketed across the finish line, and as he stopped to catch his breath, he saw runners falling out on the floor. Feeling exhausted, he held his sides, trying not to fall over as well, but he could hear the crowd cheering loudly, which made him stand with pride. He looked at his teammates and saw them jumping up and down with joy.

Coach Hunter had the timer in his hand and was looking from it to him and back with a shocked expression on his face. He slowly walked over to Dev and just showed him the stopwatch. Dev looked and then shook his head and looked again, not believing what he was seeing. By his count, it took him just a little over ten seconds to finish the race. In reality, he had just run the hundred-yard dash in nine seconds flat. That was the fastest time ever recorded in the history of his state. Maybe even in the country.

He looked up at the scoreboard to see his name in lights, and his time was being shown as a new record. He looked over at James, who gave him a small nod of congratulations before his teammates mobbed him, clapping and thumping him on his back. .

"Good race, Vanseal," James said as he walked over to shake his hand. "I'll get you next time." Casting his hand out, Dev shook it and nodded to him. Exhausted as well, James turned and walked back towards his team. Coach Hunter was shaking his head, but he wore a proud grin on his face.

"Vanseal, that was one hell of a race! You just broke every record in the world, even an Olympic one. Well done," said Hunter.

Dev looked into the stands and saw his parents standing up, clapping and cheering for him. He waved up at them and laughed at his aunt's antics, because

she seemed to be doing a celebratory dance around the stands with Tiye, Yendor, and Eve.

Breaking free of the mob, he went to take a seat next to Anthony and grab a drink of water. He could see that Anthony was still in a grim mood after his terrible performance during the long jump. Anthony looked over and said, "Great job during the race, man. I wish I could have done as good as that. I mean, wow, breaking all those records." He gave Dev a side glance. "You sure you're not using your magic to boost your skills a bit?"

Dev looked at him in shock. "No way. There is no way I would cheat like that to win," he replied angrily.

Anthony's face changed into a grin, "Yeah, I know. I was just messing with you." He looked down at the ground again with a frown. "Coach Hunter is thinking of pulling me from the four by four and putting in one of the alternates. He doesn't want me to mess up our chances of winning."

Dev couldn't believe what he was hearing. There was no way that he would allow this to happen. He got up and walked over to the coach, who was speaking with one of the teachers. "Coach Hunter, please. You can't be seriously thinking of pulling Anthony from the race. We need him."

"Sorry Dev, but we can't have a weak link holding us down. You saw how poorly he did in the jump. We need our best so we can pull ahead, and we don't have time for mistakes." The coach started to walk away.

Dev ran after him, stopping shortly in front of him. "Please, coach, I know Anthony didn't show his best today, and I don't think that it was completely his fault. I'm not just sticking up for my best friend, but we need Anthony for the race. He is one of our fastest runners, and you know we need him to win."

The coach looked up at the sky and sighed. "Fine, he can race, but he better do his best, or I will kick him back to an alternate." With that, he turned and yelled, "Pike! Get over here. You're in the race. You better go out there and run like the Devil himself is chasing you. You got that!"

Anthony smiled and leaped from his seat. "You got it, coach! I'm your man, I won't let you down, I swear!" Dev smiled at his friend's antics as he watched him go warm-up for the race. He looked over at the coach, who was watching Anthony. Even though he looked like he had a permanent scowl on his face, anyone who knew him would be able to see the small smile.

Dev's smile was soon wiped away as he felt the same mysterious force that he had felt all day. He looked around, trying to locate the source while also alerting Dagon that the stranger was close by. He looked towards his family sitting in the stands, and he could see from the worried looks that they had felt it too. His mom and Aunt were walking around the stands, trying to locate the source of the magic while his father had his eyes closed and was standing in one spot.

Dev could feel his dad's mental probes reaching out to pinpoint where the power was coming from. From the frustrated look on his face, he could tell that he was having no luck locking down the location, but he kept trying. He seemed to be able to sense his son watching him, and he sent him a quiet message, *"Dev, let us handle this. You just focus on winning your last race."*

Taking comfort in the fact that his family was there in case anything went down, Dev started stretching for the next race. He tried to push the mysterious stranger out of his head for the time being and focus on the last and final race. It was the four by four relay hurdles and would be the most difficult. The top racers from all the schools would be participating. It would be anyone's race. It was one of the reasons why he had fought to get Anthony back. If they were to win, they would need all their strongest racers in every position to pull it off.

He ran over to Anthony to stretch out with him before everything started. Coming closer, he saw the other two racers, Brandon and Kendall, already there and in the middle of warming up. He felt a sense of victory because he knew with the four of them, they would dominate this race with ease.

He looked around and saw Dagon sitting up high in the stands, still keeping a lookout. Next to him, he saw the chimp that he had mentioned earlier. He saw that she was looking over at the far side of the field, so he looked over in that direction as well. Casing the area, he saw James, who seemed to be looking in Dagon and the chimps direction. It couldn't possibly be James they were looking at, however was he a Zortegan too? In all this time, Dev had never met any other kids from Zortega. He couldn't make sense of it, so he just ignored the thought and focused on the medal at the end of the starting line.

"Dev, get your head out of the clouds and get over here so we can strategize how to take this race," said Brandon as he got into a huddle with the other two. Dev joined them as Anthony laid out the plan for how they should run. "First up, it will be Brandon, okay? You have a lot of speed, and your block time is always the best out of all of us, so I know we'll get a good start." Anthony explained. "When the race starts, just burst from the blocks and gun it through the hurdles, just be careful and don't trip yourself up, got it?" Brandon nodded in understanding of his role. "Next, Kendall will go. I know you're not that fastest, but you are way more careful with the hurdles in the turns, and we all know how you hate distance. With the gap Brandon gives you, just go as fast as you can and get me the baton." Kendall gave him a thumbs up.

"Next comes me," Anthony said, standing upright and puffing out his chest. "Since I'm the strongest runner here, I should be the anchor." He said with a laugh. The others jumped on him for a moment, telling him he was full of himself and to get his head out of his ass.

"All right, all right, back off me before coach sees us and makes us do togetherness runs," he said jokingly. "Anyway, as I was saying. I will take the baton next and keep the lead going. I'll run as fast as possible to get to Dev so he can blast away and get across the finish line. So, we all good on the plan?"

As everyone answered yes, they then went to their battle stations.

CHAPTER 20

Dev stood in position at the end of the track, breathing slowly. He saw the other participants of the race prepping themselves as well. Some were getting in a few last-minute stretches, while others seemed to be praying. Dev looked over and saw James Avery standing perfectly still with his arms crossed and eyes closed. No nervousness or anticipation was coming from him. He just radiated an air of calm. James seemed to sense Dev staring, so he opened his eyes to look at him, to give him a thumbs up and a quick nod. Dev returned the gesture and smiled. He knew this race would be one to remember. Unlike James, he was very excited and could barely contain himself while he waited for it to start. Soon he noticed the judge walking up and calling out, "Are all racers ready?"

Everyone gave a shout to show they were. Dev's excitement grew as he watched the judge raise the pistol. "On your marks!" The first set of racers moved to their positions. "Get set!" Moving to the next position, they got down into their running stances.

Bang!!

The judge fired the pistol and just like that the race started. Dev watched as Brandon took off, gliding over the hurdles as fast as he could. He gained an early lead and pushed himself to stay ahead of the others. Right behind him was Myles Thompson from Central High, and Tony Samuels from Mountainside was just a few feet behind him, with Lincoln and Porter on their toes. Bringing up the rear was Thomas Mills, and although he was in last place, he was slowly gaining on the other three racers. In no time at all, he had passed the other two and was neck and neck with Brandon.

The crowd in the stands were on their feet and cheering for their respective racer. The sound was deafening and seemed to be boosting the racers to push themselves harder. Drawing closer to Kendall, Brandon put on one last burst of speed. Kendall began running with his hand behind his back, and as soon as he had the baton, he put his head down and ran for all he was worth.

From what Dev could see, they still had a pretty good lead, but Kendall was not the fastest runner. However, he made up for it with being very careful and cautious while jumping hurdles. He did everything he could to ensure that he would make it over each one and not risk tripping and injuring himself. Kendall opened his stride and leaped over each hurdle. He came down seemingly to just push off to leap over the next one. Closing in on him was Mountainside's Frank Wylinder, who seemed to be having trouble keeping himself upright although he was being very swift. He would jump too far and come too close to knocking over the next hurdle. It made him stumble many times and almost fall on his face. Taking a look back, Dev noticed the other schools weren't fairing any better. That was why they always placed Kendall in the middle during races. He kept a clear head, and although he was excited, he still kept himself calm to perform at his best.

Within a few minutes, he had cleared the hurdles and was racing towards Anthony. Letting out a whoop of joy, Anthony started to run forward, holding his hand out for the baton. He had a massive smile on his face, but when

the baton landed in his hand, his entire face changed. A look of supreme concentration came over Anthony, and he simply took off like a bullet out of a gun. He soared over each hurdle flawlessly, his eyes focused only on Devereaux and getting the baton to him. The other three racers didn't even stand a chance of catching him, even though they tried their hardest. The gap Anthony made was just too wide. Dev looked on with a smile as his friend raced towards him, but his smile vanished in the next second. He once again felt that cold presence race towards Anthony.

Suddenly, Anthony tripped with a cry of pain and started to fall towards the ground. The crowd gasped, and some screamed as Anthony seemed to fall in slow motion. Without thinking, Dev used his own magic to dispel the dark presence around his friend. Pushing his free hand out, he used it to level himself from falling on the ground, and he flipped himself over the last hurdle. He landed on his left foot and let out another cry of pain as he buckled to the ground. Luckily for the team, he landed in the passing area, so Dev started to run towards him to help him.

"Don't move, Dev!" Anthony yelled. "We still have to win this." Dev looked back and saw the other racers beginning to draw closer. Lifting himself up, he began to hop on one leg, gritting his teeth and fighting through the pain. Soon the noise from the crowd was shouting and cheering for him to keep going. Others were saying he was out of the race and disqualified for stumbling to the ground. Dev could see Coach Hunter arguing with the referee, but couldn't hear what was being heard over the crowd. Anthony hopped closer and closer, now holding the baton out towards him, telling him to take it. The other racers sped past and handed their batons off to their teammates. Dev looked on as they all started to run towards the finish line.

Dev saw James hesitate and look back at him, but then he, too, ran off towards the end of the finish line. Dev turned back towards Anthony and saw him right behind him, barely holding himself up. Anthony was exhausted and in tremendous pain.

"Take it, Dev. They aren't too far ahead. You can still win this for us. So, take the damn baton and run!" Anthony growled. Dev took the baton, and as soon as he did, Anthony collapsed to the ground, breathing hard. He looked up at Dev, "What are you waiting for?" he asked in a soft whisper. "Don't worry about me. Get your butt moving, Vanseal!" With that, Anthony passed out cold. Dev stared at his best friend, not understanding what was going on, but he swore he would find out. With that promise, he lifted Anthony and handed him off to the coach and judge, who ran up. He turned and saw that everyone was already halfway across the hurdles. Dev shook his head and tucked his arms and began to run after the others.

At first, it was a slight jog, but then he began to pick up speed. Seeing the look of his friend's face and the determination shining in his eyes, Dev sped up faster and faster. He had no intention of losing this race after Anthony had pushed himself so hard to do his part. Dev dropped his head and raced faster than he thought possible. He jumped over each hurdle, almost seeming as if he were flying from one step to the next. In no time, he had caught up to the racers who had started to slow down because they believed they had the race in the bag.

With a loud yell, Dev raced faster to close the distance. Hearing him yell, the other racers looked back and stared in shock as he gained on them at incredible speed. They tried to pick up their pace to keep their lead, but Dev wasn't having it. One racer lost his concentration and fell over the hurdle, landing on the track with the baton on the ground. Dev pushed past him and continued to leap over each hurdle as if he was completely weightless.

The last racer to pass was James, who was almost to the finish line. Dev imagined himself running like a wolf and pushed himself to go even faster, and slowly the gap began to close. As he ran, he kept thinking of Anthony hopping towards him. He could see and almost feel the pain his friend was experiencing. However, even while dealing with all that pain, Anthony never gave up, and his faith in Dev never wavered. Anthony solely believed that by getting the baton to Dev, they would win this race. Dev wanted to make sure he lived up to his best friend's expectations. With each step, he swore he would win and then find the person responsible for that pain.

Soon, he was racing for the finish line neck and neck with James, who was pushing just as hard to win. Every second, one would pull in front of the other, a never-ending tug of war to see who would cross first. They were evenly matched, and neither was willing to give an inch as they rounded the last curve and sped towards the end.

Dev could hear the crowd cheering; he saw his teammates egging him on, yelling for him to pull ahead. With one last push and a yell, Dev practically dove forward and by a nose crossed the line, first winning the race for his team. As he came to a stop, he dropped to his knees in exhaustion, breathing hard with sweat dripping down his face. The rest of the team mobbed him and lifted him up on their shoulders, cheering loudly while congratulating him. Although he was worried about Anthony, Dev took a moment to smile and put his fist in the air, celebrating his victory.

The people in the stands were on their feet, yelling loudly about the conclusion of the race. Some were clapping and cheering from the performance. Others were still enraged at what they thought was a clear disqualification.

"Attention everyone, please. May we have your attention?" A voice over the intercom called out. "After pulling all the judges together and reviewing the rules, a decision has been made on the outcome of the race."

Everyone in the stands grew quiet, waiting to hear what the final ruling would be. Dev looked incredulously at the group of officials huddled together. Surely, they wouldn't disqualify Anthony from the race. If that happened, it would mean another race would need to be run, and Dev didn't think he had enough in him to run again.

"Our decision stands as thus. Although Anthony Pike fell to his knees, he did not allow the baton to touch the ground and could pass it. In conclusion, the winners of the race is the Reda Miles Magnet High School."

The stands erupted in cheers, and Dev's teammates threw him in the air while shouting his name. Laughing at his teammates, Dev looked around and saw his family clapping and cheering. When the others finally let him down, he started to look for Anthony to make sure he was okay.

"Hey Wolf, aren't you forgetting something?" Brandon asked. Dev turned back to them, looking very confused, but after a minute or two he heard Dagon howling in the stands. Then, with a smile, Dev sucked in a large breath and let out an ear-splitting howl. His teammates joined in as he howled a second time. Dagon was relishing in his Niyor's victory.

Running over to Anthony's side after celebrating with his teammates. Dev walked up to where the coach and the nurse's tent was and where Anthony was being treated. "Well, if it isn't jellyfish legs," said Dev to Anthony as he walked over to take a look at the leg that he was holding.

"Man, shut up and help a dude limp off this table hint, hint. A guy has to bust a move on the dance floor tonight with Katrina. I convinced her to come, but not as my date. I gotta look available if she wants to cut in," said Anthony. He winked at Dev and pointed to his legs, which indicated that he wanted him to do a magic healing spell. Looking around as the coach and nurse turned their backs to them to have a conversation on how bad his injury was. Dev quickly decided to help his friend out, but he had never done the spell without his mother before. Practicing it on humans was dangerous, and strictly only for emergencies.

So, Dev considered that him missing prom, and him being attacked by a stranger's magic counted as an emergency. Zortegans were accustomed to a limited number of feathers when they were adults, but when they were kids, they had double the amount for healing purposes. Dev had to choose wisely which conditions are worth not being able to fly in Zortega for if all of his feathers were gone.

Standing still for a moment or two, Dev reached in his pocket and produced a beige feather with a grayish-black stem. Holding the feather in his hand, he broke it in half and wrapped it on both sides of Anthony's ankle. "Advebies Dawhul." As he said that, the feather began to melt into Anthony's skin. Standing up to celebrate his instant relief, Anthony nodded at Dev in thanks and went to show the nurse he was just fine.

As Dev watched Anthony convince the nurse he was okay, he heard a message ring in his ears, "Nephew, I don't know where you are, but it's obviously not safe here for your friend. They might be targeting you through him, so get him and yourself home now. Your parents are surrounding the school looking for the guy you saw. If it was up to me, I'd ban you from the school. I think you shouldn't be going to this prom because I bet it's a trap," messaged Lesley. Dev thought she was wrong about the prom being a trap, but she was right that they needed to get out of there so they could get ready.

Grabbing Anthony by the arm, Dev gladly dragged him to the handicap locker room behind the bleachers and flashed back to the house as fast as possible. Dev knew all that celebrating had given him very little time to get dressed, and Dev had also wanted to blink Anthony home due to the mystery man messing with him. Driving in traffic would have taken so much longer with only one hour to get dressed.

After dropping his shoes, clothes, and medal at the bathroom door, Dev quickly showered. Prom wasn't a super big deal to him, but he knew how important this night was for Harley. Dev always heard her complain about the popular girls having the magic movie moments. Dev wanted to do his best to give her a night like one of the classics from the 80s.

Finishing up in the shower, Dev stepped out to his magical beauty team, ready to dry him off with a flying toothbrush ready to brush his teeth. With all the chaos of the comb and flying deodorant was following him to the dresser drawer for an undershirt. Dev wondered if his parents found any clues of who that guy was and why it was so hard to get a read on him. With his phone buzzing, Dev changed gears and saw the text message from Harley.

Hey, don't forget to wear a purple tie so we can match. My mom likes to take pictures of these things, like she's actually going to show someone one day. But don't worry. If you wanna bail on prom and we just go to Land Daski's Pizza, I'm okay with that too, text Harley.

He heard some heavy breathing over his shoulder. "So, what ya reading?" Asked Dagon.

Before Dev answered him, he wrote back.

Hey, don't chicken out on me now, I'll wear the right color. My mom went out and bought one for me, so don't worry. Hey, I saw you at the meet, thanks for coming we thought you weren't going to make it. I'm getting dressed right now, and I'll be over soon, so we're not late to see Marie and Stephanie's grand entrances. I bet Anthony has something in store for them, and then we can laugh at Kendall and Brandon deciding who's going to chase him down for hitting on their girls.

"It was a message from Harley, making sure I was still coming. Did you find out anything from that Delexi familiar about what was going on, or were you just flirting with a pretty chimp?" Said Dev as he walked out of his closet and through the suit on the hanger.

"I was not flirting. I was being a watchful familiar, looking out for my buddy while in the company of a nice lady friend who wasn't family," huffed Dagon bashfully as he disappeared into his totem. Outside the window, Dev could hear his parents pulling his car in the driveway as they parked. Walking in the door and up the stairs to check on him was his dad. Dev was very relieved he had made it back because he couldn't get his tie to tie right.

"Hey son, you ready to go?" Said Rodney.

"No, I can't seem to get this tie done, and when I used magic, it about choked me. Can you help me?" Asked Dev with a frustrated look on his face.

Laughing with a little chuckle, Rodney said, "Son, even in Zortega some things are best learned being passed down from father to son. Not all lessons are magical, and some things just shouldn't be rushed, you see. Now wrap that end-around. Perfect!" Rodney manifested a coat out of the closet that Dev could use for Harley as a friendly gesture if she were to get cold.

"Ready," said Dev as he put his earrings, watch, and cufflinks on.

"Oh, wait. I don't think you're quite ready yet." Dev's mom walked in the room with a pocket square that only the male heir to the lines were allowed to use. It was embroidered with the family crest on it. "Now you're perfect," stated Selena with a proud smile.

Looking at the time, his dad said, "Dev, you better get going before you are extra late picking up your friend. Your car is downstairs. Be safe and don't drink the punch, I bet some punk is going to spike it. Dev also just have fun tonight and remember we have put you under total protection." After tossing his keys to him, Dev double-checked that he had everything, including the tickets.

"Ah, Rodney, look at our baby. He cleans up nice. I want one group photo, and then I'll let you go," said Selena.

Rodney instantly messaged him, "Run boy!"

Taking his dad's advice, he kissed his mom on the cheek, smiled, posed really quickly, and raced down the stairs and out the front door. Before Selena could turn around, Dev had bolted out of the house.

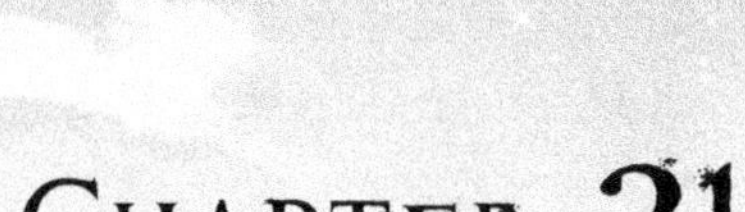

CHAPTER 21

"Ding Dong." The doorbell rings, "Ooo, Ooo, Ooo, let me get the door!" Said Axer.

"Please don't!" Said Uni.

"Oh, come on, I wanna show him who the muscle is around this place. I'll be the bad cop. Keith, you be the good cop. We'll tag team!" Axer grinned happily.

"No, buddy," said Keith. "We're just going to answer the door. Elizabeth, tell Harley her date for prom is here!" shouted Keith. Undenounced to him even before Keith could get up,

"Presenting young Devereaux Vanseal for Madam Harley," said Dominic. "Wait here, young sir. Mrs. Braymark does not allow shoes any farther into the house."

After guiding Harley's guest to the bottom of the stairs, Dominic went to retrieve the family camera and refreshments for the two gentlemen waiting in the parlor

room. When Dev entered the house, he nervously stared at the wallpaper, hoping he looked good enough. The wallpaper he noticed had a slight nautical theme to it that kind of reminded him of the beach. There were different types of sea creatures and shells in no apparent pattern on the wall. He continued looking around, hoping to find a mirror to check his suit one more time. He did a double-take as he saw a leopard statue that he could have sworn was outside, but had now it made its way into the hallway by the stairs.

Immediately confused by the announcement, Elizabeth walks out of the laundry room. "Dominic, did you say Vanseal? Why in the world would a Vanseal step foot on this property?" She scowled! "Young man is this some kind of joke' cuz I don't find it funny!" She rushed around the corner towards the front door and was blocked by a stylish size eleven-inch leather shoe.

"Now, now Lizzy," said Keith.

"Ambrose, move out of my way!" Said Elizabeth.

"Um, no... Why do we have to keep this ridiculous fight going? They're just kids, I bet he doesn't even know what happened, just like Harley or she wouldn't have picked him for her date. Wait a minute, you didn't know his last name was Vanseal, and you've basically let them grow up together? That's hilarious that miss overprotective let her daughter play with her most unliked bloodlines kid." Ambrose said with a slight chuckle. "How did we know his last name, and you didn't?" Ambrose started laughing extremely hard.

"Check you out, mom of the year," said Axer as he rolled around in the air, laughing hysterically. Ambrose was holding himself up on the wall while he tried to catch his breath.

Elizabeth glared at her brother, debating if she should blast him into the next state. "If I had known, I would have never allowed her to hang out with him!" She growled. "You know what? Never mind. Just go upstairs and get her. I'm sure if it was a trick, Links would have warned Dominic by now. I mean, he is

like our secret watch kitty." Elizabeth gave in and told the familiars to be on their toes with much frustration because the Vanseals couldn't be trusted.

Now with all the familiars concealed to the average human eye. Elizabeth went up to Harley's room and knocked on the door. "Harls, are you ready? Your date is here."

As Harley sat in her room, looking at her dress, she wondered if she should just call Dev and tell him to just forget it. "What do I look like wearing this dress?" Mumbled Harley.

"Yes, what do you look like wearing a dress, you lame?" Questioned Bowen.

"Get out of here, Bowen!" Yelled Harley.

"At least I don't have to take you like Mom wanted. I mean, how lame would that have been? Taking my little sister to prom?" Said Bowen as he giggled in the doorway.

Buzz, buzz, buzz. Harley's phone went off from a text message.

*I'm downstairs. I can't wait to see you. It's been years
since anyone has seen you in a dress.*

"So, who's the chump that gets to take my little sister out? It better not be anyone I know, or they're going to meet PULL-versus-RISE. Get it? Pulverize," said Bowen.

"Really? Then you call me lame? Hashtag wow. Now get out so I can get dressed, you perv!" Said Harley as she shut the door in his face.

"Knock, knock, Harls, did you hear me? Your date's here!" Asked her mom.

"Mom, I need your help. How do I make myself look pretty?" Harley said sadly.

"Oh babe, if a Vanseal doesn't see your beauty, then you shouldn't worry. I mean, just ask your Uncle."

"Mom, now why would I ask Uncle Am?"

"Never mind, forget I said anything. So, how do you know young Devereaux?"

"He's been in my class since first grade, and we became friends during recess, I go over to play with him and Anthony all the time. We're just going as best friends because no one asked me, and I don't wanna go alone. Why? I promise nothing is going to happen, it's just like any other birthday party. It's just I'll be dressed up for this one."

"Nothing, sweetie, I just want to know who's taking my baby out, that's all." Brushing her hair out of her face with her finger, Elizabeth smiled at Harley. "Now, there you go," said Elizabeth. She placed the brush down and turned the mirror around to show what she had done to her daughter's hair.

After her first glance, Harley was so shocked it was her. She was actually cute after she put a little powder on her face. "Oh, thanks, Mom. I look so pretty," said Harley.

Taken back by her daughter's appearance, Liz remembered the day when she went to prom with Harley's Dad and began to shed a tear. She realized she looked so much like him and had his loving spirit too.

"What's wrong, Mom?" Said Harls.

"Oh, nothing sweetie. If only your dad could see you, he'd be so proud of you and happy that...."

"I know, Mom, I wished I could have said goodbye too," said Harley. Grabbing her mom to give her a big hug, she held her close without trying to ruin her makeup. After making sure she was good, she let her go and grabbed her eagle necklace, purse, and phone before heading downstairs to her date.

Standing at the top of the stairs was Harley, trying to put her eagle necklace on. There was no way she could go anywhere without Sage close to her, even on a regular date with Dev. She had heard some weird stories about them, but she figured it couldn't be any worse than the stories people mentioned about her family. After her dad vanished, her mom tried to live quietly. She barely used her magic, and she tried to get Grandpa Keith and Uncle Am to do the same. However, after Bowen's Kaloke Ceremony, the council demanded they be taught magic because she was the heir, and Bowen was the oldest.

"I don't think he's good enough for you in my book. He better have brought a corsage. I mean, it's the least he can do," messaged Sage.

"Sage, now stay outta sight. I don't want him thinking I'm crazy for talking to a necklace." Harley smiled as she walked down the stairs.

"But Harls, there's something I can't put my finger on about him. I think he can see us, and I don't know how," said Sage.

Harley laughed at her familiar. *"There's no way he can see you, Sage. He's just a regular human without any knowledge of the magical world. Just relax, everything will be okay."* Poking her head out into the hallway, she saw Dev at the bottom of the stairs. He was looking dapper in his all-white tux and dark grey vest that deeply contrasted with his rich chocolate skin. He was scanning the room silently while Axer floated lazily over his head. The way his eyes seemed to follow Axer made it seem like he really could see him, but there was no way that was possible, he thought. When his eyes fell on her, his face broke into a bright smile, and his eyes lit up.

"Wow, you look amazing!" He said. Harley smiled, but she could swear she heard a wolf howl somewhere in the distance. Dev's hand reached up to the wolf necklace he always wore, and it looked like he spoke to it for a second.

Shaking the thought away, she descended down the stairs and met him at the bottom. She smiled at him, "You don't look so bad yourself," she said. Dev smiled down at her and, with his hands behind his back, using a little magic, produced a beautiful corsage that matched her plum dress. She gasped in delight. "It's beautiful." She then held out her wrist for him to put it on. As he put the flower in place, he heard an eagle cry in the distance. He looked around for the source of the noise and noticed the eagle pendant on her neck. He could have sworn the eagle winked at him, but dismissed the thought.

With a bow and a flourish of his hand, he said, "Shall we go, Miss Braymark?"

She laughed at his antics and batted her eyelashes while gripping onto his offered arm; she replied. "Why yes, Mr. Vanseal, we shall. First, I want to give you your rose pin before Mom starts taking thirty photos of us." Said Harley as Ambrose passed a rose pin that he had produced from behind his back.

On their way to the door, Elizabeth tried to distract both the kids by asking for a photo. "Dominic, can you hand me the camera? Okay kids, get in close, but not too close and say cheese!" Said Elizabeth.

"Ooo, picture! Me too, me too! Meeeeeeeee! I'm sexy, and I know it!" Yelled Axer as he photo bombed the picture. He landed between the two teens, striking a pose during the flash. "Axer!!" Elizabeth shouted before she could stop herself. Dev looked at her Mom, very detective-like for her outburst, while also trying to figure out if this was a joke his parents were playing on him.

"Come on, Dev. Ask her if she wants another picture," said Ambrose as he tried to cover up Elizabeth's slip up. After a few more photos, the kids start to head out the door. So Axer tried to dive-bomb Dev from the stairwell. *"Banzai!!!"* He yelled as he flew down.

Just as Dev looked up, Keith called his familiar back to his fox headed cane and placed it in the next room so he couldn't cause any more mischief. "Wow, what a lively family and friends you have." Thinking he would bring up the topic of the familiar he saw, Dev pointed at Keith with an odd look of did you see that gaze on his face.

"Hey kids, before you go, let me tell you about what happened when I went to my senior prom. I wore a white suit just like yours when I was your age. However, our proms were slightly more formal. All the men had coattails. And let me tell you, we made that shit look good. I rolled in with my fly date, and she was in the running for the prom queen, which means I was going to be the man if she won," gloated Keith.

"Oh, come on, old man. Your grandfather went to prom with his high school crush, but what he didn't know is that she was playing a prank on him. He wore an all-white suit and even saved all his money to buy her some flowers and a hotel room. Gross, right?" Asked Ambrose. Everyone shook their heads. With her mom staring at the both of them, Harley felt blushed, and Dev felt super uncomfortable as he looked away. Giggling, "What he didn't know is that she played him. Halfway through the night her actual boyfriend showed up and completely poured all the fruit punch all over his white suit. He was just covered, and he went from a clean hankie to a flamingo. Everyone laughed at him, but on his way out, a little birdy with a towel helped him dry off," said Ambrose.

"And what a little birdy she was... Said Keith wistfully. "So, to not look like a chump, I rolled back in and punched him in the stomach, and it was the craziest thing. The sprinkler system drenched everyone in the room." Winked Keith at Harley. "That asshole had ruined my rental, but it was worth the school suspension because I got your grandma in the end," said Keith.

"Sir, young Harls and Mr. Vanseal should be leaving before it gets too late," said Dominic.

Wrapping his arm around hers, Dev turned towards the door, so they could get out of this loony home with the moving animal statues. "Oh, hold up, young ones, let's remember to drive safe, which means take my car. I know you'll be safe because I have a drive home button on my car, and I'm able to come find you for keeping my niece out too late." Suggested Ambrose as he hugged Dev really tight. Leaning in, Ambrose said, "I'm the nice Uncle as long as her virtue is intact, do you understand me, son?... No means no, and trust me, you might not think I'm there, but I'll be watching." Startled by Ambrose smacking him on the butt, Harley grabbed Uncle Am's keys and Dev's hand and dashed for the garage where his new sparkling royal blue 2018, two-door 911 Porsche was waiting to be driven.

Dev's eyes lit up because there was no way he was going to drive the speed limit in this car. "Don't even think about it, boy," said Ambrose. Ambrose made sure he was being a gentleman and accompanied them around the car. Dev helped Harley get her dress in the passenger seat and placed his hands out for the keys. "Remember, I will be watching," said Ambrose ominously as he rubbed one of the snake-shaped cufflinks on his sleeve. Dev looked around again as he heard a soft hiss coming from somewhere in the garage.

"You ready to go, Dev?" Harley asked from the car as she put her seatbelt on. He smiled and nodded as he slid into the driver's seat.

Despite the weird family welcome, he couldn't help but appreciate the cool leather interior of the car and the engine's soft purring as he started it. When he put on his seatbelt, he felt it tighten to an almost uncomfortable level as another hiss echoed through the car. "Okay, am I the only one who has been hearing the bizarre animal noises since I got here?" He said, looking at Harley. "And what is up with that statue that seems to move on its own?"

She looked at him with a bit of a forced smile, "What on earth are you talking about?" She asked. She pretended to put her hand on his forehead to feel if he had a fever. "Are you feeling okay?" She laughed as they pulled out of the garage and onto the main road heading for the dance. As they drove, she looked off to the right and saw a bear standing at the edge of the road. She could have sworn as they drove past, the bear was watching them.

"I know one of you gentlemen had the great idea to send one of your familiars with them, right?" Asked Elizabeth.

Ambrose turned around and said, "Liz, just smile and wave goodbye and turn around. I got this. I wasn't kidding when I said I have a return home low jack button for that car. You will have to explain later why the car can reappear out of thin air. Also, that we're the rival magical family that been at war with his for years, I mean, just saying..." Elizabeth just sighed, and walked back to her office, praying that tonight would go well, and her daughter would be safe. Although she didn't think Devereaux would try to harm her, Elizabeth didn't put it past anyone in his untrustworthy family from trying to pull a stunt that would put her child in harm's way. "On another note." Ambrose said as he became very serious. "You two have no more excuses. It's time to speak with the council. Even if I have to drag you there myself. Now grab your coats and get a move on." He said with a growl. "Dexter and I will keep an eye on the kids."

Dev was sitting in the car, loving the leather between his fingers, but the seat belt was crazy uncomfortable. It seemed to get tighter every time he drove over forty-five miles an hour. "So, are we like supposed to hold hands or something? Prom is kinda like a date," said Harley.

"I mean, sure, as long as you don't step on my feet like you did Anthony in gym class on line dance day... Ouch...! Why did you hit me?" Said Dev.

"Because I should have picked a nicer date," glared Harley.

"You know it's not nice to hit people while they're driving. The jolt could easily make me drive into the other lane like this... Cough cough..." Suddenly the seatbelt tightened. "What is up with this seat belt? I swear it's choking me," said Dev.

Giggling in the passenger seat was Harley because she finally noticed the red stripe on the seat belt and realized it wasn't a seat belt at all. Driving on the right side of the road, Dev felt the seatbelt let go, so he looked around. Mable was in the back, weaving through the cars, trying to keep up with the car unseen. *"Did you just choke me? Go away, haven't you been sent to ruin enough dates?"* Messaged Dev.

"Boy, If I catch you, I'm choking you myself! Act like you have manners and a life to live," messaged Mable. Defiantly not wanting to explain being choked out by a bear, Dev began speeding up to get to the school a little faster. Driving into the parking lot, Dev pulled up to the Reda Miles Magnet High School and waited in line to park.

As everyone was getting out of their fancy limos to the 'Stars under the bright skies prom of 2029'. Harley looked in the mirror to make sure the top being down hadn't messed up her hair. Pulling up to the teachers that were playing valet, Dev hopped out of the car to help Harley get out like a true gentleman.

"Yo man, if I knew you won the lottery, I would have told you to get me a matching one in yellow!" Shouted Anthony.

"Like, whoa, look at that runway model. Oh wait, it's just you, Harley. My bad, I thought you actually looked like a girl." He laughed at his comment, but quickly clammed up when he saw the glare Harley was shooting his way. He began to stammer an apology to her as he backed away slowly, looking to Dev for help. Unfortunately, his best friend had conveniently turned away to look towards the parking lot and was whistling rather loudly, pretending that he had no idea what was going on.

Harley proceeded to fix her dress and said, "At least I don't look like a trained monkey in a pin-striped navy-blue suit with no neck!" She laughed back at him.

"Well, if you ask me, I think I look mighty purty," Anthony said in his best cowboy accent. "And that's a mighty fine dress you have on as well, ma'am. Be sure to save me a dance." With a tip of his imaginary cowboy hat and a wink, he headed inside. Taking a second to look each other over, Dev wrapped a coat around her shoulders and proceeded to open the gym door.

TAURUS

CHAPTER 22

Dev, being a gentleman, offered his arm to Harley, who looped hers through it. With a small bow, he said, "Shall we follow the cowboy and enjoy a pleasant night, madam?"

Harley giggled and replied, "Yes, good sir. We shall." What Dev didn't realize was that Harley was also giggling at Dexter, who was slithering close behind, keeping a close eye on the couple. Out of nowhere, he felt a heavy pressure on the tip of his tail. He looked back and saw a gigantic bear's paw holding him in place.

Looking up, he stares into Mable's dark eyes. Well, if it isn't one of the guardians of the Vanseal family and an old friend. *"Well, well, look who I caught slithering around?"* Mable inquired with some amusement.

"Dexter bowed his head in greeting to her and replied with a hiss, *"I assssume you are here for the ssssame reassson assss mysssself."*

"

With a throaty chuckle, Mable said, *"Of course. You know these children would get into all kinds of trouble without us along. Besides, I have a bad feeling about tonight. My fur has been on end since I left the house."*

Dexter nodded, *"I agree there issss a foreboding feeling in the air."* Both familiars looked around, sensing a dark presence but seeing nothing. In the end, they looked at each other and came to an unspoken agreement. Swiftly turning, they rushed inside to ensure the safety of their charges.

Stars were the first thing the kids noticed as they walked into the gym. With thousands of bright, glistening jewels twinkling against a dark background, it was stunning with how it resembled the sky. All the students looked in amazement at the scene, wondering how the student council had managed to pull off this realistic illusion. Mrs. Itza, the guidance counselor, walked over to the student council president and stated, "Good job. You guys really outdid yourselves this year." However, the president of the council was just as shocked as everyone else. She simply stated that right before they had finished decorating, one of the math teachers, the librarian, and the principal had come in and said that they would finish.

Mrs. Itza still said that the place looked terrific with everyone's help, but Aaron just stood confused on how so much got done in so little time. It was like they had called in a movie crew, but she knew they didn't have the funds. While she decided to get to the bottom of this, Anthony nudged Dev and asked. "Hey man, did you? For Harley?"

Dev looked back and replied, "Nope!" But Harley and Dev did feel magical energy. They just couldn't place it.

"Okay good. I'm going to head over to spike the punch bowl. Do you wanna come?"

Harley grabbed Dev's hand and said, "Let him get kicked out of school on his own. I wanna dance."

Anthony shrugged his shoulder and said, "Suit yourselves, chickens. I'm going to get this party started!" On his way to the punch bowl, Anthony kept getting this overwhelming feeling to stop what he was doing and to become obedient. Little did he know, Principal Weber had been operating the drink table all night, and he magically put a warning spell on the bowl. When Anthony finally made it to the bowl, he no longer had any intention of spiking the punch.

Instead, he decided to grab some for him and the others. As he went to ladle the punch into a cup, he heard a slight hissing and saw a red and black viper wrapped around the punch bowl. He almost screamed, but he took a second and looked again. Anthony recognized it as a familiar, so he figured Dev's family had sent someone to keep an eye on Dev and make sure he was okay.

He took a look around the room. Low and behold, he saw Mable stalking around the gym, keeping to the wall. She watched Dev and the others, who were currently in the middle of a mosh pit dancing. Anthony continued to ladle punch into the cups and then turned to head back to the others.

Before he left, he looked directly at the snake and said, "Dev is okay. I'll let him know you're here." Dexter, who was thoroughly surprised that a regular mortal could actually see him, hissed to make sure. In dismay at Anthony's smile, he just stared back at the boy in shock as he walked away with the punch.

Mable walked up to the table and chuckled at Dexter's expression. *"That's Anthony. He is Devereaux's best friend and, due to an incident when they were kids, he can see us familiars for what we are. Don't worry, he is a good and loyal friend."*

Dexter continued to stare and flicked his tongue out, tasting the air. *"I will take your word for it, but there'sss ssssomething off about that boy."*

"Yes, the boy lives by something they call, yolo, and tries to get us all to join him."

"No Mable hisssss blood ssssssmells different."

Back at one of the tables, Anthony set the drinks down and noticed two more familiars. The first one was a bull that looked like a constellation for the school backdrop of the prom photo booth. Then there was a chameleon that was pretending to be a very scaly meteor hanging from the decorations. He wondered if they were all here for Dev. It was weird to see more than just Mable and didn't know if it was a good or bad thing. Furthermore, Anthony knew all Dev's family's familiars, and he didn't recognize any of these.

Anthony walked over to Dev and Harley and asked if he could cut in. They just looked at him. Moving Harley out of the way, he took Dev's hand, pretending to slow dance. Whispering, he said, "Yo, man, how many familiars does one family need to bodyguard you? I know you said your kind is on red alert, but would they really come after you here?"

Stunned, Dev said, "Let me go. There's no one here, but Mable and we both know she's enough for three bodyguards."

Taking his hand, Anthony spun him around. "Look at the punch bowl, that's not a snake-shaped punch bowl holder." Spinning him again. "Look over my shoulder at the picture booth. When has there been a see-through 3D bull constellation?" Dipping him in a very fashionable way so he could see the ceiling, Anthony said, "Again, who's moving rock is that?"

Harley tapped back in, "If you two are done having a moment, I'd like to get back to my dance or is the... "Paused in thought, she saw a big brown bear checking out the stage and quickly looked for Dexter amongst the crowd of kids. With no luck on locating him through all the students, and with the bear looking this way, she became even more worried. Sage... she messaged as she held her necklace. *"I think someone's here for me. There's a bear in the corner by the stage, and I can't see Dexter. I'm scared they wouldn't kill me in front of all these people, would they?"* Harley messaged back.

No, that would raise too many problems, but stay close to Dev. He might surprise you, but I'll come out if I have to. With Sage's pendent growing warm, Harley

pulled back into focus on Anthony waving his hand in her face, "Hello! Why do both of you look like zombies?" Asked Anthony.

"GO FIND A DATE, ANTHONY!" They both shouted. Dev turned around to grab her hand for another dance.

He told Anthony to go and take a picture at the booth or something. Taking the hint, Anthony walked over to the drama kids who were just huddled around the bleachers and asked Dara if she wanted to go to the photo booth with him.

"I'm sorry about him," said Dev.

Harley tried to look engaging but couldn't keep her eyes off the bear. "It's okay. If I didn't know better, I'd say Anthony just wants to date you," Harley said jokingly.

Dev laughed as a slow tune came on over the speakers, and he took Harley's hand in his and placed another hand on her waist while swaying to the music. The atmosphere around them grew heavy with tension as their bodies reacted to each other. Dev felt his heart begin to race, and he could swear that hers kept pace with his. To Dev, Harley had always been just a friend, but tonight something in him seemed to call out to her, and he felt her respond in kind. He didn't understand it, but right now, he couldn't care less. To him, it felt as if they were meant to be together. He stared deep into her eyes as their faces came closer together. His eyes dropped to her lips, and he saw that they were lightly pursed. Almost as if they were begging him to kiss her. Dev's eyes traveled back to hers, and he felt trapped in her bright gaze as she stared back at him intently. In this lighting, Harley looked like a beautiful divine goddess, and he found himself entirely enraptured by her.

Harley stared back at Dev as her feelings and hormones pushed their way to the front of her mind. She had always had a crush on him. Everything about him, from his handsome features to his caring personality, appealed to her. She didn't even know when she started to like him, but Harley knew she did. He was everything she wanted in a boyfriend. She knew it wouldn't last because Dev was human, but she would give anything to make him hers. She watched as he bit his lip softly, his eyes never leaving hers. She leaned in closer to him and was delighted to see him draw closer too. She closed her eyes and waited to feel his soft lips to press against hers. Just as their lips were about to touch, the slow jam switched to a loud rock number, shocking them both out of their trance. They almost jumped apart in shock, their hearts beating fast and heat filling their faces. Dev looked over to Harley and gave her a sheepish grin, which she returned even though she wished the floor would just swallow her up to hide her embarrassment. She watched as he stood and looked around as if nothing had happened. Vibing to the music, he returned his gaze to hers and held his hand out to her again.

With a sigh, she wiped softly at her face to not to mess up her makeup before she took his hand and started to continue dancing. As they danced, Dev could tell something was bothering Harley and wished he could fix it.

Spinning her around, Dev dipped her just like he had been by Anthony, so she could lighten up and put a smile on her face, but by the look, she gave it only made it worse. When he dipped her, she saw the familiar jump from one decoration to the next, and it scared her so bad, she yelped, and the screech made him drop her.

"Ouch, why did you do that?" Laying on the floor, Harley looked at Dev in annoyance. "Why did you drop me?" Said Harley.

"I'm sorry. You sounded like I hurt you or stepped on your foot."

Harley was still looking shaken from seeing multiple familiars lurking around the room, especially the bear in the corner that was showing a particular interest in her and Dev. "I'm fine. I just need to run to the bathroom really fast. I will be right back." With that, she spun and almost sprinted out of the room, leaving Deveraux looking confused at her exit.

274

While watching her go, he noticed Mable watching her exit and walked over to her, pretending to lean against the wall. Other kids hooted and hollered at the music as it changed from a slow dance to party music. Closing his eyes, he spoke to Mable with his mind.

"What is going on? Why are you here, and why is Anthony showing me other familiars at the school right now?"

Mable's response came back gruff as always. *"Watch that tone, boy. I'm here to keep an eye on you because it's my job. As for the other familiars, they are here for the same reasons, which is to ensure the safety of the children."*

Dev was shocked at the revelation. *"You mean that something may happen tonight?"* He looked around, feeling a dark presence for the first time that night. At the same time, another thought occurred to him from what Mable had said. *"What do you mean children? Are you trying to tell me that there are other members of the Zortegans here?"*

Mable shook her head and looked at him as if he was simple-minded. *"Do you honestly believe that you and your siblings are the only ones, boy? There are other zodiac children here. That's how it has always been. You are all raised and taught at mortal school so that you can be monitored and guarded together. As for something happening tonight, we are not sure. We just sense a dark presence growing, and I have a feeling that something or someone is trying to harm you or one of the others. So, we are here to ensure that nothing happens."*

Dev continued to scan the rest of the gym, feeling more and more concerned for the lives of the students there. Most were his friends, and he didn't wish to see any harm come to them. With that thought in mind, he began to build the magic in him, remembering all his father had taught him about combat, ready to defend his friends should they need it. Mable could sense him building up his power, and although it worried her that he may get injured, she was proud that he was taking this situation seriously and meeting it head on. In her eyes, he was on his way to being a worthy successor to his father, and she would defend him at all costs.

As they both stood against the wall and watched the other students dancing, seemingly oblivious to the growing danger that approached. Dev's whole body tensed up as a thought ran through his head.

He ran out of the gym at a dead sprint, shoving other students out of the way, *"Deveraux?!"* Shouted Mable in his head. *"Where are you going? You need to stay right here!!!"*

His only response was, *"Harley! She's not here! I have to get her!"*

Mable looked around and saw that Harley wasn't in the room, frustrated with him running off she followed after him. She wasn't too worried because she knew that Harley had her own familiar, and Dexter watching over her. However, Mable couldn't just let him run off on his own. She knew that Dagon was powerful, but neither of them had ever been in any actual combat before. If they both just jumped into danger without knowing their enemy, they could be seriously hurt or worse.

Mable followed him down the hall as he turned the corner and headed for what seemed to be the restrooms. She heard footsteps and saw Anthony running behind her, but to everyone else, it had looked like he had ran after his best friend. Turning her attention back to Dev, Mable saw him barge straight into the girl's bathroom without any second thought. Due to his worry for Harley, she knew he was going to charge in first and ask questions later.

"Oh, My God!"

Hearing Harley shout was all Mable needed to pass straight through the door. Now inside the bathroom, Mable had stopped at his side, ready to defend him in every way possible. She let out a growl, but when she realized that the only ones in there were Harley, Sage, and Dexter, she backed down. Dexter was slithering around on one of the sinks, and Sage had taken flight at Dev's abrupt

entrance. From the way her talons were set, it looked like she was ready to swipe down and take a scrape at Dev's neck.

Both teens stood shocked and motionless as they stared at each one of the familiars that were currently in the room with them. Dev looked from Harley to Dexter to Sage, not knowing how to word the questions that were firing through his head at that moment. Harley stared back at Mable and then at Dagon, who had just materialized next to Dev, wondering if this could be real or a dream.

Finally, after a few more minutes of silence, Dev composed himself, looked at Harley, and simply asked, "Which house do you belong to?"

Harley responded, "The House of Libra. And you?"

Dev was shocked even more at the answer but replied, "The House of Capricorn."

Harley's eyes grew wide when she heard that, but then looking around at the other familiars, she decided to calm down and not react just then. "Would someone like to tell me what the hell is going on?" Groaned Dagon.

There was a knock on the bathroom door. Dev turned to open it and saw Anthony trying to peek inside. "Everything all right in there, bro?" Anthony asked, his eyes full of concern. Dev was still trying to process what he had just learned about one of his oldest friends. He looked both ways down the hall to make sure that no one was around and then grabbed Anthony and pulled him inside. Using a small bit of magic, he locked the door and then made the out-of-order sign appear outside.

Feeling better, knowing that they would not be disturbed, he turned around just in time to watch Anthony freak out at the sight of all the familiars present. "Yo, bro, why do you have so many bodyguards around you?" He asked. He saw Harley standing behind him and tried to cover up what he had just said. "I uh... What I mean to say is,"

"Relax, Anthony," she said with a smile. "I know all about familiars. This is Sage, my personal familiar." Harley pointed to the eagle that was still hovering in the air. "The snake in the sink is Dexter. He belongs to my Uncle Ambrose. I assume he is here to ensure Dev and I behave ourselves."

Although Sage was glaring at him, there was a small smile playing on her lips as she scolded him. *"I can't believe that a regular human can see us."* Said Sage with a hint of disdain as she fluttered down on Harley's shoulder.

"Yes, I can see you and hear you, little birdy. So, get used to it," Anthony shot back. He looked between Dev and Harley, seeing their familiars with them and knowing they could do magic. He felt a slight twinge of jealousy, wishing he too could be part of the group.

"Don't worry about him," Mable said to Sage. *"He has been a loyal friend to Deveraux over the years. He has known all about us and kept our secret safe. In my eyes, he is a member of the family, and we will fight for him, should he need it."*

Anthony smiled at Mable, genuinely touched by her words and the loyalty he felt from them.

Dexter, who had been staring rather intently at Anthony, chose that moment to speak up. *"We mean the boy no harm. We are here to ensssure the sssafety of the child, jussst like you are."* Mable inclined her head in agreement with his statement.

"What about those other familiars in the crowd out there?" Asked Anthony, "I saw a bull and a chameleon just hanging out, keeping an eye on all of us."

"I assume that those are the familiars of a few of the council members who are employed at this school. Just another measure to ensure the safety of the heirs that are enrolled here," Mable responded. Anthony and Harley both looked at her in shock.

"There are other heirs at this school?" They asked together.

Dexter snorted at their reaction. *"Did you honessstly think you were the only oness that were here?"* He asked. Dev and Harley both looked at each other, thinking about the fact that they were both Zortegan.

"I guess we did," said Dev.

"Yeah. It's just a little strange to find out that there are others like us here, and we don't even know who they are," Harley chimed in.

"If you were to know about each other, no doubt you would band together because you all have something in common," Mable said, *"You would spend all your time together and possibly even practice with your magic. That much magic at any one time would be a beacon that would lead any enemies we may have right to you. So, until you were able to defend yourselves, you had no idea you were so close to each other."*

Dev could feel his anger building at being deceived for so long, not knowing the truth. He looked over at Harley, who was looking troubled, but slowly nodded her head. Narrowing his eyes at her, he asked, "I suppose you agree with this?" He asked, rather harshly.

She looked back at him, wondering where the attitude was coming from. "I don't necessarily agree, and I am just as upset over this news as you are," she said calmly, trying to diffuse the situation. "However, I understand why they kept the truth from us. It was for our own safety, Dev." She placed her hand on his arm, trying to calm him down and get him to think clearly.

Seeing her smile and feeling her hand on his arm had calmed him down as he steadied himself. Busting through the door was Cindy. "Come quick! There's Kantors everywhere, and one just took over Bowen's date."

CHAPTER 23

Running back into the gym was horrifying because of the scene before them. The night had gone from a beautiful starry night to a living nightmare. All around them, students were screaming and running in terror. Chasing them were the dark forms of countless Kantors. They swarmed in from dark portals opening all around the room. Dev had never seen one before because he had only ever read about them in ancient texts. They looked like deformed and mutated versions of their original forms. They were true monsters with burning red eyes that glowed with hate and violence and sharp talons and claws. The other students, who were ordinary humans, couldn't see them, but whatever they did see made them want to escape as fast as possible.

The Kantors were having none of that; however, but they were chasing after each student to corner them. They were making it to where no one could get away by knocking things over. Then they would dive straight into each student and take over their body and mind. Everyone who was possessed grew razor-sharp fangs, and their eyes would burn with the same red light. All those possessed then turned on their friends and classmates and attacked them with a savage fury.

The screams from the gym echoed like a movie on surround sound. Harley could see her brother trying to defend a group of students who were huddled in a corner from Kantors and possessed students alike. Although they were attacking to kill, he was doing all he could to hinder them without really harming them. Harley immediately ran towards him as fast as she could to give him help, but her dress was inhibiting her ability to run.

Harley thought of releasing her Scythes but decided against it since they were still her classmates. Harley had to stop to take one of her weapons out to cut her dress open, so she could help fight better amongst the crowd. She heard someone's feet running towards her, and was quickly knocked to the ground. Harley was pinned by her arms with someone on top of her.

Looking up, she saw Marcus, he was glowing, and it didn't look normal. The tough boy exterior turned into a mature figure. Harley knew he had to have been taken over by a Kantor. The veins in his head grew with disdain for her as his eyes burned red. Marcus growled down at her as he placed his hands to her throat to strangle her. Harley could only stare in horror at the person who had been her brother's best friend gripped her neck and began to squeeze. Kicking and punching his arms, Harley tried to break free, but it seemed all her training went out the window. As she tried to fight him, the happiness in his voice echoed in her ears. Hoping for help, she gasped a deep breath to scream for Sage, but he was too strong for her to speak words. Harley's fear made it hard for her to focus and use her powers to free herself because his hands squeezed harder and harder. Soon her vision began to get hazy as she started to blackout. She could see Dev trying to fight his way to her, but the Kantor army surrounded Dev on all sides along with possessed students.

Dev couldn't believe that in a matter of minutes, all hell broke loose on what was supposed to be a perfect night for all of them. Fighting and dodging every Kantors attempt to capture him, Dev looked at Mable for help but saw her trying to help kids escape the chaos. Distracted by the fighting everywhere, David from Dev's math class came up behind him and gashed Dev's arm with a broken cake server. Bleeding in extreme pain, Dev was met with a chair to the back by Brandon with a glazed look in his eyes.

Dev felt like everyone was attacking him, but he couldn't hurt them. Deflecting David's slashing as best he could with a fold-up chair, Dev saw after a few minutes that they divided the gym with Zortegans and the possessed humans that were taken over. Dev heard Bowen cry out to Harley. He was scared by the tone in his voice as he saw Marcus strangling Harley, almost lifeless. Seeing her hanging in the air erupted a fire in every one of Dev's veins.

"Harley, hold on! I'm coming! Marcus, I know you're in there, and I swear if you hurt her..." Cried out Dev. Distracted for only a moment, some of his classmates came up behind and grabbed him. Fighting and struggling to break both arms free without hurting his classmates, Dev tried his best to use his feet to kick them off, but they swarmed him like bee's on honey. Under complete stress to resolve his issue and get to her side, he looked for a familiar, but before he knew it, slithering up behind him was Dexter. *"When I give you the sssignal, blassst them on their backsss, and I'll take it from there with my bite. Then go sssave my Niyor'sss niece."* Hissed Dexter.

On Dexter's mark, Dev exploded his anger in a burst of energy, knocking everyone in a three-foot radius on their backs. Now free to help Harley, he saw Anthony was in trouble as well. He was running around the gym, trying to get away from possessed kids. Breaking through the tables and chairs to go help Bowen save Harley, Dev was attacked from both sides and pinned to the ground by four football players. Anthony tried to go help him, but he was struggling with a girl that he had introduced to them as Katrina. She, too, was possessed and seemed to be pulling him away to some dark corner. Harley's body grew lifeless, and just as she was about to completely lose consciousness, Marcus let go of her neck. Falling to the gym floor, she laid still for a moment, and then she rolled over and coughed, trying to take deep breaths.

With Dev pinned, Bowen cornered, and Anthony captured, it looked like their only hope was Harley, but she wasn't in good shape. "Harley, get up and help me save these council members! There are too many of them and not enough of us. They're the only ones that know the spell to kill them, and we can't hurt your classmates!" Shouted James across the room.

Tyson, the bull, bulldozed his way through the gym, with James riding on him. Shooting waves of energy at Marcus, who got up to finish the job, James scooped Harley up on his way across the dance floor. Marcus wasn't just possessed by a Kantor. He had embodied a presence Dev had felt before.

Everyone watched as he walked over to the stage to open a portal next to him. With fear, silent fear on everyone's chest that more Kantors were coming through, they were mortified to see a single dark figure. He was a man of average height and a dark trench coat. A mask covered his face, but you could still see the disdain in his eyes. His roar bounced off the walls as he shot lightning out of his hands at the gym lights above.

Everyone that wasn't possessed tried to take cover from the sparks flying out of the lights. This made Dev wonder if he was the leader, but first, he had to figure out a way to get Harley out safely before he could focus his powers on him. Dev was itching to punch each football player in the face until they let him go, but he couldn't because one had ripped Dagon's pendant off his neck.

"Delexi, go help wolf boy get his totem back and..." Before James could finish, Marcus shot a fireball at Tyson, blasting them to the ground. "Requise!" Now with decorations on fire, Dev saw Principal Weber hunch over in pain at the same time Tyson fell.

"Gemini, help the kids!" Screamed Weber to his council member friend. Clinging to his chest, Principle Weber realized he was significantly hurt. Tyson had taken a significant gash out of his side, and even though he couldn't be killed, their life spans were tied to their Niyors.

As the smoke seemed to gather around Marcus, he called out to a man named Markel walking out of the portal. Marcus began to transform into a shadow figure that was more mature and regal in stature. With a barbed wire weapon around Marcus' chest, his skin smoked like a living shadow, all except his back. In the upper left corner of his body was a scar of some sort that burned in rippling discomfort for the figure. As the three walked closer to Taurus,

Gemini successfully helped Bowen put the students down into a deep sleep. Gemini looked over to see Taurus in major trouble. So, she transformed in front of everyone, which disobeyed the human rule, but this was an emergency she needed her other half for.

Adare closed her eyes and floated in the air as her body and clothes changed. She was to be met back to back with her twin self. Fully charged and ready to fight, Gemini launched her halo rings at the two intruders one at a time. Marcus placed a Kantor in each one of her halo's paths. Soon he became annoyed and displeased with the interruption of wanting to talk with the head council member. Frustrated as well, Gemini split into two beings and charged forward to attack. Markel ran to face both halves while the rest of the kids fought the possessed students.

"Hey, meat brains! That's my sister's date, and he still owes her a dance!" Said Bowen as he punched each kid in the face while Deveraux was pinned them down.

"Looked like you needed help." Stated Bowen as he reached out to help Dev up off the floor.

"Thanks, I would have taken them if he wouldn't have had my totem." Said Dev, looking around for Dagon's necklace under all the broken chairs.

"You looking for this? The chimp handed it to me on my way over. I guess she's a pretty good pickpocket. Now get up and let's go help, Mrs. Jones." Joked Bowen as he handed him the necklace.

Gemini and the man that had walked out of the portal were battling so intensely. Gemini's Zortegan battle rings cut the air as they boomeranged through the man's fire blast. While shooting a shot of lighting at her, one of the rings crashed off and into the bleachers on the wall. Ducking behind a table, the man forced Kantor after Kantor on her to force her out of her barricade. However, what he didn't know is that she had a plan. Gemini was the only council leader that had the power to call on her other half.

"Come out. Come out, or I'll pick a kid to fry," said the man as he boasted.

Waiting for her perfect moment, Gemini's other half snuck up on Markel after pulling the ring out of the wall. Wondering why she didn't retaliate, the man turned around to a sound of a Kantor racing at him. With a horrified look on his face, Markel was kicked flipped in the chest as Gemini threw her ring at the Kantor. The original Gemini jumped over the table, ready to battle some more two on one. The cross wave of kicks, jumps, spells, and swipes continued as the Kantors continued their madness over the gym.

"We gotta go help her and get him and the take down the other guy," called out Cindy.

After slicing at Kantor in half with his blade, Dev asked Bowen, "Who is that?"

"Honestly, I don't know, but she's fighting with us so just keep going. We'll investigate later," huffed Bowen.

Nodding to him, Dev, Bowen, Cindy, Harley, and James stood lined up at the half quart line, ready to put this night to an end. In the distance was a voice calling out to Harley. She tried to ignore it and help the others, but it sounded so warming. Cindy and Bowen fought the left as James charged the man to help Gemini. Dev wanted Marcus because of the feeling he gave him earlier and how he treated Harley. Raising his magical energy, Dev faced the stage where Marcus stood. Charging at him with blinding speed Dev was spell casted back so hard that he shouldn't have stood back up on his feet.

"ENOUGH!!!"

Blasting an energy ring throughout the whole gym, everyone fell back and fell silent at the intruder's voice. In his hand was his weapon. It was a metal wired chain-like sword that had a brass handle. He used it as an extension, wrapping Principal Weber up in the wire links from chest to neck. He aimed the point at his heart, which for Zortegans was in his back. Terrified of what was to happen next, everyone stood back up, frozen in their tracks. Mortified by the display,

Gemini stopped fighting Markel as the intruder made his way towards the stage with Principal Weber floating in the air.

"Now that I have everyone's attention, let's give a brief history lesson to everyone not old enough to recognize former royalty. I am the rightful leader of the Ophiuchan line, one of the most powerful in my day, and I'm demanding to be returned to my glory." Said Ophiuchan, looking out amongst everyone in the gym.

Standing tall back at the half quart line, all five kids prepared for round two. "That will never happen!" Shouted out James and Cindy as they tried to lunge forward.

Catching them mid-air. "Sit, you misbehaved toddlers, the adults are talking." Ophiuchan casted a spell, and the kids fell to their knees, ropes tied around their hands and feet. He turned back to Taurus. "This sorry excuse for a council member's ancestors banished my line during the zodiac wars over a thousand years ago. A whole line erased from existence, killed, and banished from using magic, only to deny their true nature as a dominant race."

Gemini walked closer with her halos behind her back. "Dominant race? We were all equals until your ancestors thought to pit us against each other. That one line would rule, but everyone knew the original Ophiuchan leader meant her."

Angered by her outburst, the intruder squeezed Taurus harder until his pain hurt more than his pride. "The only thing your cowardly ancestors failed to realize was that our familiar planned ahead and sent the next in line out into the future using the last of the line's powers. It was the prophecy laid out for me, and I will have that book to complete my destiny. I almost had it ten years ago, but that meddling Johnathan Braymark stopped me, and now I have a curse for a prize instead. The only way to lift it is with that book, and I will kill every member until I find it. Now the only thing missing is the Qualum, old man, and

I know you know where it is. Give it up, and I won't kill you." Suspended in the air, the dagger end of the chain moved closer to his back.

"We vowed to never let that book fall into the hands of anyone from your line, and I will not be the first to go against my destiny, Ophiuchus. So, it looks like you'll have to kill me." Spitting into the shadow's face, Taurus fell silent, proud of himself for not saying any more than a leader should. Worried for his familiar friend, he began to message Tyson.

"Goodbye, old friend. If I leave you today, remember that I love you and that you are strong. Don't let your heart turn cold. The next one in line needs you to help them lead our people." Crying out in anguish, Tyson barreled up on his feet and tried with all his might to get to him.

"You fool! Looks like you've forced me to put you and your mutt down." Jabbing the knife into his back, Tyson fell face first next to Harley.

As Gemini and the rest screamed out the principal's name. Harley heard a voice tell her to grab Tyson and hold on. Feeling some sense of warmth, she did as the voice said and grabbed Tyson. Smoke swirled around her, and she seemed to disappear from the room, but she was still there at the same time.

Looking around for the voice, Harley asked, "Who are you?"

Appearing from the shadows was a figure she had seen before, but she always thought he was a dream. The shadow spoke, "Honey, when I left you, you and your brother were only kids, but look at you now."

Chilled with hope and fear, Harley cried out, "Dad!"

Smiling at her, he said, "I have to send you away to help Tyson while Ebon and I help your friends. Only one of us can be in this pain without the spell from the book."

Looking at him with sheer confusion, she asked, "What does that mean, and where do I take Tyson?... Dad? ...Dad?"

Flashing her away from him, Johnathan stepped out of the shadows, wincing in pain. Gemini was holding Taurus, trying to protect him from further harm. With Ebon by his side, Johnathan told the kids to get out of the way. "Remember me, Xalucard? I've been waiting for this day to put you back in your cage. I know you still have the scar that connects us."

"Teath Vidacula, Teath Vidacula ..." Johnathan repeated the spell repeatedly, connecting his pain and raising it to its highest peak. As he screeched out in pain, the mark on the Ophiuchus' back began to glow and bleed along with the one on Ebon's head. Blasting fireballs at him, Xalucard realized they just vaporized around Johnathan's shadow.

Fed up with the disappointment of not knowing where the book was, Xalucard decided to recoiled his weapon and dissipated into his portal before Johnathan could get any closer. "I will be back. That you can count on. We took a little present for ourselves and boy of the Capricorn line, if you ever want to see him alive, you find me that book..." Laughing in pain as he vanished from view with a gust of smoke.

While everyone wasn't looking, the man slipped away in the portal as Johnathan fell into Dev's arms. Glowing once more for a few short minutes, Marcus laid lifeless on the gym stage, and the gym fell quiet for a few moments.

"Are you okay? Who are you?" Asked Dev.

Smiling at Bowen, Johnathan answered his question, "Thank you for being my daughter's best friend." After saying that, Johnathan closed his eyes and melted into the shadow that surrounded them. Ebon bowed at Dev, and then he, too, disappeared.

Looking around at all the chaos and destruction, Dev couldn't believe what had happened tonight. He heard footsteps and rose to his feet, ready to fight off this

new threat. The doors burst open, and Dev saw his parents rush in with the rest of his family. His dad was leading the charge, and the look on his face was one of pure rage. Dev had seen him angry before, but this was on a whole other level. His eyes burned with white lightning, and they promised pain and misery to whoever they rested on. He had his Sai knives ready for battle, and Yendor looked to have grown two sizes. Behind Rodney was Selena and Lesley, brandishing their weapons and spreading out to fend off attacks from either side. One after another, Dev's family raced in, ready to do battle with whatever enemy was present.

As they looked around, they saw a destroyed gym with students lying unconscious on the ground; soon, their anger turned to confusion. Looking around, Rodney saw Dev looking like he was going to collapse, and his blood froze at the sight. He raced to his son and grabbed him as he began to fall over. "Dev, Dev, hold on, son, it's okay." He laid him on the ground, "Gabby! Come quick! Dev's been hurt. He needs you." A pillar of light flashed into the room, and out of it stepped Gabby. When she saw Dev lying on the floor, injured and weak, her eyes became inflamed with fury, and she released an energy that seemed to suck the light out of the room. Everyone stepped back, fearful of the power they felt radiating from her. She flashed herself forward to kneel at Dev's side, placed a hand on his cheek, and began to heal his wounds and restore his energy. All the wounds Dev had received closed and healed without any scarring.

Once that was completed, Gabby stood up and looked around at the gym. With a snap of her fingers, she released a wave of energy that fixed everything in the area. Gabby healed the students who were possessed by the Kantors and replaced their memories with a pleasant night at the prom. Dev awoke for a few moments more to ask his father, "Where's Harley? She was hurt, really bad. I have to find her. Do you see her? Dad, they took Anthony. I saw them dragging him away. I have to get up and help you guys look for them."

Pushing his son back down to the floor, Rodney reassured him that they would search everywhere for them. This now was an adult matter, and he should go rest. Then with a small nod of satisfaction, Gabby levitated Dev off the ground and flashed all the kids, him and herself home.

Chapter 24

"Dad? Where am I? "Whispered Harley to herself as she clung to Tyson, terrified to open her eyes. Peeking her eyes open, Harley found herself in the most beautiful place she had ever seen. It was like a dream out of a bedtime fairytale with the most unique looking fruit and flowers, they looked like fireworks. The sky was starry as night, but it was bright and sunny and filled with laughter in the distance.

As she kneeled in the northeast corner of the grounds, she heard footsteps. In a panic, she didn't know if they were friend or foe, so without hesitation, she called on Sage to help her. *"Sage, Help me! I know you're scared, but I can't run with Tyson. He can't transform without his totem, and he doesn't look so good. Scare them away and give me some time to find a hiding spot."* Messaged Harley to Sage before she made her take off after the person coming close to her.

In the distance, all she heard was, "Hey, get back here! Rogue familiar! Kantor! Kantor!" With a whistle going off and what seemed to be more people chasing

Sage, Harley tried to lift Tyson and drag him to the door she had seen on the building wall. No one had come out of it, so she assumed that must not be where anyone goes.

After repeatedly dragging him, Harley had finally made it to the door when she felt an icy chill down her back. "If you have come to bring harm to this land, Ophiuchan, prepare to be killed where you stand," said Avi, pointing his blade at her back just below her teenage heart.

Bursting out into instant tears, Harley said, "I'm not here to cause harm. My name is Harley, I'm 15 years old, my favorite color is orange and maroon. I don't know what I'm doing here or where here is. I just met my long-lost father. I'm tired, I'm hungry, and I just had the worst prom in the history of proms, and I just want my mom." Sobbing and sobbing some more.

Avi couldn't help to ask her one more question "Who is your mother, child? Just in case she needs to die as well. Choose your words wisely, criminal. Tears are for the soft, and they do not melt my conscience."

Sniffling up her tears as best she could, she asked if she could put Tyson down before answering his question. Looking at the child in utter confusion, he circled around her carefully to see if his ears heard her correctly. The only Tyson he knew never left Taurus's side unless asked. "Guards, over here. I caught her red-handed, trying to grab Tyson. Scour the grounds for the council member! She must have killed him." With and ungraceful thud, Harley dropped Tyson and held her neck. They had caught Sage and held her so tight that she couldn't breathe once again. "So that familiar belongs to you, huh? Even better. Now maybe we can get some real answers out of you, Ophiuchan," said Avi as he called for the other guard with the eagle to cage the bird. Then he ordered the other guard to take her to be taken to the Shanket for questioning.

With confusion and chaos, every council member who had made it to the castle was suited up to defend their home. Walking in from a portal, Keith and Elizabeth got word they had caught one of the four Ophiuchan's. Rushing to

the Marti Cani Gardens on the northeastern grounds, Keith looked over the wall to take a look at one of the faces of the handcuffed Ophiuchan members. Outraged and beyond himself, Keith took his staff out and threw it to the ground below him. Terrified that a golden staff with lightning surrounding it just nailed her dress to the ground, Harley looked up and saw her grandpa.

Her mom jumped from the balcony with her fan blades unleashed, "You let my daughter go! Now! She is a future line leader. Recognize your royalty!"

Relieved to see her mom, Harley didn't care how she got here but was damn happy to see her.

"Mom, someone needs to help Tyson. The principal is dead. Dad said someone would know what to do." Harley said as she looked at her mother.

"General Avi, we have two options: one, we let my daughter go, and we handle this the right way and get Tyson help like my daughter said. Or we stand here and fight to see who wins. Your choice."

Unhappy with the outcome, Avi figured if she was her daughter, it wouldn't be smart to fight an angry mother. So, he ordered her release and hurried to the familiar's side. "Summon all the legacies here at once and get him to his constellation statue now."

After being uncuffed, Harley ran into her mother's arms. Taking a moment to embrace her and look her over for any trauma or injuries. "Hunny, how did you get here? Why did you have Tyson?" Said Elizabeth.

"Mom, as I said, it was Dad. He's alive, and he saved Tyson and me at the school from the Ophiuchan that attacked us." Turning around to look at the men and women rushing Tyson away, she asked, "Is he going to be okay?"

Floating down to Elizabeth's side, Keith looked at her with joy and confusion. "How could that be possible?" said Keith as he sheathed his staff.

Walking up was Pisces, "Well, ladies, it looks like you have things to share. How about you follow me?" Harley walked beside her mother, gripping her hand and trying to figure out what was going on. She gripped her necklace and silently hoped her friends were okay.

Meanwhile...

Back home, Dev awoke visibly startled and was surprised to find himself in his own room. Dagon appeared next to him and jumped on him. He was so happy that his partner was all right. Laughing at the wolf's antics, Dev tried to push him off, but he found he was still weak from the fight. His door opened, and in walked his mom, dad, and Gabby. They all looked relieved to see him awake and well.

Gabby rushed over and gave him a bone-crushing hug. "Oh, Dev. I was so worried about my precious boy!!" Gabby cried as she held on to him tightly. "When Mable sent me a call for help, everyone rushed to get to your school. Of course, I stayed here to protect the house, but when your father called, I rushed over." Gabby was in hysterics by this point. "When I saw you lying there near death... I've never been so scared."

Dev had no idea that Gabby felt this way and looked at his parents in bewilderment, not knowing what to do. His father walked up and carefully detached Gabby's arms from around Dev's neck, chuckling to himself. "Gabby, he's all right, thanks to your care. Now go on downstairs. I'm sure Dev is hungry after expending so much energy last night." Dev hadn't thought about it, but now he realized he was starving. Gabby perked up and rushed out the door, promising to bring Dev all of his favorites when she finished in the kitchen.

Dev laughed to himself until he noticed his parents looking at him with worried expressions on their faces. "What is it? What's happened?" He asked as they moved to sit next to his bed. They both stared at each other, silently debating on who would tell him what was going on.

Finally, his father sighed and spoke. "We didn't want to worry you right now after everything that had happened, but you need to know." Rodney stopped and composed himself. "First off, let me say how proud of you we all are that you held your ground against so many Kantors last night. You and your friends did a splendid job on keeping the other kids who hadn't been possessed safe from harm." He gave Dev a warm smile, and the pride for his son was visible. Dev, however, could still see something bothering him and was growing more and more worried. "Second, the other students who were possessed are all fine. They were healed, and their memories modified by Gabby to forget everything. Afterwards, we had them placed at home in their beds. They will wake up thinking that prom last night was a success with no issues. So, you have nothing to worry about there."

Dev relaxed a bit. He had been worried about the effects of the Kantor's possession on regular humans. Most aren't able to cope and end up going insane and hurting themselves or others. He was glad the other students at the school were going to be okay and wouldn't be haunted by that night. His dad cleared his throat to get his attention again. Looking back at his dad, he could tell that he had finally gotten to the news he wanted to tell him. His dad looked worried, and his mother was wringing her hands, which was something she only did when she was apprehensive about something.

Rodney sighed again and looked at Dev, seeming to debate with himself on if he should tell him what was going on. Dev grabbed his parent's hands. "Just tell me what happened. I can take it," he said with a smile. They both stared at him, trying to figure out when he had become such a man. His father had never been prouder and knew his son wouldn't run from this.

"First, you need to know that Harley is alive and well. She appeared in Zortega a few hours ago, bruised and weak, but she's okay, and she's with her mother, but that's not the issue. She appeared with Tyson on her back, who was injured in his own way. They transported him to his constellation statue and is healing." Dev couldn't figure out why this was a problem. As far as he was concerned, both of them being alive was a good thing. Wasn't it? Before he could voice his question, his father continued. "The issue with this is that Tyson's Niyor was nowhere around or with him. I'm sure you know by now that that was your principal, Mr. Weber, and unfortunately, he was killed last night."

Dev looked down at his bed, he remembered the scene of his principle dying at the hands of the mysterious enemy that invaded the prom. He had no idea that so many other Zortegans had been around him for so many years. What made him feel worse was he was unable to save Mr. Weber's life. He knew he was powerful, but at that moment, he felt utterly powerless. "Because Harley appeared with Tyson and he was wounded, the Zortegan guard believed that she had a hand in Mr. Weber's death," said Rodney. Dev looked up in shock, not believing what he was hearing. "There was no way that they could possibly believe that because Gemini was there. There's no way, Dad!" Dev cried out, "She was trying to help Tyson when she saw the man injured him. If they don't believe it. I'll make them believe it." He got up and started walking to his closet to get dressed. He wasn't about to let anyone railroad his friend and accuse her of a crime she didn't commit.

"Dev, wait, there are some things you need to know before you go running off." His dad said as he tried to grab him.

"No!" He cried. "My friend is being accused of a crime she had no hand in. I'm not going to sit here and do nothing!"

His dad grabbed him and pulled him back. "We are not going to do nothing, but you need to hear me out first. I swear you will only make it worse if you go there looking for a fight."

Dev relaxed slightly, but began pacing around his room while his dad continued speaking. "Right now, the lines are divided. Some think she is innocent, and others believe she is guilty. Naturally, her mother is fighting tooth and nail to prove her innocence. Also, on her side is Scorpio, Gemini, Aries, and myself. However, we are slightly outnumbered because its five to the other six." He shook his head at this. "I don't understand how the others could believe that

she was capable of this, but it's true. They think she has been possessed and is now trying to act innocent to get away with it."

Dev felt sick to his stomach at this news. He had always believed the council was wise and just, but this just sounded wrong. "What are we gonna do, dad?" Asked Dev.

"We will figure out a way to fix this and free her, son. Don't worry." Rodney replied. He then closed his eyes to prepare himself for the next bit of news he had to tell his son. "Dev, there is one more thing you need to know." Said Rodney.

"What is it, dad?" Frantically asked Dev.

Rodney took a deep breath and said. "It's about Anthony. He has gone missing, and there is no trace of him anywhere." Dev felt like someone had punched him in the gut. He had been so worried about Harley, he forgot to ask about his best friend. He crashed down onto his bed as his father tried to comfort him, but he wondered what happened and where Anthony could be.

EPILOGUE

Running in the gym behind the others, Anthony stared in horror at the scene before him. What was once a fun night had turned into an actual nightmare. Everywhere around him, he saw his friends and classmates being attacked by creatures of evil and shadow. What made it worse for them was they did not understand what was attacking. Anthony, however, could see every vile creature stalking and possessing the surrounding students. He saw Dev, Harley, and Bowen working together along with their familiars to fight back against the evil spirits. For the first time, Anthony stood amazed watching his friends being able to wield such incredible powers. What he wouldn't give to be able to stand back to back with them and defend their school.

The only thing Anthony could do, however, was grab kids and lead them out of the gym to safety. Doing all he could to duck and dodge the Kantors as they wreaked havoc across the gym, Anthony rounded up as many students as possible and urged them to run for the doors. Then Anthony heard a scream from the corner of the room and saw Katrina. She was the girl he had been hoping to impress tonight, but she was huddled in a corner with a look of terror on her face. Feeling protective of her, Anthony thought this might be his chance to be a hero, so he ran over and wrapped an arm around her.

"Hey, everything will be okay," Anthony said, trying to calm her down. Katrina was clinging to his arm as Anthony moved her to safety. Even though he was scared, Anthony rushed her to a side door. Anthony whispered encouragements to her to keep her calm when he heard a roar and turned. He saw Mable fighting her way to Dev, who seemed to be surrounded by a circle of Kantors while trying to defend himself.

As he watched her fight to get closer and closer, he felt Katrina grip his arm even tighter as she pulled him towards the door. "Okay. Okay. I'm gonna get you out of here." He turned back towards her, only to stop short at the sight before him.

Her eyes were glowing red, but instead of a snarl on her face, she smiled in evil anticipation at him. "Finally," she purred in a dark, husky voice. "You are mine!"

Before Anthony could pull away or call for help, she swung a fist towards his head. The blow connected with the force of a sledgehammer and darkness claimed him as he passed out. No one saw as Katrina quickly grabbed him by the ankle and dragged him out of the gym. Once she made it to the doors of the school, she lifted him up and opened a portal. She was delighted with her performance as she slid away to her waiting companions and carried him through.

The back of the book

As Deveraux Vanseal grows upon Earth with his friends Anthony Pike and Harley Braymark, he soon realizes there is more to his zodiac world that meets the eye. After the Zodiac wars, there was a long-kept secret in his magical

ancestry that he couldn't just learn in history class. Dev is the successor of the Capricorn line. His safe and protected life was soon coming to an end, when his friends and family are attacked on Earth. With Dagon, Dev's trusted wolf familiar by his side at every turn, will Dev be ready for the change awaiting him? Now, Dev must train in order to help defend himself from danger. With this new imminent threat declaring to overturn Zortega and the twelve council members. Dev must find a way to help the council take down the mysterious shadow figure. The Ophiuchans are real, but can Dev prove it before they charge Harley with a crime she didn't commit? Will he be able to fight the Kantors and survive? Will the prophecy of the thirteenth line finally come true after so many years? Will the answer be in this book or the next... who knows?

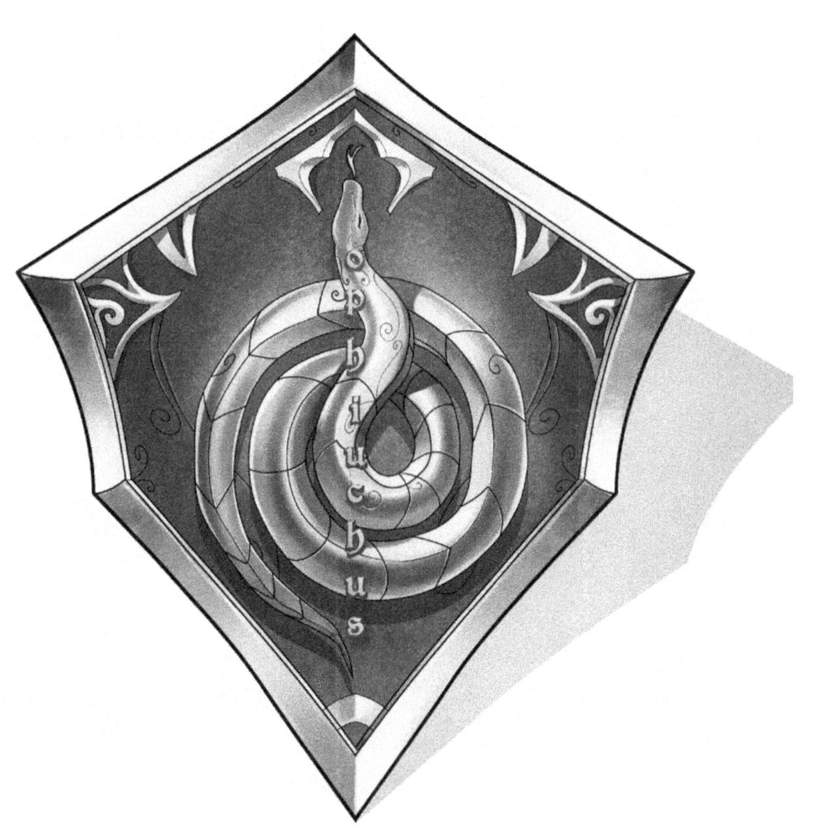

Ophiuchus

GLOSSARY

<u>Braymark Family:</u>

Elizabeth Braymark: Libra Leader and head of the Braymark Family. (Miniature Panda-Uni)

Jonathan Braymark: Husband of Elizabeth. (Panther-Ebon)

Ambrose Foster: Elizabeth's Older Brother. (Viper-Dexter)

Harley Braymark: Elizabeth's 14 year old Daughter. Heir to the Braymark Family line. (Eagle-Sage)

Bowen Braymark: Harley's Older Brother. (Raccoon-Sidney)

Dominic Cade: The Braymarks Legion, Butler, and Guardian. (Leopard-Links)

Keith Braymark: The Father of Johnathan Braymark and Grandfather of Harley and Bowen. (Fox-Axer)

<u>Vanseal Family:</u>

Rodney Vanseal: Capricorn Leader and head of Vanseal Family. (Goat- Yendor)

Selena Vanseal: Rodney's Wife and Dev's Mother. (Lynx-Tiye)

Deveraux Vanseal: Main character and heir to Vanseal Family line. (Wolf-Dagon)

Ezekiel Eliza Vanseal: Dev's Twin Little Brother. (Monkey-Semi)

Eland Joshua Vanseal: Dev's Twin Little Sister. (Husky-Simi)

Lesley Dumont: Salena's Sister, Autumn's Mother and Dev's Aunt. (Owl-Eve)

Autumn Dumont: Lesley's Daughter. (Parrot-Cadence)

Gabby Wilson: The Vanseal's Legion, Nanny, and Guardian. (Bear-Mable)

Caroline Vanseal: Rodney's Younger Sister, Warrior in the Zortegan Army. (Jackal-Ruby)

Gabriel Dumont: Selena's and Lesley's Father and Dev's Grandfather. (Gorilla-Kayli)

Delila Vanseal: Rodney's favorite Aunt and Corleejus Sister. (Ghost)

Grandpa Corleejus: Julia's Husband. (Dead)

Lady Julia Vanseal: Rodney's Mother and Dev's Grandmother. (Tarantula-Lord Websly)

Stover: Rodney's Kleptomaniac Uncle and Julia's Older Brother. Myler's and Chelsea's Dad. (Peacock-Snipe)

Cousin Myler: Stover's 16 Years Old Son. (Boar-Darmath)

Cousin Chelsea: Stover's Daughter, Age 11 (No Familiar)

Cousin Chase: Incurable horn dog that is in love with Gabby. (Ghost)

Kilo: Youngest Brother of Julia and Stover and Makayla and Bailey's Dad. (Beaver-Isaac)

Cousin Mikayla: Kilo's Youngest Daughter, Age 10 (No Familiar)

Cousin Bailey: Kilo's Oldest Daughter, Age 15 (Tiger-Nima)

Uncle Pat Dumont: Gabriel's Younger Brother. (Ghost)

Names of the Zodiac council Members and familiars:

<u>Scorpio</u>: Nikolai Avery-Real Estate Agent. (Scorpion-Celeste)

<u>Aries</u>: Armani Steel-Wedding planner. (Ram-Akyo)

<u>Gemini</u>: Adare Jones-Math Teacher. (Chameleon- Myuka)

<u>Virgo</u>: Rochelle Lema-College Student. (Dove-Yera)

<u>Sagittarius</u>: Renee Long-Humanitarian. (Horse-Lovett)

Capricorn: Rodney Vanseal-Bank manager. (Goat-Yendor)

Aquarius: Taylor-Rose Mason-Nurse. (Seal-Quinn)

Leo: Donovan Sipher-Mobster. (Lion-Callen)

Cancer: Daymon Erickson-Detective. (Crab-Chandler)

Taurus: Levi Weber-High School Principal. (Bull-Tyson)

Pisces: Geno Smarts-Mail Man/ (Shark-Denton)

Libra: Elizabeth Braymark-Librarian. (Panda-Uni)

Ophiuchus: Xalucard the main bad guy. (Python-Raymyth)

Extra people:

Anthony Pike: Dev's Best Friend.

Remy Phillips: Dev's 14 years old high school crush.

Olivia Tyler: Anthony's 16 years old date at the Rollie.

Lynette Itza: School Councilor.

Avi Erwin: General Paratar Solider.

Katrena: Anthony's Prom Date.

James Avery: Dev's Track Rival. (Lemur-Deluxi)

Coach Hunter: Former drill Sargent turned Track Coach.

Marie and Stephanie James: The mean Cheerleader Sisters.

Mr. Houston: History Teacher.

Brandon: Extended Track Friend.

Kendall: Extended Track Friend.

Kedra McCurdy: Sraw's Mother. (Ghost)

Safire McCurdy: Sraw's Wife. (Doe-Capri)

Cousin Ralston: Straw's Son, Age 12 (No Familiar)

Sraw McCurdy: Rodney's Bestfriend and Ralston's Father. (Cayote -Cypress)

Marcus Gore: Bowen's Bestfriend.

Simone MacAroy: Remy Prom Queen Rival.

Cindy: Classroom Student.

Places:

Nova Castle: The Zodiac Castle in Kalebulax City.

Moonlight River: The place where the crescent turtles live.

Rochella City: The name of the city on earth they live in.

The Rollie: The name of the skating rink.

Kalebulax city: The Capitol of Zortega.

Marti Cani Gardens: Garden on northeast side of the castle.

Slaven: Council Meeting Hall.

Reda Miles Magnet: Dev's High School.

Mountain Side High Mustangs: Dev's rival track school.

Gravite Caverns: The Zortegan's max security prison.

Shanket: Nova Castle's jail.

Lex Meadows: The emotional lake in Zortega.

The Dipper: The Faux Loc's matting lands.

Red Jackson's famous BBQ: Dev's favorite place to eat.

Prickson City Police Department: Detective Erickson (Cancer's) job in Oklahoma.

Rockbelly Bellows: Special place for Elizabeth.

Land Daski's Pizza: Harley's favorite hangout spot.

Terms:

Zortega: The home planet of the Zodiacs.

Zortegans: The Name of the people.

The Qualum: The most powerful book of spells.

Xlatherus key: The twelve-sided key that opens the book.

Legion: Original Zortegans. The most powerful Guardians of the family lines.

The Kaloke Ceremony: Coming of age ceremony where Zortegans meet their familiars.

Niyor: Term familiars use for their partners.

Suniva: The Zortegan term of battle fighting.

Triquetra Vinculum: Meaning a magical triangle bond between three people.

Vamperous: Stone/charm that drains the powers of anyone it comes in contact with.

Emphanalt: Stone/charm that enhances the powers of all who wear it.

Holju: A healing star brings one person back from the dead.

Faux Loc: Snake Dragon looking creature.

Espi: Planet like animals that assist the Zortegan Council members.

Paratars: The name of the Zortegan Army.

Lagesse: Sour Purple Peppermint Candy.

Jeuhra: The famous Zortegan battle game.

Sparkle bombs: Magical exploding bombs.

Kantor: Bad familiars.

Novalo Gama: Releasing their max power.

Nupqrawls: Zortegan money.

Yolwery: Means wedding proposals.

Fricdaraw: My almighty leader.

Vewanic Armor: Zortegans most majestic metal.

Jalacken: The toughest leather.

Spells:

Rollinka: Wind spell.

Raquise: Fireball spell.

Aduka: A laser beam spell.

Leapa: Charm Transformation spell.

Teath Vidacula: Cure of the falling star activation.

Advebies Dawhul: The spell to activate the feathers healing powers.

Rogoca Enel: Spell used to enhance hearing.

Alocknic: Spell used to unlock Lex Meadows.

Chichen muileti da cend ta phecy: The spell to create the soul version of their familiar.

Poe'lin Cambrtic Goursha Obeyo: The spell to transfer the pure soul energy into a totem needed to house there familiar.

Geairco Los Pricela: To call forth.

About the Author

Darryl Johnson Jr. & LaGina Weaver happen to be a married couple that was established in June of 2013. They have three beautiful girls named, JaLissa, NaShayla, and SaRiyah. Along with one handsome son named Darryl Johnson III and two fur babies. Darryl is a United States Army soldier with many years under his belt as an active duty member. LaGina is a former medical caregiver with many avenues of medical education. They both work very hard to be role models and entrepreneurs in their businesses. Darryl's favorite past time is reading books, listening to records on his record player, and smoking a good cigar. LaGina's favorite pastime is listening to music, watching tv and movies with her family, and arts and crafts. Writing this book was pure joy for them. "We explored a new partnership in our marriage, so we hope you like it as much as we enjoyed writing it."

9 781952 982606